Hell's Belles

by

Jon LaForce

For Frank Strahorn.

On an otherwise normal day in Sebastian, Florida, Frank Strahorn put himself between an evil man bent on murder, and a restaurant full of innocent bystanders, shepherding them to safety at the cost of his own life. His actions were in keeping with the highest traditions of the Marine Corps and the US Naval Service.

Frank Shelton Strahorn, USMC
5 July, 1985, - 19 June 2020

Chapter 1

Here We Belong, Fighting For Survival

The next time Grandpapa tells me something is best avoided? I'll listen to him, Sylvie Lyons told herself from her spot in the front of the Coyote tactical vehicle. The truck wasn't even idling, just sitting in place near the front gate as she ruminated on how much she thoroughly despised the Northwest Frontier.

It can't be that bad, Grandpapa. People don't really live like that. Not in the twenty-first century! She had protested in his study.

Now she knew better. After a month here, Sylvie looked forward to sitting down with Grandpapa and telling him she was so very sorry for ever doubting him.

Still, we must keep up appearances. Would be bad for morale if the troops heard their sergeant whining about our current predicament. She looked back once more, scanning for helmets and counting as she went. *One, two, three, four. Three lasses and a lad. Wonder how they're taking the daily mushroom treatment?*

"Join the Army they said," Private Albrecht declared from his spot in the machine gun turret just behind Sylvie's seat.

"It'll be fun they said," Godfrey sighed.

"See the world they said," Chevasse said idly in the seat beside Godfrey. Both women were positioned behind Albrecht and could hear everything the machine gunner said.

"The fooking recruiter never mentioned sweating me arse off in the middle of nowhere Afghanistan!" Albrecht declared.

"Well Albrecht, I'm sure the Ministry would be right happy to send you to the Arctic," Sylvie snarked from the front left-hand seat. As the senior Sergeant, she was both section leader and vehicle commander.

"Sergeant, that would be a relief. Leastways then I wouldn't be drowning in me own sweat!" Albrecht replied.

"Nah, but we'd have to listen to your whining about the cold. And shoveling snow. And having to get the vehicle unstuck from snow," Godfrey declared.

Sylvie rose in her seat and looked back at the soldier sitting in the machine gun turret mount. "At least until the cold froze your mouth shut. Then it'd be peaceful."

"Oh, Sergeant. That's mean! How could you say that?" Albrecht protested.

"Aye. But we would na be listening to a bloody Welshman who gets up in a huff about everything," Godfrey announced.

"Okay, so I'm picky. So what?" Albrecht replied boldly.

"Picky? And you joined the Army? Are you mad or daft?" Sylvie demanded.

"Ummmm..." Albrecht struggled for an answer.

"Lyons! Go ahead and move on out!" Staff Munro ordered over the radio.

Sylvie's section was responsible for bringing out the first sets of lights purpose built for the new airstrip they were building at FOB Bourne.

Damned if we aren't a motley looking pile of ass Sylvie considered as they rolled out through the serpentine barriers.

Their company was an amalgamation of three separate units. First Platoon was combat engineers, odds and sods from across the Corps of Engineers. Second Platoon was all Air Support types, from the 8th Engineer Brigade specifically. Third Platoon, Sylvie's, was composed entirely of electricians and mechanical engineers yanked up from their regiments without warning. The company staff came from eight different regiments, with the orders "make this work, you're deploying in two months' time."

She didn't know how it happened, or why. There were loads of rumors surrounding the matter. Nobody seemed to know what was 'really' going on. The day they'd flown out, there had been speeches and politicians which still explained nothing. The company didn't even have a regiment to call home! The unit simply existed as "Number 1 Company, Engineers, Support Command."

Not a single bit of which mattered compared to the immediate reality of their job here in Afghanistan- getting an airfield built and a Forward Operating Base rebuilt, in Dishu.

The walls of the FOB hadn't been expanded this far outwards. The surveyors who'd laid out the plans explained that it was best not to do so in case "anything comes up which we haven't planned for." Most of Number One Company's personnel had translated this to mean "I don't want to be responsible when things go wrong."

But orders were orders. So Sylvie was out here with the electricians, laying in lines for landing lights. Up ahead, she could see Farquharson in his dozer, scraping the ground to make it level and filling in divots. He waved and blew them a kiss.

"That man is bored to tears," Lance Corporal Noel declared.

"What makes you say that, Noel?" Sylvie asked.

"He said as much this morning during chow. Ain't got a radio in there for music, and his iPod won't charge anymore."

"Sucks."

"I tell ya Sergeant, if I ever have kids, I am not buying them a sandbox," Albrecht admitted.

"Oh?"

"I'm bloody sick of it all."

"What about the locals?"

"Almost sick of them too."

Less than a hundred yards to their front, a man stood upright, holding a short stubby tube over one shoulder, his face shrouded behind a shemagh. In an instant, smoke filled the air behind him as a fiery dart flew towards the massive dozer. It plowed into the ground, just left of its intended target, throwing up rocks and dirt in a massive spray.

As if a puppet on strings, he dropped down, disappearing.

"Action front, ten o'clock!" Sylvie shouted.

Albrecht started to swivel that direction when a second man appeared. His arms also held an RPG. Before Albrecht could complete the turn, the new assailant had launched another rocket at the dozer.

This time, the aim held true and his round struck the side of the dozer solidly. Farquharson threw open the door of his cab, preparing to jump when the first rocketeer reappeared and sent another deadly lance downrange. He was also dead on target this time, the warhead flying past the twisted armor plates to bury itself within the dozer's guts before it exploded.

Farquharson screamed, the explosion ejecting him from the cab. His body struck the ground, bounced, striking once more as he crumpled with all the stillness of a child's broken doll.

Sylvie didn't wait to be told instructions. Her left hand stabbed the button controlling the grenade launcher. Eight separate cylinders ejected from their tubes on the front of the Coyote, smoke filling the air as they flew along to land on the far side of the now-damaged dozer.

"Noel, put us on the left side of the dozer! Godfrey! Chevasse! Get to Farquharson, see if we can put him in the lorry bed!"

Albrecht, to his credit, had begun laying down suppressive fire, alternating between both locations. "Come on you dirty sons of bitches!" he screamed shrilly as the steady bursts slammed out in reply.

Behind him, Godfrey and Chevasse rolled out the right hand door, headed for where they had seen Farquharson go flying.

All around them she could hear AK rounds bouncing off the Coyote's armor plates as Staff Munro gave orders and tried to keep control of both squads. The air strip no longer mattered. Nor did the burning dozer. Now they had to get their people back inside the safety of the berms and call for dustoff. If the man caught in the dual RPG blasts was going to live, he needed immediate care.

"Found him!" Godfrey reported over her radio. *"It doesn't look good!"*

"What's he got?" Sylvie asked.

"Looks like burns, shrapnel and multiple broken bones!" Godfrey responded.

"Can you move him?" Sylvie asked.

"We think so!"

"Well for the love of Jesus and Mary, move your asses dammit!" Sylvie screeched, fighting to be heard above the roar around her.

"On it!"

Above and behind her, she heard Albrecht call out that he was reloading. Then he gave an inhuman shriek and Sylvie turned to see blood spurting from his left arm.

"Noel, once they have Farquharson onboard, take off, don't wait for my say-so!"

"Aye, sergeant!" Her driver responded.

Unbuckling, Sylvie clambered up and over the roll cage bars to where Albrecht was struggling to staunch his wound.

"Holyshitballsthisfookingburns!" the machine gunner screamed, followed by a manic stream of curses.

"Easy now!" Sylvie ordered, pulling bandages from the first aid kit on his armor. "Let's get you bandaged right quick."

Albrecht grimaced but she managed to get the bandage in place, dumping quik clot into the wound channel before she tied it off.

"There, now can you shift ammo?" Sylvie demanded.

"Aye, I'll try," Albrecht admitted through gritted teeth.

"Good lad."

Standing, Sylvie turned her attention to the L7A2 resting in its cradle on the pintle mount. Albrecht had managed to get the new ammo can in place before he went down. Grasping the linkage with her left, she fed it into the still-open feed tray on top, then slammed the lid shut. While her left hand took hold of the trigger, her right ripped the charging handle to the rear in a violent motion, cycling the first new round into the breech. Hands switched positions and then she began to fire.

BAM BAM BAM BAM BAM

Red tracer fire lashed out into the confusion. She did not notice Farquharson being shoved up and into the bed of her tactical vehicle. Nor that McMasters, his ground guide, was beside him, right arm hanging loosely.

Three men in dishdashas and turbans came staggering out of the smoke, coughing and gasping for air, not paying attention to what they were doing. She was almost willing to ignore them as poor locals caught in the crossfire. Except that they held RPGs in their arms. There were only two options at that moment and Sylvie was too mad to care.

BAM BAM BAM BAM BAM BAM

The long burst of rapid fire cut through all three. They died where they stood.

Beneath her feet the Coyote tactical vehicle began to move, shaking everything. She held on, even as she recognized Albrecht beside her, hauling a new ammo can up and linking cartridge belts together so she could maintain suppressive fire.

Noel stayed on the accelerator as they wound their way through the serpentine. Godfrey and Chevasse kept trying to put bandages on but nothing held still long enough for them to get a good grip as Sylvie kept scanning for targets.

"Medic! Somebody get me a gods-be-damned medic!" she shouted as they cleared the serpentine.

"I'm already here, Lyons!" Doc Gnem declared, vaulting into the Coyote's bed, followed by an engineer with a radio.

The engineer took one look at the mangled burnt body and promptly puked over the side of the truck, screaming in terror. Gnem looked up from his task and slapped her.

"Dillon! Get a grip girl!"

"But he's dead!" Dillon protested.

"Not yet he ain't!" Gnem roared. "If you canna do it, just hold down the button, let me do the nine-line damn it!"

Dillon retched again, but this time held the radio out as Gnem began a process he was all too familiar with since coming to Bourne.

Sylvie watched it in a weird, detached way, trying to regain her equilibrium.

"Jesus save us, that was good shooting Sergeant," Noel said slowly.

Sylvie sank back against the turret ring. "Sure. Sure thing." She croaked, fingers fumbling on her canteen lid as she tried to quench the awful thirst.

What the hell? She asked herself. *What the hell happened? How the blazes are we gonna survive this place? Why am I not dead yet?*

\#

From where she stood, Captain Natasha Fitzsimmons could see all of Forward Operating Base Bourne, and its immediate environs. She could also see why her blood pressure kept rising. Black smoke still rose from the hulk of what had been a functioning bulldozer. She was amazed nobody else had been injured in the disastrous morning.

"How bad is the damage, Sergeant Major?"

Stirling Mayne, Company Sergeant Major for Number 1 Company, Royal Corps of Engineers, sighed as he observed the columns of smoke rising. The medevac chopper could no longer be seen winging across the sky towards Camp Bastion.

"Hard to tell yet ma'am. Gallagher's handling damage control right now. Says it'll be at least an hour."

"Any word on Farquharson or McMaster?"

"Nothing yet. We won't know until the doctors get back to us."

Fitzsimmons swore something particularly vile. "I'm going to send a message to Higher. Keep me apprised."

"Yes ma'am."

Stomping down the steps, Natasha left the roof and returned to her command post. She had a message to write, much as it hurt her pride, because for all the world it would sound like her people had failed.

They haven't failed, Natasha told herself. *There just aren't enough of us to get the job done like we need.*

Message to Regional Command- Southwest

Two lads injured, possibly dead. As of this writing, I now have twelve KIA and twenty-seven wounded still in hospital. Taking contact daily. ANP of no use. Troops exhausted. Cannot hold at present this way. Need reinforcements. Mission to rebuild Bourne and properly install airfield in danger. Need reinforcements.

#

"Fire mission!"

The field phone's tinny scream could be heard clearly across the long length of the gun line, shattering the still of the night. Men began running to and fro, in a dance they had come to know quite well over the previous months. The steps were intimately familiar now, a whirling dervish whose only end came in death.

"Special instructions: adjust, at my command!"

Handwheels spun rapidly, six thirty-four hundred and twenty pound barrels rising on their trunnions as men bearing massive green-painted projectiles ran forward, deadly cargoes held up in their arms.

"Battery, three rounds in effect."

TANG-TUNK.

Steel bit into the brass obturating band, conforming the softer metal to the hardened rifling's grooves.

"Ready Five!"

"Five is ready. Standby, fire!"

On Gun Five, Sergeant Hondo Cassidy moved through the motions of his profession. A husky man of medium height, he possessed broad features, and angry green eyes. Right then, even as his brain processed the fire command, he was giving his own signal to the crew, left arm slashing down while he bellowed.

Beagle, the Number One man, rotated in place, snapping the six-foot cotton lanyard tight as he did so. The howitzer belched fire and smoke in a thunderous BOOOM that would have deafened the unwary. Billows of dust launched through the air in a choking reek of burnt powder. For the Marines on Gun Five, it was part of how they earned their living. By the time their round found its way back to earth, they'd be reloaded and ready to shoot again.

Battery F, Second Battalion, Twelfth Marine Regiment had been moving from their patrol base at Zaranj on the Iranian-Afghanistan border, back toward Delaram Air Base. Then they got a hipshoot call and found themselves deploying to the right of Route 606, gun barrels training south, toward the deep desert. Behind them, covering the road, were the smaller crew-served machine guns, watching for threats from the rear and flanks.

Hondo Cassidy knew all of this, and processed it accordingly. As the Gun Chief for Five, he had to, and so would his Assistant Chief.

Brian would be a damn fool not to, Cassidy told himself.

The Missourian had been playing the soldier's game for far too long to not process everything around him in that clinical, detached manner and start making judgments about hows or whats. Such thoughts and behaviors were a normal part of everything he did.

Dust fell back down to the earth as Five's report echoed across the still-hot sand. Rodd, the Number Three Man, was already replacing the massive swab in its bucket on the left hand side of the gun, even as Bath threw the next round onto the loading tray and spun out to his left. Thompson and Logan ran forward with the ramrod, driving the heavy projectile up and into the open breech. By instinct they knew to turn as one, sprinting backwards and out of the way. Powder increments followed. Rodd's arms came up clear of the breech before it slammed shut, interrupted screw threads locking tightly into place.

"Ready on Five," Huerta announced through the handset.

"Five is ready, the battery is ready."

Kramer saw all of this and nodded at Cassidy who checked a shot clock on his belt. "Five point three-eight seconds! Good work guys!"

"Hell yeah!" Thompson whooped. "Fast Five out here making that dollar!"

"Damn right. We're adjusting gun for a reason," Kramer declared loudly.

"And we prove why every single freaking time!" Cassidy announced as he stepped forward to examine the olive green projectiles over either of Kramer's prodigious shoulders.

They were two of a kind, thick in the chest, shoulders and arms, focused as their job was on extreme upper-body strength. Slightly slimmer in the waist, Cassidy stood easily a hand and a half taller, with a pronounced jawline and mustache the wrong side of regulation length, hazel eyes seething at the world as if he wished to watch it all burn. Kramer had features more akin to a hobgoblin, brooding brown eyes and short-clipped red hair to match his persistently volatile temper. The Sergeant and Corporal got along well together, thus their platoon commander had no problem keeping them joined at the hip.

Cassidy slapped both rounds as he verified them with the recorder, Lance Corporal Huerta, then stepped back.

"Looking good, guys," Cassidy proclaimed.

"Roger that, sergeant," some of the Marines chirped.

Behind Kramer, a smaller Marine bent backwards to keep a single large green projectile off the ground.

"Ow," the Marine said as he adjusted his grip.

"Don't set it down, Bath." Cassidy ordered. He knew what the younger man was struggling with. And still he expected him to hold.

"It's not. Heavy. Sergeant! Promise!"

"Sounds like you need some more pushups in your diet, son."

"Maybe. Sergeant," Bath grunted.

"Step in front of Kramer. I want you out of his way and resting your arms first chance you can."

As Bath moved to the fore, Cassidy began verifying the round, just as he had done so with the projectiles Kramer held. The slowest part of any fire mission was the ammo train. With the projectiles verified and stacked up, they could be thrown onto the loading tray without unnecessary delay. The same was true for the trio of powder monkeys standing to the left of the gun. Each of those worthies held a select number of drum-shaped charges, to be verified before use.

All we're waiting on is FDC. Then it's off to the races, Cassidy told himself.

"Battery, cancel special instructions: 'at my command!' Special instructions: 'when ready!'" the radio shouted.

They'd been hoping for exactly this call. Whoever they were shooting for, the forward observer had been at it intermittently all evening. Now, after much trial, error, and not a little patience, they were finishing off the target. And doing so at their own speed.

BOOM BOOM BOOM

As fast as Thompson and Logan could set and run the ramrod, they'd gotten all three of their rounds off.

"Shot Five!" Huerta declared over the radio set.

"Rounds complete on Five!"

"Damn you're fast tonight," a new voice declared over the radio loop.

"Solid copy on Five, thanks Gunny!" Huerta said cheerfully.

"FDC this is Gun Three, can somebody tell Five Actual he needs to lay off the steroids!"

Cassidy motioned for the handset and Huerta passed it over.

"Gun Three, what I hear you saying is you're weak and you can't hang."

"No it's not."

"You need to come lift with me," Cassidy admonished into the mouthpiece.

"Negative Gun Five, kiss my ass," Three's Chief replied.

"Sorry, Three, your mother is too busy staring at mine. She'll get mad and demand child support if I leave," Hondo retorted.

Laughter filled the position at Three's expense. Then the Marines went back to silently waiting in the dark.

"Gun Line this is the Captain. Assessment from the observers says we got a massive weapons cache and the IEDs placed around it. Whoever was guarding it got caught in the secondaries. We are cold tube. Prepare to march order."

A new race began then. Not the dervish of death, but the celebratory joy of victory. They had shot, shot well, and now could continue onward with their drive through the starry night. It was eighty-three miles from here to Delaram Air Base, and all of these men wanted good sleep after three months living in shallow trenches day and night.

Barrels dropped as the massive carriages rose, gloved hands grabbing for the muzzle to attach tow hookups. Staying in such an exposed position was hazardous. These men wanted to be gone shortly.

"C'mon assholes, Delaram is still two hours away. If we hurry we can catch midrats!" Kramer excoriated.

"What're midrats, Corporal?" Bath asked.

"Midnight Rations! The last good meal we can have before breakfast! It is The Reason you move faster!" Cassidy growled behind him.

"Yes, Sergeant!"

"Hooked up!" Thompson yelled, slamming the pintle into place as Huerta grabbed the cotter pin to secure it in place. Kramer checked air lines, and Cassidy inspected the handbrakes on either side of the howitzer.

"Mount up uglies!" Cassidy ordered, satisfied with their work.

Men swarmed into their respective trucks, doors and tailgates slamming shut with finality before the big diesel engines roared to life and they launched forward, surging through the sand like sharks hunting prey through the surf. Six massive wheels propelled them forward, slinging dust across the dark night. Then they were gone, and save for the tracks those wide tires left in the reddish sand, one might have never thought they were there.

Chapter 2

How'd You Earn Your Living Boy?

When Colonel Michael Roach stepped out of his office and into the common area of the Regional Command-Southwest Headquarters, he was surprised to find people still hard at work, despite the late hour. Person rather: Colonel Christian DuBois, the British Army liaison. The two men enjoyed a friendly working relationship, to the point that when others were not present, they went by first names with each other. Mike, as the regional commander's chief of staff, was always grateful for the calm which his British counterpart displayed.

As he looked at the man, Mike realized something was amiss. Christian's face was ashen, and he appeared to be entirely distraught about something.

"Mike, I need help.'" Christian said despondently, dropping his pen on the desk.

Crossing the space as quickly as his compact frame allowed, Mike sat down beside his friend. "What's going on, Christian?"

"I've got an engineer company busting their asses trying to rebuild FOB Bourne. But they're taking it in the teeth."

"That's down south, right?"

"Yes, down in Dishu. It's the engineer company," he sighed, "and a platoon of Afghan police."

Christian DuBois' handsome face had managed to regain some color but Michael Roach knew the British officer was seething. He'd lost too many men to Blue-on-Green fire from unfaithful locals, and the idea of trusting his people's safety to potential threats once again did not make him happy in the slightest.

"I suppose that might be a slight problem," Mike admitted.

"Just slightly." His voice grew lower and darker. "I found out after the fact — most of that company are women."

"How many is most?" Mike asked just as quietly.

"Nearly three-quarters."

"What?!?!"

Mike's shout was heard by the duty sergeant who came out his seat, hand on his pistol in alarm. Mike waved him away, then returned his attention to DuBois.

"Who does this, Christian? Why?"

"It was an experiment pushed forward by Parliament on the Ministry of Defense to prove that it could work. What few men the company has are simply holdovers at this point. When they return to barracks at the end of this trip, the last men will leave and it will be the first entirely female engineer company in the British army."

"And your government wanted to let Afghan police near them?"

"All in the name of progress and diplomatic good will. I have been told to give them maximum support." He sighed. "And to stay completely hands off."

Mike snorted disdainfully as the enormity of what his friend was saying took effect.

"Why not use your own troops?"

"Parliament committee says it would ruin their self-determination."

Mike's face twisted as he tried to consider the information he'd been given. "And when they start losing girls to IED attacks like they've lost men? Or worse? You'll be hung out to dry!"

"Quite. You see my dilemma?"

"I do. Think your bosses would mind if I sent an American unit into the area?" Mike asked aloud as he stared at a large wall map of Helmand Province and thought a great deal about it. As Chief of Staff to the regional commander, he had wide latitude to act as he saw fit.

"Likely not. Parliament's the ones giving me fits, but I doubt the General Staff will mind."

Mike nodded. "Let me check with Operations. I can scrounge up at least a platoon of something."

"I appreciate anything you can get me, Mike, thank you."

#

Mike Roach had wracked his brain all the next day, and part of the following morning trying to figure out who he could grab bodies from, to run security for the engineers at Bourne. It had been nearly forty-eight hours since DuBois accepted his offer of assistance, but the Colonel still had no idea what to do.

Pulling squads piecemeal to form a new security platoon had been suggested by his staff and discarded. Too many personality conflicts engaged in dick measuring contests that way. Oh sure, the Marines would say 'Yes sir' and double time off to do the job, but that would last approximately three weeks. Then the discipline issues would start. Mike needed a platoon already sorted out and ready to fight.

He was still thinking about the problem when he, a security team, and two aides, stepped off their Super Stallion helicopter and onto Forward Operating Base Delaram. Mike made it a point to visit every location where he had Marines operating, which included tiny patrol bases. It kept him constantly in motion, but he preferred that, and it gave him a means of providing thoughtful input to his boss, the Regional Commander. Sitting idly behind his desk did nothing to make life better for his Marines. Even if the constant traveling did give Gunnery Sergeant Pililaau and the rest of his security team fits.

Wish I knew how to fix the issue of Dishu, Mike told himself for what had to be the hundredth time. The handsome Irishman from New York City hated not having answers when his people needed them.

"What are gun bunnies doing out here?" Gunny Pililaau demanded loudly.

The question snapped Mike out of his self-critique.

"What was that, Gunny?" He asked.

"Look sir." Pililaau pointed in the direction of the motor pool. "Those are howitzers. When did we have cannon cockers assigned to Delaram?"

"They're from Twelfth Marines. They sent us a battalion to replace First Battalion, Eleventh Marines."

Pililaau squinted. "Can't see any guidons. Sorry, sir."

"Prael," Mike called out.

"Sir?" the aide, a lieutenant, stepped forward out of the colonel's shadow.

"Here's my card, you know the PIN. You and some of Gunny's marines go to the PX, grab me six dozen cans apiece Monster, Red Bull, and Rockstar, a carton of Marlboro 100s."

"Should they get some Cope too, sir?" Pililaau suggested.

"Good call Gunny, couple logs of tobacco, maybe some chew too, Charlie."

"Where do you want it delivered to sir?" Prael asked.

"Look for the gun barrels," Mike directed. "Come on Gunny, let's go for a walk."

"Aye aye, sir," Pililaau declared, motioning with his head for the security team to move out.

In any event, the slender aide wound up commandeering a forklift to carry the entirety of the purchase from the PX to the distant motor pool. When they arrived, Mike Roach was sitting between the trails of a howitzer on a makeshift chair of MRE boxes. Around him, in a school circle, were the marines of Fox Battery, drinking water as they talked.

Seeing his diligent aide, Mike held up a hand and pointed at the fork lift.

"Pass the Cartons around, we've got enough for everybody to have one, and share the logs of Cope. NCOs, pass out the energy drinks."

In short order, and much happier for the gifts, Mike and his Marines continued where they had left off.

"I don't get it," Prael said quietly to Pililaau. "Why do all this?"

"After he made Lieutenant Colonel, the man got bounced around in staff jobs. He finally got a battalion, and it was One-Twelve in Hawaii. Fox Two-Twelve was attached as a weird leftover, from when the rest of their battalion was stood down," Pililaau explained. "They had just come back from deployment. Previous commander left a lot to be desired. Cousin of mine who was a platoon sergeant said they had the lowest reenlistment rate in the Corps — not even two percent. It was a real mess"

"Oh dammit!" Prael muttered in shock

"Yeah, but the Colonel fixed all of that. Took him six months to get most of the kinks worked out. My cousin swears by the guy, would follow him anywhere."

"Wait, is this the battalion Roach left to come here as a Colonel?" Prael asked.

"Yeah. And word on the street is that higher strong-armed him into doing it."

"What a rotten deal."

"His Marines requested Mast and filed written complaints with the entire chain of command."

"How many did that?"

"All of them. Whole battalion. Rumor has it their letters wound up on the Commandant's desk."

"It's like that?"

"Yeah. He knows these marines by name. Everybody except the newest privates."

"And they clearly remember him well."

"Good colonels are a precious treasure and a joy, sir," Pililaau intoned.

"That they are," Prael agreed.

#

Metal screamed as it buckled, shattering into fragments popping all over the interior of FOB Bourne. Men and women sought cover or hit the ground, hoping and praying their body armor could stop the flying shards of steel.

Sylvie Lyons had just stepped out of her shop when she heard the sound of metal pinging against the cinderblock side of her machine shop.

"Well crap." she took a pull from the plastic bottle of water in hand. *Sounds like a hydraulic arm.*

"Sylvie, you hear that?" a female voice behind her asked. Sandra Collier, her friend and one of the unit's mechanics, stepped outside to join her.

"Aye. I'm hoping it wasn't that lift we fixed this morning."

Sandra sighed, drank from her own bottle. The younger woman had grease everywhere still from that particular work order. It was even in her fiery red hair.

"Ready to go look?" Sandra asked.

"Not really."

"You too?"

"Yeah." Sylvie finished the rest of her bottle, tossed it into a trash can, then grabbed her rifle off the rack near the open bay door. "Let's go have a look, Sandy. I have a feeling somebody owes me an explanation," Sylvie directed.

"Aye. Let's do that," Sandra agreed.

#

"Criminy! Wadeson, the hell did you do with the lift?" Cornelius Coughlan asked his fellow Private.

A head appeared out of the cab as Richard Wadeson slowly extracted himself from the vehicle he was attempting to drive. "Sorry Coughlan, but I think the hydraulics are shot."

"Oy, get it over to Lyons, she knows how to fix everything."

"Get what over to who?" a voice asked with a deadly calm.

Both men whipped around at this, and saw one of the most beautiful women to have graced the British Army with her presence walking towards them.

Strike that, Wadeson realized, *she's stalking towards us.* The muscles in his butt cheeks reflexively clenched tighter.

Normally, the very lovely Sergeant Lyons was a welcome sight at any occasion. This was not a normal occasion however. Lyons was the senior machinist in the company. She and Corporal Collier from the mechanic section had just fixed the lift Wadeson currently occupied.

"Didn't I tell you to watch what you were doing with the lift and be careful how quickly you put it under load?" Sylvie scolded.

"Yes, Sergeant!" Wadeson replied.

"Well?" Sandra demanded.

"We was trying to finish early," Coughlan confessed, suddenly feeling incredibly embarrassed and trying to look away. "It was only a few more feet," he muttered.

"So you rushed it?" Sandra said angrily.

"Yes." They looked down at their feet again, embarrassed.

"Ground guide the lift over to my shop," Sylvie said coldly. "You get there after I do, you'll be worse off." She stomped off, leaving only frustration in her wake.

Long minutes later, Sylvie arrived at the bay door of her shop as Sandra finished parking the lift inside, with Coughlan and Wadeson standing at attention, quietly waiting.

Beckoning them over to where she stood, Sylvie waited as they ran to her side.

"Now, O'Grady and Logue are running a new field phone over here so we're not constantly using the radios. What do field phones need?"

Both men's faces screwed up as they processed her question.

"Wire, Sergeant," Wadeson volunteered.

"Very good, Wadeson. Can we have exposed wire lying around, Coughlan?"

"No," he said loudly, trying not to fidget.

"That's right. You're going to dig a trench from right here," she drew an 'X' on the ground with her boot toe. "All the way over to the command post," she pointed at the concrete and sandbagged cluster of buildings nearly forty meters away

"Yes, Sergeant."

Both men made to leave and she stopped them.

"Where in the blue blazes do you two fatherless sons of camel ticks think you're going?" Sylvie demanded.

"We um..."

"We need shovels."

"Yeah, Sarn't. Shovels. To dig."

"I'm aware of what shovels are for, Wadeson," Lyons replied coolly. "Hold up your hands." She ordered. "What do you see?"

"I think I've got dirt under one of my nails, Sergeant."

"I see shovels," Sylvie replied.

"Sergeant?"

She patted their upheld hands for emphasis. "Shovel, right, one each. Left, one each."

Both men gaped, unable to hold their bearing.

"Dig fast with your shovels, privates. Or I might decide O'Grady and Logue need more trenchline dug for wire."

Oh this is going to suck, Wadeson scolded himself.

As Lyons strode back into her shop, Wadeson felt his body relaxing by degrees.

"I hate my life," Coughlan declared sadly.

"Look on the bright side, mate."

"What bright side?"

"We get to watch the prettiest woman in the British army make fatigues look outstanding."

Coughlan considered this, then the object of Wadeson's attention, and shrugged. "You're not wrong, mate."

Her ash brown hair hung down to her waist when it wasn't wound into a bun or tied into a braid, and she possessed a figure that even camouflage fatigues could not conceal. It was rare for any of the men to see her smile, dedicated as she was to her work. Those who had witnessed the event swore it was worth waiting for.

"She's an ice-hearted ball breaker who's all Army, every single damned day. But God as my witness Coughlan, she's a lovely sight to behold," Wadeson elucidated.

"And it beats the alternative for me," Coughlan admitted.

"Wuzzat?"

Grunt. "Shoveling coal in North Yorkshire."

"Didn't know you was from North Yorkshire. Me dah came from there, though he's more inclined towards Liverpool these days."

"Ah, prefer a good ocean breeze does he?"

"That. What I'd give for one right now." Wadeson confessed.

"Still better than shoveling coal."

Grunt.

"Ya know, as tempting as she is to look at mate, there's no way you could convince me to stay with her. An hour? Sure. A night? Maybe. But nothing longer. She's way more woman than I could ever handle."

Grunt.

"The man who marries her will be hell on wheels." Coughlan relegated his thoughts. "Wadeson."

"Yeah mate?"

"I hate digging," Coughlan said with finality.

\#

Much later, in the cool of the Delaram Air Base Headquarters building, Mike Roach sipped water from a tepid bottle as Colonel Baumer, the Delaram base CO spoke with him about the present situation and needs.

"We're gonna be a little snug with that extra battery on deck, but we can make it while they're helping us with that training mission." Baumer explained.

Huh. I hadn't thought about it. I wonder, what would happen if they suddenly gave up a platoon? Mike asked himself.

"Baumer, do you know how long that battery has left?"

"I think three months. Yeah, that sounds right."

"Perfect. Hmmm… are they geared for split battery ops?"

"I believe so, yes."

"Good. What if we took one of their two platoons away for a support mission."

"Support?"

"Assisting allies elsewhere."

"I don't see why not. Their captain really only needs one platoon of go-getters for the training mission. Does that sound right to you, Sergeant Major?" Baumer asked the large man in stiff cammies sitting next to him.

"It does sir. Probably want to let them get a full resupply first."

Mike nodded at this input. "Sage as always. Good Sergeants Major are a treasure, make note of that, Lieutenant Prael."

"Yes sir."

Minutes later, in the common area of the HQ, Mike motioned for Prael to sit while he dictated.

"I want orders cut for Second Platoon, Fox Battery, Second Battalion, Twelfth Marines. They will move to Dishu forthwith. They are to be extended in-country by sixty days. Once that is done, I want you to go back to them, find Captain Anness and First Sergeant Torrez. Bring them here."

#

Sweat beaded his forehead as he walked alongside the perimeter wall. Hondo tried hard to pay it as little of his attention as he could. Having divested himself of his boonie hat and camouflage blouse, he now carried a dumbbell in either hand. He was not unarmed though. A hefty rifle slung across his back rested muzzle-down, thumping lightly against his leg as he walked.

With the battery posted on a tiny patrol base, it had been virtually impossible to perform sufficient cardio the way he liked. Delaram however, had an interior perimeter measuring a smidge over 4 miles in length. Weights in hand, he was trying to walk that distance at least two times, all the while maintaining positive control of the weights and proper walking form. Known to the weightlifting community at large as "Farmer's Walks," it was an activity Hondo enjoyed. Grip strength and concentration mattered in this exercise. Which gave out first remained to be seen.

Once now, he had gone around the interior perimeter, thirty-five-pound dumbbells in hand. He could feel the slow burn in his shoulders, along the back of his forearms, edging into his wrists. Soon enough, his legs would feel the strain as well.

A twinge in his left arm caught his attention, starting from the wrist and spiking up to his shoulder. Hondo grunted, redoubled his concentration on ignoring the pain.

Not done yet, he reminded himself. *Still got one more left turn to go.*

Barring the runway, the longest portion of the base was the main drag along which the transient barracks were located. As he rounded the corner, Hondo could see them, still over a thousand feet away.

One step at a time, we earn our way there. That's how winning is made.

Closing the distance, he could feel cramps building in his calves.

Nope. I didn't hear no bell. Not yet. I didn't hear no bell.

A figure down the road waved at him. Hondo quickened his pace slightly.

The figure moved towards him at a trot. It was Kramer, looking worried. "Hey Cass, Gunny needs us."

Out here, without no one else around, the two men dropped all pretenses of rank or pack drill. Theirs was a friendship running back four years and a pair of deployments with Eleventh Marine Regiment. Hondo had been a junior Corporal on the gun back then, and Brian right behind him, as Senior Lance, butting heads. Eventually, the two men had settled their differences at a bar in Korea while deployed under the "Thirty Worst" Marine Expeditionary Unit. First they'd been swinging at each other. When a Korean army squad tried to step in, it pushed the two marines to clear the bar with violent abandon.

Such behavior was a tale old as mankind itself. Whilst they disappeared down an alleyway, MP sirens howling behind them in the dark Korean night, a friendship soaked in bloody knuckles and bruises was born. The years and miles and memories since then had become fertile ground for what made the duo successful running a gun crew.

Brian refrained from saying more until Hondo had come to a stop, dropping the dumbbells into the sand so his stiff fingers could flex and stretch. Greedy lips sucked water through the hose of his camelback, Spitting, he cleared away the sand and grit which had accumulated in his mouth during his walk, then drank more.

"So, what's Gunny want?" Hondo asked.

"Captain and First Sergeant got called into Base Headquarters, maybe twenty minutes ago. Gunny told us to recall everybody and stand ready."

"We meeting over in the Staff-and-O hooch?" Hondo asked.

"Yeah."

"Roger that. Let me get my blouse and we'll do that thing."

Grabbing one of the dumbbells, Brian walked alongside him back toward the area where they were billeted.

"What do you think happened?" Brian asked.

"Something stupid. Something monumentally idiotic," Cassidy replied cynically.

"We are Marines. It's our job to fix the disasters others cause."

Brian's comment was a statement, rather than a question. In the two-hundred thirty-eight years since the Marine Corps had come into existence, it had become a preferred solution for dealing with the mistakes of others. Especially when the application of violent force needed to be applied. Both men understood that business quite well. They called it "job security."

Hondo dropped the dumbbell beside the front door of the hooch besides several other dubious looking pieces of exercise equipment, then stepped inside, enjoying the cool air within.

"Ya know, it occurs to me that I still haven't decided what to do with my leave time when we go back to Hawaii," Hondo admitted.

"Elisha wants to go back to Missouri for a visit."

"She always was a glutton for punishment."

"Hey now, it's not my fault Hawaii ain't got KC barbecue or her sisters," Brian protested. "And I'd really like to catch a Cardinal's game."

"I know, I know," Hondo admitted. "I'm thinking I'll spend ten days at home, fly back to Hawaii and sit on the rest of my leave."

"That's right, you're leaving Hawaii at the end of next year aren't you?"

"Nope, year after next, April of 2015."

"Still, you gotta make some decisions soon."

"Yeah."

"What do you want? One-Eleven and a relaxing stay at Las Pulgas?"

"I — I don't know."

Cassidy pulled on the worn FROG blouse, mulling over what he'd said. It was the truth- he didn't want to get out, but he wasn't sure if he wanted to stay where he was at. A lot of things weren't clear right now.

"I'm trying to avoid a B Billet for as long as I can," he said as he finished dressing.

"You don't want to be a Drill Instructor, Recruiter, Embassy Guard, or Security Forces?" Kramer teased.

"Absolutely not!" Hondo snarled. "The friggin' idea I need to step outside my specialty and take up a secondary job for an entire enlistment, just to prove I'm a good Marine, is a collection of lies sold by those spoiled brats at Manpower and Personnel because they're too stupid to figure out a better way to fill those billets."

"I know," Kramer replied. "But you better hurry up, you know spots will be limited by February."

"Yeah, you're right. Let's go find Gunny, see what all the fuss is about."

Fortunately for the foot-bound Marines, the massive quonset-hut style tents which Fox Battery had been placed in weren't far away from each other. Just like so many generations of Marines before them, they had promptly named their home "the hooches." One each for officers and Staff NCOs, another for all the sergeants and corporals, and lastly the Junior Enlisted.

"Cassidy, where the hell have you been?" Nealen bellowed when he saw both non-commissioned officers walk into his tent on the far side.

"Exercising, Staff Sergeant!" Cassidy shouted back.

"C'mon Nealen, did you expect him to skip a day?" Gunnery Sergeant Moore teased as he threw back another handful of ranch-flavored sunflower seeds. "He lives in the gym. I'm surprised he hasn't traded in his cot for a weight bench already."

"It'd be comfier, Gunny," Cassidy said politely as they joined the circle of NCOs lounging and standing wherever space afforded, chewing on sunflower seeds, dipping tobacco, or drinking still-hot water from plastic bottles as they waited.

Some things don't change in the Marine Corps, regardless of the job field, Nealen noted. He had come to the artillery after leaving the Recon community on medical advice.

"You're not gonna make it long on those knees son," the *medical officer had told him seriously. "You can't kick doors forever."*

"But I want to do at least twenty!" Peter had protested.

"Son, you're twelve in years. If you want to see retirement, you need to change jobs. Something with less running and ruck marching."

Artillery was definitely different, and certainly easier on his knees. If an artilleryman couldn't ride to the fight, he had no interest in going to that place. Which, to be fair, was smart. One did not want to try towing five-ton guns up a mountain by hand.

Rather than four platoons like a Recon Company, the Batteries were organized into two platoons, with a lieutenant and staff sergeant in charge of each. The focus centered around guns — massive one hundred fifty-five millimeter rifled cannons, each towed by a seven-ton truck. Six guns to the battery, three per platoon. First Platoon was full of senior Sergeants for chiefs in charge of each gun. These had brand new corporals as their assistants, learning the trade properly. First Platoon was nothing but old men leading very young boys, given how they'd received most of the new men during the last delivery from the school house.

In Second Platoon, at Gunny Moore's insistence, Nealen had one Sergeant; the other two guns were chief'd by senior Corporals, all three of whom thought they walked on water. Which, to be fair, they did. Nobody on their respective guns possessed a higher billet, and if Nealen became a casualty, his position would be filled by the 0811 with the longest time in grade — in this case Cassidy on Gun Five. Cassidy's assistant chief would then step into his former role as the Chief of Five. Each gun was set up that way specifically for such moments.

Cherney and Samuels on Four, Cassidy and Kramer on Five, with Tolliver and Shockley on Six. But if the gun chiefs were juniors in terms of rank to their First platoon counterparts, they had a slew of experienced junior enlisted to call upon. What the Corps called "senior" lance corporals. Every gun section had at least a half-dozen seasoned men training only a few new marines per gun. This left Nealen with far less in the way of hand holding day to day, as the lance corporals knew their jobs and did them well.

The few boots we've got are shaping up nicely, Nealen told himself. *And thank God I have solid chiefs on each gun.*

Tolliver, always enthusiastic and motivated by his dedication to the Corps, with the gangly, relaxed Shockley following along behind. Cherney, the easy-going boy from South Dakota, balanced out by his omnipresent Floridian gorilla: Samuels. Kramer had done a hitch with the Army before coming over to the Corps. *By the end of deployment, he'll be eligible for re-promotion to Sergeant, his old Army rank. Right alongside his best friend.*

This last caused Nealen to look for the perpetually brooding man from Gun 5 — Hondo Cassidy.

He's only happy when he's fighting. Gunny Moore warned me about him — 'Cassidy will request transfer just for the sake of deployment. He did one at Lejeune and one while he was at Twenty-Nine Palms and another at Pendleton. Keep him usefully occupied. Please.'

"We catch you in the middle of a workout, Cass?" Gunny Moore asked loudly

"No, Gunny. Just finished."

"Good. Good. How much are you deadlifting right now?"

"Four-sixty-five," Cassidy cocked his head to one side as he considered the weight. "Heavier than Shockley's last girlfriend."

"Not by much it ain't!" Tolliver declared. "That girl strikes oil when she wears stilettos!"

The room fell over laughing at Shockley's obvious discomfort and he signaled his reply with an upright middle finger. "Screw all of you. Twice."

"What about them weird ass walks I've seen you do before?" Gunny Moore asked, turning his attention back to Cassidy.

"Farmer's walks. They're light workouts for off-days. Great for grip strength and making my arms bigger. That's what I was just doing."

"Yeah, like you need bigger arms. Any bigger we won't be able to fit you in cammies, son," Gunny Moore suggested.

"I'll bet I can find a tailor in Oki," Cassidy said with conviction, referring to the Marine bases in Okinawa, Japan.

"True, we're slated to go to Oki next year. You get Mamasan some Yen-jamins? She should be able to hook you up."

"I hope so. But what do we do about body armor?" Hondo asked.

"Son, at this point, I think bullets bounce off of you," Moore suggested.

"No thanks Gunny, I've already done that twice."

The door slammed open, ricocheting off the wall.

"Gunnery Sergeant, we got all our Second platoon NCOs?" Captain Anness demanded as he stormed into the hooch followed by First Sergeant Torrez, the battery's senior enlisted man. Neither looked especially pleased.

"Yes sir."

"Good, saves us having to say this twice, sit-kneel-bend!" Torrez commanded

Torrez only waited long enough for them to get partially seated before he continued speaking.

"Originally we were all going to stay here at Delaram. Living up the good life for four months or so. Second Platoon, your vacation has now been canceled."

"Where are they going sir?" Gunny asked in surprise.

"They're going all the way down here, to FOB Bourne. Near Dishu," Anness declared as he laid out a map at the foot of his cot.

"Might as well say the Pakistani border, sir," First Sergeant Torrez said nonchalantly.

"You're not wrong, First Sergeant," Anness agreed.

"Is there anything down there?" Nealen asked.

"A FOB. Intel claims the Taliban have training camps down there. The FOB is being put up so we can run in more units and supplies to shut them down. RC-Southwest sent an engineer company down to rebuild it plus install an airstrip."

"When did they send Seabees down there sir?" Staff Sergeant Brady asked, referring to the US Navy's construction battalions.

"Actually, it's not them. The Seabees are tasked out already and our engineers are busy providing daily route clearance."

"Thank you God. Thank you so much for no Seabees!" Cassidy snarled.

Anness peered at the younger man. "Something you care to add, Sergeant?"

"The Seabees cut and ran during a firefight on our last deployment, sir. Sergeant Cassidy gained a serious allergy to AK ammo because of it," Kramer answered.

"This true, Cass?" Gunny Moore asked.

"Yes, Gunny," Cassidy snarled.

"Well in this case you got nothing to worry about," Torrez assured. "These are British Army engineers. Their headache is that the FOB is in serious disrepair, and the engineers keep getting attacked. The engineers say they need more bodies pulling security so their people can catch a break, and get the job done on time."

"What do they have right now, First Sergeant?" Moore asked.

"A platoon of ANP. The engineers don't trust the ANP."

"Hell sir, I wouldn't either," Nealen declared soberly. "Girl Scouts are more reliable. Least they bring cookies."

"How long are we gonna be there, sir?" Lt. Harper asked as he wrote furiously in his notepad.

"Rest of the deployment and then some. RC-Southwest is extending us by sixty days. You're going there specifically to stand posts and cover for the engineers," Anness declared.

"Are we flying or driving?" Nealen asked.

"Driving. You'll be re-mounting your trucks but leaving the guns here. RC-Southwest doesn't think you'll need them. Sergeant Johnson, I need Motor-T to prep the trucks."

"Walsh, how's the maintenance coming along?" Johnson snapped to a marine behind him.

"Just got the hundred-twenty day PMCS done, Staff Sergeant" the rawboned lance corporal from Kentucky declared. "Everything's up and ready to move if we need it."

"Well done, Motor-T!" Torrez declared. "Johnson, Battalion truckmaster says we'll have permission to refuel at FOBs along the way."

"Good cuz it's a long walk to 7-Eleven from here sir," Johnson quipped.

This brought a moment of levity to the Captain's dour pronouncement and he waited for them to refocus before he continued.

"You leave the morning after tomorrow, by zero-six. You'll be following a route clearance team from here down to as far as Garmsir. After that, follow the river all the way to Dishu." He looked up at his Marines, checking their faces for questions. "Oh and Harper, you're not going."

"Sir?" Harper asked worriedly.

"Nealen, you're taking this one."

Harper looked crushed and Anness took this into account. "I argued with RC-Southwest for ten minutes, Harper. No go. However, if you wish to submit a written protest on the matter, I will happily endorse it. I think he's wrong to keep you out of this, but he insisted the best place he could use a solid lieutenant was instructing artillery to the Afghanis."

"I'll take you up on that, sir," Harper said. "These are my Marines, damnit!"

"I know, and like I said, RC-Southwest wouldn't allow it," Anness reminded.

"Damnit."

"Nealen, is there anything you need before you go?" Torrez asked.

"They got a PX of any kind down there, or are we on our own?"

"Higher didn't say. I'd let your boys hit the PX tonight. They'll be too busy prepping tomorrow, and it may be months before they see one again."

"Roger that."

"If nobody's got anything else, you're dismissed. Carry on with your plans for the night," Anness ordered.

\#

"Man, my wife is not going to be happy, but it's whatever for me," Scott Cherney said casually as all three Marines made their way out of the hooch, toward one of the chow halls which dotted Delaram's massive site.

"Why would Darcy be mad?" Kramer asked.

"She was looking forward to regular skype visits and all that trash when we talked earlier. Bet they don't have any internet connection at Dishu. None at all."

"You're probably right. Means more time you can come lift with us you skinny bastard!" Kramer teased.

"What do you think, Cass?" Cherney asked.

If the larger man heard them, he said nothing, lost as he was in the swirl of thoughts. Reaching up, Cassidy ran a hand through his short dark brown hair. Every man in the platoon had shaved his head before they hopped aboard the flight to Afghanistan. What Cassidy had now was bristly and not quite curling over as it normally would when it grew another inch. Kramer recognized his friend's tell and stopped walking, just waiting for Cassidy to collect himself.

Delaram has a very nice gym, Cassidy told himself. *But now I'm going back to war proper. Thank you God.*

"Cass? Earth to Cass? Hello?" Cherney repeated, trying to get the other man's attention as he gazed southward toward the far distant horizon.

"Don't bother," Kramer ordered. "I know that look. He wore it when we were on our last deployment."

"Weren't you getting shot at?"

"And missed. Don't forget that part. Not getting hit is important," Kramer chided.

"The Seabees didn't really run did they?" Cherney asked nervously, suddenly remembering what the two had brought up during the briefing.

"Yeah they did. Next time he's got his shirt off, check his right side."

"Scars?"

"Three of them."

"Well they appear to suck at shooting, seeing as he's still alive. What happened to the Seabees?"

"Haven't run across them since."

"So what is this look he's rocking now? He looks happy."

"Cuz I am happy," Cass growled. "I'm going somewhere I can fight!"

"Lyons, what are you doing in here?" a male voice asked from the door of the machine shop.

Leftenant DiResta walked in, followed by Staff Sergeant Keating, Sylvie's platoon sergeant.

Looking up from where she'd been busily working on cutting bar stock with an oxy-acetylene torch, Sylvie cut off the flame. Only once it was entirely out did she remove the welding hood covering her face.

"I'm sorry, sir, I just need to get this last set of cuts finished so I can go in for the night!" Lyons protested.

"Christ Almighty," Keating proclaimed. The stout Scot had been busily examining Sylvie's work. "How long have you been working on this, Lyons?"

"I started around thirteen-hundred, Staff Sergeant. Work needs to be done so we can get the airstrip up and running."

"You did all of this on your own?" DiResta demanded.

"Yes sir."

"Do you know what bleeding time it is?" Keating demanded.

"No, Staff, I don't," Sylvie declared.

"God help me it's damn near midnight, Lyons," Keating replied. "When was the last time you ate? Noon?"

"Yes," she admitted sheepishly.

DiResta and Keating shared a look, and DiResta held out his hand, rubbing thumb and forefinger together. "Pay up, Keating. I won and you know it."

"Aye, I hate losing." Keating passed him a five-pound note. "But at least it's not to a fooking no-account Sassenach. Sir."

"True." DiResta smiled.

"Lyons, I think it's time we had a little heart to heart," DiResta admitted.

"Sir?"

DiResta set his rifle on the rack then hopped onto an empty table space and made himself comfortable. "You came to the company as a senior corporal, rolling into your second hitch. A lot of people questioned your fitness to be here. Tonight just proved otherwise ."

"He's not wrong, Lyons," Keating injected. "At a glance, if we weren't bogged down by problems with the Taliban around here, you'd have us a week ahead on the airfield. That's damn fine work."

"Thank you gentlemen. I don't know what to say," Sylvie admitted, unsure of why they were even having this conversation.

"You should be proud of this," Keating replied. "I've been in other companies where the machinists gaffed off because they could. Or the birds tried to pawn off the work onto their mates."

"Which leads to my next issue," he continued. "Since then, you've been all work and damn near no play. Ever. It recently came to my attention that you completed a degree in art history."

"Art History, sir?" Keating asked.

"Aye. Our Sergeant Lyons is not only an artist, to judge by the copy of her portfolio forwarded to me by St. Andrews, but an expert on the Baroque period."

"Well whatever the blazes "baroque" is, good on you. I'm just grateful I know me own history and that all the best things come from Scotland. Like whisky."

"Quite," DiResta sniffed, causing his mustache to jostle about. "Oh and I forgot to mention her other degree, from Imperial College of London, in Metallurgy."

"Two degrees? I don't even have one!" Keating wheeled on Sylvie. "Where did you ever find time to finish two degrees?"

"Colour Baker back in Hobart Barracks didn't mind me taking classes on the side so long as I had all my work done."

"But that's still what, three years work?" Keating asked pointedly.

"They accepted my certifications from the Army, and some other places."

"Ah. That would do it."

"Sounds simple enough you could do it, Staff," DiResta suggested.

"No sir, not I. I like being a soldier. Academics is not my cuppa," Keating said staunchly.

"Fair enough. Now, back on topic — our educated young Sergeant is seeking approval to begin a research degree. Which I have no problem with, save that in speaking with the rest of the platoon I'm now learning that you're not just an introvert, you're practically a recluse. Something's riding you, and I'd like to know what happened. I also know about how you modified the welding storage out in the materials yard," DiResta's face grew dark. "What in the devil's got you so worked up?"

Sylvie bit her lip. This was not a conversation she expected to be having right now. Much less with her platoon sergeant and platoon commander. *And they know about the shop! Dammit, I'll have to tear all of it down now.* She felt her frustration grow as she stared at them, angry at all of it.

"Easy now, Lyons," DiResta said calmly. "I'm not putting you on report. Just tell me what happened."

"Oh. Well, okay, sir," Sylvie admitted. "My third year at Uni. My fiancé wanted something I wouldn't give him. Then I caught him in bed with a known local hooker."

"Oh jeez. What a wanker," DiResta snorted.

"It was near to Christmas, so I went down to London on holiday," Sylvie continued. "Figured I could get roaring drunk at my — with family. Saw the changing of the guard at Buckingham and thought maybe the Army was a good place to be. Withdrew from school and took the bus to Pirbright in February."

"Good, but that's what, six years ago?" DiResta asked.

"Just over seven sir," Sylvie corrected.

"And what happened after that?" he asked nonchalantly. "Because that kind of pain only lasts so long. Something's happened since then, hasn't it?"

"How'd you know sir?"

"I have three older sisters and a passel of aunts. I've learned a thing or two," DiResta admitted smoothly.

"Did somebody grab you?" Keating asked. "Cuz if they did I'll see the worthless mother's son sent to Wormwood Scrubs!"

"Not like you'd think Staff," Sylvie confessed. "I was at 6 Battalion, Delhi Barracks This was back in 2011. I'd started to go out with the squaddies and have fun again. One of the corporals, a bloke named Parduhn, took a real shine to me."

"What did you do?"

"I was lonely sir. But not that lonely."

"Fair enough. Continue."

"At some point, I realized Parduhn was gaslighting me. And grooming me. I didn't like being touched that way. Leastways not without a wedding ring. I transferred out to Hobart Barracks and re-enlisted."

"Smart thinking, it got you out of that brigade entirely." DiResta sighed. "It is an unfortunate truth that even the Army has its fair share of assholes."

Keating grunted in agreement. "You're not wrong, sir."

"We have a few things to do then, Staff."

"I agree sir. Think I need to call around a few friends of mine over at 6 Battalion and see if they know Mr. Parduhn. Want to make sure he's not grooming new victims."

"While you do that, Lyons, we need to handle your issues. You need sleep, and at a guess, your shop is the only one that's ahead of schedule."

"Likely sir."

"Good, tomorrow you're going to stand Post Three from noon to eighteen. Between now and then, I do not want to see you awake before zero-nine and nobody is authorized to wake you without my permission. You need the rest."

"Thank you sir."

"Additionally, your request to pursue a research degree will be authorized and countersigned by the Captain, shortly. Your name will also be going up to brigade for the meritorious board. Hard work deserves proper credit. Sound fair to you, Staff?"

"Aye it does sir," Keating replied.

"As for your little retreat in the yard, do you go there often? Aside from when you need welding supplies?"

"Just when I need to get away from people sir. I really hate people invading my space. I do take a radio with me in case something comes up," Lyons informed.

"What's this shop you're talking about sir?" Keating asked.

"Well I could be wrong but I believe she's making something. She has more than the spare welding gear and tanks in there. Looked like a workshop, though I couldn't follow all of the diagrams on the walls," DiResta admitted.

Keating stared at the young woman. "Whatcha making lass?"

"Staff, I design and engrave custom blades for paying customers."

"With what tools?"

"She does it by hand, Keating, files and the like."

"Very well. Why though?"

"I just need some place without people where I can make art. This stuff" — she waved a hand at the workshop's furnishings — "this isn't pretty. Oh sure it works, but it doesn't look nice. I'm making fluted grips for a dagger right now, with aged bog oak and silver wire."

"How?"

"Bladesmiths ship the blades to me, I do work as I'm able, then send it back out. It's what I do in barracks too. One client's work ended up as my senior capstone for the Imperial College."

"That pay well?"

"It's decent money. The army gives me stability and I'm able to expand my professional portfolio."

"Good lass. I'm impressed. In that case, sir, why don't we have it marked for no unauthorized entry without the permission of yourself, sir, or Colour Gallagher? She can keep the keys for it on her person," Keating suggested.

"I agree." DiResta turned to Sylvie. "So long as your shop stays on top of its business, you may feel free to go in and decompress as much as you need. Lord knows we all need a break after the last several weeks."

"Thank you sir!"

"Now, let's get this shop secured and we'll walk you to the mess hall, see if we can't get Herfy to roust up something edible for you at this hour."

"Why are you doing all of this sir?" Lyons asked, worried for a moment.

"The only way the Army succeeds is if we look after our people. Loyalty is a two-way street," DiResta lectured. "You demonstrated loyalty by going above and beyond to get work done. I am demonstrating it by helping you get your life improved."

"Thank you again, sir."

"That's the proper way to go about it, Lyons," Keating declared solemnly.

Chapter 3

How'd You Earn Your Pay?

Twilight still held a tenuous grasp on the sky, refusing to surrender to the rising sun when the first men mounted their vehicles preparatory to rolling through Camp Delaram's gates. Cassidy and Kramer had done their final walk-arounds together, inspecting the two vehicles which constituted their segment of the convoy.

"We good?" Nealen asked.

Cassidy threw him a high sign. "Green, green up, Staff Sergeant."

"Good trash. Listen up, you two. Cassidy I want you up front. As soon as y'all and the FDC truck are fueled up at Garmsir, you'll be on the road and moving. Do not wait for us. Brady's been told the same thing already by me."

"Something wrong, staff sergeant?" Kramer asked with a frown.

"Nah, but this smells bad. I need eyes and ears up front."

"Roger that."

"Doesn't matter that we're dismounted. Cassidy is in charge as senior oh-eight until I arrive. Brady will establish FDC as if we brought the guns with us. I want you two to get tents and an ammo pit set up. Jimenez will start walking the perimeter to make sure everything is kosher."

"Can do."

Both men turned to go when Nealen stopped them, latching hold of Kramer's vest by the rear grab strap.

"How are there grenades in your chest pouches?" he asked seriously as he looked at Kramer.

"Yes, Staff Sergeant," Kramer admitted.

"Does not answer my question," Nealen pressed. "Where did you get them?"

"We acquired them."

"Obviously. How though, is a matter which I need to know. Especially given the new directive from the RC-Southwest commander that we are not to have such in our possession."

"Staff Sergeant, did you know that there are Army route clearance teams based out of Delaram?" Cassidy asked.

"Which has what to do with these grenades?" Nealen demanded.

"The army boys don't fall under RC-Southwest."

"Oh?"

"Yes, Staff Sergeant. These belong to a command all the way down in Iraq," Kramer added.

"I wouldn't have guessed that," Nealen admitted.

"Did you know that soldiers really like playing poker, Staff Sergeant?" Cassidy said cheerfully.

"We're not supposed to be gambling money in-country. Falls under General Order One," Nealen ground out through clenched teeth.

"Right alongside no alcohol and no sex," Cassidy admitted. "We remember the briefing from CID, Staff Sergeant."

"They should know, they are the most crooked personnel in the Corps," Kramer groused.

"I am about to butt stroke the two of you chuckle fucks if you don't stay on topic."

"There was no money on the table, staff sergeant," Kramer assured.

"Go on," Nealen growled

"Well while this totally free poker game was going on, would it surprise you to know that soldiers will gamble supplies if they can't cover bets they're not making with money they never had?" Cassidy asked.

Nealen closed his eyes. "I think I'm not hearing something I would definitely dislike."

"The honest, upright soldiers of the US Army would never bet cases of forty millimeter grenades," Cassidy quipped.

"Against what?" Nealen demanded. "One of our seven-tons? A .50-cal?"

"There were never Krugerrands passed across the table," Cassidy solemnly declared.

"You know, the gold coins from South Africa," Kramer added helpfully

"I know what they are. What I want to know is how you got them. No. Wait." Nealen held up his left hand to forestall a comment. "I'm better off not knowing."

"Yes, Staff Sergeant. And all five grenadiers in the platoon are not carrying six rounds to use as necessary," Hondo assured. "Nor are we holding rounds in reserve in case everything goes sideways with a quickness. Like we know it's going to."

Nealen slowly opened his eyes. "We are going to pretend this conversation never happened. We are going to pray to Almighty God that there never emerges a need for the use of these grenades we never obtained. And when we leave country?"

"There better not be any coming back with us?" Cassidy suggested.

"Get out of my sight before I stab you in the throat," Nealen ordered.

"Yes, Staff Sergeant," the Marines parroted.

As they mounted their trucks, Nealen struggled to control his spiking blood pressure.

You're all crazy! Utterly fracking nuts! I swear you assholes are going to put me in an early grave. He breathed.

"Dammit! I'm gonna need to spend a day in confession saying Hail Mary's and Our Fathers till I pass out at this rate."

He breathed again. *Damn I love this job.*

\#

Sylvie Lyons ascended the guard post steps carefully, trying hard to keep the cardboard trays and steaming styrofoam cups of tea properly balanced.

"Oi, Sergeant Lyons, that you?" a tired voice called out from atop the guard post.

"It is, MacIntosh. Brought you and Carter some lunch and a fresh cuppa apiece before you go off post."

"You're a saint!" MacIntosh crooned. Grabbing one of the cups he sipped deeply. "Oh that's lovely. By the by, have you heard the good news?"

"The Taliban call it quits and decide to go back to buggering goats permanently?" Sylvie asked.

"I wish but nah," MacIntosh said.

"The mullahs finally decided to treat the testimony of women as equal to a man's?"

"Too much to hope for," Carter opined.

"How about the right to vote and the right to drive unescorted or be seen in public without a male family member?"

Both men shook their heads negatively.

"Well then I'm all out of ideas!" Sylvie groused.

"Somebody paid attention during the cultural education briefs," Carter muttered.

"Normally, I'm inclined to make a joke about women's lib," MacIntosh said earnestly. "Right now I get the distinct impression that would be a bad idea."

"You've only got two testicles, MacIntosh. And I've got a thirty-round magazine." Her smile turned glacial. "Care to try your luck?"

"Not on your life, Sarn't. Mariah wants to start a family when we get home. Hard to do when me Crown Jewels 'ave been shot to Timbuktu!"

"So, what is the good news?" Sylvie asked far more lightly.

"Captain Fitzsimmons called higher, and they finally got back to her with word of reinforcements."

"So?"

"We're getting reinforced by Marines!" MacIntosh exclaimed.

"Why on earth would they send a bunch of Her Majesty's Jollies down to this shite heap?" Sylvie asked.

"God loves us?" Carter suggested.

"Eh. I mean I could see a company of The Rifles. Buncha riflemen would be nice around here. But bootnecks? That's almost overkill!" Sylvie exclaimed.

"I wouldn't complain about having overkill on our side for once," Carter said dourly as he finished off his lunch.

"Still beats the blazes out of getting a pack of Rockapes," MacIntosh opined. "I'm certain they could screw up a wet dream."

#

Midday post was boring. Sylvie preferred it because she had the post to herself, with nobody to bother her. Grease pencil in hand, she could find ways and means to keep herself entertained, as she looked across the sprawling red-tan vista.

Sylvie turned to see what her fellow soldier was pointing at. Coming up over the ridge by way of Route Blue was a sand-tan up-armored vehicle. Further behind it, rising into the sky was an impossibly large cloud of dirt and sand.

"Ops. This is Post One," Sylvie declared.

"Send it, Post One."

"Vehicles approaching over Route Blue. Look like up-armoreds."

"Can you get a count?"

"There's two, make that three in sight. Hard to see behind them with all that dirt and dust."

"Flying any flags?"

"One moment, let me check."

Sylvie looked down to where the two gate guards had their own post in the entrance to the serpentine. "Wadeson, get up here!"

"Aye, Sergeant!"

As he scanned the area, Sylvie continued to give her report.

"Post One, any word on markings?"

"Wadeson," Sylvie said impatiently.

"I'm looking," Wadeson declared, peering at each vehicle through his high-powered binoculars. "Wait, is that... Sergeant, tell me what you think that is, middle vehicle, on the turret."

The black flag which greeted her gaze flapped cheerfully. A white skull over crossed cutlasses, popping in the wind stream of the big truck's passage.

"A pirate flag," Sylvie proclaimed.

"That's what I thought. But aren't we a little far inland for pirates?" Wadeson asked.

"Ops, this is Post One. Only flag in sight is a pirate flag."

"Not funny Post One."

"I'm not joking."

"Echo Five Lima, if this were anybody else, I'd tell you to put yourself on report."

"Well best hurry, they look like they're coming straight for us."

"Ops copies all."

"I hope to God it's friendlies. Wadeson, get back down there and prepare to receive company."

#

"Sergeant, what's the plan once we get there?" Corporal Logan, Cassidy's driver, asked as their vehicle bore down on the gate of the FOB. Behind them, two more vehicles, a seven-ton Oshkosh and a massive Cougar MRAP, carried the rest of the advanced party.

"I'm gonna go talk to them."

"That works for me."

"Glad to have your approval," Cassidy harrumphed.

"Why are you always mad, dammit!" Logan demanded.

"What do you mean? I don't feel mad."

"How? Don't matter what we're doing. I've seen you angry at breakfast!" Logan protested.

"So?"

"I know brothers who are hard all the time. But even they need time to warm up! Meanwhile, you over here beefing with bacon!"

"So?"

"How can you be angry all the time?" Logan exasperated.

"It's a gift," Cassidy growled. Lifting the radio, he clicked the talk button. "FDC, this is Five Actual."

"Send it."

"I'm gonna hop out and go talk to the gate guards."

"Roger."

"While I do that, watch for tangos. Somebody had to have seen us driving this way."

"Given our numbers, they'll think we're easy targets." Kramer finished.

"Exactly. Five Actual out." He dropped the handset back in its cradle, listening as Kramer began snapping orders at the vehicle crews.

"Wait, you really are gonna go play diplomat?" Logan said worriedly, half paying attention as he slewed the truck around so that the vehicle's bulk was between Hondo and the open desert beyond.

Next to them, a hundred meters away, Kramer's vehicle did the same, followed by the FDC truck. Under normal procedure, they would've formed a herringbone. With slight modification, what they had done provided an ideal form of defense. Each truck was broadside on to the open desert on their flank, allowing not only the crew-served weapons but the riflemen in the rear cargo compartment to present arms at any possible threats.

"Who me? Diplomat? Perish the thought!" Hondo said lugubriously.

"Who thought this was a good idea?" Logan demanded.

"Me," Hondo said more conversationally as he removed his Kevlar helmet. "I want this done right. And Staff Sergeant ain't real particular about how the job is done. So long as it gets done."

"But — but — but, why you?" Logan said exasperatedly.

"I used to live in the UK. Know the culture, and the language."

"They speak English," Logan pointed out.

"Nah. It's different," Hondo insisted.

"How?"

"Remember high school Spanish class?"

"Yeah."

"That's Castellano. The proper stuff they speak back in Spain."

"So what do we speak?"

"American English is more like the Spanish you hear construction workers use."

Logan mulled over this for a moment. "So nothing proper about it?"

"Hasn't been proper since seventeen seventy-five. Watch my back and be ready to move when Kramer tells you," Hondo ordered.

#

What sauntered into Sylvie's view looked odd. She'd watched through her rifle scope as the large tan vehicle slewed around, so it was facing mostly away from FOB's serpentine. A door opened, slammed shut. A man appeared, walking towards the gate, rifle casually held just forward of the mag well. The symbol on the center of his chest looked like the Marine emblem, but what gollywog rifle was he carrying instead of a proper L85A2?

"Afternoon. Is this FOB Bourne?" he asked loudly in a very proud *American* accent.

"Aye, but who are you to be asking after it?" Coughlan asked.

"Name's Cassidy. Me and my buddies were told to come lend y'all some help."

"You're Americans!"

"Yeah. Last time I checked. And you are?"

"Coughlan. This one's Wadeson."

"We were told we'd be getting Marines!" Wadeson protested suddenly.

"You were?" Cassidy asked casually.

"Uh huh. Why'd we get the American bleeding Army on our doorstep?"

#

"*Ops, this is Post One.*"

"Send it Post One."

"*We need Sierra Mike Mike at the front gate ASAP.*"

Within the command post, personnel looked at each other. Colour Sergeant Gallagher glanced at Mayne, who cocked an eyebrow before returning his attention to the still-steaming tea he was sipping.

"Why?"

"Because we've got an angry American beasting the bollocks off Coughlan and Wadeson. And I haven't finished deciding if I need to shoot him."

Sergeant Major Mayne choked and coughed, showering not only the table but Captain Fitzsimmons, with hot tea.

"Of course the bloody Americans decide to show up and ruin tea time! Because why wouldn't they?" Mayne grumbled as he stood. "Impertinent colonial upstarts can't just leave a man in peace, can they?"

Mayne wasn't the only person who came over to see what all the noise was about coming from the gate. What the crowd saw when they drew near was almost comical. Coughlan and Wadeson were in the front leaning rest position, alternately driving their legs towards their chest while a very irate American bellowed at them in a voice that sounded entirely too *Welsh* at times. Dust flew every which way as he jumped around, knife hand punctuating his statement. Even from several meters away Mayne could hear him quite clearly.

"I don't know what planet you two gob shite wanking pieces of monkey filth came from, but we're on Earth! And nowhere on planet Earth does an eagle-globe-and-foul-weather motherfracking anchor equal the Allah-damned US Army! Are your legs getting tired *seu filho de puta?*"

"No!" Wadeson whined.

"They must be, you're not moving them very quickly! We'll fix that! On your backs, leg lifts, begin!"

As they complied he bent at the waist so that all three men could clearly see each other.

"Do you see my chevrons?" Cassidy demanded. "How many are there?"

"Three!"

"That's fracking right and don't stop! I didn't give you permission, Clown Shoes!"

Legs began to rise once more as he continued his lecture. "Now, who knows what three chevrons means?"

"That you're a Sergeant?" Coughlan shouted.

"That's right, laddy! I'm a bleeding Sergeant! Better yet, I'm a Sergeant of Marines! Not some army dog who has to ask permission to piss before he raises his leg!"

"This is slightly amusing," Colour Sergeant Gallagher admitted drolly as she walked up on the scene and stood beside Mayne. Nordic, stern, and a hair too trim or fit to ever be mistaken for "svelte," Morgana Gallagher would not have looked out of place amongst a band of battle axe-wielding einherjaren. She was also incredibly competent and capable in her duties.

For this, Mayne and Gallagher got along very well. A great deal of respect passed both ways — she left him to handle the personnel and logistical matters, Mayne left to her the matter of training, and rarely if ever did the two find a matter to disagree upon. Captain Fitzsimmons was the company commander, no doubt about it, but if pressed, every soldier in the company knew who the Queen was.

"Ain't it though? I put these two on gate guard for screwing up that lift yesterday. Figured some time in the sun would be good for them," Mayne admitted.

"Oh, that is ironic. Should we rescue them yet?" Gallagher asked.

"Not quite, I think he's just getting warmed up."

"Aye, and it's lovely to hear a Sergeant give a proper arse chewing," Gallagher admitted.

"Just wish this had happened before breakfast. Imagine this while enjoying your morning cuppa?"

"Sounds grand." Gallagher looked at the swelling crowd of onlookers. "Pistol is looking a tad antsy."

She pointedly did not look in the direction of Number One Company's lone sapper. Sergeant Henry Pistol had strong opinions on everything, up to and including his elaborately waxed mustachio, the tips of which curled around neatly to give the well-muscled sergeant the appearance of an old-time circus strongman.

"Aye." Mayne stepped forward. "Can't be having Pistol take a swing at our visitors now, can we?"

"No, that wouldn't do. Not at all." Morgana looked from Pistol to the American.

On second thought, that one looks like he can take a punch from Pistol she reconsidered. *And my Pistol is not a small lad either.*

Mayne started walking forward, whistling a wordless tune he'd learned long ago on Malta as a young boy.

"Afternoon, Sergeant, how can I help you this fine day?" Mayne asked

The American stopped moving and looked toward Mayne before jumping to parade rest.

"Good afternoon, sir!"

"American Marines," Mayne shook his head. "When in doubt you will call a lamp post, sir."

"Yes, sir. Bad habit, sir. Will happen again, sir."

"It's Company Sergeant Major, which is the same as your First Sergeant. Sarn't Major will do just fine in the meantime, lad."

"Sarn't Major, I —" Coughlan began.

"Shut up, Coughlan. The adults are talking," Mayne ordered.

"Yes, Sarn't Major!"

"Now, how can I help you, Sergeant?"

"My platoon was told to assist your company as best we could by standing guard posts, and shooting everybody that needs to meet God."

"Is this your whole platoon?" Stirling asked.

"No, Sarn't Major, just the advanced party. We're a single Gun plus FDC."

"What kind of unit are you?" Mayne asked, puzzled by his answer.

"Artillery, Sarn't Major. We left the tubes behind, but kept all of our men and —"

"Contact! Twelve o'clock!" the younger man's radio snapped, only a moment before rounds began cracking overhead and sparking off the seven-ton trucks' up-armored hulls. The Marine turned to assess the threat before he was warned off by that same voice.

"Go handle the fracking Limeys! I got these assholes!" a man's voice bellowed out of the radio handset. The mic was still keyed open as he turned his attention to the marines firing at their assailants from open ports on the starboard side of their respective trucks.

"Pour it onto 'em you sons a bitches!" he ordered. *"Make your guns talk!"*

One soul, braver than his comrades tried rising up, RPG in hand. Before he could let fly, the combined fire of several rifles struck him, shredding his body into bloody gobbets across the red sand.

"Remember, boot to ass. Do not piss on them," Hondo barked into his radio.

An RPG arced outwards, followed by a contrail of smoke. It tipped over, coming down well short of the marines.

"Teach yo' grandmammy to make biscuits!" the same voice replied.

KA-THUNK THUNK THUNK THUNK THUNK.

The Mark Nineteen mounted on the FDC truck made itself heard. Each high-velocity grenade, itself the weight of a beer can, was a marvel not only of modern engineering, but what the gunner manning it could achieve. These reached their target, dropping down and into the shallow swell where the Taliban had ensconced themselves, before erupting as their fuzes triggered.

Mayne watched the firefight and the marine sergeant standing in front of him. He calmly waited, watching as the men on the trucks engaged the Taliban with a withering fire. Not one of the three trucks had moved before the grenades erupted. A secondary blast lit up the afternoon sky and Mayne smiled.

"They won't be using those RPGs anymore."

"I agree, Sarn't Major," the marine replied, holding an open bag towards him. "Care for a piece? It's moose jerky."

"Moose?"

"Big ass deer with attitude issues."

"Ah. Very well. I'll try a bite." Taking a chunk, Stirling bit into the meat, delighting at the flavor.

"Very nice." He arched an eyebrow as Hondo continued to watch the machine gunners blaze away, occasionally asking questions over his radio. Finally, he lifted the strange rifle he was holding up to his shoulder, scanning the area back and forth. "All elements, all elements this is Gun Five Actual. Victor Charlies, sound off."

"FDC loud and clear. Green green up."

"Ammo, green green up."

"This is Lexus, green green up."

"All units, maintain watch for nasties, and reload. Good work."

He turned to face Stirling. "Sarn't Major, would you happen to have a use for a buncha heartbreakers and lifetakers?"

"How many of you are there?"

"One Staff Sergeant, seventy-nine NCOs and enlisted, one Navy Corpsman. Eighty-one of us all told."

Mayne blew out a breath. "We were told we'd be getting Marines and assumed it was a squad or two of Royal Marines. We did not prepare for a platoon of American Marines."

"I can see how that'd be a problem Sarn't Major. If it helps, we brought our own tents and such, we didn't know what you'd have on hand."

"You have them with you?"

"Yes Sergeant Major. On the 7-ton back thataway." Cassidy gestured for his benefit and Stirling smiled tightly.

"Oh good. That makes this far simpler. How much time do we have till the rest of your unit arrives?"

"Probably a couple hours at most, Sarn't Major. They stopped in Garmsir for fuel but Staff Sergeant Nealen ain't the kind to waste daylight. We'll also need an ammo bunker."

"For what?"

"Small arms resupply. It's all on pallets. Spread the load across the platoon."

"How much are we talking about?" Mayne asked, puzzled.

"Fourteen tons of small arms stuff. Figured you'd need some extra."

"I can appreciate that."

"Oh, yeah, forgot, we'll need some extra space for the big stuff," Hondo added hastily.

"Big stuff?"

"Call it a hundred-twenty, mebbe a hundred-thirty-ish rounds of one-five-five."

"On top of the fourteen tons of whatever else you brought?"

"Uh-huh."

"You drove all the bloody way across Helmand with that fooking load? Why don't ya just run through a house fire with detcord in your hair and bangalores in your arms?"

Cassidy gave a positively Gaelic shrug. "Marine, Sarn't Major. If I was a sensible man I'd be home in bed, getting a leg over."

"I'll give you that one," Mayne admitted. "But why the artillery ammo? There aren't any guns out here."

"The ammo point at Delaram couldn't fit anymore in, so we had to keep it with us."

"I'll bet you a hundred quid the lazy buggers had room, they just didn't want to fill out the paperwork."

The ghost of a smile passed over Cassidy's face, "Sucker bet, Sarn't Major. I wouldn't touch that, even at five to one."

"How about seven to one?" Stirling suggested.

"Nothing less than twenty," Hondo countered.

"Ah. Bugger that for a lark." Mayne breathed in, smiled, letting his thoughts collect themselves as he determined the best course of action. "Still, enough about that for the moment. Why don't we get all of your trucks inside the perimeter then go pick out spots for quarters?"

"Thank you kindly, Sarn't Major."

"Colour Gallagher!" Mayne shouted.

"Yes Sarn't Major!"

"We need spots for —"

"Five tents."

"Five tents, and a full platoon of vehicles in the motor pool. The rest of them should be along shortly."

As Gallagher began snapping orders to heavy equipment operators, the American signaled for his driver to come through on ground guide. Mayne turned to go when he noticed both Wadeson and Coughlan staring in shock, looking for all the world like tourists on holiday.

"Oi, you two, what are you doing?" Mayne demanded.

"Thought we was done —" Coughlan began.

"Did the Sergeant give you an order?"

"Yes, Sarn't Major!"

"Then I suppose you better keep moving! I'd hate to think you were weak and tired already, Coughlan!" Mayne clucked his tongue disapprovingly. "What are they doing at Pirbright these days that you two graduated?"

Chapter 4

Now We Call It The Cadillac Ranch

Captain Fitzsimmons felt much better about the tactical situation two hours later as she watched a long stream of olive-drab and tan vehicles rolling over the horizon toward her position.

They're not Royal Marines, she told herself. *Which would be very nice indeed.*

"But they'll do. Because it's all we've got. They'll have to do."

"Ma'am?" Lyons asked, from a spot beside her in the guard post.

"Just musing aloud Lyons."

"Yes ma'am."

"Tell me, what did you think of the Americans?"

"I can't say as I liked that one Sergeant."

"I detect a "but" there. In your tone."

"Coughlan and Wadeson rather deserved the beasting ma'am. Saves one of us having to do it later."

"Indeed. Think they'll fit in? The Americans?"

Sylvie thought about the attempted attack and the swift reply which had ended it.

"Can't hurt to try ma'am. God knows we need the help."

\#

"Echo-Six November, this is Gun Five Actual."

"Send it!" Nealen announced over the radio, happy to be in range of the gun chief once again.

"We've got space made in the motor pool, engineers are assembling an ammo bunker for us right now. All tents are up and ready to go. With power."

"That's good work."

"Soon as you drop the units we can hook up the A/C and we'll be set."

"Outstanding, that's what I like to hear."

"Echo-Six November, roll over."

Shifting the radio's channel knob over to a prearranged private channel the two men used to discuss business, Nealen keyed the thumb button again,

"Five Actual, this is Echo-Six November, how copy?"

"Solid Copy. Did anybody mention to you that this site is full of wookies?" Cassidy asked seriously.

This question surprised Nealen, and he frowned.

"Say again your last."

Nealen could've sworn he'd just heard the Corps' unofficial slang term for "Woman Marines." A phrase verboten elsewhere, but entirely common to hear in an all-male combat arms unit.

"Echo-Six November we got whiskey oscar oscar kilo india echo sierras all over our position. We need to have a chat with the boys pronto when y'all get here."

"Echo-Six-November copies all." Nealen set down the handset then began mentally swearing as he contemplated how he was going to handle this.

Some days, I really hate this job.

\#

Trucks surged down the road, barreling for the gates where men waited, rifles slung across their backs. Sylvie had heard mutterings, enlisted men complaining as such are wont to do when they have time on their hands, and then that angry Sergeant came back, the one who'd berated Wadeson and Coughlan so badly. He wore neither helmet nor body armor, simply a floppy boonie cover and that severe scowl. She watched him pull a bag of something from one pocket, pour its contents into his mouth, then drop the bag back into his pocket. His cheek had swollen precipitously and she watched him move his tongue around before spitting something onto the dirt.

One of the Marines asked him a question that disappeared on the wind. What she did hear was a snarled reply: "Push boy! Beat the ground to death with that filthy face of yours!"

"Cheerful sort of fellow, aren't you?" Sylvie asked herself sarcastically.

"Hey Post! Guard Post!" he bellowed.

"What?" Sylvie retorted.

"See any Taliban in need of shooting?"

"Not yet. We'll let you know if that changes," Sylvie assured.

He turned back to the marine who'd addressed him. "Recover, numb nuts."

"Yes, Sergeant."

"Now if Ali Baba and the Forty muthafrackin' Taliban get so close they can shoot me in the chest with an AK, we got problems. In the meantime, I ain't wearing a flak and kevlar unless I need to." Something crunched in his mouth and he spat onto the dirt. "And I don't see any fracking need, you feel me?"

As trucks rolled inside the gate, they were greeted by their respective guides, each getting the particular driver's attention then sprinting toward what Sylvie's fellow engineers were already calling "MarineLand" as some wag had put up signage declaring. Colour Gallagher busily directed the engineers putting finishing touches on the new tentage. The Marines, it was rumored, were even bringing extra air conditioning units and loaded fuel trucks, all of which would be appreciated.

The rumors would survive the first few weeks, at least. She didn't care. Even if it meant some eye candy, which all of the women were getting excited about.

Don't have a man, don't need one. Though that one Marine is a nicely proper bastard, she admitted. *Besides, he probably calls football "soccer" and couldn't keep pace with rugby. Like every other damn colonial.*

#

"Platoon, formation on me!" Nealen ordered.

In front of Nealen, all the sections drew up in neat ranks.

"Report!"

"Gun Four, up!"

"Gun Five, up!"

"Gun Six, up!"

"FDC, up!"

"Comm, up!"

"Motor-T, up!"

"Supply, up!"

"At ease, gents, welcome to FOB Bourne. This is home now."

"Kinda ugly, Staff Sergeant!" Sergeant House, the comm chief declared.

"No argument from me. We're at the edge of the Rigestan. You wanna know what that is, go ask Cassidy."

"He knows everything, Staff Sergeant!" House replied.

"Not everything!" Johnson argued. "He doesn't know how to eat pussy!"

This kicked off a round of laughter amongst the Marines and even Cassidy smiled at his fellow sergeant's wit.

"Be careful Johnson, Cass is smiling," Nealen cautioned.

"Don't you put that curse on me, Ricky Bobby!" Johnson shrieked.

More laughter followed and Nealen smiled. Marines who could still laugh and joke were in a good place mentally. He also saw what looked like officious persons walking towards the platoon.

"Lock it up and listen good!" Nealen ordered, then paused, giving them a moment to comply. "There are women here. We do not need woman problems. We don't need international trouble neither. Keep your hands, and your rude comments to yourselves. We understand?"

"Yes, Staff Sergeant!" the Marines echoed.

"Good. Remember this — if you are dumb enough to put a hand on a woman here, and she shoots you, it's your own damn fault. If any of you rape a woman, it's a big damn desert and you won't be missed, except on paperwork. I certainly will not miss you. Not at this range. Understand me?"

"Yes, Staff Sergeant!"

"Good. Starting tomorrow, we begin position improvements. Jimenez!"

"Yes, Staff Sergeant?"

"You are local security chief. I want a roster for all guard posts by lunch tomorrow. Corporals and below will stand watch. Sergeants and above will handle Sergeant of the Guard. You are in charge of it all. Understood?"

"Si, Staff Sergeant!"

"Bueno. Cassidy, you've lived in England, for what, two years? You've got two minutes to give a hip pocket class on differences between England and America. Get your ass up here and start talking!"

Cassidy ran in front of the formation then faced the platoon.

"Item the first, it's called football or footie, not soccer. The diehards get pissy about this. Either way, it's overrated. If I wanted to watch men fail to score for hours at a time, I'd follow you clowns into a gay bar on ladies' night."

This brought on laughter from the men, and sideways glances at erstwhile offenders.

"Item the second: a lot of them call us colonials. Never mind that my Injun ancestors were raiding the Plains before Elizabeth the First sat on the throne. Roll with it and smile."

"They use a lot of words we don't. One is this word."

He said it, causing the platoon to goggle at him. Cassidy was not known for being explicitly profane, or anywhere near that vulgar.

"This word is normal," he explained. "It does not carry the same significance which we ascribe to it. Men greet each other using this word. Just the same way we use 'devil' or 'devil dog.'"

"Are we Brits?" Nealen asked from the side.

"We're Americans!" Johnson announced.

"Damn straight. Anytime you drop that, you will be dropped. We tracking, devils?"

"Yes, Staff Sergeant!" the platoon sounded off.

"Good, carry on Cassidy. What's something we say that would offend them?"

"Thank you Staff Sergeant. Fanny — don't use it. We think it's normal. That's how you get buttstroked. Also, tea time is normal. Good manners dictate that they invite us to participate. Roll with it and be polite. Remember we brought plenty of coffee for us."

"'Merica!" Tolliver shouted.

"Oh yeah, junior officers are Leftenants. Not Lieutenants. And the head honcho I talked to earlier with the red mustache is the company-level Sarn't Major. Same as a First Sergeant, different title."

"Customs and courtesies still apply, use them," Nealen cautioned. "I can always find use for new sandbags."

"At this time, are there any questions?" Cassidy surveyed the platoon. "Going once, going twice, We're done, Staff Sergeant."

"Good trash, give him one!"

"ERR!" the platoon shouted as Cassidy ran back to his spot in the formation.

"Afternoon, Ma'am. Sir." Nealen greeted the Brits standing near him.

"Do American Marines not salute officers any more?" Fitzsimmons asked.

"Ma'am, they're under arms," Mayne declared. "Marines believe saluting under arms is a signal to snipers as to who needs to be shot first."

"Oh, I wasn't aware you did that. My apologies," Fitzsimmons declared.

"No worries, ma'am, it happens." Nealen put forward his hand. "Peter Nealen, Staff Sergeant."

"Thank you Staff Sergeant."

"Would you like to address the men, ma'am?" Peter invited.

"If that's alright with you."

"By all means."

The Marines looked her over as she walked to where they'd all hear her. Short brunette hair, short of height, trim, and fit. She looked competent— how she held up to that expectation remained to be seen.

"Afternoon lads. I hear you had a nice drive down here."

"It sucked, ma'am!" a voice called out from the crowd.

"I'll bet. My name is Fitzsimmons. I'm the Captain in charge here at Bourne. We've been taking it in the teeth for nearly two months straight. I already have multiple dead and wounded. Two more went to the hospital at your Ramstein Air Force Base this week. We don't know if they'll survive. We need your help. Tomorrow, we'll start working on getting you up to speed. Tonight, you're welcome to dine with us in the mess and settle in. Thank you for coming down to help."

"Give her one!" Nealen barked.

"Errr!"

"Staff Sergeant, if you'd care to join us in the CP, we'll discuss the situation with you," Fitzsimmons politely invited.

"Roger that ma'am, what time is chow at?"

"Evening dinner should be at seventeen-thirty."

"Cassidy, Johnson, I want the platoon formed up outside the chow hall no later than seventeen twenty-five."

"Oorah, Staff Sergeant."

"Dismissed!"

Sergeant Johnson waited until Nealen and the Brits were well out of earshot before he called out to his fellow non-coms. "Hey NCOs, gather on around heah on me."

As men circled up, he lit up a cigarette.

"Whatcha want, Okie?" House, the bespectacled comm sergeant, asked good naturedly.

Johnson took a long drag. "Well Tex, I don't know about you, but I feel like putting on a show."

"Yeah, what are you thinking, Sergeant?" Tolliver asked.

"Ever heard about how the young bull and the old bull scored themselves a whole herd of sweet heifers? It's my favorite story," Johnson rejoined, then explained his plan.

#

"Seen any of the Yanks yet?" Sandra asked cheerfully as she stood in line waiting for evening chow service.

"Nope. Well aside from that one angry bastard while I was on the front post, nothing."

"Wonder if they're as wild as the rumors say?" another woman declared.

"What rumors are those?"

"Well apparently they're all sex-starved psychos who'll do anything for a good roll around."

"Sure. That's what they all say," Sylvie replied cynically.

"Oh come off it Lyons! You just need a proper bloke to sweep you off your feet already."

"No I don't, I'm too busy for that nonsense," her cynical voice declared. "And that's final!"

Further away from them, in the smoke pit, the Company Sergeant Major was getting acquainted with the new Platoon Sergeant assigned to him.

"How long have your lads been out here now?"

"Just over three months."

"Enjoying yourselves?"

"If we're being honest, yeah. Mostly."

"Mostly?"

"Don't get me wrong, they're good guys, my devils."

"But they have their moments."

"Yes. And trying to keep some semblance of civility is hard. Ever watched puppies playing in mud?"

"One of the little buggers starts up, and soon the whole damn litter is tracking mud all over your clean floors," Stirling chuckled at this.

"Ah, a man experienced with such actions."

"Indubitably."

"I'm glad you understand." Nealen replied.

"One does what one must."

"Some of their mustaches are so out of control it's like watching an '80s porno!" Nealen groused.

"How'd they get around Delaram?" Mayne asked.

"Carefully. And we weren't there for more than forty-eight hours. Otherwise some pissy SOB with a starched cover might've come after us."

"Quite."

"It was a president's wife who said it real well."

"Oh?"

"The Marines I have seen around the world have the cleanest bodies, the filthiest minds, the highest morale, and the lowest morals of any group of animals I have ever seen." He gestured toward the compound where he'd left his platoon. "Just wish they'd quit living down to bad expectations."

Nealen stripped the remnants of his cigarette apart and dropped it in the smoke butt. "I really don't know what's going to happen between now and December."

"Your left! Your left! Your left, right, left!" a voice bellowed and as one the body of personnel waiting for chow turned to see its source.

They came out across the motor pool, marching in time with their weapons held at port arms. Tanned and burned faces staring straight ahead, their boot heels struck the ground in a procession of thunder as they moved.

The earth was hard packed from constant traffic. No dust rose to obscure the view of eighty men moving in metronomic procession. Corporal Tolliver, ever the drill enthusiast, had taken charge of the platoon, putting them through the various close-order commands.

"Well. That's impressive," Stirling admitted.

As the platoon drew nearer, Nealen thought something seemed off, though he couldn't place a finger on what was different —

"Good Lord, they even shaved!" Nealen breathed. "I don't see a mustache amongst them."

"Maybe they're living up to the hype?" Mayne suggested.

"It'd be a nice change of pace."

"Think they mean to give us a show?" Sandra asked.

"What could they possibly do that would be entertaining?"

"Tolliver, give me a cadence!" Nealen called from the smoke pit.

"Aye aye Staff Sergeant!" Tolliver seemed to take in the crowd watching before he drew a breath.

"When I get to hell, Satan he will say
How'd you earn your living boy?
How'd you earn your pay?
I'll reply as I point to my bod
Earned my living on a killing squad!
I'll reply as I point to my chest,
Earned my living in the leaning rest!"
"Platoon! Halt!"
"Double arm interval, move!"
"Open ranks!"
"Stack arms!"

"Half right face. Pushup position, move!" Tolliver ordered. "We don't need slack fat bodies. Your first exercise will be Marine Corps pushups! I will count the cadence, you will count the repetition. We will do many of them. Ready? Begin!"

After twenty four-count pushups, Tolliver had them recover to the standing position.

"Sergeant Cassidy, front and center," Tolliver announced.

Groans accompanied this announcement. The new exercise began, and the onlookers watched with mounting curiosity as arms still sore from pushing beneath the bright sun began performing what the now-infamous Sergeant Cassidy called "Sun Gods."

"I'm not entirely sure if that's healthy," a woman noted.

"Cooper, I don't care if it's healthy," another engineer declared as she watched the men in action. "After four months in garrison getting lectured at and two months here, I'm ready for anything that doesn't involve batteries. Especially if they're as good at fighting as they are at marching."

"Which one do you think you'll go for?" Sandra asked.

"Oh I don't know, depends on how hungry he looks. What about you, Sergeant Lyons?"

"I think you're all insane."

"Oh come on, what's the worst that could happen?" another woman asked.

"Finding Mr. Right in Afghanistan. Sure. Like that could ever happen outside one of your cockamamie smut romances!" Sylvie snorted derisively.

"Platoon, atten-hut!" Tolliver ordered. "Unstack arms."

The men snapped to attention, rifles now held at their sides.

There was space between each of the marines, who looked forward with sharp, silent miens as they went about their business, aligning to the man on their right.

Sylvie noticed for the first time that many wore extra magazines, either on their belts or in thigh rigs. They also carried bayonets in belt sheaths.

Are they serious, or trying to show off thinking some macho bullshit will impress us? She wondered.

When the marines finished adjusting, Tolliver made an about face.

"Belligerent Second formed for inspection, Staff Sergeant."

"Sergeant Major, would you care to join me?"

"My pleasure, Nealen."

Trooping up and down the lines, they found nothing seriously wrong. Returning to where Tolliver stood, Mayne made his approval known.

"Tolliver, give me a final cadence," Nealen ordered.

"Model A Ford and a tank full of gas!"

At once, the platoon repeated the line, bellowing it in reply.

"Mouth full of pussy and a handful of ass!" Tolliver yelled.

They must have known this was coming as the rejoinder fairly echoed across the FOB.

"See?" Sylvie said in disgust. "What did I tell you? Barbarians! The whole lot of them!"

Chapter 5

Let The Bodies Hit The Floor

Silent figures moved in the half-lit dark, headed toward the guard posts in groups of two and three men. All nine posts needed to be handled simultaneously.

Nealen watched the figures moving, seated as he was on the roof of the Command Post. Whoever had sited the building put it on the only elevated position in Forward Operating Base Bourne, with a protected observation point on top of that. Beside him, Cassidy had binoculars in hand as he examined the area. It was just light enough that a patient man could find a great deal as he studied the terrain. Whatever his personal issues, when a task came along, the burly man knew how to get it done. Which was also how he trained his section.

So many times Nealen reminded himself. *So damned many times the Taliban came at us, down at Zaranj thinking they could get the jump on us. And every time they learned the hard way to leave us alone.*

He smiled thinly, lighting up a cigarette as he listened to the guard posts reporting their status over the field phones.

The boys know their jobs. Just like I know mine. Thus my LT leaves me be.

Nealen groaned internally as he considered how much he missed Lieutenant Harper. His tall, well-cultured platoon commander had known to ask questions before and after, not during a task. Harper had been a welcome change from when he had first come to the battery nearly two years ago.

Jacob Hudson is the most miserable excuse for an officer I've ever seen after fourteen years in the Corps. He still takes the cake for "Walking Pile of Ass with Lieutenant's bars." I genuinely didn't know God and the Big Green Weenie could stack shit that tall or drunk, he reflected.

Not that Leftenant Balcombe seemed to be the bad sort. But she let her curiosity get the better of her, asking too many questions when he needed to be concentrating on his job.

"Echo-Six November, this is Local Suck. Everybody's up," Jimenez reported.

"Good work." Nealen eyed his watch. "Two minutes sixteen seconds. We can be faster, but that'll come with time."

"Aye aye," Jimenez said.

"All Sections, all sections, hydrate and wait for all-clear," Nealen announced into his handset.

Clipping the radio back to his vest, he smiled as he turned to face the eastern horizon.

Nearby, he could see the GBOSS camera dome slowly rotating in place as the FDC morning shift scanned an area beyond where normal eyesight could make out fine details, searching for possible enemy action.

"You lads normally do this?" Balcombe asked.

"Every day, ma'am."

"Why?"

"The best times to attack a position are after sunset, and just before dawn, when human reaction times ebb to their lowest."

"How do you prevent the enemy from doing that?"

"You're not going to stop an attempt to attack. That's why it's called an attempt. What you can do is prevent him from walking away afterwards. That's why they man the positions for one-half hour after dark, and one half hour before dawn"

She pursed her lips, mulling over what he said. "You're forcing the body to do something unnatural then."

"Eh, lots of things are unnatural."

"So you can respond to threats which never materialize."

"It ensures we have security when we need it the most," Nealen countered.

"Are you lot looking for a fight?" she asked after a moment.

Nealen watched Cassidy silently bristle before he shoved his binoculars at Nealen.

"Staff Sergeant, mind taking a look please?"

"What's up?"

"See that funny bush out there? Looks like a two-hump camel facing west. Yellow flowers on it. Sitting about eleven o'clock?" Hondo indicated, careful to keep his arm movement behind cover.

"Lemme see with your glasses — huh, yeah I see it."

"Go maybe a hundred meters beyond that. Something is moving around out there."

"Huh." Nealen scanned carefully. He could tell Cassidy was agitated, both by the scenario and by the Lieutenant's comments. *He does not suffer fools, my young sergeant*

He was almost ready to give up looking when he caught the flash of light.

Rather like that time in Ramadi when I caught that Chechen sniper looking at us through his scope.

Peter Nealen did not consciously realize his voice had shifted, or how his breathing had slowed, simply that he was back in *that* place.

"You see that, Cass?" Nealen asked the younger man, who by now was scanning through a spotting scope.

"Uh huh."

"How far is the range?"

"Laser says a monkey's testicle hair under one klick."

"What's your zero?"

"I'm set for eight."

"Roger. LT, take a seat, ma'am."

"Whatever for? You don't seriously think somebody is out there right now, do you?"

Nealen ignored her question. "FDC, this is Hogfather, need you to check a location."

"Send it."

"From my location," Nealen glanced at the range card Cassidy had drawn in grease paint for this particular area. "Bearing is tree-four-niner, range one klick."

"Roger that, we're on it."

Silence prevailed in the thick morning heat. Nealen made a gimme-motion to Hondo, taking his long rifle and tucking it into his shoulder, taking in the terrain as his mind began to run through the math involved.

At such a range, words such as "coriolis effect' and "ballistic arc" could be mentioned. The further one was shooting, the more factors came into play. He was fighting not only the light wind gently twisting through the brush, but Earth's gravity, the slight beat of his own heart, temperature, humidity, the fact that he was firing at a downward angle from an elevated position.

Thankfully, the M110 is chambered in 7.62 NATO, the same caliber as my M40A3. Now it's time for the Hogfather to go to work. Thank you, Oh Lord, for I have missed this. He smiled coldly. *Hogfather to Chicago, we are weapons free.*

Running a platoon was all fine and dandy, but Peter Nealen had come up through the ranks as a sniper. He missed being behind a rifle scope.

Might as well teach Cassidy how to do this stuff while I'm at it. He listens.

"Cassidy, what's my wind call?" Nealen asked.

"Two miles per hour," Cassidy replied.

Peering down the scope, Nealen concurred with the younger man's judgment.

"Good. It's a half value, so only half a mil click adjustment on the scope. What's our elevation?"

"Probably twenty meters."

"Sounds about right. If the range to target were under five hundred meters, we wouldn't need to adjust significantly enough to talk about it. This is, for all purposes, a thousand-meter shot. We're gonna need to set our point of aim low. Why?"

"Because the bullet will rise before it drops by the time it reaches the target."

"Exactly. Now, how many seconds of flight time do we have on this?"

"Ummm, I don't know."

"What're your mags loaded with?"

"Sierra MatchKings"

"Hundred seventy-five grain competition ammo?"

"Uh huh."

"What primer?"

"Federal Gold Medal."

Nealen rotated his head slightly so as to spare a glance for his younger charge. "I don't recall NAVSea Crane giving away crates of Mark 316 Mod 0. Or did you find this in a poker game too?"

Hondo, long used to angry glares, gave a positively Gallic shrug. "Internet is a vast place, staff sergeant."

"Uh-huh. Anyways. Projectile's flight time is ten seconds. 7.62 NATO is, by and large, slow compared to newer stuff."

"Newer stuff being .338 Lapua or Norma Magnum?"

"Exactly. Also, whoever tries to tell you that using those on people is a war crime —"

"They're lying or ignorant?" Cassidy suggested.

"Very." Nealen paused, glanced toward Cassidy. "Who told you that?"

"Remember during deployment work-ups when I had to go to Camp Pendleton after Mojave Viper, for the Designated Marksman Course?"

"The one I told the Ops-O you didn't need, because you'd already been a Designated Marksman since you were a Lance? And he ignored me?"

"Yeah, that one. Still good training." Cassidy shrugged. "Anyway, we had this Chief Warrant Officer Five, the one who ran the range, come and talk to our class. He mentioned that."

"What was his name?" Peter asked, suddenly curious.

"Curtis. Had a thick gray mustache —"

"He also have a strong southern accent? Loved driving fast cars?"

"Yeah, matter of fact he drove on to the range in a brand new Cadillac. You could hear the V-8 rumbling from half a mile away," Cassidy admitted, suddenly suspicious.

"I remember when he was the CWO-Two running the Sniper Instructor School in Quantico. He drove an Impala SS then. Car was damn fast," Nealen declared.

"He what?" Cassidy said in surprise. "Jeez, how long has he been in?"

"I won't say that Chief Curtis is older than dirt itself, but he might've given God the recipe for making mud."

"Shucks." Cassidy sat back in his seat, chewing thoughtfully on a piece of jerky he'd produced from somewhere on his ballistic vest.

Taking his time adjusting the magnification so he could properly see his target, Nealen identified what he thought might be an enemy sniper's position.

Canny little bastard, wonder if he's using a periscope to see from behind cover?

It wasn't a bad way to operate, the Germans and Brits had both used the technique in the trenches during the First World War.

But you've still got to come up to take the shot. And coyotes don't hunt where there's nothing to eat.

Cassidy must've been thinking the same thing as his platoon sergeant. Grabbing the four-pack of water bottles sitting on the deck, he took his helmet off, carefully placing it on the pack with the helmet's face open away from the space they'd been examining, and wrapping his green keffiyeh around it.

"Bait is set, Staff Sergeant," Cassidy declared as he resumed looking through the spotting scope.

Nealen's radio crackled.

"Hogfather, we've got somebody but he's playing real smart, recommend you keep an eye on this one."

"Understood."

Just as Hondo took his binoculars back, there came a *crack!* Water sprayed the observation post, dousing the inhabitants.

"I really hate when you're right like this!" Nealen shouted above Balcombe's terrified shrieks.

Balcombe started to rise before Cassidy clamped a hand on her shoulder and shoved her to the ground.

"Stay down!" He ordered.

Neither man followed this counsel though, taking positions so as to remain covered, rapidly searching for their quarry once more.

"Got him! Right where we thought he was!" Cassidy barked.

"Roger that."

The sound of a radio being used was loud, but Nealen pushed it aside, focused as he was.

BAM.

A heavy caliber round thumped into a wooden beam, causing Balcombe to scream, more likely from shock than pain.

Nealen felt, rather than heard the sound of Cassidy pulling Lieutenant Balcombe back down once again. If she protested further, he heard nothing. Nealen had learned well down in Zaranj — he didn't need to worry about Cassidy in a fight. If absolutely necessary, tell the man what you needed, but often enough, he could figure things out for himself.

"Cassidy, bait!" Nealen proclaimed.

"Aye, Staff Sergeant!"

Moments later, Nealen felt Cassidy slapping his thigh. The bait had been set.

"C'mon you pissant bastard, take it. Take it like you know you want to," Nealen muttered.

A long rifle barrel poked up over the edge of the hillock, slowly settling into place. It also gave Nealen exactly what he needed. Timing the flow of blood through his elbows with his breathing, he gently squeezed the trigger backwards. Something slammed into the observation post and he felt, but did not acknowledge the scraps of material which pattered against his face. There was a voice yelling. His ears failed to articulate the sound as anything more than merest background noise.

KRAK.

Through the scope, Nealen watched. Waited. Counted.

Seven Mississippi.

Eight Mississippi.

Nine Mississippi.

The still-visible rifle barrel jerked upwards, then fell back down. What blood spray he could see was minimal.

Fucker's likely using a ghillie suit of some kind, if he's not in a hide, for insurance.

Looking up from the rifle, he surveyed the holes in the heavy timbers.

It damn near worked.

Pushing on the rifle's safety, he passed it over to Cassidy, then retrieved his carbine.

"Toothless, this is Hogfather, I need two vehicles with the reaction squad mounted. On the double," Nealen announced into his radio.

"Roger that, they'll be ready at the gate," Johnson replied.

"Oscar mike." Nealen looked over at Cassidy.

"Sergeant Cassidy, I'm gonna go secure that asymmetrical asshole's gear. Don't want to leave it where the Taliban can get any ideas. You have the platoon till I return."

"Aye aye, Staff Sergeant."

Lieutenant Balcombe had not risen from her spot on the deck. Given that Cassidy had seated himself on top of her so she couldn't move, Nealen approved. It was hard to get up if you had most of two-hundred seventeen pounds of man and gear sitting on your rear end, stubbornly refusing to listen to any orders you gave him.

Either they'll decorate him, or court-martial him, Nealen declared, echoing a sentiment famous throughout the history of soldiering. *And today, I severely doubt it will be a court-martial.*

Balcombe's face held a flabbergasted look, brunette hair spilling everywhere as she stared at the marines in horror while Cassidy described the scene for her, in a deliberately calm voice.

"By your leave ma'am," Nealen declared.

"Yes, yes of course," Balcombe muttered absently.

Nealen started to walk away then stopped. "Sergeant, I wouldn't say the danger has passed, but there's no reason to keep the poor Leftenant on the deck."

Cassidy leapt to his feet, trying hard not to smile as he reached a hand down to help the Leftenant up.

"Probably bad for international relations, Staff Sergeant."

"Highly likely," Nealen agreed.

It was only as he trotted down the steps that Nealen realized why he'd seen her hair — the material which had rained down around him as he'd pulled the trigger was from the Leftenant's helmet.

Hondo Cassidy had forcibly removed her helmet to make a new bait for the enemy sharpshooter.

Peter Nealen had earned a living in his native Montana, shooting coyotes for farmers and ranchers to protect their herds. He understood exactly how one went about hunting for predators. And how one taught them to stay far away from potential prey.

Bait makes the coyotes come calling. Bullets make them die.

\#

"Well Mike, your lads made it there safely," Christian DuBois announced as he strolled into Michael Roach's office.

"Oh?"

"And by all accounts they've already gotten busy dealing with the riff raff giving us trouble."

DuBois dropped the papers he held onto Mike's desk.

"Read this."

Dropping into a chair, DuBois drank from a water bottle as Mike quickly scanned the report. When Mike set the papers down, Christian took them back.

"What do you think?" DuBois asked.

"Well, taking out the trash is one way to improve international goodwill."

"Quite. I'd like to buy your man Nealen a drink. Nice shooting. Especially as I've already watched the GBOSS footage."

"They caught it on camera?" Mike asked.

"Aye. And a lovely piece of work it was too." DuBois smiled. "I'll also add that helmets are a far sight cheaper than a new Leftenant or Sergeant."

"That they are. We can send out replacements from Supply on the next mail truck."

"Will you put him in for anything?"

"Nealen? Nah. Not for this. That'd be a cheap move. He already has a chestful of awards."

DuBois raised an eyebrow and Mike smiled cheerfully.

"He's a former Recon Marine. Rather like the Special Boat Service. He already spent the last decade and then some running around playing the younger man's game."

"Ah. Top draw that."

"Very. What I can do is award him an extra week worth of leave."

"Really?"

"Entirely within my remittance. And I have yet to meet an enlisted man who didn't like a few extra days off."

"Would you mind if I added a letter of commendation?" Christian asked.

"Not at all."

DuBois stood to leave then stopped.

"Mike, if this is what your lads can deliver, day in and day out, I will be very grateful indeed."

"We aim to please, Christian."

#

"I do not believe that Shamil will be returning."

The men spoke in hushed tones, even within the confines of the tent.

"The British killed him?"

"Worse. There was shooting from the FOB this morning."

If the group leader heard him, he said nothing as Aziz continued to speak, simply pouring tea for both of them.

"Not long after, vehicles emerged from the base and went to where Shamil had established a hide."

"Was he taken alive?"

"Unknown." Aziz sighed. "There was no way to see properly."

"The British are growing ambitious."

"Group Leader, I do not believe these were the British. Their uniforms looked distinctly American. And they carried M16s rather than Enfields."

"What color were the uniforms?"

"House. A light brown, almost like sand."

"Did they blend in well?"

"Far better than I saw up in Kunduz or Tora Bora."

The Group Leader set his teacup down.

"This is an unexpected development."

The Group Leader sighed.

"It is a very unwelcome development," he continued, trying to remain calm.

"Oh?"

"Those were definitely Americans."

"Why are you saying it that way?"

"Because I really wanted this particular group of Americans to stay far north of here."

He gestured toward the half-closed tent flap.

"There was always the possibility we'd have to deal with them, inasmuch as we're in Helmand. But here?" He snorted grandiosely. "It was supposed to be nigh unto impossible."

"I do not understand."

"Basayev, you were with me in Al-Anbar."

That worthy spat on the ground. "Would to Allah I never returned, it would not be soon enough!"

"Several of my fighters have been with me since before First Chechnya. They endured Fallujah and Al-Anbar with me. Those are American Marines out there."

He spoke the name with venomous rancor. "If you told me that the Americans emptied out the worst of their jails and prisons for fighting men, I would not be the least bit surprised. But those —"

He shook visibly. "They are vile men. The very servants of Shaitan. If Shamil has been captured, then he is in Allah's hands and we can only pray that he dies before they can interrogate him."

The Group Leader mulled over this.

"Send for a courier, we must make our situation known to the Emir."

#

After taking the man's fingerprints and what pictures they could for a forensic analysis by others, his remains had been cremated with an incendiary grenade, the marksman's hide filled in over his ashes.

The rifle, along with its attendant bandolier of Russian-made ammunition however, were retained.

Fitzsimmons had wondered why right up until she walked into the mess, where Nealen and several others were busily engaged inspecting the rifle.

"Looking for something, Staff?"

"Yes ma'am. We're taking this apart and giving it a once over."

"Why?"

"I don't think that fella was from around here."

"Oh?"

"His clothes were fine, but his appearance was all off. Figure I should give the intel monkeys something to work with before they make their voodoo sacrifices and see what the dead chicken entrails say."

"Think they'll try reading tea leaves too?" a Marine volunteered.

"Hard to read those. They're at the bottom of Boston Harbor," Hondo declared.

Others at the table snickered, while Balcombe glowered at Cassidy.

"What are you thinking, Staff?" Fitzsimmons asked patiently.

"I'm thinking Chechen. I've dealt with them before," Nealen stated.

"Where?"

"Iraq. Lots of 'em drifted down as part of the Jihad against the Great Satan."

"Oh, joy."

"Yes, ma'am. Counter-sniper work can be both relaxing and stressful all at once."

"Noted. What can you tell me about the rifle?"

"I'd have to call a friend who knows such things, but I think this is an anti-material rifle. His ammo is a hair bigger than .50 BMG."

"What do you think it is?"

"At a guess, it's maybe leftover soviet stocks. I don't recognize the headstamps at all."

"Hmm. It remains a mystery for the moment. I'm sure the intelligence lads will appreciate the task."

"Yes, ma'am."

"I am curious, where did your callsign come from? Is it something you came up with?"

"When a marine graduates Sniper School, we're given a Hog's Tooth."

Reaching inside his shirt, Nealen pulled out a bullet on a length of paracord for her to see. "HOGs are Hunters of Gunmen. I spent nine months playing hide-and-go-shoot with urban snipers in Al-Anbar province, during my first deployment. The company I was attached to started out calling me by my last name, but their Gunny changed that one night after a marathon of watching the Godfather movies. He thought 'Hogfather' described me pretty well."

Fitzsimmons raised an eyebrow.

"I make the 7.62 NATO offer that nobody can refuse."

"I see. Well, carry on, Don Hogfather."

The laughter she heard in her wake made the Captain smile.

Maybe we can make the impossible happen on this godforsaken heap of shite.

Chapter 6

Cooking Raw With The Brooklyn Boy

"Section heads, is there anything you need to report to me before I speak with the Captain?" Nealen asked.

It was 0830 of their third day onsite. Morning chow had already wrapped up, the new guards were on post, and the off-coming guards had just finished their personal hygiene. Peter Nealen stood outside the chow hall tent as several men standing around him lit cigarettes or threw in their first dip of the day.

"Staff Sergeant, I need to get out and walk the perimeter," Jimenez announced.

"What're you talking to me for?" Nealen asked.

"Going outside the wire. Something ain't jiving. I need to take a closer look at our exterior perimeter."

"Ah. How much help do you think you'll need?"

"Not a whole squad. Just a fire team or two that'll keep their mouths shut and let me do my thing."

"Grab who ya want and go for it."

"Thank you, Staff Sergeant. Appreciate it."

Jimenez made his way toward the newly thrown together gym. Not that any sane person would call the heaps of scrap metal spread across the small patch of dirt a proper gym. But, like junkies in need of their next fix, the gym rats would willfully make do with whatever was on hand. Music thumped out of it loud enough he could clearly hear the words as he approached.

Oh boy. More Sabaton. He really loves that heavy metal crap turned up loud. At least it's about fighting battles and winning. Jimenez grinned. *Ain't no hippies sticking around when he cranks that up.*

It's kinda like how I love Asian girls, the stocky Puerto Rican boy from Queens told himself as he continued along. *Wonder what Cassidy likes? From what Kramer has said, he's never had much luck with a girlfriend.*

Who knew what the future held though? Maybe being in close proximity to all these British women would be good for him.

Jimenez walked into the gym space, noticing that there were several people already in the area lifting.

"Menez, you finally made it to my church of iron! Come to worship with me?" Cassidy announced cheerfully from his spot by the benchpress.

"You wish," Jimenez replied. "Doctor's orders. Slowly, with the brace and nothing but what he assigned me."

Cassidy shook his head sadly. "What terrible news."

"I know. How much longer you think it'll take the doctors at Crippler to figure out I'm over here when they said 'no'?"

"No idea. Bureaucracy is a fickle creature." Cassidy said as he sat up.

"Ain't it? Especially after S-One made sure I was on all the rosters.

"I wonder how that happened?" Cassidy asked absently.

"I call it a Christmas miracle," Jimenez remarked.

"Whatcha in here for?" House asked.

"I need a fire team, going for a perimeter walk."

"Huh, who ya thinking of grabbing?" Cassidy made a contemplative face.

"Two from you. One from Cherney. One from Tolliver."

Cassidy turned to two Marines at the dumbbell rack nearby. "Bath, Thompson, follow the Corporal. You're his for the patrol. Menez, where you want them?"

"Form up the front gate in 20 minutes for inspection. Camelback, ammo load, the basics. We're traveling light."

"Hey, Menez, you might wanna grab somebody from Comm before you go. Take a real radio with you. And one of them Motor-T boys too. Our drivers are looking soft around the middle again," Cassidy suggested in between reps.

"Hey, that's a good idea. Thanks." Menez turned and called to another Marine doing tricep extensions in the corner. "House, you mind if I borrow Shiver?"

"Shiver, you bout done for now?"

"Yes, Sergeant."

"Good, git your crap, grab a 148 and get to the front gate!" House ordered without taking an eye off of his plate.

"Aye Sergeant!" Shiver dropped his dumbbell into the dirt, then moved it with another heave onto the makeshift rack.

Jimenez turned to the last NCO in the gym and called out, "Moore, who can I take from you?"

"Scarbro," he called back.

"Sounds good," he said with an approving nod.

As their names were called the four men dropped their respective tasks to go gear up. Jimenez surveyed the makeshift gym one last time and then left. Samuels looked beside him to where Cassidy loaded more plates onto his bar without a small amount of curiosity.

"I'm surprised Cass, why didn't you volunteer yourself to go along?" Kramer asked.

"It's Jimenez's show. Not mine. Every man's gotta learn to lead a patrol sometime."

"Fair enough."

"Besides, if they need help, who better to bail them out?"

#

"Good to see you bright and cheerful this morning, Nealen. Fitting in well?" Staff Sergeant Keating asked as the former sniper stepped into the Command Post.

"Nobody's dead yet and my lances aren't organizing a beer run to India," Nealen casually admitted.

"Oh, are we concerned about such things?"

"Only on days which end in 'Y'," Nealen assured.

Keating carefully considered his next move, then invited Nealen to sit down at a small table in the Operations Center.

"Staff Sergeant, I've had the pleasure of working with Americans before. Army though, not Marines. What makes you different from them?" Keating asked.

"We're...odd, Staff. Marines are very odd."

"So I noticed."

"Think of us as a cult, and we make more sense."

"Like sacrificing virgins under a full moon?"

"My Marines would call that a waste of a good virgin, sir."

The female Private sitting behind Keating at the radio, one Joanna Bellmore, let her head whip around to stare at Nealen in surprise, as Keating's cheeks took on an odd shade.

"Well then," Keating said politely. "You've been in-country for how long?"

"Four months as of this week. Been shot at nearly every day of it."

"And you're still intact?"

"We're Marines. We like to fight," Nealen assured. "And when we can't find an enemy worth fighting, we'll fight each other."

"That sounds somewhat hazardous."

"Ehhh," Nealen shrugged dismissively. "It has its moments."

"How do you get anything done?" Lieutenant Balcombe asked

"The best way to get my boys to do something is tell them they can't. The ballsy little shits will damn near kill themselves proving otherwise."

"That seems horribly counter-productive."

Nealen shrugged. "Welcome to ground combat arms. I've got a platoon worth of heartbreakers and life takers. They'd drink kerosene if they thought that would make them piss napalm."

"Please tell me you're joking. You've got to be joking," Balcombe breathed.

"Not even slightly. There's an army colonel who explained it best: 'From Imperial Rome to sceptered Britain to democratic America. He is the stuff of which legions are made. His pride is in his colors and his regiment, his training hard and thorough and coldly realistic to fit him for what he must face and his obedience is to his orders. He has been called United States Marine.'"

"You sound like a vicar preaching to a choir," Keating breathed.

"Marines imbibe the history and deeds of our Corps like mother's milk. The Irish do the same thing, except their babes have thoughts of rebellion and whiskey."

"Lord do the Irish ever. My father served during the end of the Troubles and the —"

"Yankee Patrol to Bourne, we are under fire, taking contact from hostiles! Vicinity patrol point Becky."

The wiry Staff Sergeant came off his chair with a lurch as he grabbed his M4 and clipped the sling point into place.

"Of course Becky. It just had to be fucking Becky."

#

"Dude. Baltierra. You know it's taken us three hours to walk this perimeter twice?" Thompson complained.

"Yup,"

"It's almost noon."

"Uh-huh."

"Dude, what are we still doing out here?"

The terrain remained relatively flat, occasional low spots punctuated by large bushes and scrubby trees. The river's presence here in Dishu meant more plants could survive. Indeed they had seen farms of some kind as they drove in, and even a few groves of what looked like palms.

The July heat seemed to suck the life out of everything. Here in the Rigestan, it didn't bear much thinking about. The river's presence meant the area was slightly cooler, but not by much.

"I dunno. Why don't you ask the Corporal?" Scarbro suggested.

"Hey Corporal, what exactly are we doing out here?" Thompson asked.

"Easy, you're pulling security. I'm writing down terrain features."

"Why?"

"Because you can't see everything from the posts."

"But they're like twenty feet high, how can you not?"

"Curvature of the earth? Maybe your eyes are crap. Should send you back like we did Robinson."

"No, thanks, I know how not to fall ass first into barbed wire," Thompson countered, then fell silent.

"This wadi isn't on the range card for the post." Jimenez said it smoothly, matter-of-fact, a calm entirely at odds with the nature of his statement.

"What?" All six marines looked back at him now, glancing toward the empty creek bed he was examining.

"I made copies before we left. This wadi isn't on any of them," Jimenez explained.

"We're only like 300 yards away!" Beagle said unhappily.

"295.9 to be precise, according to my laser range finder. This is easily inside M4 range. Hell, Tommy Taliban could set up mortars here and shoot at us all day long. We don't have anything with indirect capabilities except for our 203s and the Marks."

"Corporal."

"Yes, Thompson?"

"I hate this damn country."

"You're not the only one," Jimenez said as he finished his sketch and write-up of the wadi.

"Why couldn't we go to war in some place with good beer that isn't balls hot?"

"Because God doesn't love your whining, Thompson," Scarbro pointed out.

As the others laughed, Baltierra produced a cigarette and passed one to him.

"Still, you gotta agree — this place is ugly," Shiver said calmly.

"I dunno, this place makes me think of West Texas and all the stories about the old Comanche raids. We stick around long enough, Quanah Parker is gonna come riding on up and try to take our scalps!" Scarbro suggested.

"Yeah sure, whatever you say man. Anybody got a light?" Thompson asked.

"Yeah one sec," Beagle replied as Thompson leaned over.

CRACK

A single bullet ripped across the back of Thompson's body armor, skipping across the face of his back plate and into the water bladder there. For a moment, it seemed as if somebody had just slapped the whole team with a massive water balloon.

The angry *crack* of a bullet was a sound they had become intimately familiar with. After four months of dealing with raids and car bomb attempts, an AK round out of the blue was nothing new to them. All seven men hit the ground with their weapons aimed outboard as more bullets cracked through the air around them.

"Corporal, I really hate this damn country!" Thompson shouted as the Marines began returning fire.

Over on the light machine gun, Bath saw movement coming from a bush ahead of them. Through his optic he saw two men wearing djellabas and bandoliers of bullets, struggling to move a Russian-made machine gun into position.

"Action front, crew serve team one o'clock!"

"Shiver, call it in!" Jimenez barked.

"Yankee Patrol to Bourne, we are under fire, taking contact from hostiles! Vicinity patrol point Becky," Shiver drawled out. "

Bath began making his machine gun talk in a slow, sustained fire as Scarbro watched his right flank and Thompson covered the left.

BAM BAM BAM BAM BAM

Both of the enemy machine gunners went down. Shifting slightly, Bath started to take up the slack on his trigger again when something smacked into the receiver of the Russian-made crew serve. Metal spanged and sparked. A second shot. A third. The receiver twisted, bending to the impact of the rounds striking it.

"Well, nice to see our designated marksman is earning his pay!" Jimenez shouted.

A man arose from the ground holding an RPG and fell back, cut down by the same precise fire.

"Cassidy you bastard, save some for us!" Jimenez yelled.

"Who cares Corporal? We're winning so far!" Scarbro suggested.

"No maldigas pendejo!" Jimenez bellowed in reply.

"Yankee Patrol, this is Echo-Six November, how's it hanging?" the radio Shiver was carrying squawked. Jimenez took the handset from him as he studied their immediate area.

"Down and to the left. Can you see anything on GBOSS?" Jimenez asked, referring to the telescoping boom-mounted camera the Marines had brought with them.

"One second... There's a cluster of men about a hundred meters north from your position. May be winding up for something bigger. Can you make it back to the gate?"

Jimenez looked at the terrain around them for a moment, considering his options.

Fight them now, or fight them again later? "Echo Six November, do you see this wadi I'm next to?"

Silence. Rifles barked. Jimenez' trained ear differentiated between his Marines' M16s, and the sharper crack of enemy AKs.

"Local Suck, we can make out the edges of it. Looks like it runs south, then doglegs west. Ends maybe ten meters from where the bad guys are hunkered down.

"Walls to climb or a slope?"

"We don't know. Can't see."

Hell with this, I am not fighting them again Jimenez decided.

"Send the response squad to where they're hunkered down," Jimenez directed. "We'll be there and waiting."

"Roger that! Out!"

"Bath, can you keep their heads down, make 'em think we're all still here?" Jimenez asked.

"Hell yes!"

"Make it happen!" Jimenez ordered.

"Oorah!" Bath smoothly increased his rate of fire to rapid, chewing up earth and plants alike with furious intensity.

"Baltierra, Thompson stay with Bath, watch his back. Fire team, into the wadi!" Jimenez ordered, slithering down into the sandy bottom as his men did likewise. "I've got point. Follow me and keep quiet."

It was hot down inside the wadi, heat reflecting off the dirt walls and onto the tired, sweaty Marines as they half-ran, half-walked, wondering if the wadi had been wired with booby traps.

"Dear Mrs. Jimenez, his head began to recite as his hungry eyes looked for any signs of tripwires. *We regret to inform you that your son, Raymundo Vasquez de Cordoba Jimenez was killed in action."* Knock that off, you got other crap to worry about!

Ahead, he saw the wadi split into two paths, one of which sloped upwards.

Going belly down in the soft, hot sand, he wriggled up the slope snake-like.

Bet I can drop a 203 round on 'em and they'll get quiet real quick. Just can't see enough. Screw it, I'll stand up, shoot, drop back down. They'll never know what hit them.

Carmen Jimenez's son stood, in time to see a large knot of djellabas proned out in firing positions perpendicular to his line of advance. Some of them wore RPGs across their backs, but all had AKs. He stroked the grenade launcher's trigger.

TOONK

Till the day he died, Raymundo Jimenez swore he saw the 40mm grenade round curve to the left as it flew through the air. Straight toward the mortar tubes, even as some other part of his brain recognized that there were rows of uncased mortar projectiles lined up on either side of the tubes.

Oh —

A fireball erupted in his vision.

Jimenez felt himself thrown to the ground and all he saw was black.

Strong hands lifted him up as his vision swam. A man on either side. Somebody else was shoving him upright.

Everything sounded weird, a ringing sensation he'd never experienced before.

What happened?

He was flat on his back at the bottom of the slope.

Explosion must've knocked me back down.

"Corporal, what do we do?" Scarbro shouted.

Jimenez shook their hands away and fumbled at his belt as he stood on his feet.

"Fix bayonets!" he barked

"Wha —"

"Orale cabrones! Fix bayonets!"

Stumbling forward, he managed to grasp the hilt and pull it, socketing the stout blade onto the warm muzzle end of his rifle. He waited just a moment for the rest of his marines to do likewise.

"Shiver, you got a starburst ready?"

"On it, Corporal!"

"We taking prisoners?" Rodd asked.

"Si chico. If their hands are up, we don't shoot. They get stupid, we send them to God." Jimenez looked his men in the eyes. "Do not take an unnecessary chance. We are too far from home for that nonsense."

It hurt getting up the slope, and he was damn sure his doctors back at Crippler Medical would be furious if they saw him right now. But it was too late for any more consideration. "Vencomigo pendejos! Charge!"

#

"Staff Sergeant, we got a runner! Five hundred meters or better!" Hondo declared as he sighted in once more from where he stood, rifle nestled in place.

"Where's he headed?" Nealen asked as he came up the stairs.

"Straight outta Dodge." Hondo didn't bother to look up from his position. "Fella ain't never heard of a serpentine at all."

"So it appears," Nealen agreed, peering through his own ACOG at the figure rapidly moving away from them.

"You can't shoot that man!" a female voice shrieked.

Hondo didn't move, but Nealen did, and saw Leftenant Balcombe had joined them.

"Why not ma'am?" the staff sergeant asked.

"He's disengaging," Balcombe declared.

"Really? Is that why he's still carrying his rifle?" Nealen replied.

"Shooting him in the back would be a violation of the laws of war," she insisted.

"Since when?" Nealen said.

"Since —" Balcombe stopped, struggling for words. "Since the Geneva Convention was signed."

"Staff Sergeant, range is just about six hundred meters. I can still catch him," Hondo declared.

The edge in the younger man's voice caused Nealen to be concerned.

He's trying not to snap on her. I don't blame him. Nealen chuckled. *Or her. Her heart's in the right place but she's out of her depth on this one. Hondo too. He's got little tolerance for people who he thinks aren't staying in their lane.*

"Ma'am —" Hondo started to say, stopping as he felt Nealen's gloved hand come to rest on his right shoulder.

"Sergeant Cassidy, you remember what I said long ago, about teaching moments?" Nealen asked.

"Yes, Staff Sergeant."

"I need to have one of those right now. Take Sweetwood and Ostrovsky with you, go get some water."

The firm command in his voice helped the younger man come back down from the mental fight he was then grappling with.

"Come on guys, let's go," Hondo declared, none too gently grabbing both junior Marines by the strap across the back of their flak jackets

"Aye, aye, sergeant," both younger marines chirped, eager to be out of sight before any further conversation took place.

Nealen waited till they were well out of earshot. "Ma'am I understand where you're coming from, but that was really bad timing."

"I'll say, we could've had a war crime on our hands. The International Criminal Court —"

"Has no jurisdiction over US military personnel," Nealen retorted.

"But —"

"Who are they gonna send that would make us do anything?"

"Umm." She let out a breath. "When you put it like that, I guess nobody."

"That's right. Now, on to timing. If you wanna establish rules of engagement, it needs to happen before the troops are engaged. A firefight is an awful place to write policy."

"Oh. Yes." She had the good graces to look a little embarrassed as realization sank home. "I see your point. But, still. How do we not end up being the bad guys?"

"Well for starters ma'am, we're not randomly burning down villages just 'cuz they looked at us funny."

"Oh."

"That was the Russian method of handling matters."

"Ah. Yes, let's not do that."

"Second, we're not tricking little boys with Autism or Down Syndrome into wearing suicide vests."

She paled considerably. "You've seen that?"

"In Kandahar and Al Anbar," Nealen said stonily.

"That's vile."

"Yes, ma'am. And I'll bet good money that my young sergeant has seen some of that as well. Likely all of my sergeants if I asked."

"He doesn't seem to care much for the Taliban or Al Qaeda."

Nealen shrugged. "As he has said more than once in my presence, 'we don't have to worry about the Taliban if they're all dead.'"

Balcombe silently mulled over his words, and Nealen returned to scanning the area for any hostile threats.

"Damn country looks the same as when Moses was alive," Nealen muttered.

"Staff?"

"Talking to myself ma'am.

"Ah. At any rate, I hear what you're saying, but I still worry. Is there any way we could do a class or two on rules of engagement, and laws of war?"

"I think that's a great idea ma'am."

"I'll get right on it then." She turned to leave, then stopped. "Staff, should I apologize to Sergeant Cassidy?"

"No, ma'am. Best I talk with him. "

"You sure?"

"Positive. The boy's single-mindedness is often handy."
He gestured towards the bodies of the dead machine gunners."

Balcombe gulped.

"Quite," she said after regaining her composure.

"But when he gets wound up too tight, he needs a strong hand to help him come down."

"Very well then, I leave it in your capable hands."

"Have a good afternoon ma'am."

Turning, Nealen looked over the post, made note of the range card, then went back to watching the scenery as the reaction squad performed a post-battle sweep of the engagement zone. Marines moved about, stacking bodies and captured equipment for disposal, joking as they did so.

Nealen watched them, lit up his own cigarette, and smiled. "Pays to be a winner, sucks to be a loser. You pissants ain't nearly good enough to beat us."

#

"Everybody come take a look at what the Americans did!"

Sylvie had just put the final touches on a dozer blade in need of repair when the door flew open, banging against the wall and slowly bouncing backwards as Coughlan forced his way inside the shop, yelling to be heard above the various machines in operation.

"What's happening Coughlan?" Staff Sergeant Keating inquired.

"The bloody Yanks got in a firefight and decided to go stab the bastards, Staff!"

"You've got to be kidding me."

"God's my witness, they did it. That survey patrol they sent out took contact and went to work with a vengeance!"

"Uh huh sure."

"Honest, Staff! I watched it happen on the GBOSS camera!" Coughlan swore. "They're coming back on a couple trucks right now."

Keating grabbed his rifle and threw on his patrol cap. "Fine, I'll come take a look, but if you're blowing smoke up me arse boy, I'll make you dig trenches for Lyons all over the damn desert."

As Keating left the shop, others joined him. Outside, Sylvie saw that they weren't alone. The whole of the company had been informed of the firefight and were coming to gawk at the sight of the marines as they returned.

They'd used the large Cougar up-armored vehicles to fetch the patrol, men standing on the running boards as they rode through the serpentine, whooping and hollering the whole way.

"Bloody loud lot, ain't they?" Keating observed, lighting a cigarette and slowly dragging on it.

"Nasty business what they did," Mayne opined as he joined the growing crowd. "Got a light, Keating?"

"Aye Sarn't Major," Keating extended a lighter over.

Puff-puff-puff. The cherry glowed brightly.

"Did it really happen like Coughlan said?" Keating asked as he took the lighter back.

"With bayonets?"

"Uh huh."

"Indeed," Mayne stated calmly.

"Nobody uses those things anymore! Hasn't in ages!" Keating protested.

"Thirty minutes ago, you'd have been right."

Keating's eyes widened as he contemplated those words, then watched the men clambering off their rides while more from within the vehicles emerged, carrying litters loaded with what had to be evidence, and seized weapons. Keating noted the bayonets still mounted on rifles.

"Well ain't that a change?"

"Aye."

"Think the locals will take the hint?"

"I hope so. Otherwise, the Americans might have to do it all over again."

"They'll be heartbroken at the prospect."

"Utterly devastated."

Chapter 7

Shenanigans?

"All stations, how copy?" Cassidy spoke calmly into the radio.

The radio handsets assigned to each pair of guards in the seven posts squawked simultaneously, and just like on gunline, Cassidy waited for their reports. They'd been here eleven days now, and in the eight since Jimenez had decided to end an immediate problem at bayonet point, it was quiet around FOB Bourne.

Cassidy wasn't surprised about that either. Exactly one of the shooters had made it out alive, running hell-for leather across the desert.

Nealen had been right though, if the week of silence had been anything to go by. According to Captain Fitzsimmons, the engineers were getting real sleep for the first time since they'd arrived in Deshu.

Right then, Cassidy was standing the midday watch as Sergeant of the Guard.

"Thought you lot didn't read, not unless it was a picture book?" A soldier named McSweeney said loudly as he walked past.

"What made you think that?" Cassidy asked in a voice suspiciously calm.

"Well everybody knows American Marines ain't exactly what you'd call the best or brightest of the lot!" McSweeney guffawed.

"I suppose every poor boy makes his own way in life how he will." Cassidy said, then returned to his book, as if McSweeney weren't standing in front of him.

"What's that supposed to mean?" McSweeney snarled.

"You're so smart, you tell me."

"I bleeding asked you —"

Cassidy slammed the book shut on the table, skewering McSweeney's acne-scarred face with a contemptuously malevolent gaze as he began to speak.

"By the old Moulmein Pagoda, lookin' eastward to the sea,
There's a Burma girl a-settin', and I know she thinks o' me;
For the wind is in the palm-trees, and the temple-bells they say:
"Come you back, you British soldier; come you back to Mandalay!"
Come you back to Mandalay,
Where the old Flotilla lay:
Can't you 'ear their paddles chunkin' from Rangoon to Mandalay?
On the road to Mandalay,
Where the flyin'-fishes play,
An' the dawn comes up like thunder outer China 'crost the Bay!

In the silence of the mess, nobody spoke, least of all McSweeney, who stared hotly as he tried to decipher what he'd just heard.

"What nonsense is that?" McSweeney demanded. "Something you Yanks came up with when you weren't out making trouble for honest folks?"

Cassidy continued in that same baritone voice, pushing the sound out to every corner of the mess as he spoke, with an intensity that seemed to rise out of the very ground where he sat.

"'Er petticoat was yaller an' 'er little cap was green,
An' 'er name was Supi-yaw-lat -- jes' the same as Theebaw's Queen,
An' I seed her first a-smokin' of a whackin' white cheroot,
An' a-wastin' Christian kisses on an 'eathen idol's foot:
Bloomin' idol made o'mud --

Wot they called the Great Gawd Budd --
Plucky lot she cared for idols when I kissed 'er where she
stud!
On the road to Mandalay . . .

"It's called Kipling, you insouciant lout," Sergeant Pistol declared as he roughly shoved McSweeney aside to sit down opposite Cassidy. "If you'd spent even a tenth of the time studying your country's history as you did shoving your head in your teacher's fanny to pass the damn class, McSweeney, you'd be twice as smart and half as poor as you are now."

The serious look on Pistol's face disappeared, his nostrils flaring and his mustache seemed to grow even larger before he leaned forward on either tattooed forearm and began to recite.

"When the mist was on the rice-fields an' the sun was
droppin' slow,
She'd git 'er little banjo an' she'd sing "Kulla-lo-lo!"
With 'er arm upon my shoulder an' 'er cheek agin' my
cheek
We useter watch the steamers an' the hathis pilin' teak.
Elephints a-pilin' teak
In the sludgy, squdgy creek,
Where the silence 'ung that 'eavy you was 'arf afraid to
speak!
On the road to Mandalay . . ."

Turning his head to face McSweeney with that blinding grin on his dark face, Pistol smiled. "Shut your gob and sit your ass down McSweeney, it's time you learned a thing or two. Fooking embarrassment to honest Scots everywhere. I swear." Then he turned back to Cassidy. "Your move, Yank."

#

"Hey Lyons, you in here? I've been looking all over —" Sandra announced as she stepped inside the mess.

"Shhhhh!" somebody hissed at her.

"What?" Sandra asked, confused to receive such a response.

"Pistol's reciting poetry!" Jones replied excitedly.

"There was not a man but carried his feud
with the blood of the mountaineer.
Ha' done! ha' done!" said the Colonel's son.
"Put up the steel at your sides!
Last night ye had struck at a Border thief —
to-night 't is a man of the Guides!"

Pistol's strong voice rang through the packed mess. His blue eyes twinkled with a previously unseen joy. The real surprise, to Sandra's mind, was Lyons. Sylvie had seated herself to Pistol's right, near the tent wall. Given the position, she'd be able to see both men easily.

But her attention was solely on the Yank across from him — Cassidy.

Odd, Sandra thought. *She normally doesn't have any interest in men. At all. Especially not since Parduhn tried to "tame" her. Wanker.*

Sandra checked again, listening to Cassidy's voice as he spoke, but watching her friend carefully. *Yep, she's eyes on him, facing him, staring at him like she's going to eat him for dinner. You can fool others with the Ice Queen act, but I know your tells. This one has got you riled up.*

Sylvie Lyons felt entranced. Possibly even bewitched. Of all the shenanigans she'd come to expect from the Marines since they'd arrived here a week prior, hearing one of their number recite poetry was not on the list. Especially not poems her grandfather had rocked her to sleep with as he recited them to his eldest grandchild. For the first time, Sylvie noticed the scarring on that American's hands, the knuckles swollen like so many knots on one of the ancient oaks scattered about her grandfather's property.

I've seen those hands before, but where? How? Why?

What mattered in this confusing, wonderful, horrid moment, was the measured cadence of his baritone voice as he orated in a way she'd never have expected him capable of.

"Oh, East is East, and West is West,
and never the twain shall meet,
Till Earth and Sky stand presently
at God's great Judgment Seat;
But there is neither East nor West,
Border, nor Breed, nor Birth,
When two strong men stand face to face
though they come from the ends of the earth!"

In a scene fit for a Hollywood production, both men stood, eyes still locked on the other like dueling gun turrets, as Pistol extended his right hand to the other man.

"Well done. Cassidy. It's nice to see somebody in your lot's got a civilized bone in his body."

Cassidy took the broad man's hand with equal fervor. "Appreciate it. Always felt a classical education was the best way to go."

Muscles flexed. Sylvie winced as she considered the force they were exerting on each other. Veins stood out against taut flesh as the tension increased. Neither man backed down, both grimacing.

"Nice to see a strong handshake once again."

"You too. Flabby ones annoy me."

Tension released. Now the smiles were unfeigned. They had reached an understanding of each other that the other men in the room understood on a primal level.

Pistol looked over his left shoulder at McSweeney. "The next time you think to run your mouth at them, I want you to remember how this Yank schooled you with our Empire's bard. Schooled you like you wasn't even dirt beneath his boots. You understand me?"

"Yes," McSweeney said weakly.

Pistol looked at Cassidy and smiled. "That was fun, Yank. Might have to do it again sometime."

"Aye. Shall we teach them about well-worked rushes on the GBT?"

"We might have to do that very thing." Pistol chuckled, then stomped to the far side of the mess, leaving Cassidy to sit back in his seat, one hand grasping a water bottle to pull a drink from and quench his parched throat.

"That was impressive!" Sandra declared. "You have a great voice for speaking."

Cassidy smiled, fingers spreading across the table.

Brabham! Sylvie thought suddenly.

She'd seen those hands on her grandfather's Welsh gamekeeper, Brabham, a man who came from the Army to join him. They were the hands of a working man. Grandpapa's hands bore similar scars, though not quite as pronounced. He had left behind a workman's tools after his career in the Army was over, though if his arms' room was anything to go by, he hadn't left all of his tools behind. But the scars and memories remained.

I wonder what Brabham and Grandpapa would have to say about this Cassidy? She thought as she examined Cassidy intently. His dark hair, like so many of his fellows, was close-cropped to the skull, and his dark eyes flashed as they scanned the room, never stopping their movement.

"Thank you, Collier. Appreciate your saying so."

"I think Lyons enjoyed it too, didn't you?" Sandra asked.

Sylvie tried to hide her displeasure at being put on the spot like this. Sandra knew how much she wasn't interested in men. *Why are you doing this to me?* Sylvie thought with a great deal of anguish.

"I appreciate the audience. Thank you ladies, for enjoying the show," he said politely.

"I don't suppose you've got a copy of Kipling handy," a stern voice declared from behind Cassidy. It was Sergeant Major Mayne, looking slightly perturbed even with his mustache tucked behind his mug.

"Evening, Sarn't Major," Cassidy said calmly. "I might, I'll have to rummage through my library and see what I brought."

"How many books did you pack along, lad?" Mayne asked curiously.

"A couple dozen, I can't remember if Kipling is one of them.

"Why so many?" Sandra asked.

"Because books don't run out of batteries. And I like to read."

"Very well," Mayne replied. "Let me know if you do. Pistol!"

"Yes, Sarn't Major."

"You're going to give McSweeney the education his teachers failed to impress him."

"With pleasure, Sarn't Major."

Somewhere in the back of the mess, Cassidy thought he heard McSweeney whimpering.

#

"Hey Sergeant Cassidy, you lived in England, right?" Thompson asked inside their hooch. For a moment, it was quiet, with no need to shoot people in the face. The Marines were enjoying a slow reprieve from the heat, reading or napping in their tents.

"Yeah, what about it?" Cassidy asked.

"Do they have like any good shows worth watching that aren't Doctor Who?"

Cassidy chuckled. "Actually yeah, come by the mess later tonight. We'll see if we can't get something going on my projector."

"You brought a projector?"

"Well yeah, didn't you?"

"How?" Thompson asked, slightly awestruck.

"This ain't my first rodeo bubba, hell it ain't even my second."

As the burly sergeant began rummaging through his rucksack, Kramer smiled behind the pages of his worn-magazine.

This should be amusing, the Missourian told himself. *God in Heaven only knows what Cass will pull out. Maybe it'll be the latest edition of Big Rugby Hits or Bare Knuckle Boxing.*

#

After evening chow had been cleared, the first movie night was held. Marines, by and large, will watch anything at least once, with little regard for how objectionable the content might be, if only because they are bored. Those not on watch filtered into the large mess hall, taking seats and drinking water as Cassidy went about setting up his projector and speakers.

"Whatcha playing, Sergeant?" a marine asked.

"Ever heard of Nigella Lawson?"

"No, I haven't, Sergeant. Who is she?"

"Well it's time you learned, bubba," Hondo pronounced.

"The peaches really are so very lovely and give such a voluptuous look to the whole dish."

On camera, Nigella smiled as she spoke, whilst the marines watched, entranced, as she went through the motion of prepping her chosen fruit for the dessert she was making. The dark-haired woman with perfect features was making magic. They were convinced of that.

"Sergeant," a hand went up in the front.

Cassidy hit 'pause.' "Yes, Thompson?"

"What's voluptuous mean?"

"Curvaceous. Possessing pronounced curves."

"So if Webber says 'Shawty in the blue got a fat ass,' I could call her voluptuous and sound cooler than him," Thompson mused.

"Yes. Yes, you could."

"Cool."

Cassidy clicked "play" and the video resumed.

In the back of the mess, Morgana Gallagher wanted to laugh at the amusing tableau.

"This is patently absurd," she declared to Stirling Mayne.

"Aye, but imagine how much trouble they'd be getting into if they weren't busy watching Nigella," Stirling countered.

"I know. But still —"

"What's the worst that could happen?" Stirling suggested.

#

Camille Balcombe was quite thoroughly done. For the last two days, she'd had to listen to the Marines use every ten pound word they heard Nigella bloody Lawson drop, and she was done. D. O. N. E.

"I swear to Christ, the next person who says 'voluptuous' or 'lovely' is going to get butt stroked!" she loudly swore as she made a strong cuppa for herself before she went into the FDC for her turn at night shift.

Private "Herfy" Pilsen, the cook's assistant, leaned out from the kitchen to look at her with a worried expression on his face. "Everything alright, ma'am?"

Before she could respond one of the marines inserted himself into the conversation.

"Hey Herfy, I'm about to go on post. What are the challenge and pass of the day?" Barrasco asked loudly.

"Lovely and Voluptuous," Herfy volunteered.

Balcombe's hot gaze swung from Barrasco to Pilsen as she growled low in her throat.

Near immediately three rifles were extended towards her, buttstocks first.

Glaring menacingly towards the owners, she wondered why it seemed so familiar. A memory bubbled up from her uni days, an evening spent drinking beer and watching a horrid movie about getting outrageously high.

I walked right into that. Breathing in deeply, she sighed. *Maybe I need to relax just a hair.*

"Shenanigans," she muttered

"Ma'am?" Pilsen asked, confused.

"Just thinking about shenanigans, Private."

"Yes ma'am."

"You three, put those damn things away. You'll poke your eye out," she ordered the Marines.

"Yes ma'am!" the marines said, smirking as they did so.

Crazy weirdos. She smiled at the long-ago memory. *One day at a time, we'll get through this.*

Chapter 8

Looks Like Another Tequila Sunrise

Hondo Cassidy wondered what was going wrong now. The Marines were standing posts daily, nobody had girl trouble, and until that random medevac appearance earlier, he'd have thought his boys were enjoying a machine gun-laden vacation on taxpayer dime.

That was before Doc Gnem and Doc Knighton had been called to the mess for an emergency. Before a medevac chopper had arrived, taking with it somebody on a stretcher.

Now we've got a section heads meeting in the CP he thought to himself. *I wonder what for this time?*

As he stomped into the command post, Hondo felt his doubts and insecurities speaking even more loudly.

"Cassidy, good you're here," Nealen said curtly.

"Staff Sergeant, what's going on?" Hondo asked.

"Ever thrown a cow pie into a fan?"

"Not intentionally."

"Well it just happened," Nealen assured.

Cherney stomped into the post, followed by Tolliver.

"We're up, Sarn't Major," Nealen announced.

"Thanks." The declaration did nothing to alleviate Mayne's graven unhappiness.

A few more personnel entered the command post, and Mayne began to speak "Corporal Daggett, our cook was on the medevac. It looks like ulcers and extreme stress."

"Oh dammit," a Brit muttered.

"Preliminary reports says he is not coming back to us."

"Why?"

"Doc Gnem?"

"With ulcers the best method of treatment is a low-stress environment and a complete change in diet," Doc Gnem admitted.

"Neither of which happens if he's stuck in here," Knighton added.

"Yeah, that might be a problem," Nealen agreed.

"Daggett kept good books and did what he could. He managed to squirrel away half a year's worth of tray-rations and MREs for us."

"Oh joy," Hondo growled.

"Aye. The troops can eat that just fine. They'll make do," Fitzsimmons declared.

"Herfy, how many weeks supply fresh food do we have on hand?" Mayne asked suddenly.

"Four, Sarn't Major. Corporal Daggett made sure to keep plenty of stock on hand."

"Excellent. We'll shift over to those stocks as much as we can. Between whatever we have, and what the Americans brought along, we should be just fine, right?"

"Yes, Sarn't Major," Herfy agreed.

\#

Hondo Cassidy stood at the wash station, carefully shaving his face. Nearby, Sergeant Pistol carefully combed his luxurious testament to the highest traditions of the British Army. Both men were shirtless as they went about their task. Indeed both could be accused of preening, if only because they seemed to take an inordinately long time at their morning ablutions. That they were doing so only after they had exercised, as well as ensured that their troops were fed, watered, and prepared for the day was never mentioned.

"Sergeant Pistol, are you in love with pilchards?" Hondo asked as he began the process of toweling his face clean.

"No, Sergeant Cassidy, no I am not."

"Are you sure?" Hondo reiterated.

Pistol let his eyes wander left to his fellow sergeant. "Whatever gave you the impression that I was?"

"The Cook."

"Herfy?"

"The very one."

Pistol's face soured as he looked toward his fellow non-commissioned officer. "What balderdash is that filthy disgrace to the uniform of my Queen spreading now?"

Cassidy waved dramatically. "Oh nothing like that, it's just, well, I figured he was doing it for somebody."

Pistol made a face.

"Don't get me wrong," Hondo continued. "I enjoy sardines, as we Americans call them. They can be quite good any number of ways."

"Grew up on 'em meself. Council flat in Tower Hamlets." Pistol stopped, then clarified. "East end of London. Not exactly posh. Nor even proper."

"Go home much?"

"Not since I buried me mother. Dad died of cocaine before I went to Pirbright. Mum died in a house fire." Pistol patted his cheeks dry. "I was a new lance corporal by then. The Army's been me family since."

"I understand. On a very personal level."

"I'm sorry you do. Which still doesn't explain your line of questioning. Or pilchards," Pistol said after a moment, as he patted his cheeks with aftershave.

"Now, I am going to guess that while you enjoy our briny little friends, marinating as they are in tomato sauce, you do not enjoy having to eat them every meal."

"No, I do not," Pistol said testily.

"Well I did not know this, and I thought I should conduct an informal poll."

"Beginning with me?" Pistol asked.

"You have divined the very platonic essence of my course of thought, good sir."

Pistol chewed on this further. "Refresh my memory, my fine American friend, what did we have for dinner last night?"

"Rice. With pilchards."

"Lunch was rations. Breakfast was —"

"Eggs and pilchards on toast. Just like today."

Pistol's eyes narrowed. "I seem to recall a dinner the night before last that involved pilchards-and-alphabety spaghetti."

Cassidy zipped his hygiene bag up, then pulled on his shirt. "Far be it from me to suggest there's an issue, but that's at least four meals in two days with sardines."

"He's only been in charge of chow for what, four days?"

"Five." Pistol started to look around with a frown. "Wonder what he's up to right now?"

"Would it surprise you then, if I told you that on my way here, I saw ol' Herfy cracking open more cans of pilchards into a stock pot?"

Pistol paused, mental wheels spinning as he considered the information presented. "What else was he putting in the pot?"

"I believe that was it," Cassidy said.

"No pepper? Salt?"

"None that I saw," Cassidy said.

"Sergeant Cassidy, would you care to accompany me for a walk?" Pistol asked in a voice which betrayed nothing of his own thoughts.

"A walk?"

"Aye. A walk."

"Have anywhere in mind?"

Pistol inhaled sharply. "I'm still debating that. My feet have a tendency to yonder."

"Yonder?"

"Yonder. Which as it happens, is a word I picked up from a Yank."

Hondo smiled. "Well then, Sergeant Pistol, let us yonder."

Grabbing their rifles, the two men sauntered forth out of the shade into the bright mid-morning sunshine.

\#

"Morning, Sergeant Major, anything happening about which I should be aware?" Captain Fitzsimmons asked as Stirling walked into the Command Post.

"No ma'am. I've walked the posts. I've walked the shops, the motor pool, the excavators. Everything's Sir Garnet, ma'am."

"Marvelous, simply marvelous. I love it when a plan comes together."

"Yes, ma'am." They exchanged pleasantries, speaking about a few new items of business that had come up. With nobody shooting at them for the moment, it was relatively easy to get work done at FOB Bourne.

A veteran campaigner, Stirling Mayne enjoyed the simple pleasures in life. And right then, with nothing else on his plate, he realized he could sit down and relax.

I do believe it's time for a choice cigar. Yes, yes it is.

Excusing himself, he stepped back outside and made for the smoke pit.

Be nice to dip it in Brandy while I'm smoking it. If only —

Two A-frames had been lashed together with tow straps, and a beam placed on top, between the frames. In the middle, standing on an MRE box, was Herfy, looking horribly worried. He wasn't saying much right then, given how his mouth had been covered with a length of duct tape and his wrists bound together with zip ties. No, Herfy was not saying much of anything right then.

Given the stout lads on either side of him have thrown a tow rope over the cross spar and secured the other end to the pintle hook of a 7-ton truck, I very much doubt Herfy will be saying anything in the future.

The small but growing crowd around them parted as Stirling stepped forward to inspect the handiwork.

Lashings look neat, zip-ties are just tight enough to restrain, why they even remembered to tie his feet together. Oh I do love working with professionals, they make my life so much easier.

Stirling smiled within himself, then stepped over to the smoke butt. Carefully clipping one end off the cigar, Stirling struck a match from the book he kept handy in his left sleeve pocket, then puffed appreciably on it.

Cuban cigars and Cuban coffee. Thank whatever Gods may be for them. Would be fantastic in St. George's Bay, watching the sun come up, listening to the gulls winging about.

But first we have to survive this mess. Which means determining why exactly, two NCOs are engaged in what appears to be the long overdue execution of that filthy disgrace to the Army which is one Joseph Pilsen aka "Herfy."

Smiling cheerfully, as a Sergeant Major ought to when a good joke is occurring, Stirling looked from Cassidy to Pistol.

"What's the story, gents?" Mayne asked casually.

"We're going to hang Herfy, Sarn't Major," Pistol explained.

"Well yes, I can see that." Stirling paused to puff on the Romeo y Julieta. "I was wondering why."

Pistol fixed Herfy with a coldly gimlet eye as he ripped the tape off the young private's mouth.

"Go on, Herfy. Tell the man," Pistol ordered.

"S-s-sarn't major, I didn't want to open a new pallet of meal boxes before we'd finished all the supplies left over from the previous weeks."

"What were those supplies, Herfy?" Stirling asked curiously.

"P-p-p-pilchards, Sarn't Major. Daggett didn't like 'em so he pulled them before issuing. I thought now was a good — *urk* — time to use all of them."

"All of them?" Stirling asked.

"Uh huh," Herfy confirmed.

"At once?"

"Yes. They're — *urk* — taking up a lot of space."

"Hmmmmmm. Haul away lads. I'd best go inform the captain we need a new cook."

Stirling turned, puffing on his cigar, waiting for the odiferous stench to strike his nostrils before he turned around, cigar in hand as he held it up.

"Hold on lads, hold on a minute," Stirling commanded.

"Yes, Sarn't major?" Pistol and Cassidy asked at once, looking for all the world like two foxes in a hen house.

"Herfy, do you understand how your poor choice of actions has brought this on?"

Sniffle. "Yes."

"Good. I should hate to think we'd need to repeat this lesson."

"Yes. Sarn't Major."

"Let him down gently now lads. Musn't lose our new convert."

"Convert?"

"Aye. Just like Saul on the road to Damascus, I believe our mister Herfy is now a firm believer."

"In what?" Cassidy asked.

"Proper meal planning, prep, and service." Stirling leaned in closer to the terror stricken young man. "I do have that right, don't I?"

Herfy's head bobbed up and down. "Yes, Sarn't Major."

"Excellent."

\#

Cassidy was waiting for him when he came out of the latrine.

"Show me your hands, boy," the sergeant ordered.

"What?" Pilsen replied.

A rough hand slapped the back of his head causing Pilsen to stumble forward.

"That is a non-commissioned officer. Address him by his rank, boy!" Pistol ordered.

The confused private held up his hands. "Here, Sergeant."

Cassidy scanned them critically.

"See that? That's dirt under your nails. Fix it. Now."

Bending over the washbasin, Joseph Pilsen began vigorously scrubbing with a boot brush as they watched him. Once his hands received Cassidy's approval, the two men looked over the rest of him.

"Private Pilsen, you are a shocking, awful disgrace to my uniform," Pistol declared.

"Yes, Sergeant." Pilsen looked down at his shoes.

"Sergeant Cassidy and I have been talking. Your days of being such are numbered."

Pilsen swallowed.

"Firstly, you will no longer be allowed to slouch about and act the fool. No more beer for you. Not even from that still you've been hiding."

The boy's eyes widened and he started to speak.

"Spare me, boy-oh. This isn't my first tour. Nor my last. I've smelt it on yer breath. Yer done making alcohol," Pistol said.

"Yes, Sergeant."

As if to emphasize the point, Pistol took away the hygiene bag Pilsen had in one hand, and began rummaging through it.

"Ah, there it is!" and pulling out a large bottle of mouthwash, Pistol uncapped it. "Take a sniff of that, my fine American friend."

"Smells like vodka, my fine British friend."

"Don't it just?" Pistol's smile grew wider as he upended the bottle, dispensing the bottle's contents across the sand. When he finished, he put the bottle back into the bag and roughly thrust it into the private's chest.

"No more 'Herfy.' You are Private Pilsen. You are a soldier in the British Army."

"Yes, Sergeant," he resigned.

"Secondly, Sergeant Cassidy is taking over the mess."

"He's what? He's not allowed!" Pilsen exploded.

Pistol smiled thinly.

"I'll allow you that one, I expected it. Show him, Sergeant Cassidy."

The American reached into his pocket, producing a series of stamped steel cards. "See these? They authorize me as a food handler. And an inspector. I possess both military and civilian licenses."

Pilsen licked his lips as he read the cards whilst Cassidy spoke. The conversation had just taken a far more painful turn than he wished.

"Ha — Hu — how?" Pilsen muttered.

Cassidy checked his watch, ignoring the question. "It is currently zero-nine-seventeen. At eleven-hundred, I am walking into my kitchen. I expect to see a menu for tonight's dinner service. I will then inspect my kitchen. If it is up to standard, I will allow you to begin cooking the menu you've written up. If it is not up to standard, you will finish the cleaning of my kitchen while I prepare the evening service. Do you understand?"

"Your kitchen?" Pilsen challenged.

"Yes, Private, My kitchen. You want to make an issue out of it?

"As a matter of fact I do!"

Cassidy allowed him space to set his things down.

It was all the time Pilsen received before he was speared and bodily knocked into the ground. Even as his mind adjusted to the fact that he'd been hit, he felt strong arms flipping him around and about. One of those arms wrapped around his neck while another covered the back of his head. He was bodily hauled up so he could see himself in the mirror over the washbasin.

Behind him, grinning like death's head, was Cassidy.

"I can knock you unconscious right now, just by flexing. You're no challenge. None at all."

"Ack."

Cassidy pushed him away, letting the man regain his breath and his senses.

"You're a shit excuse for a man and a soldier, Pilsen," Pistol intoned. "But between me and Cassidy, we're going to fix that. No more 'Herfy' drunken and disorderly. No more slop, no more sloven. No more excuses, shitty or otherwise. Understand?"

"Yes. Sergeant."

"Good. Now clean yourself up and get Chef Cassidy's kitchen ready for inspection."

#

"This has been an excellent meal!" Morgana Gallagher declared as she finished up the last of her mashed potatoes and gravy.

Private Pilsen was nearby, cleaning up a table.

"Well done, Herfy," Stirling said.

"My name is Private Pilsen, Sarn't Major. I am a soldier in the British Army."

Stirling blinked. *Where had this come from?*

"Very well. Carry on, Private Pilsen."

"Yes, Sarn't Major."

He headed back through the double doors of the kitchen at a march, highly unlike his previous slothful slouch. Stirling watched him, lips pursed.

Methinks it's time for some skullduggery.

Dinner was over when the Sergeant Major went for a walk, enjoying the lower temperature as the sun disappeared from sight. Behind the chow hall he found them, working away merrily as they finished rinsing out the trays from dinner. Pilsen diligently scrubbed a pan as Sergeant Cassidy loaded the bucket of a bobcat with trash bags from the mess. Pistol had a cigarette in his mouth, cherry blazing as he relaxed against the side of the bobcat.

"After that rousing performance, what do you have planned for the rest of the week?" Pistol asked cheerfully.

"Whatever I tell him to cook," Cassidy replied. "I know enough cuisine to use everything we've got in stock and then some."

Leaning up against the wall where he'd remain concealed, Stirling listened intently.

"Private, tell me something."

"Yes Sergeant?"

"What do you actually know how to do in a kitchen?" Cassidy asked.

"I'm good at baking," Pilsen confessed.

"Explain."

"I grew up next door to a bakery shop. Learned a lot from the baker."

"Why'd you join the Army, boy? Why not stay there and earn your living?"

"Matter of a stolen car and bad timing," Pilsen shrugged. "I ran out the door before Old Bull could come calling."

"What can you bake?" Cassidy asked.

"All types of bread. Even posh stuff for toffs. I can do magic with flour, sergeant."

Cassidy shook his head, smiling ruefully. Pistol had an eyebrow cocked and a glare on his face.

"Well we need that. Know what bread is good for, Pilsen?" Cassidy asked.

"It fills yer belly, Sergeant?"

"Exactly. Complex carbohydrates are good for troops in the field and on maneuvers." Cassidy looked to Pistol. "Imagine having fresh bread in-country, Pistol?"

"That'd be right proper it would. Especially with a helping of butter or some hot bangers." Pistol glared at their charge. "Why was Daggett holding this out on us?"

"I can't say Sergeant."

"Noted." Pistol cracked his knuckles. "Remind me to beat his ass back into the hospital when we get back to the world."

"Yes, Sergeant." Pilsen hesitated. "Is this your first deployment, Sergeant?"

"Who? Me or Pistol?" Cassidy asked.

"Either of you."

"It's my second in Afghanistan, did two prior in Iraq before this. How about you Pistol?" Hondo replied.

"Same. I'd have killed for good bread the second time in Iraq. Got stuck on a patrol base for eight months. Tray rations and the like the whole time." He spat on the ground. "Go ahead and put that pan up, Pilsen. Then get your blouse on and come over here."

"Yes, Sergeant."

Properly attired once again, Pilsen stood in front of Pistol. The elaborately mustachioed man stepped forward, taking the cigarette out of his mouth as he spoke and inspected the uniform.

"Do you understand what's expected of you now?"

"Yes, Sergeant."

"Good. Now, do we have enough for you to make bread here for us?"

"Yes, sergeant. I'll just need more yeast at some point."

"We can get yeast, lad. Sergeant Cassidy, what time would he need to be up in the morning to handle making bread and getting breakfast ready?"

Hondo looked skyward, thinking through the process.

"Zero-four," he declared.

"Corporal Jimenez will be informed to come look for you tomorrow morning at 0400 hours." Pistol tapped his chest.

"What about post standing?" Pilsen asked.

"You're not doing that anymore. You're on assignment." Hondo declared.

Pilsen looked askance at the comment.

"Don't worry about Staff Munro. Talking to her is Sergeant's business," Pistol explained.

"Yes, sergeant."

"Do not get here after Sergeant Cassidy, you understand?" Pistol threatened.

"Yes, Sergeant."

"Off with you now."

For an instant, Stirling worried that the private would walk towards where he stood concealed. Instead Pilsen went left, toward the far side of the Mess facility and Stirling relaxed. He had a strong idea of what was going on. But he needed to make sure he didn't undermine the two men handling the mess.

"You think the Captain'll mind?" Cassidy asked as he finished securing a few items.

"Nah, I don't think so. I don't think she'll mind at all," Pistol suggested.

"Mind what?" Stirling asked loudly as he walked around the corner.

"Evening Sarn't Major," both NCOs replied as they continued about their tasks.

"Good evening. Which doesn't answer my question." Stirling leaned against the wall long enough to strike a match and light his cigar. "What did you do to Herfy?"

"Private Pilsen wishes to be a good soldier, Sarn't Major," Pistol replied.

"Do tell."

"Nothing to tell," Pistol said, flipping empty trays onto the drying rack. "Herfy was shown the door, and Private Pilsen walked in."

"Who made dinner?"

"He did," Cassidy assured.

"Bullshit. I've tasted his cooking. Who cooked dinner?"

"Private really cooked dinner, Sarn't Major," Pistol assured.

"This time he had proper oversight," Cassidy groused.

"And how on earth did you do that?" Stirling asked mildly.

"It helps not having that fat twat Daggett around," Pistol griped.

"Quite. What else?"

"We just explained the facts of life to him, Sarn't Major. Man does not live by pilchards alone."

Both Sergeants smiled at this and Stirling worried as he saw that devilish grin.

Slap matching mustaches on them, they'd be twins. Sweet Christ preserve us, as if either of these meatheads needs a twin. The world does not deserve such agony.

"Cassidy, you should show the Sarn't Major, like you did Pilsen."

"Fine," Cassidy sighed. "I will."

"He won't leave us alone until you do," Pistol intoned.

"It goes like this Sarn't Major — before I came to the colors, I worked in hotel kitchens. Even did two apprenticeships before I was eighteen."

"Isn't that a little young to be doing so?"

"Sort of. Daddy started teaching me when I was young, and I listened."

Reached into a sleeve pocket, Cassidy produced the same cards he'd shown to Pilsen. "These authorize me as a food handler. And an inspector. Everywhere I get stationed, I get new certs, and then maintain them. I have military and civilian licenses."

Stirling read the cards carefully as Cassidy continued to speak and point at different cards. "These are the civilian kitchens I'm authorized to work in, as a Chef de Partie."

"Partie?"

"I can run all the stations in the kitchen."

"Nice work."

Cassidy held up a black card trimmed with gold in a clear sleeve. "Sous Chef. I only use it when I'm on leave, but it's in case of lawyers."

"I didn't know restaurants had these."

"The hospitality company I worked for implemented them, so that staff could prove they were properly trained on how to do certain functions in the kitchen."

"Very pretty. What part of the kitchen was your apprenticeship in?"

"The first was culinary arts with a specialization in large group service."

"Sounds like cooking for crowds," Stirling suggested.

"I've done weddings for three-hundred before."

"That's impressive."

"It was, when it was all done," Cassidy admitted.

"After you stopped us from hanging him, Cassidy and I had a talk betwixt ourselves. The way we figure it, everybody has been so busy running all helter-skelter that we didn't have time to handle all the things that needed doing."

Stirling made a face as he thought over that tidbit. "I am loathe to say it, but you're right, lad."

"When Pilsen's in the kitchen, Cassidy takes care of it. I handle him the rest of the time."

"You sure?" Stirling asked.

"Positive. No more hiding in the kitchen being a dumb shit. He's got a schedule, he knows that he will be in my kitchen by a specific time," Cassidy declared.

"If he's not in the kitchen, he's with me, learning to be a soldier. You mentioned the road to Damascus. We took you seriously," Pistol added.

"Putting him on the straight and narrow." Stirling said it more as a statement of fact than a question.

"Very," Pistol agreed.

"Cassidy, you're still gonna have to sell the captain on this. There's things that absolutely must have her signature."

"Understood, Sarn't Major. Can I hold off on it for a little bit?"

"Why?"

"I hate paperwork."

"Fair enough."

Chapter 9

We'll Have Big Fun On The Bayou

At Staff Call four days after his departure, Colour Gallagher confirmed the doctor's final prognosis on Daggett.

"He's not coming back. Doc says he's too screwed up to consider any option besides a return to England."

"Well isn't he so lucky?" Munro muttered *sotto voce.*

"Which doesn't change the fact that we've got nearly two weeks of fresh food sitting in the reefer. We need a cook," Gallagher admitted. "Do any of your people have kitchen experience?"

"I think a couple of mine worked as burger flippers at a McDonald's," Tolliver suggested. Faces crinkled in mixed horror.

"Beyond fast food, please," Gallagher hastily added. "They'll get no extra duties and free reign when it comes to making a menu so long as they can cook. Decently even."

Cassidy felt a smile coming on, and he tried to contain himself. *They're not going to believe me. Not a single damn one of them!* He studiously avoided looking at Pistol or Mayne, both of whom seemed poised to speak if he didn't.

Giggle.

Cherney looked his way for a moment, then turned back towards Mayne.

Snort.

This time Tolliver looked his way, cocking an eyebrow. "You okay, Cassidy?"

Guffaw.

Now Nealen was staring at him, wondering why Cassidy was holding his sides as he laughed, unable to contain himself any longer.

"Sergeant, control yourself!" Gallagher ordered,

Slowly, he slowly unbent, as the entire room looked at him, wondering how he'd lost his mind.

"You have something to add, Sergeant?" Gallagher asked, lips pursed in disappointment.

"Yes Colour Sergeant, one moment." He lifted his radio. "Goblin, this is Gun Five Actual."

"This is Goblin, send it Gun Five Actual."

"Report to the Command Post with my tool kit. Lo-right-a-lay-oh."

"On the way!"

Nobody is going to believe this. Save for Sergeant Major or Pistol. At least we won't have to hide what we're doing to fix Pilsen! Cassidy told himself with no small amount of glee.

"What tool kit are you talking about?" Nealen asked in the quiet room.

"Staff Sergeant, it's better if I explain after Kramer gets here."

"If you say so." Nealen paused. "I've never asked this, but how long have you known each other?"

"I was the new corporal when he showed up at One-Eleven, did a MEU with them, jumped over to Third Battalion for a deployment at Sangin up north. Call it four and a half years and you're probably right."

"I didn't know that," Nealen admitted.

"Part of why we get along, Staff Sergeant. This is our third trip somewhere together."

"Still doesn't explain why we're waiting on Kramer," Gallagher said impatiently.

"I trust my brother not to muck about with my stuff, Colour Sergeant. Everybody else knows I'll beat 'em with my axe handle."

"That's fair."

"Good afternoon ladies and gentlemen!" Kramer loudly exclaimed as he ran inside the mess, two large black rolls stuffed under his left arm.

"Kramer is here. Perhaps now you can explain to us your undignified outburst, Sergeant Cassidy?" Gallagher demanded.

Cassidy's face curdled as he sharply turned to face Nealen. "Permission to speak freely, Staff Sergeant?"

"Enlighten us," Nealen ordered.

"Daggett is a cocksure idiot who doesn't know a pig's asshole from beef tenderloin when it comes to cooking and meal planning. He can microwave something. I'd even trust him to boil water without burning the pot, but don't ask for more than that. Three-year-olds run pillow fights better than the meals he puts out. He's outside his depth, overworked, and likely losing his mind trying to keep up. God bless him he can organize. But he gets lost making soup."

"You think you know how to run a mess?" a staff sergeant from the British side charged.

"He does," Kramer insisted

"I can't imagine you working in a kitchen," Nealen admitted.

"My father runs a series of Michelin-star rated restaurants," Hondo informed the crowd. "I grew up assisting him with inspections and audits."

"Anything famous us lowly mortals would know?" Fitzsimmons asked.

Hondo cocked his head to one side, thinking for a moment. "Biggest one so far is the Grosjean Marrick Hotel."

"The ski resort in Verbier, Switzerland?" Fitzsimmons asked in surprise and Cassidy nodded affirmatively.

"I honeymooned there when it had its grand opening," she exclaimed. "A hundred fifty euros for a rack of lamb is criminal I tell you! Utterly criminal! And that was before we added sides!"

Cassidy's eyes shined brightly as he began to speak. "A notch under a kilo of dry-aged Highland lamb, double cut. Served rare with a balsamic fig glaze drizzled across it. Best paired with parmesan fingerling potatoes, caramelized onions, and a glass of Chapoutier Hermitage La Sizeranne, 2001."

"You're doing good so far," Fitzsimmons assured.

Cassidy's lips quirked and his head inclined slightly, noticing how her stance shifted. It was a small thing, but it was something Daddy had taught him to watch for.

"Make that two glasses of Chapoutier for the new bride. She'll have rushed through the first to calm her nerves. The second will be savored more slowly as she works through her serving of the lamb. Assuming the sommelier is still Romain Jolles, the waiter will discreetly check the lady's cheeks to see how well she's handled her wine thus far. If she's wearing it well, the waiter will politely encourage a third glass of Chapoutier, otherwise, it's sparkling water to 'refresh the palate.'"

"Refresh the palate?" an onlooker asked.

"Slow down the drinking. We don't want an unsteady drunk disturbing the dining room."

"Makes sense. What next?" Fitzsimmons asked.

"Waiter will bring the dessert menu, and politely wait for the guests to order, before they lose their courage."

"Lose their courage?"

"To spend money on dessert," Hondo said in a voice full of charm and goodwill.

Morgana felt the need to reach for a purse she hadn't worn in months, if only to check for her wallet.

"A separate menu for dessert?" somebody interrupted. "Sounds frigging posh."

"Ayup. Daddy deliberately made it that way, used the corporate board's wives and those ladies' toff girl friends for his guinea pigs. Three options: first is the raspberry limoncello tiramisu topped with italian meringue. Second, passion fruit parfait with mango mousse." He held up a third finger. "French cotillions on chocolate sponge."

By the look on her face, he was hitting the right notes with the Captain, whose eyes widened at a memory.

"Which one do you think we picked?" Fitzsimmons queried.

"We?" Cassidy laughed. "We?" His derisive snort made clear what he thought of the question. "I've watched you at work for the last few weeks ma'am. We all know who told the waiter your dessert order. And it certainly wasn't your husband. The two of you drank Fonseca Ruby Porto, probably 92 or 95, in between feeding each other bites of cotillion." He paused, weighing his words. "After ordering a bottle of bubbly for your room, you made it to the elevator, which is when the shameless kissing started —"

"Okay I'm convinced!" Fitzsimmons interrupted. "Damnit, now Chris is gonna need to take me there for our anniversary."

"You're welcome ma'am," Cassidy said cheerfully. "Do try the scallop carpaccio this time."

"How many of the Crown Jewels does that cost?" Munro derided.

"With or without the gold flakes?" Hondo retorted with a smirk.

"Are you taking the piss?" Munro swore.

"You wish, Staff. Dessert is forty euros. Per serving."

"Bloody hell," Keating declared.

"What's the tool kit you told Kramer to bring?" Mayne asked, trying to steer the conversation away from dangerous waters.

"Tools of the trade, Sarn't Major." Placing both on an empty table, Cassidy unbuckled then shoved them gently. The black fabric unwound itself, revealing gleaming stainless steel knives and a variety of implements. His second roll contained small containers, each neatly labeled.

"Are those spices? Did you bring your own spices?" Fitzsimmons demanded.

"Yes, ma'am. I also started hitting the market in Zaranj with our terp to get more." He declared, holding an open shaker out. Fitzsimmons walked towards him in disbelief and took a whiff. Her eyes widened.

"What the hell, Marine? That can't be real!"

"You can get spices by the kilo in the souk," Hondo said cheerfully.

"By the kilo? Sounds like you're running a drug deal," Balcombe snapped.

"Yes ma'am. But these bricks won't piss off the DEA. I've got a bunch of stuff stashed in our truck," Cassidy said. "Which doesn't include what I mailed home while we were at Delaram."

"Which was?" Nealen asked, suddenly concerned.

"A kilo of pure Afghani saffron."

"Drug deal," Balcombe declared in a sing-song voice.

Hondo grinned at her. "Considering that I'm probably the only person here who knows three good ways to cut a kilo of heroin, I'd say that makes me highly qualified in the matter."

"Anyway," Mayne interrupted before the conversation could go further astray. "Call it professional curiosity, what does saffron go for, back in the world?"

"Three thousand for pure Spanish, if it's cut into thirty-four bags each weighing twenty-eight grams."

"And Afghani?" Munro said tentatively.

"Ten thousand."

"What's that in pounds sterling?" Keating asked, slightly awed.

"Um — Cassidy closed one eye as he tried to remember exchange rates. "I think it comes out north of six full bags."

"What did you pay?"

"Twenty dollars."

The room collectively gasped.

"Wait, is this why the culture lecture we had talked about the program trying to replace heroin production with saffron?" Nealen asked in disbelief.

"Yes, staff sergeant. I called Daddy's spice distributor after class. Saqib said the Taliban made roughly two hundred million dollars selling heroin illegally."

"What if they switched to saffron?" Nealen asked.

"Saffron prices are better than double over heroin. Possibly even four times as much. Nobody has ever figured out the top end for the market on quality saffron."

"Ya know, this really makes me hate the rotters that much more," Keating declared sourly. "They could be swimming in pools full of gold sovereigns from here to Timbuktu, and I could be home, enjoying a pint watching footie on the telly, but no! These assholes had to go making a mess of it all."

"How come you never told anybody about this, Cassidy?" Nealen demanded.

"I have no interest in peeling potatoes when there's fighting to be done," Cassidy said doggedly.

"Nonetheless, it is what we need, Sergeant," Fitzsimmons said, trying to keep tempers from flaring any further. "With Daggett not coming back, Herfy needs somebody to keep an eye on him."

"I really do not want to leave my gun, ma'am," Cassidy persisted.

"Does it matter that much to you?" Balcombe demanded.

"Ma'am, if I may?" Nealen interjected.

"Go ahead," Balcombe said.

"It takes a minimum of three-and-a-half years' work, if you're squared away, to become qualified as a gun chief, but even then you've got to wait for a slot to open up. And it really is about the best job you can ask for in a firing battery. Giving that up is a death sentence."

"I see," Fitzsimmons stated flatly. "We've got two weeks of fresh food which needs to be used up before it goes bad. After that, it's just tray rations, excepting what Leatherneck sends us as resupply. I hadn't intended to take you away from your gun permanently, but I can see how that would be a concern."

"Can I have your word on that, ma'am?" Cassidy asked.

"You have my word, Marine."

"Then I'll do it, ma'am."

"Anybody else have questions?" Gallagher asked.

"Will you need help?" a sergeant asked.

"I'll need to see what I'm working with. We've got what, two hundred something people?"

"Sergeant Brady, what are my counts?" Gallagher demanded.

"Seventy-nine Marines, one sailor, one-hundred thirty-seven enlisted, four officers."

"Two-twenty-one," Cassidy said after a moment.

"Is that with or without Daggett, Brady?" Fitzsimmons inquired.

"Without. Updated since we got the call from the doctors at Bastion."

"Fair enough," Fitzsimmons said. She turned her attention back to Cassidy. "After we get through dinner, we'll talk. From here on out, you are my Mess Sergeant. And whatever you say about the mess is what goes. Understood?"

"Yes ma'am!" Cassidy said excitedly.

"You'll need these, lad," Mayne lobbed him a set of keys on a ring. "Try not to lose them, yeah?"

"Understood, Sarn't Major."

"I expect dinner ready no later than seventeen hundred. I suggest you make the best use of your time," Fitzsimmons informed him.

"Errah ma'am!" Cassidy cheerfully declared, rolling his bundles back up, then breaking for the door at a speed even Fitzsimmons found impressive.

"Staff Sergeant Munro, you seem slightly shocked," Nealen suggested as he surveyed the room.

"Is there anything that blasted bugger can't do?" Munro demanded derisively.

"Can't keep a girlfriend to save his life," Nealen declared solemnly.

"Oh. Jeez. Really?" Munro scoffed.

"He ain't exaggerating," Kramer emphasized. "Sergeant Cass has had two since he's been in. Both times they tried to control him. The first one dumped him for going to Iraq and getting shot at."

"And the second?"

"Told him if he loved her he'd get out and work a real job. He reenlisted out of spite."

"That seems to be a common theme of his," Balcombe muttered.

"I wouldn't say you're wrong, ma'am," Kramer admitted. "But things have a tendency to go that way around him."

"You're okay with that?"

"Well ma'am, I ain't bored." Kramer's face took on a cheerful grin. "Sides, if'n it comes down to pulling pistols or whistling Dixie, I know which way he's a-gonna jump."

"Do tell."

"I wouldn't suggest Sergeant Cassidy purely sucks at singing." Kramer's grin grew wider. "But he has been kicked out of several karaoke bars. And he was stone sober every swingin' time."

#

"Wonder what's for dinner tonight?"

"I'd be partial to steak and kidney pie right now."

The Brits chatting were but two of the many personnel clustering around the doors to the chow hall. With two minutes to go, a crowd was gathering and nobody knew quite what was happening.

The door opened, admitting Cassidy into the late afternoon sun.

"So, what's for dinner, Sergeant?" a Marine asked.

"Food," Cass replied.

"Uh —"

"Privates and PFCs to port, Lance Corporals, Corporals to starboard, Sergeants and above to the rear! Make it happen!" Cassidy ordered.

"Oy, this is new," Munro muttered to Gallagher.

"Aye, but it could be worse. Do ya want to be eating pilchards right now?" Keating challenged.

"Well no, but —"

"Shut up and move then," Gallagher hissed.

Up ahead of them, lines were forming.

"Ladies by rank first, do we understand?" Cassidy commanded.

Mutters and acknowledgements greeted his ears. "Grab what you can eat. Waste nothing. Also, where is the Local Suck at?"

"Right here!" Jimenez announced.

"Menez, I have trays prepped for the guard posts. Grab a Humvee, back it up to the rear doors and you can carry everything off at once."

"Appreciate it, Sergeant Cassidy. Thanks."

"You're welcome." Cassidy surveyed the hungry crowd, mindful of the eyes watching him. "Rule number Seven: If the chow is good enough, the grunts will stop complaining about the incoming fire. Rub a dub dub, Lord bless this grub! Yay God! Amen!"

Turning on his heel, he strode back inside the chow hall.

Munro's eyes grew wide as she looked toward Gallagher. "Did he?"

"He did."

"Afternoon ladies, how's he doing?" Nealen asked as he walked up, sniffing the breeze.

"Staff Sergeant Nealen, that is a very odd young man of yours," Munro declared, crossing herself feverishly.

"He has a gift for that," Nealen said nonchalantly.

Munro scanned the sky nervously. "I'm still waiting for the lightning bolt to hit us."

Nealen chuckled.

"Give it time, you may even learn to like him."

"I do like the smell of whatever is coming out of the mess," Gallagher confessed.

"Hey Perez, what'd he make?" Nealen called out to a Marine near the front.

"Cheeseburgers, Staff sergeant. With fries."

"Oh hell yeah!" Johnson crowed.

The lines of men and women moved with surprising speed, and Colour Sergeant Gallagher quickly found herself inside the cool chow hall, grabbing food from the line Cassidy had set up.

"Well it certainly smells good," Munro admitted, apprehension ebbing away as she studied the spread. "At this point, what can it hurt?"

"Oh snap! Sergeant Cass, you made cookies!" Lance Corporal Moore joyously shouted from the other side of the serving line as he reached for the tray.

"Oi, you mean biscuits?" a British engineer said in exasperated fashion at the head of the line.

"What are you talking about?"

"This, with the chocolate chips in it!"

"Well it sure as shooting ain't a damn biscuit!" Moore replied.

"Yes it is."

"Biscuits get covered in gravy. When in the hell would you ever dip a chocolate chip cookie in gravy?" He asked.

"Biscuits. With gravy? You lot are mad!"

Cassidy smiled as he stepped forward, then looked down at the engineer, whose high cheekbones didn't come up past his sternum. "Little Miss, this may be a British base. But this, by God, is an American kitchen. These are cookies. Have one." He put a chocolate chip cookie in her open mouth. "The only Queen we recognize is Freddie Mercury."

#

A door into the mess had been propped open and as Sylvie walked closer, she saw a glimmer of light. Her stomach rumbled but she refused to quicken her pace.

We'll get there when we get there!

She'd been busy working on the next project and things got away from her. At nearly 7pm, she'd finally noticed that she was the only person left in her shop. Shutting down, she quickly secured her things then ran to the chow hall. The sight of lights and propped open door gave her hope that maybe there'd be leftovers still when she arrived.

Inside, the tables had been cleared and all she saw was Cassidy, sweeping the floor. Music blared as he moved about, almost dancing to the tune as he worked. She could also see that the warmers had been emptied. There was no food left.

Oh well, guess it's MRE time she told herself. Grabbing one from a pile of boxes in the corner, she grimaced. *Patty, beef, one each. Oh joy!*

Sitting down on a bench at one of the tables, dark thoughts ran through her head as she imagined her recruiter's face.

Join the Army they said. It'll be fun they said. See the world in the Army they said. Nobody ever mentioned getting stuck in Satan's asshole eating warmed over horse smegma!

With every thought, she proceeded through the steps of "cooking" the MRE. *Now I just need water to activate the heater pack —*

"Why on God's green earth are you eating that in my chow hall?" Cassidy demanded.

He stood in the kitchen doorway, torso somehow filling the otherwise empty door frame.

"I uh… I um… missed dinner!" she stammered.

Why am I acting like this? Sylvie asked herself.

"Well ain't that something," Cassidy said gruffly.

"Where's the water at? I need to get this heated," she blurted.

He eyed her up and down, the same way he had the first time they met, his expression guarded, clinical. His mouth quirked, curiously, as if trying to say something.

"Water?" he shrugged finally. "Follow me."

Inside the kitchen he pointed at the sink. "That one is in operation," he said brusquely.

"Thanks," she replied, stepping up and turning on the faucet. "Hey — what are you doing? I'm eating that!"

As she had turned away from him, Cassidy had stepped behind her and to the left, then reached down to pluck the heater bag out of her hand and tossed it into an open trash can.

"MREs. In my kitchen? Puh-lease. You want a real meal?"

"If you've got it, yes! I do!" Sylvie demanded.

"Good! Sit down right there and watch a man work!" He enthusiastically directed her.

Taking a seat where he pointed, Sylvie found herself able to watch him at work on the waist high prep table, hands and knives moving in rapid time as he began to talk.

"Ya know what the real problem with that Daggett kid was?" Cassidy asked her as he went about his craft.

"What?"

"No imagination. Being a good cook, a good chef, isn't just about producing food. There's gotta be a certain amount of soul and imagination to what you're doing."

"What does imagination do?"

"Take this beef patty," he said, holding one up on his palm. "Today it was a hamburger. Normally these are flashboiled in the big pots behind me. It's easy to do, and it'll mean mass production is very simple for all 221 of us."

He threw the patty onto his cutting board, letting the knife slash and chop through it with ease.

"But boiled beef is nasty in taste, and almost never gets seasoned right. Ideally you want this on a flat top or a grill of some kind."

Sylvie made a nasty face, remembering a hamburger she had tried at Camp Bastion on her way here. "Thanks no, I don't like burned meat."

"Yeah well that's the other side of your problem — you need somebody who does it right."

"I suppose you know how?"

"Watch and find out. You want one patty or two?"

Her stomach rumbled, loud enough Cassidy could hear it and she cringed from embarrassment.

"Sounds like two," he said with a chuckle, throwing a pair of thick, raw, red patties onto the cooktop, followed by two more for himself.

He didn't stop talking or moving the entire time, prepping both of their plates as he explained the steps he went through, and the spices he used on the meat.

When he finally presented it before her she was astonished at how good it looked and smelled.

"Go ahead, take a bite," he urged her.

It's a just a burger, it can't be that —

Sylvie felt her mind stop, not with a slam, but in a cacophony, hurried and confused. The spicy morsel of beef rolled across her tongue, the narrow-focus of all her attention. The spices amazed her as they played across her senses, a symphony of paprika, garlic, salt and whatever else she could only guess at. Sure Cassidy had told her what he was doing, but she'd partially tuned him out. In this moment, she regretted it.

Oh this is incredible!

Greedily, Sylvie began gulping down larger bites, enjoying all of the flavors as they serenaded her taste buds.

"You like?" Cassidy asked, his voice far more playful and considerate.

"Yes. Ohmygosh this is delicious!" she blurted, speaking around a large chunk of beef and tomato.

"I'm glad you enjoy it." He grinned for her, then dug into his own plate.

"You haven't eaten yet?"

"Habit from when I worked in a restaurant," Cassidy explained.

"Oh."

"Lyons, right?"

"Yeah, thanks for remembering," Sylvie said.

"You're welcome."

"So you're the new Mess Sergeant now?"

"That's what the captain says. And she be da boss," he intoned.

"What meals?"

"She was saying something about breakfast and dinner. Everybody can eat MRE's for lunch, at least until we run out of fresh stuff, then we switch over to t-rats." His lip curled in a sneer.

"How bad are those?" Lyons asked, unsure she really wanted to know the answer.

"Pretty awful unless you spend some time fiddling with them."

"Fiddling?"

"You know, experiment."

"Oh, Experiment! That I understand." She eyed him over a french fry. "You Americans have the strangest colloquialisms."

"Well, thank you. We try."

Sylvie shot him a baleful glance. "You're succeeding."

"You're welcome."

"But I didn't say 'thank you!'"

He waved a hand airily. "No need. I thought I'd spare you the trouble."

"So why are you doing this?" Sylvie asked.

"Because I like getting a rise out of you."

"Not that!" Her cheeks blushed furiously. "This. The mess. Why'd you switch over to do this?"

He sighed. "For starters, I hate what Daggett was cooking. It really sucked. Except the rolls. Those were pretty good. And now we know Pilsen was making those."

Picking up a dill spear, he took a bite and crunched thoughtfully. "The oldest rule of being the cook — he who holds the knife picks his cut."

"Never heard of that," Sylvie admitted.

"Let's just say that I have a sweet tooth and a fondness for proper baked goods. Have you ever considered croissants stuffed with nutella?"

"I like croissants. I like nutella. Where do you get off combining the two? And where did you find the butter out here to make it happen?"

Cassidy smiled. "I have my means."

"If it gets out that you have chocolate or Nutella, there's likely to be a riot!"

"Well then, we'll just have to keep it our little secret, won't we?"

"You are a bad man, Mister Cassidy."

"Thank you, Miss Lyons. It's a gift."

Chapter 10

The Heart is a Lonely Hunter

Brian Kramer stepped out of the back door to the kitchen and squinted at the bright sunlight that assaulted his eyes.

Damn desert. If there is Hell on earth this might just be it.

He let out a heavy sigh of hot, dusty air and let the door slam shut behind him. He was making his way towards the guard posts, to make his rounds as corporal of the guard, but didn't get very far before a head popped out of the mechanic bay and a feminine voice called out to him.

"Hey Kramer!" It was Lyons. "You busy?" she asked.

"Just doing my rounds, what's up?" he called back, pausing to see what the woman wanted. Lyons glanced back into the mechanic bay briefly before stepping through the door and jogging up to him. He watched her as she closed the distance, how her braided hair swung back and forth behind her, the easy, lithe way that she moved, how whatever she wore could never fully hide the contours of her curves.

Cass, you might just have struck gold this time, Kramer thought. *Not only is she gorgeous, she's wicked smart too.*

"I was hoping I could talk to you. I have a few questions," she said when she got close enough, slowing down and eventually stopping in front of him.

"Okay. Come with me on my rounds, we can talk while we walk." Kramer started walking again and Lyons fell in line beside him, matching his stride unconsciously.

"You're Cassidy's best mate, yeah?"

"You mean his best friend? Yeah, you could say that."

"Mate, friend, same same," she paused briefly, choosing her words carefully, "I... I don't usually get along very well with my fellows. They say that I am," she paused, "too brash, too lacking in subtlety. So I usually keep my mouth shut and say nothing, because it's easier that way. It's where I get the 'recluse' reputation from, if those rumors have spread far enough into your camp for you to hear them. Thing is, I can't very well tolerate beating around the bush, as you say." She let out a sigh, "I suspect I fit in much better with you Americans than with my own countrymen, they don't like it very well when a woman is as direct as I am. Which brings me around me to why I requested to speak with you, being direct that is. Cassidy, what can you tell me about him?"

Brian smiled. *We're gonna get along just fine, girlie.*

"That depends on why you're asking," he said lightly, glancing sideways at her "and what you want to know."

Lyons smiled back, "Sounds like you know all his secrets."

He let out a bark, "Just about girlie. He's about as close to a brother as a man can get without being blood."

Brian held up his hand as they approached the guard post. "Post Three, report!"

"All clear at this time, Corporal. Nothing moving except flies and those weird white ladybugs."

"How are you for water?"

"Got a dozen bottles and two MREs."

"How much ammo?"

"Four cases for the 240."

"Good trash. Carry on, I'll see you in a while."

They started walking again and a dozen steps further and he spoke once more. "So, tell me, Lyons. What secrets are you interested in trying to twist out of me?"

"Not secrets, those are his to keep or not, I'm more just trying to figure the bloke out. He... baffles me. Apparently he's always angry like a fooking gorilla during mating season."

"But on the other hand, he reads things like Kipling, and recites it from memory," Kramer continued for her.

Lyons nodded, "And the way he recites it, you can tell there's real thought and passion behind it," she paused, recalling the battle of words between Pistol and Cassidy, "There's a big difference between just reading something, and really pouring your heart into it. And when Cassidy had that showdown with Pistol in the mess? You could tell that nothing else existed for him in that moment, that he had a great passion for the words you don't hear from most men."

Kramer smiled to himself, having been a victim of Cassidy's rants about the obscure topics the man was 'passionate' about more than once, "That's Cassidy for ya."

"Yes, and I don't get it! It doesn't make sense. What kind of a man is he that those two things live side by side in him?"

"Well first thing you gotta do is stop putting the man in a box."

A sharp laugh escaped her at the mental image of trying to squeeze the hulking marine into anything remotely box-shaped.

"They make boxes big enough to hold him?" she jested, turning and grinning at Kramer.

"Only in your mind," he grinned back, but his message was clear.

"Hm." *He's right. When you get down deep enough,* most *people don't fit into boxes. And even then, Hondo Cassidy is not most people. Not even a little bit.*

They walked along in silence a bit further as Lyons mulled it over. "He's complex," she stated finally.

"Just a little."

"Here's my real concern, Kramer," she stopped walking and he paused to turn and face her. She looked straight into his eyes as she spoke, her gaze intense and serious, "He seems to be honest. I've had my fill of men who seem that way, but hurt me when they don't get exactly what they want. I am not a little girl."

No, you're definitely not 'little.' Or a 'girl.'

"I want to know if your best mate is a man of his word. A good man. Or have I got this all wrong and he's too good to be true?"

Oh, I like her. Kramer thought as he gave her a cocky smile. *No bullshit with this one.*

"You're in luck, Lyons!" he turned and started walking again. She fell into step beside him once more, body language still intense and focused. "You're not gonna find a better man in all of Helmand. He's more honest than me even, and that's saying something," he looked over at her, his tone deeply serious, "When he takes a notion as to something, the only one that convince him otherwise is him, and he don't like taking orders from people who ain't in charge of him," he looked away and then grumbled as an afterthought, "If only his previous girlfriends would actually have believed him, it could have saved him from suffering a world of pain."

"How do you mean?"

"Hold that thought," Kramer ordered. "Post Two, report!"

"All clear, Corporal. I got a cold case of water and three MREs, two belts for the Mark!"

"Roger that. Anything moving?"

"In about 20 minutes my dick if The Taliban don't gimme something to shoot at."

"Boy, when did you find time to break out tweezers and a microscope?" Kramer teased.

The Marine on post looked down, face showing a hurt expression. "I'll have you know that I keep my girlfriend very happy."

"How? Growing cucumbers?"

"You're a dick, Corporal!"

"No shit, son. Carry on, I'll haze you later."

"Aye, aye Corporal!"

Sylvie grinned at the easy camaraderie between them, a sign of the good morale and easy manners the Marines had among themselves, quite a bit different than how things were run in the British Army. This foreign culture of theirs felt like some piece of home that she'd been missing her whole life, and made a part of her ache to belong to it. They walked out of hearing distance before Kramer spoke again.

"Listen, the man's history is his own, and it ain't my place to go telling his life everywhere, even to somebody that's interested in him."

"That's fair, and I appreciate your forthrightness in this. Again, it's a refreshing change of pace."

"We may be loud and uncivilized according to all y'all folks, but we tell it how we see it. Any other questions for me?"

"Yes, but I think I'll ask them another time," she paused briefly, thinking through her next words. "Do you think he'll mind if I go asking him about his personal life?"

Brian shrugged, "Certainly won't hurt. But if he doesn't want to answer he'll tell you so. He's not hiding anything, just doesn't want to talk about it right then."

"As it should be. Thank you."

"No problem."

They were approaching the trash pile that happened to be between Post Two and Post One, and Lyons grimaced inwardly as she caught a whiff of it. It had started off as a pit that the engineers had dug out, but now the pit was filled in with refuse with more refuse piled on top. And it was always burning. Not an ideal way to handle trash, but there were no other reasonable options open to them.

"I'm unfortunately not busy at the moment," she piped up again, "waiting on a machine to get fixed. Think he would mind if I bothered him?"

"Gotta be honest, I don't think he would say no to some company from a pretty thing like yourself."

She felt her heart jump slightly at the compliment. As welcome as their plainness was, she was still unaccustomed to how casually direct the Americans could be.

"You're too much," she managed to say, "Where would I —"

"Find him? He'll be over in the chow hall right now. Use the back door. Front is locked up," Kramer suggested, then added, "You know what, I'll walk you there so that I can avoid passing by the trash dump."

"I appreciate it."

They walked in silence back up to the chow hall, Lyons was lost in her own thoughts, Kramer not minding the quiet between them. It was interesting that she had come to him, much less this quickly. Women either ran away from Cass or tried to lasso him, like he was a bull in a field.

And this little filly came along asking about his character he mentally smiled, recalling her exact words. He wasn't sure if she was high-falutin with these five dollar words by nature, or because she was British, but it certainly made for more interesting conversation.

She really is pretty, that's for damn sure. And I haven't heard anybody say a bad thing about her. Side from the fact that she's colder than my mother-in-law's heart.

When they got to the kitchen, Kramer lifted a hand to knock on the door but stopped halfway and looked seriously at her.

"Lyons, do me a favor will ya?"

"Perhaps."

Never make a promise before you know what it is you're promising, her grandfather's words echoed through her mind.

He paused, considering his words, "This is the happiest I've seen the man in a while. Don't go playing games with him." There was an earnest plea in his voice. He looked back towards the kitchen door where Cassidy was and added more quietly, "My brother doesn't deserve that."

Sylvie smiled softly, every failed relationship and mistake flashing through her mind.

"I've had my fair share of being played. I have no intention of inflicting that on anyone else."

Kramer gave her a nod and started to knock on the door again but something stopped him.

"What's up?" Sylvie asked, concerned.

"Can you hear it?" the corner of his mouth turned up in a half grin.

"Hear what?"

"Listen closer. He's got music playing."

Sylvie put her ear against the metal door and Kramer watched as her eyebrows rose in surprise when she recognized the tune, "Is that Britney Spears?"

"Right in one!" The grin he gave her was filled with mischievous glee.

"Huh. Why?"

"Because he can," he shrugged, "Means he's in a good mood."

"Alright, well," she paused a second, trying to decide what she felt about it, then looked back at Kramer inquisitively, "Could he even hear us if we knocked?"

"Yeah I don't think so," Kramer lifted his radio to his face, "Echo Four Kilo to Five Actual, come in?"

Cassidy's voice crackled back a moment later, *"This is Chef, send it!"*

"Roll over to Channel Nine."

"Sure thing."

The music stopped and moments later the door opened wide to admit both visitors inside the cool dark kitchen. They stepped inside and Cassidy shut the door behind them. Lyons savored the fresh cold room and the relief it provided her.

"So what's up Kramer? Carrot fall outta your ass?" Cassidy demanded with a playful smirk on his face.

"Yeah, so I could shove it up yours, sideways."

True friendship at its finest, Lyons thought, her face taking on an amused expression.

Cassidy's eyes narrowed with suspicion, "If you think you're getting more Rip-It's, you best think again, cuz that ain't happening."

Kramer's grin widened, "Nah, nothing like that," he barked out a laugh. "Don't need Bath trying to taste sound again!"

"Or trying to get buzzed on non-alcoholic beer. *That* was a night."

"I didn't think he'd ever stop running to the piss tubes." Brian hooked a thumb at Sylvie and gave an impish grin, "Sergeant Lyons here was trying to pry your darkest secrets out of me, but I ain't no rat, so I came to report on her."

Sylvie put her hand to her chest and looked at Kramer with mock shock and accusation, "Corporal Kramer, I would never! Cassidy, this man is a scoundrel and a liar and you cannot believe a word he says."

Cassidy lifted an eyebrow in amusement and looked between the two of them.

"Well aren't you two just the picture of innocence and piety?"

Kramer snorted and Sylvie grinned.

"Excuse me while I piously beat your ass!" Kramer retorted.

Cassidy held his hand above Kramer's head. "Sorry, you must be at least this tall to try physical violence." Cassidy inclined his head to one side, grinning. "Looks like you come up short. Again."

"You're making me homesick for Missouri," Kramer retorted. "Anywho, I figure I'd leave Lyons here with you and let you answer her questions."

"Sounds good. I'll see you when you're finished."

"Roger that." They clasped arms for a moment, then Brian disappeared out the door, slamming it shut with an ominous click.

Cassidy looked her up and down, expression unreadable.

There was a challenging air about the boisterous man. As if he were daring her to question his examination before he'd finished. She wasn't surprised in the least by that. Firstly, because she knew how she looked and the effect she had on men. Grandmere had been quick to instruct her on that as she blossomed into young womanhood.

Since his arrival at Bourne, she had watched him move about with all the ease of a winter storm, tossing about all which came into his path.

And yet, I don't feel threatened by him. I know predators, I've seen them in action. He moves like one, but he isn't, she reminded herself.

His icy cold grey glare always moved about, watching for anything which might threaten his well-being. It was enough to unnerve a woman. But in this place, she found that glare relaxed, playful even.

Why is he relaxed? She asked herself. *Is he comfortable in here?*

"Can I get you anything to drink?" he asked finally.

"Some tea would be wonderful."

"What kind, we have breakfast, darjeeling, oolong, and chai."

"I'll go with chai." Her face took on a strange look. "Wait. Daggett never mentioned having chai tea. That cheeky bastard!"

Cassidy only smiled slyly and turned to start preparing the tea.

"Milk and sugar too?"

"There's actual milk?"

"Well, sweetened and condensed. Until we run out."

"Oh so we're living the toff life now! Yes, I'll have a spoonful if you don't mind."

Cassidy set about making her tea while Lyons took the same seat she had sat in the night before.

"So, whatcha wanna know 'bout?" Cassidy asked from across the kitchen.

Sylvie sighed, "Not secrets, as Kramer implied. I — Just — Wanted to know more about you."

"Well, he was right about one thing, it's probably best to ask me yourself rather than to try to find anything out through the rumor mill. I don't mind."

"That's not a thing I'm accustomed to being able to do. British men are different, not so forthright. It's a refreshing change of pace, I have to say. If a bit strange."

"I'm not surprised, they spend so much time trying to see who can do dry understatement better than the next moron."

"And you know this how?"

"Spent two years living in England. Western side of the country, out by Wales."

"West Midlands?" She asked, curiosity piqued.

"Aye. Traveled all over there."

"That's where I'm from!" Sylvie exclaimed happily.

"No kidding!"

"How'd you end up in the West Midlands?" She asked.

"Decided I wanted to travel," Hondo said casually.

"Which is how you wound up in England, in the middle of nowhere?"

"Yep!" He positively beamed as he carefully filled a styrofoam cup with fresh tea.

"Is that why you were the first one we dealt with? Your superiors figured you knew the culture well enough?" She took the tea from his hands, enjoying the fresh smelling steam rolling off the top. It smelled majestic.

"More or less. Though most folks didn't think it was the smartest move at the time."

"Why not? Do they doubt your skill as a diplomat?"

"Just a little."

"You did make quite the entrance," she said over the rim of her cup before she took a small sip.

Oh now THIS is a proper cup of tea!

"Like Will Rogers always preached: 'Diplomacy is the art of saying 'nice doggie while you reach for a bigger stick,'" he explained.

"So what does that make you, the big stick?" Sylvie asked, taking another sip of her tea.

"That's what she said."

Sylvie snorted then coughed, looking up at him indignantly. "Next time, warn me, why don't you?"

"She said that too."

More coughing and sputtering followed before Sylvie regained her composure.

"Dammit Marine!" She growled.

Cassidy shot her a winning smile and turned back to his chopping block where he had items laid out for dinner that evening.

"What are you making?" Sylvie asked finally.

"Clown Shoes had a metric buttload of tortillas for some reason, so tonight it's King Ranch Chicken."

"Huh, he normally tried to do a taco bar, just for variety."

"Oh, come on! Did nobody teach that boy about meal planning in a high stress environment?" Hondo complained.

"What do you mean?" Sylvie asked.

"What's easier to serve and carry, taco fixings, or a single scoop casserole with everything already inside of it? Furthermore, which of those can easily be shoveled down with a spoon?"

Sylvie considered the matter. "You make a fair point."

"Yeah. Also, it cuts down on how much energy is used to produce it. We're in the middle of nowhere, our entire supply line is wholly dependent on what can be trucked in or flown in, and flying stuff is super impractical."

"You take this stuff seriously."

"I try to."

"I'm glad we have you around. And in charge of the food now, too."

"I like cooking. It's fun for me. I can do it. But I didn't want to spend the rest of my life peeling potatoes."

"Why not?"

"I like being a professional soldier. That, and, well — there's a story there."

"Oh?"

"I was... I think twenty-one. Yeah. I'd just finished busting the brakes off this absolutely drunk pissant who came into the dining room of the Sorrel House."

"Sorrel House?"

"The hotel's fine-dining establishment."

"Ah, not the place to be ill-mannered then."

"No, no it is not. Boy's father and I had never crossed words afore. He looked at me though, after I tuned his son up and said to me 'you're so tough with that name and all that money behind you, but you ain't earned nothing on yer own account."

"That's a helluva thing to say.

"It is, ain't it?" He ran a hand through his short black hair. "I was so mad I walked into the Marine recruiter's office the next day and asked how soon I could go to boot camp."

"That's one way to go about proving folks wrong," Sylvie admitted.

"Yeah. Funny thing is, I never got to shove it in the old man's face," Hondo said.

"No?"

"Died from a heart attack behind the wheel of his farm truck while I was doing the Crucible March."

"Damn."

"Yeah. But I love my job, and I love what I do. Gives me a sense of purpose," Hondo said

"You want to stay till retirement?" Sylvie asked.

"I'm leaning that way. I'm already nine years in. I might need to get an education though."

"Enlighten me as to why," Sylvie said.

"Because in America anybody who wants to be an officer needs a college degree."

"What about your warrant officers?"

"Same thing."

"So your Company Sergeant Major is just an enlisted man?"

"First Sergeant Torrez? Yeah. Straight enlisted."

"How weird!"

"Right?"

"Is that what you want to be, a First Sergeant?"

"Nope. And I don't much feel like being a Master Guns either."

"A what?"

"Master Gunnery Sergeant. Enlisted technical expert in a given field. Every regiment has one for each job field, as necessary. I'm an oh-eight-eleven. Field artillery cannoneer. At Twelfth Marine Regiment, we have an oh-eight-eleven Master Guns. Same for Comm, and Motor-T."

"Sounds tiring to keep up with," Sylvie said.

He shrugged casually. "Can be. I've been living it for so long it comes easy to me now."

"I can tell. What do you want out of it?"

"Honestly? I'm not sure. I'd like to think that having my own battery would be cool. I wouldn't even mind staying in Hawaii. Most guys don't, but I like it there. Good weather, nice people, great food. And best of all — no snow."

"No snow? Why does that matter?" Sylvie asked.

"Ever tried to shovel it?"

"I never got the opportunity," she confessed.

Which was the truth. Last time she'd tried building a snowman, Grandmere had had Brabham come around with his shovel to help.

"Shoveling snow sucks. Even snow blowers are a pain," Cassidy continued.

"Where'd you live that fostered such a hatred of snow in you?"

"Wyoming. Little place called Thermopolis. Ski resorts, cattle ranches and hot springs."

"Where's that in relation to Jackson Hole?"

His face took on a facetious mien. "Ah yes, Jack Ass Hole. It's about two hundred miles away, maybe a notch over three and a half hours drive time."

"I take it there's no love lost between the two?"

"Jack Ass Hole is full of pretentious snobs and Californians with more money than sense, and damn near no class."

"Noted. What does your family do in Thermopolis?"

"Daddy's head chef for a hotel and hospitality company based out of there. I was his helper starting from about age eight."

"That's awfully young! Why did he do that?"

He spat into an open trash can. "Kept me from thinking about my birth mother and how much I hate her guts."

Her face took on a slight pained expression. "I'm sorry."

"I'm not." He said quietly, his voice suddenly gruff and angry.

Her eyebrows went up in surprise, "What happened, if you don't mind my asking."

Cassidy let out a deep sigh, "Teenage pregnancy turned into one really bad night when I was seven. After that, Uncle Anthony adopted me."

"Did you get to travel with him?"

"Yup. Not counting the military, I lived in seven countries and a half dozen states by the time I turned eighteen. Every summer we traveled to different resorts in the company performing inspections and training events."

Sylvie waited but that seemed to be all he wanted to say on the matter. She noticed that his posture and movements had become tense and barely contained, his knife coming down in sharp staccatos on the cutting board in front of him. She cleared her throat.

"Again, I'm sorry. I lost my parents when I was ten," she offered quietly, "They went out to hike K2 and... never came back."

Cassidy looked back at her, hands around her cup of tea and staring off at something far away from where they were. She turned and looked at him and he saw deep grief flash in her eyes for a brief moment.

"Turns out they died on my birthday. Pretty shitty day to die, ya know?" The corner of her mouth turned up in a resigned sort of smile and she leaned back in her chair.

Cassidy's face took on a severe, calculating look, and he glanced at her a moment longer before turning back to the chopping block.

"Can't argue with that. Guess that makes us both orphans."

She took another sip of tea and savored the flavor. It felt like it had been a long time since she'd had a cup of tea this good. And especially being out in the field and being shot at so often, and things breaking down or going missing, a good cup of tea at a time like this was like a soothing balm to her soul.

"Is the tea up to your standards?" Cassidy inquired casually, his movements having lost their severity. He seemed relaxed and comfortable once again, though she couldn't fathom entirely why.

"Oh the tea far exceeds my standards. And with how stressed I've been lately this is exactly what I need."

"What's got you stressed?"

"Oh this and that breaking down and going missing.

"Do tell?"

"Things keep breaking. Or disappearing. We never see them again."

"That does sound fishy."

"Fair enough but some of my lasses are blaming your Marines because it only started once you showed up."

"Nah couldn't be us."

"Tell me why."

"Everything we've kept so far has been from that big scrap heap. And we go over to your workshops to borrow tools that we put back." Hondo grinned. "Even my boys understand that it's hard to be charming when a woman with a gun is mad at you"

"This doesn't make sense," Sylvie admitted.

"I've got a gut feeling you're right. And so am I."

Sylvie considered it, "That would be odd."

"But not impossible. Local Suck, this is Five Actual," Cassidy spoke into his radio.

"Send it Five Actual."

"What is your position?"

"Out in the motor pool. By the gym."

"Stay there, en route to you."

"Roger that."

"Miss Lyons, it's been a pleasure. Unfortunately I must go speak with a man about a horse."

"Likewise, Mister Cassidy."

"Please come back around sometime. I'd appreciate it. Private Pilsen!"

"Yes, Sergeant?" the younger man said as he walked out of the back.

"Finish dicing the onions, then check the chicken trays. If those are ready, prep the mixer for shredding."

"Yes, Sergeant."

"How did you accomplish that miracle?" Sylvie asked as they stepped through the door and dogged it shut.

Hondo's lip curled around in a proud sneer. "I am a charm for making riflemen from mud."

Sylvie glanced slyly at him. "Will he Maxim his oppressors?"

"It is as a Christian ought to do."

Her laugh made him smile within himself to hear it. "Good day Miss Lyons."

"Good day to you, Mister Cassidy."

\#

Rifle slung across his back, Hondo moved through the bright sunlight across the motor pool toward where the Marines kept their vehicles parked. Music played loudly from the gym space as a crowd cheered on somebody he couldn't see.

Decent day. Nobody's shooting at us right now. Wonder what the hell they're doing over here?

Closer toward the workshops, he found Jimenez.

"Whatcha wanted to see me bout, mano?" Jimenez asked quietly as Cassidy walked up.

"What are they doing?" Cassidy asked, gesturing with his chin.

"Dance off. Didn't take much to handle PMCS."

"Figures, we ain't driven a whole lot lately. It's all foot patrols for us."

"Who ever guessed we'd get paid to go for long walks?"

"On waterless beaches?"

"In the meantime, the guys're screwing around between patrols, letting off some steam."

"Good. They need it."

"Yeah. So. What you want?"

"You heard any complaints about stuff going missing or being broken?"

"A few times. Nothing big."

"I'm hearing it more."

"Yeah?"

"Si. Some asshole. Maybe assholes are breaking stuff."

"You think our guys?"

"While I wouldn't put it totally past them, they're being really well-behaved."

Jimenez snorted.

"Okay. Mostly well behaved."

"Yeah."

"We both know who we don't trust." Hondo cast his eyes toward the ANP compound.

"Uh-huh." Jimenez chugged from his water bottle, looking toward the compound as well.

"What gave you that thought?" The New Yorker finally asked

"A severe lack of willingness on their part to eat with us."

"So?"

"Bread and salt. It's a cultural and religious thing for them. Once they eat bread and salt with somebody, they're honor-bound by the Quran to not betray them."

"So no bread or salt, they can act how they want?"

"Uh huh."

"Damn."

"Yeah. We might want to move to a two-by-two policy after dark."

"I hear you, I'll see what I can do to get the Brit's to sign off on it."

A scream rent the air and both Marines looked toward its source in time to see McCrae running away from the dance off.

"Jesus, Mommy save me from the big black man!" he shouted, disappearing into the collection of workshops where several soldiers stared at him weirdly.

"Come back here! I wanna hug!" Shockley shouted, following him as fast as he could shuffle step with his trousers around his ankles.

The visual spectacle might not have been so horrifying were it not for the massive snake which appeared at Shockley's pelvis, bouncing up and down with every step.

Lieutenant DiResta, sitting in the entrance of a workbay as he read through a technical manual, looked up in response to McCrae's cry of terror. Shockley, working hard to keep pace with the terrified lance corporal, flopped past not a foot away from the startled officer's face. DiResta slowly raised the technical manual higher, trying to hide his revulsion. Around them, Marines laughed uproariously while many of the soldiers looked at each other in shock.

"Well. I think I'm gonna go have a chat with Sarn't Major," Jimenez announced.

"I hear my kitchen calling me."

"Sure it's not a new girlfriend?"

"Shut your whore mouth. Or I'll tell Shockley how much you love anacondas."

Jimenez subtly flipped him off, causing both men to laugh before going their separate ways.

#

Lyons had slipped out of the mechanic's bay what felt like hours ago, and Sandra was starting to get concerned. Granted, their crew didn't have anything to do now that, yet again, something important was broken, but it was still unusual of Sylvie to be gone. Sandra picked at her nails and glanced towards the door for what must have been the third time in a minute.

"Ye've been starin' at tha' door past 20 minutes like yer expecting trouble to come walkin' through it," Lance Corporal Hope Aitken chided lazily. "What're ye so worked up about?"

"Lyons disappeared, didn't tell anyone where she went, and she ain't been back in a while. It's not like her," Sandra replied, grimacing as she investigated a scab on her thumb.

"Well it's not like we 'ave much in the way of things to do at the mo'. If yer so worried 'bout 'er, go find 'er. And don't ya need to be working on that busted Coyote anyway?"

Sandra glanced over at the younger woman who was lounging in a chair, fanning herself with a folded piece of paper as she stared absently at the useless fan above her.

"Ya sure you'll be fine here?"

"Don't cha worry Corporal, I'll hold down tha' fort here, go find Lyons. I'll call for ye if any of us can't manage to put two brain cells together to figure a thing out. Off with ye!"

"Well then by your leave, Lance Corporal!" Sandra made a mock bow.

Aitken grinned, still staring at the fan, "No, no Corporal, by *your* leave!" she jested while making a shooing motion with her hand, "Ah'm gonna do my best to whip this fan into shape, bloody shorted circuits."

Sandra chuckled and made her way out of the back door of the bay, towards the tents. She squinted at the harsh sunlight and closed the door quickly behind her. Although the air conditioning in the bay was hardly there, it still did something to take the edge off of the heat of the Afghani desert, and was thus preciously guarded.

She made her way over to their tent, wondering if perhaps Sylvie had gone to take a nap, only to be greeted by an immaculately empty cot. She put her hand on her hip and sighed.

"Ye can't go changing up yer patterns on me Sylvie," she said disapprovingly to the empty cot, "Mah fair skin ain't made to keep walkin' out and about in this desert."

Alright, not in her cot, not reading a book, not in the bay, not on duty... where in the blazes has this girl run off to?

Sandra stepped out of the tent and looked around, surveying what she could see of the base and trying to decide which direction she might have the most luck in. It wasn't impossible that she was in the kitchen. She had talked this morning about the Marine, Cassidy, having made dinner special just for her the night before.

I'll start there then.

She started walking parallel to the motor pool, planning to loop up and around to the kitchen.

One of the interesting things about Sylvie was that, due to her honest nature, nearly every emotion was written clearly on her face. She tried to hide it of course, but to someone who could read people well, Sylvie was no challenge. Sandra was very, very good at reading people. And what Sandra read on Lyon's face this morning, when the woman was chattering on about the previous night, was that she had a major crush going on.

About time too! Maybe she'll have better luck with an American man than with a British lad. Poor girl.

She recalled the last time Sylvie had a crush on a man, and how utterly south that debacle had gone when he found out that she wasn't some wild horse that he could tame. No, Sylvie was less like some sort of horse and more like what her name implied, lion-like. But of course, every young buck who came along and laid their eyes on her only saw a pretty woman, and not the unyielding strength prowling just beneath her skin.

Pricks, the whole lot of 'em. None of those chaps deserve a woman like Sylvie. Sandra sighed heavily. *But really thinking about it, it ain't a smart idea, getting mixed up in any sort of romance out here. We're getting shot at near every day.*

They'd already sent too many friends home in body bags, romance out here seemed too much like playing Russian roulette with firecrackers. Even something as harmless as a crush.

Sandra was startled from her thoughts when a sudden ruckus arose from the motor pool. She couldn't catch any of the words at first, but whatever was happening, it was loud, and it was getting closer. Sandra placed a hand on her rifle instinctively, expecting trouble.

She watched as one of the Marines sprinted out from the motor pool, running pell mell as he shrieked and screamed in abject terror. "Jesus! Mommy! Save me from the big black man!"

Sandra stared at the odd spectacle, wondering what he was going on about when she saw what he was hotly pursued by: one of the Corporals was half-waddling, half-running, with surprising dexterity given how his pants and boxers were at his ankles. The man seemed completely disinterested in covering himself, but entirely focused on seeking revenge on his fleeing compatriot.

And there, hanging right where you expected it to, was the most magnificent thing Sandra had ever seen. Before this instance, she wasn't even aware that they really existed that big in real life. Sandra had always thought it was just a trick of camera angles but no! It was real!

As if in slow motion she watched the object of her desires, the great certainty of her most closely guarded fantasies bouncing freely with every step as he turned left and disappeared behind the building.

"Come back, McCrae! I need a hug from my favorite white boy!" the pursuing Marine shouted.

"Good lord, that was more than I ever wanted to see in a lifetime."

Sandra's head whipped around to the voice to see Lieutenant DiResta still seated by the open door with a stack of papers in his arms, looking at where the two Marines had disappeared, a somewhat traumatized expression on his face.

"Sir!" The greeting came out as a squeaked exclamation and she cleared her throat before speaking again, "Lieutenant DiResta, I didn't see you there!"

"Bunch of bloody hooligans, the whole lot of 'em."

"Hooligans, yes. Certainly. The absolute worst." Sandra parroted while she tried to calm her suddenly erratic heartbeat.

"Not even the decency to try and cover himself in the presence of a lady!" He turned and looked at Sandra, "You alright there, Collier?"

Sandra was frozen in place with her hand still idly on her rifle, eyes wide and looking very much like a deer in the headlights. DiResta mistook her expression to mean that she was traumatized by the experience and placed a comforting hand on her arm.

"I'm sorry you had to see a thing like that, how about you go get a cuppa and... oh bloody Yanks, look away Collier, they're coming back around." He grimaced as they rounded the building they had disappeared behind and started coming back their way.

Sandra stared until the man finally managed to pull his trousers up and started pursuing the miscreant in earnest. They disappeared back between two trucks in the motor pool and DiResta sniffed with indignation.

"Completely uncivilized. No wonder we let the colonies go."

"Yes, uncivilized. Sir." Sandra parroted again, still staring at where they had disappeared.

"Collier, you really look like you're in need of a nice cuppa."

"Cuppa... sure..." She mentally shook herself, "Wait no! I'm looking for Lyons. She disappeared a while ago and hasn't shown up back in the bay."

"Oh. She passed by here a second ago, headed toward the motor pool."

"Motor pool? Oh thank goodness, thank you Lieutenant!" She turned and started walking briskly towards the trucks.

"Sure you'll be alright there Collier?" DiResta called after her.

"Yes sir! Just fine sir!" she called back over her shoulder. There was a sudden bounce in her step and DiResta cocked his head to one side as he watched her walk off.

Never a dull moment with those Yanks around, he thought grimly to himself before he turned back towards the command post. *Must go speak with the Captain about this.*

Never a dull moment with those Yanks around! Sandra thought enthusiastically, gears turning furiously in her brain as she tried to figure out how to go about enacting her plans without being caught. *Because I know what the trophy is for winning. I want it all to myself. Oh yes.*

Chapter 11

It's Raining Men

"Good morning ladies, gentlemen," Hondo announced as he walked through the serpentine passageway and into the command post.

"Mr. Cassidy, this is a surprise. To what do we owe the pleasure of our new chef?" Leftenant Balcombe asked from her desk.

Short, and so bubbly Hondo would've sworn she was secretly a blonde at birth, Camille Balcombe had a wonderful head for keeping track of tasks, which Cassidy supposed was perfect given her billet as the company's Executive Officer. Even if she was still mildly pissed at him for sitting on her.

"Well ma'am, that would be the problem." He held up a sheet of lined paper covered in neat script. "I've got a list of supplies I'd like to request, but I'm not sure who to submit it through, or what my limits are." He shrugged. "I'm not even sure who I report to around here."

"Oh, well that definitely goes through me," Balcombe confirmed. "As for who you report to, Colour Sergeant, I think he's yours?"

Gallagher sighed. "Aye, it's likely."

"Well I approve supply requests anyway, so why don't I handle this directly?"

"Sounds fantastic, ma'am. Thank you."

Balcombe made a come hither gesture at Cassidy. "Gimme."

Cassidy handed over the list and Balcombe began to read.

"What is all of this?" she demanded after a moment.

"Well ma'am, it's like this. People need food. We can both agree on that, right?"

"Absolutely."

"But what people really want is food they enjoy. How much do you like Yorkshire puddings and roast?"

"Love it. Especially for Sunday dinners."

"How would you like it if I made that some Sunday next month?"

"I'd think you were a damn genius." Her eyes narrowed. "Wait. You know what Yorkshires are?"

Cassidy smiled. "I lived in West Midlands for two years."

"How much practice do you have at making them?" she said more seriously.

"Better question ma'am: How many pounds of roast do you think your guys and gals could consume?"

Balcombe's face scrunched up as she thought about what he'd asked. "I don't know," she admitted at length.

"That's the thing — I do. Hundred kilos of beef divided by two-hundred twenty-one people is a shade under half a kilo per person, and allows for loss during cooking. By the time it's cooked and done, you're looking at roughly a third kilo of beef per person."

"You've got my attention, what else is involved?"

"Fifty kilos of flour, ten dozen eggs. Barrels of beef tallow" Hondo pointed to lines on the form. "That's all of this."

"Oh," Balcombe blinked as she reexamined the form. "And what's the rest?"

"More meals planned. I tried to do a menu for the rest of the deployment, with an eye towards improving morale. One hot meal in the day, one MRE, one T-rat. One week, breakfast t-rats, another week dinner t-rats. Should be enough diversity to keep people from going crazy."

"That's a lot of food," Balcombe said, slightly shocked at the volumes he wanted to obtain.

"Yes ma'am, there's a whole bunch that goes into feeding the troops."

"I see. What about these items?"

Cassidy glanced where she was pointing at. "Oh yeah, that. We don't have enough spices here, ma'am."

"Why do we need more than salt and pepper?" she asked, bewildered.

"Did you eat the eggs this morning ma'am?"

"Yes, they're very nice."

"That's onions, coarse garlic, a pinch of paprika, red pepper flakes, and celery salt."

"I'll see what I can do, but I make no promises," Balcombe assured.

"Understood." He scratched at his chin, then lowered his head and spoke much more softly. "Ma'am, is our sat phone working?"

"Why do you ask?" She said, understanding intuitively that he was trying to keep the matter quiet.

"I have an idea. I just need permission to make a few calls."

"Inside the privacy booth. Keep it short."

"Can do. Will do."

\#

The first time the unknown number tried to call through on his personal cell phone, Anthony Cassidy let it run to voicemail. The tall, collected Head Chef of the Marrick Corporation was reviewing his audit schedule. Speaking with a telemarketer held no interest for him.

His office phone rang, and he let this run to voicemail as well.

"Hey daddy, it's me. Pick up your cell please when I call again."

This time, he was quick to answer. "Hey, boy are you?"

"I'm alright, Daddy! How are you?"

"I'm doing well, Hondo, What's new?"

"Not much. Thought I'd call and say hi."

"Well thank you. I appreciate it. I thought you were in Afghanistan?"

"Oh, I still am."

Anthony Cassidy's eyebrow rose.

"They let you take your phone with you?"

"Nah. I'm using the Iridium — satellite phone that is."

"Oh. Sure, sure. So what's going on?"

Cassidy gave a brief summary of events, including the number of people he was feeding.

"Well. Seems you're in a bit of a bind," Anthony said mildly.

"Yeah, it do look that way," Hondo admitted.

"Let me see what I can dig up for you. What's transit time?"

"About thirty days."

Anthony *tsssked* unhappily. "Such a shame. I've got a new supply of black truffles I think you'd enjoy."

"When I get back, daddy. When I get back."

"I know. And I know it's what you love doing, but I will be glad when you're no longer deploying all the time."

"I know daddy. Oh, did you enjoy what I sent you?"

"That kilo of saffron? Yes. Thank you," Anthony said enthusiastically. "Abbu also told me that he appreciates being told of a new potential supplier."

"You're welcome, love you daddy."

"I love you too boy. Run along now, and have fun doing what you do."

The line clicked and Anthony sighed, then looked up to the wall above his desk. Hondo's face covered that wall with multiple glossy images across two decades' worth of life together.

"Son, you always did have a will to wander. I just wish you'd settle down a little, even for a minute. I'm not getting younger. And I'd really like grandchildren at some point." He sighed.

Still, I could do far worse than have Hondo for a son. Even if it was only by adoption.

Anthony began writing a plan of action, considering what he had sent in the past as care packages, and what Hondo needed now. When he finished, Anthony realized his office door was open. Sophia Marrick, his boss's wife and the company Director of Operations stood in the entryway. He started to greet her when he realized she was crying.

"Sophia, ma'am, what's wrong?"

"Look at this card Hondo sent me!" Sophia declared, thrusting it into his hands.

"When did this show up?" Anthony asked.

"Three minutes ago. It was delivered along with flowers from Mr. Reimer's shop in town. He says Hondo called in the order from Afghanistan, and dictated the card too!"

Oh good job, well done my son Anthony told himself. *Here I was, worried about what Sophia would say if you didn't call her too, but you thought ahead. Well done.*

Seeing the concern on Anthony's face, Sophia hurriedly dried her eyes.

"What's wrong Antony?" She said, dropping the "h."

Even after two decades of living in America, her accent would pop into her voice when she was truly concerned.

"Ma'am, I got to hear from the boy today. He called asking my advice on running a kitchen."

"Don't they have cooks in the military?" Sophia asked.

"They do, but where he's at, he's the only one who knows how," Anthony said, then explained what Hondo had shared with him.

Sophia tried not to laugh as she listened, and having failed in that, let her bell-like peals fill the air. "It serves the hellion right, my sweet boy is getting what he deserves after all these years. Karma é uma puta."

"True, true, ma'am, though now I'm wondering what we can do to help him."

Anthony paused, waited, popped a piece of venison jerky into his mouth, enjoying the peppers dance across his tongue in fiery tracks. Pushing Sophia to make a decision made the gaucho girl from the Pampas staunchly dig her heels in hard. Letting her come to a decision, however, worked wonders. She commanded the thing be accomplished, and it was. Sophia Marrick had a way about her in such matters.

"Señor Cassidy, would you care to accompany me to the warehouse? I need to inspect our backstock."

"Doña Marrick, I would be happy to assist you with that matter." Anthony assured her, pausing to snatch up a pen and clipboard as they headed toward the onsite warehouses.

\#

Every day at noon, Cassidy drove around to each of the guard posts, making sure those on watch had an MRE for chow and sufficient water. Jimenez didn't mind the assistance one bit, given Cassidy had been removed from the watch roster to handle chow duties.

For Cassidy, this enabled him to keep a reasonable accountability of their supplies. Running out of water was fatal in the desert. And he certainly didn't want to end up like a staff sergeant he'd known on his first deployment who'd thought the unit had too much and started destroying water stocks.

Because God alone knows how much I want that headache. Might as well go back to dating Monica. Hell to the no!

"Hallo the post! Whatcha got for chow?" Hondo called out.

"Nothing," an unhappy female voice grumped.

He perked up immediately, recognizing Sylvie. *Be nice to talk with her for a minute. And it is the duty of a Sergeant to ensure that all is in proper order.*

"How about water?"

"Half   a   case.   Maybe."

#

Sylvie had been late to post when she arrived, out of breath and pissed off that she had forgotten it was her turn up here. With lunchtime looming closer, her stomach didn't need encouragement to start chastising her either. *Hey, asshole, you forgot about me!* It had rumbled incessantly as she tried to think about anything besides the empty, ugly desert vista she was stuck in the midst of.

Hearing the Humvee pull up was a surprise, as was hearing Cassidy's voice. Her stomach started speaking again. *Wouldn't it be nice if he had Nutella and some decent bread for sandwiches?* At this her mouth began to water. Fresh bread didn't keep well, or for very long out here. *A good sandwich would be lovely.*

Thud. Thud. Thud.

Cassidy appeared at the top of the stairs, a case of water held on one shoulder and a pair of MRE's in hand.

"How we doin'?" he asked politely as he passed her water.

"Better now that you're here," Sylvie admitted. Breaking the plastic, she pulled a bottle from the pack and held it against her forehead. "Oh that feels nice. So cold."

"Fresh from the reefer," he assured her.

Removing the cap, she poured half of it on her face, and the other half down her throat.

"Getting hot are we?"

"Nah, I did that cuz I'm chilled in the midst of this frigid Afghan winter we're enjoying and I needed warmed up."

Cassidy laughed. "I do enjoy dry British wit. It's so much fun to hear again."

"Glad you appreciate it." Her stomach gurgled. "I don't suppose one of those MREs is for me, is it?"

"Thought I'd eat one and burn the other. Seemed the gentlemanly thing to do."

"Touché," Sylvie replied.

Cassidy held up both for her to read. "Pick which of these will make you puke less."

"Uhmm — this one sounds decent," she declared, grabbing the tan plastic-wrapped container labeled 'Chicken Pesto-Pasta.' "How bad can it be?"

"Better than Cheese and Veggie Omelet."

"That just sounds disgusting," Sylvie said.

"If you don't have salsa or hot sauce to go with it, you are so screwed. And not in the fun way."

"Blech."

"The only people I'd willingly feed it to are POWs," he admitted. "Oh and anybody who's pissed me off lately."

"That might be a war crime."

"Only if there's witnesses."

She nodded at the other MRE. "What flavor is that one again?"

"Chili Mac. Wanna try a bite?"

"I might. First I need to see how awful this Chicken Pesto thing is."

"Fair enough."

She paused, watching as he took a seat in the corner of the guard post and began to tear through his packet.

"Have you not eaten either?" Sylvie asked.

"Nope."

"Why not?"

"Figured I'd make the chow and water run first, then sit down in the chow hall and relax."

"You'd eat alone?"

"Force of habit. I can if I need to. Don't mean I want to. Especially right now with company so nice."

"Oh. Thank you." Heat rose in her cheeks and she fought against the desire to blush.

Dammit all! How does he get under my skin so well?

She realized with a start as she studied him that he wasn't wearing body armor. No ballistic plates, not even a helmet. Just his floppy-brimmed boonie hat and camouflage fatigues. That gollywog rifle was worn across his back on a short sling and she realized for the first time that he also wore a pistol on his upper thigh.

"Why no armor?"

"Didn't need it just to drive a humvee around the interior perimeter. Still ain't got a replacement helmet either. And I ain't much worried about getting shot."

"Why not?"

"Personal reasons."

He left those words hanging in the air, and Sylvie chose not to press him further on the matter. Looking out once more, Sylvie saw something moving in the breeze. "Huh."

"What's 'huh'?" Hondo asked, suddenly concerned.

"I swear I just saw fabric. Flapping around. Like those man-dresses the locals wear."

"Where'd you see it?"

"By that low hill right there. The one about —" she checked her range card. "Maybe 400 meters at our 2 o'clock."

"Huh. Where is the village at?"

"Way over thataway." She gestured to the southeast and he followed her gaze intently, cocking an eyebrow as he considered the relative merits of each location.

"So it's definitely nowhere near town."

"Not even close. Unless you're in a Ferrari."

A smirk turned into a smile and he stared at her, beaming. "What?"

"The way you say that word sounds so lovely."

"Ferrari?"

There you go again. Marinello should hire you to make their commercials."

Heat blossomed in her cheeks once more and she mentally cursed the man.

Damn his impertinence!

She looked away from him, embarrassed, waiting for him to speak once more.

"Given the distance, means it's not somebody's laundry that got loose and is flying around," she remarked.

WHAP! WHAP!

Rounds slapped against the weather-hardened sandbags on the exterior of the post as more whined off into the sky above them and Sylvie dropped her MRE pouch in shock.

"The hell was that?" she shouted as she began grabbing at the weapon in front of her.

"That is the AK-47 assault rifle, the preferred weapon of your enemy; and it makes a distinctive sound when fired at you, so remember it." He said it with a calm she couldn't believe, casually unslinging his rifle and bringing it up to his shoulder.

Downrange, as Sylvie watched, a man popped up from behind a low hillock.

BAM!

Even with a suppressor installed, Cassidy's rifle made her jump. Far away, the man shooting at them pirouetted awkwardly as he dropped to the ground. He'd managed to pull the trigger though, and at least three of his rounds smacked into the guard post, kicking up dust and splinters where they struck. More AKs appeared, pointed in their direction, muzzles flashing fire as rounds exited rifle barrels in a way that made Sylvie's guts churn.

She was spraying bullets all over the landscape when Cassidy slapped the back of her helmet.

"Short bursts! Use the ditty!" he commanded.

"What the hell is a ditty?"

"Hold the trigger down, say 'Die little bastard! Die!' Then you release the trigger and start over!"

"What?"

Shoving her aside, Cassidy demonstrated exactly what he meant. "It's so you don't run through your ammo too fast or overheat the barrel!" he explained.

"Oh!"

"Now, start shooting where I shot the other one!" Cassidy ordered, stepping back and up with his rifle in hand.

She tried the ditty, neatly stitching a five round-burst into the ground, watching the green tracer sizzle into the dirt.

"You're short!" he barked. "Try again!"

"At what?"

"The Taliban! What else? Your fairy godmother?"

She could still hear the crack of AK rounds overhead. Through it all, Cassidy stood beside her, watching through his scope.

Dirt kicked up where her shots landed and she adjusted upward again. Dimly, she heard Cassidy speaking into his radio.

"Post 2, Post 4, watch your sectors! The goat lovers will be waiting for you to switch fire and your attention over to here!"

"Post 3, FDC, do you need backup?"

"Just send ammo! Don't scramble QRF until we're sure this is it!"

"FDC copies all. Ammo on the way."

A man stood to shoot at them, not realizing he had stepped directly into the path of Sylvie's sights. A quick burst before he could drop back into cover caught him. His body jerked where he was hit and he fell backwards.

"I got him! I got him!" She shouted, terrified and elated all at once.

"Good! That's the way you do it!" Cassidy slapped her back plate. "Don't stop!"

Turning her attention forward, she resumed shooting. As she did so, she noticed everything else around her fading away. Dimly, she felt the vibration of footsteps pounding up the stairs. Something clunked as it impacted to the left side of her feet.

Sparing a glance she saw one of the marines on his knees, ripping open ammo cases and linking belts together. Then the ditty she was reciting to herself was over and she was shooting again.

Men came off the ground, moving at a run. Three of them, AKs in their arms and what had to be RPGs sticking up behind them, on their backs. Their appearance caught her off-guard. Not that it mattered. Before she could swing the muzzle around to take them down, Cassidy was firing.

BAM

The man in the center fell, arms outstretched as he tumbled.

BAM

Man on the left, in a brown dishdasha, had turned about and was trying to fire his RPG. Even as he pressed the trigger, his chest caved inward and his left arm went slack, pointing the tube at his feet. The warhead exploded a moment later and his body disappeared from view.

"Cleanup on aisle three!" Cassidy loudly chanted. "Cleanup on — Que merda! Seu filho da mae!"

"What's going on?" Sylvie shouted.

"That's the one Balcombe told me not to shoot. Son! The house limit is one!"

She saw the man he was referring to, now. He had turned at the sound of the RPG explosion, slipped and fell. As he started to rise, Cassidy let out a breath. Sylvie looked back to the man in the dirty blue vest. He was sprinting hard, arms pumping, his legs driving forward with furious intensity.

BAM

The man dropped again, tumbling as he fell. Dust flew into the air around him.

"Is he dead?"

"I ain't paid the insurance on him," Cassidy said calmly as he focused down range. "Until God takes him, or I've paid the insurance, I don't assume nothing."

Blue Vest tried to rise once more, but something in his legs wasn't working right even as he pointed his AK back at them.

BAM.

This time Cassidy's shot took him in the spine, just below the neck and he dropped with all the composure of a child's forgotten rag doll.

DING. Sylvie had never heard brass strike against metal quite that way as it bounced off the spent linkage. She watched the shell casing bounce around and spin before coming to a stop.

When it finished, she looked back up at Cassidy, surprised to see that his eyes had never left the target. Nor were any of the other men they had shot moving. Silence reigned, save where she could hear the reaction squad mounting a vehicle to go clean the site.

Slowly, reaching with his left hand so his right never left the trigger, nor his eyes the scope, Cassidy brought the radio to his face. "FDC, Post 3. I think that's all of them."

"Post 3, this is FDC. Thiess is sweeping with GBOSS. Nothing else in sight. You are clear."

"Roger that. Post 3 out."

Cassidy's breathing became regular. "Lions nill, Christians 5."

"Yeah, it is that." Sylvie agreed.

They cleaned up the post in silence, kicking empty cartridges and steel links out of the way. Matter settled, they returned to their lunch.

Sylvie poked at her food while Cassidy ate with intensity.

"Not hungry?" He asked.

"Not really. I get queasy every time, afterwards."

"So this isn't your first gunfight?"

"No. It's my third since we came here."

He paused, licked the spoon clean, then dropped it in the empty plastic pouch.

"Well for it being your third time, you did good."

"Is that why I feel nauseous?"

"Nope. That's a side effect. But totally normal."

"It is?"

"I know guys who piss themselves as the bullets start flying. Every person's body handles stress differently. The cortisol, the adrenaline, the dopamine hit afterwards. It is what it is."

Stomping down the stairs to the Humvee, he came back up holding two squat metal drink cans.

"Here, try a Rip It," he said, offering one to her.

"What is it?" Sylvie asked, confused.

"The sponsor of the Global War on Terror," he said, in a tone entirely too light for the occasion as she took it from him. "Energy drink. The company sells them by the metric buttload and we drink them just as quickly. I prefer Yellow over Blue. Red are delicious but not as easy to come by."

She looked askance at him, concerned.

"Why should I drink this?" she asked.

"Caffeine goes well with adrenaline." He shrugged. "And it's carbonated. Bubbly drinks are for celebration."

"What exactly are we celebrating?" Sylvie asked.

"Being alive."

"Why are you so cavalier?" she asked as he settled back into place.

"I could lie and say it's cuz we're a buncha hard pipe-hitting bastards," he paused long enough to swallow a spoonful. "But that wouldn't be the whole truth."

"It's not?"

He produced a further pair of the strange energy drinks, handing her another.

"Nope. We've got more time down range than y'all. Taken that much more contact too."

Tapping the lid of the can twice, he grabbed the pull ring and popped it open.

"That's not all of it though, is it?" Sylvie asked.

"Nah. We planned for this kinda stuff, trained for it. It's what we live for."

He half-grinned as he held up his can in a salute.

"Well some of us do," he said.

"You mean you do," Sylvie corrected.

"Aye. Fifth deployment in nine years."

"Fifth?"

"Uh-huh. Life as an enlisted man is a lot easier over here than it is in garrison."

Sylvie finally cracked open the can, took a whiff of the strange citrusy smell, then drank. Her face contorted.

"Oh that is…"

"Strange? Cloying? Hefty? Sticky?"

"Just slightly."

He gently knocked his can against hers. "Here's to living. And good company."

"I'll drink to that."

Chapter 12

Get Your Back Up Off the Wall

Good Lord what I wouldn't give for a beer right now, Corporal Clarence Shockley thought to himself as he walked down the steps of the guard post. The sun had nearly finished setting, and he was enjoying the coolness of the dark desert spread out before him. It was quiet again tonight, like it had been for the past few nights.

If the Taliban were smart they'd stay the hell away. He thought. *Kind of a shame they ain't all that smart. They'll be back.*

"Hey Shockley, whatcha gonna do now that you're off?" Domine asked.

The handsome corporal from Minnesota had just come off duty from Post Five down the wall from Shockley.

"Probably go play spades with Tolliver," Shockley admitted.

"Man loves him a good game of spades, don't he?"

"That and making money off of it."

"Think maybe them British girls would be willing to play?" a charming grin crossed Domine's face at the suggestion.

"It's a tempting thought, but if Staff Sergeant caught us we'd die."

Domine let out a heavy sigh and stared wistfully into the distance, "Yeah. You've got a point. Some of them are starting to look really cute though."

"You ain't wrong."

"Catch you later."

Walking slowly, Shockley started making the long trek from Post Five back to his tent. All things considered, Bourne wasn't a bad assignment. *At least we've got cots instead of dirt like at Zaranj.* And nobody had come to investigate them for the missing air conditioning units from Delaram. Better than that, there were girls here! Sure, you couldn't sleep with them, but at least they were pretty to look at.

Shockley was lost in his thoughts when a female voice called out to him.

"Hey! Marine!"

Shockley looked towards the voice to see one of the British girls jogging up to him. He looked around to see if there was anyone else she might be talking to. *Nope just us in the motor pool.*

"Me?" he asked, surprised, pointing at his chest.

"Yeah you," she approached and stopped in front of him, "I need some help moving some stuff around in the storage unit. It's a two-person job, think ye can help me out real fast?"

Normally, if he weren't tired, he'd be interested. But it was twenty-hundred, it had been hot all day, and he just wanted to get out of the heavy flak jacket he wore. Then she smiled at him. A brilliant, sweet smile. Framed by freckles all over a very lovely face. *She's a redhead too. How many souls has she stolen?* He briefly tried to count the freckles then gave up. And besides, the curves she seemed to pack underneath her camo uniform looked too good to be true. *Pretty girl with a nice body and a good smile asking for help? What's the worst that can happen?* He told himself.

"Uh, Yeah. Sure. Lead the way." He turned and followed her towards one of the prefab buildings.

"You just got off post?" she asked over her shoulder.

"Yup."

"I hope I'm not messin' up any of yer plans."

"I was thinking of maybe playing cards or bugging Cassidy for a snack."

"He isn't a bad cook."

"No he ain't. And he ain't so mad now that the Captain put him over the chow hall. But nah, I ain't got nothing planned."

"Oh good, I didn't pull ye away from anything important."

"Nah you're good."

She looked over at him with a smile before unlocking and opening the door, "I really appreciate you doing this."

"I do my best."

The door swung open to reveal a storage room filled with racks of tools and several shelves. A small lantern sat on top of the battered desk, filling the room with a dim, warm light. A diligent A/C unit kept the cinderblock room reasonably cool. *At least she's got A/C in this brick oven,* Shockley noted. *Could be worse.*

She unslung her rifle, leaning it on a rack near the desk before walking over to a large, unlabeled crate. Shockley let the door shut behind him and placed his rifle beside hers on the wooden rack, then slowly peeled out of his armor.

"Looks heavy compared to mine," she admitted.

"I imagine it's like taking a bra off. Can't wait to get out of it."

She laughed and he thought he saw her cheeks fill with color for a moment.

Nah, that's just my mind playing tricks on me.

"It's these right here. I need to get to the unit behind it," she placed a hand on top of it and looked around the room, "We'll move it over there," she pointed to a stack of crates in the back corner.

"Alright."

Sandra moved to the other side of the crate but before she got her hands underneath, Shockley had lifted it up and started to walk toward the corner she had indicated.

Well isn't that nice? Sandra told herself. *Who would've guessed King Kong Dong was that strong?*

Shockley put the crate down with a huff. It was heavier than he expected and he rolled his arms for a second as he looked back towards the girl. *What is her name?* He wondered. Fortunately, she had her back to him and he could see "Collier" embroidered over her back pocket tag.

And isn't that a nice set of hips for a woman, much less a white girl to have? Mmmm-mmhmmm.

She helped him with the second crate, placing it beside the other he'd moved, but he still couldn't figure out what was bugging him. He looked at the stacks of boxes and crates in the corner a bit closer and realized something wasn't quite normal about them. Nothing he could put his finger on, but some instinct in the back of his mind told him that it merited investigation.

Not my supply room, not my problem.

"Phew! I'd not 'ave been able to do this meself. Good thing ye came along when ya did… Shockley? That how you say yer name?" She pulled out a water bottle and extended it to him.

"Clarence Shockley. What's your name?"

"Sandra Collier," she extended her hand and gave him a firm handshake before taking a swig from her own bottle.

"Anything else I can do for you, ma'am?"

She studied him for a moment, expression unreadable, before finally speaking.

"Tell me Shockley, you got a girlfriend back home?"

"Nope. I'm still as single as the day I was born," he sat down on a crate opposite her and pulled out his own water, "Yourself?"

She shrugged, "I've had a fling here and there, but nothing serious for a long time."

He nodded and took a drink from his own water. *Why's she bringing this up?*

She looked away from him and off into the distance. She was silent for a moment and Shockley waited patiently for her to speak again, he was in no rush to get back to his tent. He was alone with a woman and he was going to savor the moment for as long as he could.

"Here's the thing, I've got somethin' else I need help with."

He cocked an eyebrow at her and she turned back to look at him. Her expression was serious and her gaze was, frankly, scarily intense. An uneasiness arose in his stomach and he swallowed hard.

"I guess that depends on what you need help with," he said cautiously, resting his elbows on his knees and looking up at her.

A small, sly smile crept across her face.

"See, thing is, I've got an itch that needs scratched. I ain't shared my bed with neither man nor woman for what feels like the longest dry spell of my life. The itch is driving me stark ravin' mad. I've been able to ignore it, up until the other day."

"What happened?" His curiosity was piqued.

"When that boy McCrae pulled his little stunt on ye," she was looking him straight in the eyes, grinning knowingly.

Shockley's face took on a deer in the headlights look.

"You... You saw that?" he managed to stutter out, completely taken aback.

"Every glorious bit," she glanced down between his legs and then back up to his eyes again, smile widening as she did so.

He blinked at her, then smiled. "I hope you enjoyed the show."

Clarence had not expected this to happen, much less in Afghanistan, but hey, a man took what he could get and certainly there was nothing wrong with a sexy ginger.

"Enjoy might be too weak a word for it. And what I saw got that itch screaming at me in a way I can't ignore anymore." She continued to stare him down, that sly smile still adorning her face.

His eyes narrowed as the full comprehension of those words registered with him.

"You didn't grab me by random, did you," he queried.

"Maybe, maybe not," she shrugged. "Either way, the question still stands, are ye able to help me out or not? I'm sure there's another Marine in yer platoon who wouldn't mind… *helping*." She watched, nervous, pensive and apprehensive all at once.

"Collier, If I'm getting this right, you'd like to take me for a ride."

He strode to where Sandra stood, and braced a hand on the crate behind her, his face inches from hers. A cliche move, he knew, but she seemed to have no problem with it.

She looked up at him, her grin salacious, "Seems ye aren't as dense as they make ye out to be."

"Nah, we can be real quick depending on what you're looking for."

She grabbed his hips and pulled him tight against her, a dare in her gaze. Any restraint that Shockley had had before that moment completely disappeared and he leaned down and kissed her hard on the mouth, months of loneliness crashing down around them in a rush.

There was a mad fumble of fingers and lips as she sought to take his shirt off, his hands simultaneously assisting her in the matter.

"You know," Shockley said, pulling away from her, "if we get caught, we are gonna be in some deep crap."

He did not feel like facing Nealen if they were found out. The desert was awfully big and he didn't wanna find out exactly how big Nealen could make it.

She was breathing hard, chest rising and falling in a way that drove him crazy. A chest, he realized, that didn't have anything to restrain it beneath the drab undershirt. And stood out quite prominently.

"First, this is my tool room. The only keys are on my desk right now," she responded breathily. "Second, the rules be damned. Those bastards handing down the rules killed my friends when they sent us out here. Give me one bloody good reason why I should follow their rules?" She spit the words out with contempt and pain before pulling him back to her and swiftly claiming his mouth again.

Woman's got a point, to hell with the rules.

\#

"Ma'am, we need to discuss our defenses," Nealen declared.

He'd just wrapped up an NCO call, his Marines scattering to the four winds with a quickness. He, the captain, Colour Gallagher, and Sarn't Major Mayne were sitting in the Observer's Post, surveying the darkening landscape.

"How so?"

"Ma'am, how many rifles did we bring to bear when Jimenez's patrol got attacked?"

Natasha shook her head. "I couldn't say."

"Just what was in the towers," Nealen said.

Natasha and Stirling considered his words as they drank tepid water, listening to the wind and the sounds of the night. The red glow of cigarettes stood out in the darkness.

"How many men do we have on post in daylight?" Natasha asked.

"Two per, ma'am."

Nealen drank from his water bottle. "After the shooting started, my sergeants rushed another man up to each with extra ammo."

"Good thinking," Stirling said.

"Thank you."

"Why would more rifles matter? Weren't the Taliban outside of range?" Morgana asked.

Nealen's strange look caught her off guard.

"Why are you giving me that stupid look, Staff Nealen?" Morgana pressed.

"Ma'am," he said after a moment, "What range do you qualify with your Enfields at?"

"Three hundred meters. Just like everybody else who's not infantry," Morgana informed.

Nealen's look queered, as if sniffing something unreasonably foul. "What range do infantry qualify at?"

"Four hundred meters," Stirling said patiently..

Nealen crushed his empty plastic bottle. Dropped it into his dump pouch.

"That'd be the problem right there. My boys can hit point targets out to five hundred yards with their M16s."

"That's a hair past four hundred meters," Stirling said as he considered the conversion.

"Or three hundred for that matter," Natasha said glumly.

"If we could build some sorta fighting step tall enough for my boys to see over–"

"Jimenez would've had that much more support during the engagement."

"Yes, ma'am."

Morgana regarded him coolly as she considered his words. "Even if we built a rampart, how could you get them on the walls in time to contribute to the fight?"

Nealen's smile reminded her of nothing so much as a Death's Head, angular and bony as he grinned broadly.

"Leave that part to me. They'll be able to find their way to the top half-dead or fully drunk."

"I'd say Hesco is likely our best bet," Stirling added after consideration.

"I like it. I doubt our lads and lasses would complain about doing some internal work for a short bit," Morgana suggested.

"You'd have them help us with that?" he asked cautiously.

"Well who else would you have drive the dozers?" the Captain said patiently.

"Dozers nothing. I figured my boys'd be out there digging with shovels," Nealen suggested.

"I won't lecture you on how to kill Taliban, don't you fret over how I build things," Morgana lectured.

Nealen held up his hands. "Easy enough, Colour Sergeant."

Morgana continued making notes on a pad with her grease pencil. "I can't guarantee we'll get it all done in one go. Even internally, that's a fair chunk of space."

"And we'll need a hefty bit of fill dirt," Stirling added.

Natasha shrugged as she looked at the matter. "Dig a three-meter wide ditch around the exterior, perhaps?"

"Moat without water won't slow down much, ma'am," Nealen opined.

"If we flood it, Nealen's lads might go skinny dipping," Stirling teased.

"Couldn't hurt. At least they'd smell better after a bath," Nealen groused.

"Quite."

Morgana's face betrayed her thoughts as she looked back from where she'd been surveying the stacks of supplies they had on hand. "How deep should we make the ditch? Meter?"

"Closer to two, I'm thinking," Stirling said. "We'll need several metric tons of earth to fill the Hesco."

"Caltrops," Morgana declared.

"What about them?"

"They'll put the kibosh on anybody trying to run the moat, or jump it."

"I like this. What would you make them from?" Stirling asked.

"If we bend rebar, weld the pieces together so there's always a point facing up, then cut the ends with angle grinders or chop saws to put on an edge, ." Her smile became dazzling. "If your marines bend the rebar by hand, it'll go that much quicker."

Nealen considered the request. "Not a problem at all."

"Should keep them occupied for a week or two," Natasha suggested optimistically.

Now it was Nealen's turn to laugh. "Ma'am. If it were any normal pack of twenty year-olds, you might be right." He pointed toward MarineLand where even now she could hear steel clanging against steel as men laughed and worked. "Those are cannon cockers. My boys earn their pay via brute strength in the chest, shoulders, and arms. We sling bullets heavier than some of your engineers. Bending all that rebar is three days' work. At best. And a whole lotta betting going on while we're at it."

"Betting?"

"We're inveterate gamblers. Oh sure, maybe not money, but they'll bet pushups, shifts on watch, bragging rights. Cans of chewing tobacco and cartons of cigarettes."

"Rather like prison inmates," Stirling chirped.

"Yeah. It do be like that," Nealen said cheerfully.

"Oh." The Colour Sergeant looked down at her notes. "If you say so."

"Morgana, if you drop a couple rolls of razor wire in the bottom of the trench after sunset, the locals won't know any better," Stirling suggested.

"Especially if they try to attack after dark," Nealen snickered.

"We may not have everything on hand," Morgana cautioned.

"Doesn't matter, I like this plan," Natasha declared. "Build what you can, I'll keep requesting more supplies until RC-Southwest gives us what we want."

"Thank you, ladies." Nealen stood. "Appreciate the help."

"Not a problem, Staff Nealen," Morgana declared aloud. Mentally though, she was deep in thought, considering changes necessary for the defensive structures. She'd joined the engineers to build. And she liked the ideas that Nealen's very practical request had spawned. *I wonder if they'd mind crenellations?*

Chapter 13

First Time for Everything

"Let's grab lunch," Sandra Collier said as she stepped up to Sylvie's workbench where the taller woman was hard at work on welding pipes.

The welding hood came up and Sandra saw that same smile she'd been wearing for the past day.

Who put that there, and how? Sandra wondered.

"Wonder what it'll be today. Bangers and mash or mash and bangers?" Sylvie asked.

"Don't forget the pink bug juice," Sandra reminded her.

"Of course not, mustn't forget that. Quite important to remember the bug juice," Sylvie agreed.

The Americans, unsure of what to bring, had simply grabbed everything they could lay hands on when they came down. It had taken a goodly while since they first arrived to sort out all of the supplies.

Sometimes they make absolutely no sense, Sylvie told herself. Slinging her rifle, she made for the door behind Sandra. *Which still doesn't explain why they call it bug juice. What made them pick that name?* She wondered.

The two women came out of the reasonably cool machine shop, into the blistering midday heat, and were thrown into a state of confusion when they were greeted by the sight and sound of a furious man.

"Don't drop my bar, you inbred sacks of donkey smegma!" A familiar voice bellowed as three marines drew near, two of them carrying a stainless steel bar over their heads.

Two of those three wore green shirts and brown desert camouflage pants drenched in sweat. The third left little to the imagination, dressed as he was in PT shorts and shoes, with no shirt on. In the stark heat, covered in a sheen of sweat, the musculature of Sergeant Cassidy's well-developed back was on prominent display. Lyons couldn't help but stare at the marine in front of her, wondering what those muscles might feel like underneath her hands. His form seemed to possess no softness whatsoever.

Was it more like stone or steel?

She blinked in surprise at her thoughts and quickly tried to focus on something else.

Where the hell did THAT thought come from?!

"Dumbo, Clown Shoes, get back here!" The marines holding the bar trotted backwards to where they were facing Cassidy.

"Did you see the ladies, Perez?"

"Yes, Sergeant!" Perez wheezed.

"Did you see the ladies, Swanger?" Cassidy repeated.

"No, Sergeant." Swanger blinked rapidly, trying to clear away the sweat rolling down his forehead.

"Well, you're both morons. But we already knew that! What do privates give to any NCO they meet?"

"Proper greeting of the day, Sergeant!"

"So you do know better!" he stated loudly.

"Yes, Sergeant!"

"I'm waiting!"

"Good afternoon, ladies," both men gasped, trying to gulp air down in the miserable heat.

"Good afternoon, lads," Sylvie replied, somewhat amused and intrigued by the spectacle before her, having by now recovered from the shock of her reaction to Cassidy.

"See boys, that's how it's done. All the time, every time. Set my bar down and do buddy ups! Perez first!"

While they scrambled to obey, Cassidy looked toward the two surprised women.

"Apologies ladies, their drill instructors failed to teach them good manners."

"Oh, I understand completely," Sylvie demurred. "Sometimes the troops just need a reminder or two."

"Yes, they do," Cassidy agreed. "I imagine my seniors might've said the same thing when I was a boot."

"So what did they do to deserve this rousing session of motivation?" Sandra asked in a rather bemused tone.

"They bent my only olympic bar doing Motor-T things. Johnson left me free to fix them. Speaking of which —"

He shoved the toe of his running shoe under the center of the bar, violently kicking it up into his hands.

"Dumb, Dumberer, get over here!"

"Yes, Sergeant!"

"Take my bar, hold it above your heads. Now, get in a squat and walk like ducks to the chow hall. You will quack the entire way there."

He stood there, watching the marines with malevolent eyes as they wearily stepped and quacked in time.

"Faster, Crotch rots! You do not impress me!"

It was an odd sight, but one the British soldiers were slowly becoming accustomed to. The Marine platoon assigned to FOB Bourne was neither quiet nor dignified, unless they were asleep. From sunrise to sunset, the men communicated by shouting at each other, even across the FOB. And the belligerence they demonstrated towards each other was obscene!

They weren't wholly bad though. Who knew that American Marines liked to sunbathe? Sylvie had walked onto Post Three and been utterly gobsmacked by the sight of roughly six dozen grown men, on cots, lounging about in only their PT shorts just before midday. It was a daily occurrence too. And Sylvie's fellow soldiers enjoyed it, enough so that not only had they refused to pass off that particular post to the Americans, goods were being bartered to pay for the privilege of standing watch!

Colour Gallagher had only put a stop to the bartering yesterday after a fight broke out between competing bidders. Once informed as to why the fight was occurring, she'd gone up the ladder just to see what the women were talking about. She came back down later, far more sympathetic to the issue. That evening a written watch schedule for Post Three appeared right next to the Marines' published roster in the chow hall. Short of the Captain's direct order, nobody was going to argue with Colour Sergeant Morgana Gallagher about who stood watch, or when.

Sylvie hadn't been as devoutly invested in the matter, although she did agree with Sandra's comments about this particular American, Cassidy. He'd intrigued her from the moment he first arrived, to now.

But what do I say to get his attention? She asked herself. *Why do you want it?* Another part of her mind argued. *You haven't really been interested in a man since Randall!*

"I think I can fix that bar," Sylvie declared as she studied the severe bend.

"You can what?" Cassidy asked, turning to better face her. "Did I just hear you say you might be able to fix that?"

"No seriously! It's easy!" Sylvie said enthusiastically. "We cut the bend out, add in new bar stock, then weld it into place with the TIG welder. Oh sure we could use the MIG but TIGs are lovely and I want to try out the new rig we got."

"But doesn't it need a heat treat or quench?"

She waved casually, as if unconcerned.

"Not hard to counter so we don't ruin it. And Sandy's a dab hand with a grinder for cleaning up the welds."

"Sergeant Lyons, you are a blessing." Cassidy replied. He turned back to his charges. "All right Dumb and Dumberer, turn around and face me!"

"Aye aye, Sergeant!" His victims moaned.

"You will loudly say 'God save the Queen!' as you duck march your way back to me. If at any time you stop, come out of the squat before you get to me, or I can't hear you, you will start over. Do we understand?"

"Yes, Sergeant!"

"Begin!"

The matter attended to, he faced Sylvie and Sandra once more.

"Ladies, might I interest you in performing a charitable act of community service?"

"I think we could do that," Sylvie assured him. "But I will need something in return."

"Depending on what, that can be arranged," Cassidy promised.

"Great. But first let's get your bar into my shop shall we?"

Perez and Swanger came to a stop in front of Cassidy, utterly spent. He snatched the bar away from them, holding it steady at the fulcrum, which he examined at length before he spoke again. This time, his voice was far calmer.

Rather like a school teacher than a sergeant, Sylvie considered.

"The next time either of you think to yourself 'Hey this sounds like a great idea', run it past one of your seniors. That's why they're there. Unless we are taking contact from a thousand screaming assholes with AKs, somebody is bleeding out, or there is a big damn fire, you have time to ask thoughtful questions and clarify matters. Do we understand?"

"Yes, Sergeant."

"Get back to Sergeant Johnson."

"Yes, Sergeant."

"Move."

They struggled to do more than a slow jog but Cassidy seemed content with his handling of the matter and turned his attention back to Sylvie. It was the first time she had seen him without a shirt on, this close, and it was obvious that the time he spent in the gym was worth the price. He resembled a particular statue of Heracles she'd studied at uni, all bulky muscle.

With surprisingly no tattoos she told herself. His torso had scars though, plenty of them, including a distinct star-shaped pattern. As if he'd been shot before.

"Ladies, where would you like this?" he asked in a tone Sylvie could almost say was charming. The snarl had gone out of his voice and he sounded oddly cheerful.

"If you don't mind carrying it back to the shop, and putting it on my workbench, I'd appreciate it," she directed.

"Sure thing. Mind showing me where in your shop to put this?"

He was quiet until they got inside the shop, eyes blinking as they adjusted to the dark room.

Work tables rested against the walls, with a series of lathes, drill presses, and assorted machinery he could only begin to guess at occupying the central space.

"Nice set up," he complimented.

"It does the job."

"So, which one is yours in all this?" His eyes fell on the corner over which hung a familiar green and white banner. "The Red Dragon Passant?"

"You know your flags."

"It's a gift," he shrugged. "I tried to learn as much as I could about the UK and its parts while I lived there."

"I can see why that would be wise," Sylvie muttered. "So where did you find all that exercise equipment?"

"We acquired it."

"Acquired?" She smirked. "How do you spell that? Ess tee ohh ell eee?" Sylvie teased.

"Oh nothing so dangerous as that. Everybody knows that there's only one thief in the Marine Corps."

"Only one?"

"Yeah, everybody else is trying to get their stuff back," Hondo said.

Sylvie let out a laugh and he grinned.

"You do smile!" she said brightly.

"It happens. Now and again," he confessed.

"Not if your lads are to be believed. Heard them talking about you in the mess. Said you're always mad about something."

"Maybe they should give me a reason to smile. Like you did."

"Me?"

"A few minutes ago I thought I would have to spend the rest of this deployment without a proper Olympic bar. Then a super smart lady came along and offered to fix it. I'd say that's something to smile about."

Their eyes met for a second and Sylvie smiled back at the angry marine, who didn't seem so hostile anymore. His deep gray eyes possessed a hazel tint she hadn't expected. She looked away quickly, the shared look a tad bit too vulnerable to sustain. He turned to leave.

"Hey, can I see your gym?" Sylvie asked, then kicked herself.

Way to go, that didn't sound desperate at all!

"Sure. Why?" Hondo asked.

"I have an idea, but I want to see something first."

"I've got to go finish dinner prep right now, and I have NCO call at 2000. After that, I'm free."

"I'll be waiting," Sylvie assured.

"Where can I find you?" he asked.

"In my shop, still working through the backlog of broken parts."

He was halfway out the door when he stopped walking.

"Lyons?"

"Yes?"

"Your eyes are incredible."

"My eyes?"

"One's blue, shot through with white in the iris. A prismatic blue that stops a man faster than a knife to the heart. The other is brown like rich chocolate. The kind a man wants to drown himself in and never come out of." He paused as if considering whether to keep speaking.

And promptly disappeared through the machine shop door.

In the quiet, Sylvie looked at the empty doorway, wondering why he'd said all that to her.

#

"You lift? With this?" Sylvie protested as she walked around the iron pit.

"Yeah. Why?" Hondo asked.

"It's horrid! Most of this should be condemned as health hazards!"

"Marines still need to lift."

"You are begging for tetanus!"

"Eh." He shrugged his shoulders. "We got shots for that."

Sylvie eyed him critically, examining him for defects.

"You people have serious issues. The lot of you need counseling." Her lips formed a moue. "Some of you clearly more than others."

"What gave it away?" Hondo asked nonchalantly.

In the semi-starlit dark, she switched her headlamp on and stepped closer to get a better view. What more she saw did not amuse her.

Stepping toward a ramshackle pull-down machine, Sylvie threw on one of her leather welding gloves then grabbed the cable and pulled hard. Rusted steel wire gave way, metal clanging loudly as it fell downward. She followed this up by mule kicking the weight bench with a particularly savage strike, leaving Cassidy to watch as the entire structure fell apart.

"This stuff is heinous!" Sylvie exclaimed.

"Clearly."

She let out a breath. "Do you have any bottled water around here?"

"Indeed. Cold water too."

"Even better. Lead on."

Sitting beside the refrigerator unit, Sylvie greedily gulped the cold water down in the dark, then reached for a second bottle. "I'm shocked you brought one of these," she said, tapping against the metal side with her knuckles.

"We acquired it," Hondo confessed.

"Same way you acquired the gym?"

"In a manner of speaking. Nobody was guarding it, we managed to get enough power runs to it that we could ensure it worked, and then we drove away with it. Nobody stopped us in the process."

"What else did you take that way?" she smiled.

"Generators, AC units, few other odds and sods and the like. I think McCormick swiped most of the chow hall's condiment selection," he said as he smiled back at her.

"You sure they won't try to clap you in irons? This all sounds like a recipe for investigation."

"Who are they gonna send after us?"

"Umm... provost marshal?" Sylvie ventured.

"We were given orders to outfit an artillery platoon and move south as fast as possible. Nobody said we couldn't take what we wanted. And beyond serial plate numbers, which we absolutely swapped the heck out of, there's no proof we took anything."

Sylvie considered this as she finished gulping down more cold water.

"Is this how all Marines do business?" she asked finally.

"If you're ground combat arms, yeah. We're usually under-equipped and under-manned."

"That sounds less than ideal."

"It can be," he admitted. "We take what we need on the run. And keep running."

"This explains so much," Sylvie muttered.

"Glad to hear it. Now, why did you want to look at our gym, and what are you thinking?"

"We did not bring any gym equipment with us," Sylvie explained.

"That sucks."

"It does. I think I can repair all of what you brought, with our supplies."

"What if you run out?"

"We'll order more material from Camp Bastion."

"Okay."

"I do not feel like walking all the way to MarineLand just to lift."

"So relocate the gym closer to y'all?"

"If we're putting materials forward for it, yes," Sylvie affirmed.

"Okay. We can do something about that," Cassidy promised.

"Awesome." She looked at him, hesitated. "I've seen you working out. More than once. Do you train people?"

"I can. I'll need something in return."

Please please please don't screw this up, she told herself. *Please be the man your reputation says you are.*

"What are you using for showers?" he asked.

"We ran pipes from the river back inside the walls, to a filtration system and then to a shower unit."

"Can you build a smaller set up for us? Nothing crazy like the dozen slots y'all have. Just say... four shower-heads in separate stalls and space to get dressed."

"Are you tired of using nappies?" she teased as a cool relief filled her.

"So y'all *have* been watching us!" he accused.

"I'm not gonna lie, it makes the midday guard mount much more interesting. And pleasant."

"I thought women weren't visual learners?" he teased.

"There are some things worth looking at," she said coyly.

"Really?" he asked.

"Uh huh."

"What do you like to see?" he asked, a note of apprehension in his voice.

She let herself slowly touch the olive drab fabric of his tee shirt as she stepped in closer, hands slowly riding up and down across his pectorals, a gentle caress that raised goosebumps even in the late evening heat.

"We like shoulders."

One set of nails went down his left arm, making contact with the bare skin of his tricep. "And strong arms."

There was a hint of challenge in her eyes as she looked at him, realizing for the first time how close in height they stood.

"How about you?" she asked.

"Men aren't just visual. Contrary to popular sentiment."

"Oh."

"There's things we need to hear. Need to know."

"What does a man need to know, besides 'yes please' and 'I'd like some more'?" Sylvie asked.

Those intense eyes never left hers as he began to speak. "We like seeing a woman who knows her craft and works hard at it."

He leaned in close, fingers deftly manipulating the bun in her hair to let it down so those same fingers could slide through the light brown strands with a gentleness she had not expected.

He breathed in deeply. "Love watching her pretty mouth when she laughs."

She'd stopped breathing aloud, just concentrating on his voice as he spoke. It was loud, in the quiet desert, yet so soft only she could hear him.

"Listening to her laugh too. It sounds like music to my ears."

When had his hand gone from stroking her hair to gently holding her chin as the pad of his thumb stroked her lower lip?

Don't know. Don't care. It's right where I need it.

Years had gone by since a man talked to her this way.

And this one treats me as an equal.

"I want," Hondo said in a quiet voice, "so very badly want, to kiss these beautiful, sweet lips, and taste the music they hold, I want to know everything they can tell me about her."

Sylvie said nothing, not wanting to break the moment.

"Would love to know what the fruity-flowery smelling shampoo she uses in her hair is. And how she always looks so well-put together. Like a lady should." He breathed in deeply once more. "Would cheerfully buy her more of that shampoo so I could keep enjoying that delicious scent."

"Where did you learn to charm like this?" Sylvie asked dreamily.

"It's a gift." He smiled again, then leaned in close. "Does that answer your question, Sergeant Lyons?"

"Almost, Sergeant Cassidy." Her lips devoured his and for a moment, he seemed shocked at her advance. Then he was pulling her into his lap, arms clenching her tightly to him as he returned her desire fourfold.

"Is this the real reason why you waited till dark?" she gasped.

"Nope. I really had all those other things to do."

"Does anybody else still need you tonight?"

"No," he assured.

"Then shut up and kiss me, you impertinent man."

Out beyond the perimeter, jackals howled as high overhead the Milky Way Galaxy revealed itself in all its splendor.

#

Dawn came far sooner than Sylvie Lyons cared to consider. Over seven years in the Army, she still hated getting up in the morning. And after a very pleasant night spent talking with that wonderfully charming and thoughtful man, she had no interest in getting up and out of her cot.

Just five more minutes.

"Come on lazy! Get outta bed!" Sandra kicked her cot especially hard.

"Mmmmph!"

"You'll be late for breakfast."

"Don't care."

"Would you prefer cold tea?"

"Fine!" Sylvie came up, groggy eyed and hair askew.

"Good morning to you, too, sunshine."

Grumble.

"You shouldn't scrunch your face up like that, otherwise it'll get stuck that way."

Grumble.

"Your American won't like kissing you if your face is scrunched up awful," Sandra said quietly.

Sylvie's eyes slammed open. "Woman, I will stab you!" she hissed venomously.

"So that was where you were last night. What's his first name?" Sandra said idly.

"In the taint, woman. I'll do it!"

"Relax, I wasn't gonna say nuthin'," she admitted quietly. "Not after —" Sandra paused and Sylvie stared hard at her.

"You didn't."

"I admit nothing," Sandra said quickly,

"You dirty slut. Who was it?"

"I'll show you mine if you show me yours."

They glared at each other, bursting into laughter after a moment.

"Oh I needed that," Sylvie admitted.

"No doubt, though I think you need something else."

"We just kissed."

"Which set of lips was he kissing?"

"You are still inside arm's reach," Sylvie menaced as she pulled on her camouflage blouse.

"And we're missing breakfast. Come on."

Finally, only slightly disheveled and being pushed along, Sylvie made her way toward the door of the tent and stepped through, into the bright Afghani sun.

"Iz so bri —" Sylvie started to complain.

"Put your backs into it you apes!" You wanna be done sometime before noon, you better move with a purpose!" a very familiar voice bellowed.

In the exact spot where she and he had talked about putting up the new gym, Cassidy had assembled the majority of his platoon. There seemed to be three teams going all at once — two dozen men with shovels filled sandbags, as a busy pair walked along hunched over and tying the same bags shut. The largest group by far was a chain of men, moving the sandbags into position against what looked like t-posts. The wall itself was already hip high, with many more parts and pieces lying nearby as the marines bent to their tasks with a will.

"What the hell are they doing now?" Sandra asked in surprise.

"It's supposed to be a gym," Carter declared as he walked past under a load of empty sandbags still shrink-wrapped in plastic.

"Why in the world would they build a gym? They've already got one way the hell over there!" Sandra gestured.

"I asked them to move it closer to us. So we didn't have to walk as far," Sylvie admitted in shock and surprise.

"How'd you convince them to do this?"

Sylvie and Sandra jumped. Neither had expected Colour Sergeant Gallagher to walk up behind them.

"Morning, Colour!" both women parroted.

Morgana brushed away their greeting with a wave. "Yes, yes, now did I hear Carter correctly and this is supposed to be a gym?"

"Yes, Colour."

"And Lyons, you're the reason for it being moved?"

"Yes, ma'am."

"Care to explain how you pulled that off?"

"Um... I um... I asked nicely."

"Uh huh. Asking nicely somehow got the majority of our security platoon out of their racks before sunrise to fill God alone knows how many thousands of sandbags. So we could have a gym. Near our tents." She fixed Sylvie with a gimlet eye. "Do we see my problem with this?"

"Maybe," Sylvie admitted.

"And what are you doing in return for them?"

"We're repairing all of their rusted, worn out, shoddy gym equipment. Which is getting our entire machinist section certified by the end of the month."

Gallagher looked at her over the rim of her Styrofoam cup. "Well isn't this a wonderful boon for Anglo-American relations?"

"Yes ma'am, I thought it was."

"May I assume that it's being moved so we can all use it?"

"Yes ma'am. Sergeant Cassidy plans to put up a sign saying 'Don't be dumb.' It's his only rule for the gym."

"I see." A slow sip. "Will it have overhead cover?"

"I don't know Colour," Sylvie admitted. "You'll have to ask them."

"I think I shall. After my second cuppa. I am not nearly caffeinated enough to deal with all of you fillies. Much less a pack of American Marines who seem to think the ass-crack of dawn is The Perfectly Acceptable Time to be making stupid noise."

"Little yellow birdy with a little yellow bill!" Corporal Tolliver bellowed.

This brought on a swelling of replies, the end of which made all three women blanch.

"I rest my case," the Colour Sergeant said through clenched teeth.

"Yes, ma'am," Sylvie replied.

"Carry on."

Chapter 14

Satan, He Will Say

They lay in wait, hidden amongst the low scrub brush as they watched their intended target moving along. They had watched, studying the route the Americans took as they pushed out security patrols. Only one had been constant — the morning patrol was always spotted at the same time, using the same path. Hell, Achmed bin Salah could set his watch by it, he'd seen it so many times.

Today, we strike back.

The mujahadeen needed a win. Three engagements, three losses, with nothing but destroyed equipment and dead fighters to show for it. Once the Dishu Battalion's commander had verified who and what they were fighting, certain patterns made sense. Americans expended ammunition gratuitously. Oh sure, it was accurate, but one didn't need to worry about being precise when the volume they were sending at their opponents was in vast quantities.

Achmed bin Salah hated American logistics. He'd known of it, having spent time in Saudi watching the spread of wanton decadence there. A petroleum engineering student who lacked the patronage to get ahead, he'd decided to take part in the Jihad after his family's money ran out and he couldn't continue his schooling at university.

Looking to his left, then his right at the men on either side, he smiled slightly. *Here I am in Helmand, fighting a war I never expected to participate in.*

Joining the Taliban had filled him with purpose, and listening to the impassioned speeches in the madrasas had enlightened him on how he could help turn back the tide of godless westernism.

Allah be merciful, we shall see it in our lifetimes he told himself.

Try as he might to hate it though, he couldn't help but respect it. Americans came to win, every time. Victory though, would see the Dishu Brigade given validity and standing amongst the various factions. Victories in the Rigestan could push the Americans back, would give the Taliban control of the routes into Pakistan through which heroin could flow.

Right then, he had a dozen well-armed fighters spread out, covering the American patrol's route of march as they moved through the desert at a plodding pace.

There were no mortars this time. For reasons that nobody, not even the lone survivor had understood, the mortars sympathetically detonated while still being set up, devastating a previous attack squad.

Aside from Beroj, absolutely none of our fighters came back from that. We don't know that anybody even survived Achmed fretted. Certainly none of their sources, either within the British base or elsewhere had panned out.

The lack of armored vehicle support meant Achmed's squad would not be carrying RPGs this time, though some of his fighters did have grenades in their possession. Indeed, the plan for today involved several Russian RPDs, all of which would open fire as soon as the explosive device signaled that this patrol was inside the kill box.

Patience, the man from Saudi told himself. *Just like Group Leader Aziz councils. Lots of patience.*

Looking toward his intended target, Achmed sighed. *Come on you handless cows, get inside the killzone already! Allah may have all day, and the Group Leader can be as patient as he wants. I need a bath and a pot of tea already!*

#

Brian Kramer had a love/hate affair with dawn patrols. He loved to hate them. To that end, if he had to be on one, he ran it with efficiency. Getting back to base with all of his people in one piece, and no screwing around. He wanted to be back in his rack, relaxing.

Come on, I know you're around here, he told himself. *We know the IED is buried up ahead. We watched you do it on GBOSS. You picked your position to cover where we'd be when you set off the device.*

The squad's radio chirped loudly in the early morning silence. "*Echo Four Kilo, this is Hogfather, put Spaniard on. How copy?*"

What are we doing now?" Brian asked himself.

\#

Within the CoC, the tense atmosphere was palpable. Men and women alike watched, waiting to see what would become of their plans.

Nealen took an awful gamble trying to lure the Taliban into believing we were stupid enough to run a patrol like this.

"Wish there was some way we could get the crew-serves in on this," Tolliver voiced aloud.

A slapping sound came from across the room and several heads turned to see Sergeant Brady facepalm before he began throwing crates around as he desperately looked for something.

"Theiss, where's my firing tables?" Brady demanded.

"That crate over there, Sergeant. With the red and orange spray paint on it."

"Something wrong, Brady?" Morgana asked, concerned by the normally calm Texan's frenzied burst of activity.

"Shores, find my mortar board. Now!" Brady ordered.

"On it!" Shores replied.

Brady upended a crate onto the table, dumping spiral bound notebooks all over. Snatching them up, he began discarding those he didn't want into the crate, before tossing one, then another at Theiss.

"Hold those, Theiss," Brady demanded, sweeping everything back into the crate as Shores came over, holding the requested equipment.

"Uh huh."

"Theiss, give me the grid point where the IED team fell outta sight."

The lance corporal lazed,then recited a ten-digit grid which Brady plotted on the map, double checking his data as he went along.

"We know where they disappeared. We know roughly where they reappeared. Guys have to be expert at this. Or at least more expert than the ambush team. It's why they headed back to wherever the Taliban are hiding around here. They don't want their best bomb guys getting wasted in an ambush. Goons can do ambushes, but you need nerds to make sure the bombs get laid right. Where's the spot they reappeared, Theiss?"

Lazing the spot with the GBOSS's systems, Theiss waited, then provided the second location.

Brady drew a box with the two points on opposite sides..

"Somewhere inside here is the ambush team."

He drew a circle to the west.

"Over here, in the tail of a wadi, is Samuels with the counter-ambush team."

"Right."

"Which means they're safe from what I'm about to do."

"Which is?"

"Turn our fifties on to 'em."

"What?" Fitzsimmons said, shocked at the suggestion. "That's a direct-fire weapon! They're outside of range!"

Brady didn't acknowledge her though. He'd already turned to the mortar board, plotting out lines with a slide rule and quadrant as he made more markings and filled in the data. Before Natasha could disturb him, Nealen pushed her arm.

"Let him concentrate ma'am. Promise, Brady's worth it."

"This is ludicrous!" Natasha protested.

"No ma'am, it's weaponized math," Brady declared, holding up the board for all to see his notations. "If we mount our fifties on sandbag piles under the front tripod leg to give us the elevation, we can sweep the grid square where we think the Taliban are."

Natasha paused looking over his math. "You're sure this will work?"

"I ain't saying it's perfect, but I would bet the ranch on it."

"How do we get the marines on patrol to stop without making it obvious?"

"Who all is out right now?"

"Kramer is in charge, with Jimenez as his assistant."

"Huh. That would work," Brady said casually. "Bellmore."

"Sergeant?" the petite blonde looked up from her radio set.

"Tell Jimenez I need him to take a knee and start talking into the radio like his mother is on the phone."

"Sergeant?"

"He'll understand."

"Yes, Sergeant."

#

Achmed heard a low whistle from a lookout, who pointed in the direction of the patrol. Looking he saw the man indicate that the patrol had ceased walking, though he was unsure why? Repeating the hand gestures, Achmed walked on all fours over toward the lookout, careful not to break the plane of the low hills which concealed their position. It took time, but as the Dishu Brigade's commander had stressed repeatedly — "We have time on our side. Make the most of it."

By the time he made it to the lookout, Achmed was sweating and cursing that he had to move at all.

"What do you see?"

"The patrol stopped moving."

"So?"

Voices reached him, and he wondered at what he was hearing. Achmed possessed a passing familiarity with English, but this was not it. Something far more rapid-fire, and angry if the speaker's tone was anything to go by.

"Do you think they saw us?"

"I —" Achmed paused. *Do I admit I have no clue? Will it make me look weak? Fuck it, what do I care about these illiterate pashtun savages?*

"We have nothing to worry about."

"They say the americans can see the farts a camel makes at night."

"So? Is he pointing at us?" Achmed said.

"Um —"

"Well?"

"No."

"Then don't worry about it," he reiterated.

Getting back into the dirt, Achmed slowly crab-walked back to the main body of the ambush team.

"What's going on?"

"I don't know. Sounds like an argument between the patrol and their leadership."

"Americans. Pah. May Allah always bless us with stupid and simple-minded enemies."

"True."

"You hear that?"

"No, what was it?"

"It sounded like that big crew serve the Americans always carry. The fifty."

"But there's no other attacks planned for today."

"Maybe they're showing off for the British."

"Could be," Achmed ruminated, stroking his beard as he did so.

Allah dammit but I'd love a break from all these flies! He swore mentally.

A sound filled the air, like so many locusts in flight.

A man screamed. Before Achmed could move towards the offending soul, another man screamed. Some part of Achmed's mind recognized that multiple members of his carefully laid out machine gun teams were screaming in pain, bleeding from injuries as he stood trying to assess what was happening.

A sound like so many locusts in flight filled the air.

Something thumped into his chest and he fell to the ground.

"What's happening?" he asked. The frothy red blood dribbling out between his lips went entirely unnoticed.

#

"FDC, this is Spaniard. Rounds on target. Repeat. I say again, Repeat."

Peter Nealen peeked outside the tent flaps, watching as his cannoneers went about their craft, joking all the while.

"The lads seem quite amused at this whole affair," Mayne said lightly.

"Happiness is a belt-fed weapon, Sarn't Major," Nealen politely pointed out.

Stirling scratched his chin. "You may have a point. Think we could make this permanent?"

Nealen shrugged. "Not my bailiwick, Sarn't Major. I think so, but I'm not big on construction if I can help it."

"Colour, a moment of your time please?" Stirling called out.

Morgana joined them in the doorway. "What's going on, Sarn't Major?" the cool blonde asked.

"You're the building expert, how could we make those improvised positions permanent?"

"Just a minute please," Morgana asked as she watched the gunners adjust azimuth of fire on their tees before they let loose another volley.

"This is an odd sight, to be sure. I didn't know you could do this with crew served." She squinted. "I thought Brady only mentioned the fifty cals?"

"Yes ma'am. They require more work than the Marks to get on target," Nealen said.

"Ah. I see now," Gallagher said.

"How long do you plan on letting them carry on like that?" Stirling interrupted.

"Brady has the gun line performing sweeping zone. As soon as they're done giving Tommy Taliban and company plenty of forty millimeter and fifty cal reasons to stay dead, Kramer will sweep through and ensure they're all dead," Nealen explained.

"What about Samuels?" Mayne asked.

"In reserve, in case the Taliban try something funny," Nealen told him.

"And then?" Morgana asked.

Nealen shrugged. "They'll stroll on back and we'll talk about what to do different next time, versus what worked, and what didn't. Oh and we are keeping up patrols after this."

"Why?" Balcombe asked.

"It's part of maintaining a solid defensive posture. Security patrols ensure that our enemies cannot, do not, re-establish themselves within our perimeter."

"I like this plan," Morgana admitted. "Think they'll take the clue."

Nealen shrugged casually. "Never can tell with zealots. Personally, I wish these ugly motherfrackers would."

"Fair enough, now what about permanency, Morgana?" Stirling asked.

"Hmm.. Probably best we get them off the deck. And we'll need a spot for ready ammo, won't we?" she mused.

"I imagine so," Stirling said lightly.

Pulling a notebook from her pocket, Morgana began to sketch out a design.

"Ammo like so."

"Don't forget overhead cover to keep the sun off."

"Do you not enjoy random cook offs in the middle of the day, Staff?" Morgana asked innocently.

"I find them terribly inconvenient," Nealen replied in a bored voice.

"Rather like unwanted guests at tea time they are," Stirling added.

"Quite," Morgana said, pencil still scratching out the design rapidly.

"We'll set each inside their own horseshoe of sandbags, with a ring of sandbags backed by railroad ties outside of that."

"Might want to throw up a couple t-posts covered with reflectives for after dark," Stirling suggested.

"Easy enough." Morgana held up her notebook. "Like that, Nealen?"

"Good enough for government work."

"I'll have the lasses get right on it."

"Eh, let 'em take their time," Nealen advised.

"Whatever for?" Morgana asked.

"Happiness is a belt-fed weapon," the marine explained.

Morgana looked back towards the Marines at work, watched them going about their business, cigarettes clenched between their teeth as they let loose a new volley of fire. They were laughing even, joking in between shots, needling each other as they carried on.

"Hey Sergeant Cass!" Tolliver yelled from his position.

"What's up, Tolliver?" Cassidy asked.

"Bizz-ness. Is. Good!" Tolliver pronounced.

All around them, Marines howled, as if it were the funniest joke imaginable. Even Nealen was smiling.

"Well then. No reason to disturb the lads when they're at play," Morgana declared.

Chapter 15

Work Sucks, I Know

"We're most of the way through reconstruction, and with the distinct lack of enemy contact, we should be back on schedule by the end of the month, ma'am," Staff Sergeant Keating declared as he checked his notes.

Captain Fitzsimmons tried to keep a semblance of normalcy about the FOB, to include a Sunday staff meeting after morning chow, in the mess.

"Thank you, Staff Sergeant. Thank you, all of you. Please make sure you tell your people how pleased I am with their performance. Frankly, I only have two points to go over and both of those are for the green side of our house."

Now that was unusual. Nealen and his Marines straightened up in their seats.

"Sergeant Johnson?" Fitzsimmons asked.

"Ma'am?"

"You're the instructor when the lads are doing hand-to-hand, correct?"

"Yes ma'am. It's called MCMAP, comes with belts and certifications for each of them," Johnson explained.

"Because of course Marines would have an organized system for beating each other's asses."

"Why not? Doesn't everybody?" Johnson asked innocently.

"No," Natasha deadpanned.

"Gentlemen, killing is my business! And bizz-ness. Is gooooood!" Tolliver said in a loud, whiny voice with a tinge of falsetto. The marine side of the room started laughing uproariously at this.

"Is that a movie quote?" Gallagher asked politely.

"*Major Payne*, Colour," Tolliver answered. "It's loaded with motivation!"

"There is something seriously wrong with all of you," Munro asserted.

"Don't encourage them, Munro," Mayne advised. "20 year-old alcoholics with machine guns do not need encouragement."

"Too bloody right," Munro groaned.

"Getting back on track," Fitzsimmons declared. "You call it MickMap, Johnson?"

"It's the next step after a paddy whack but before a tally whacker," Cassidy deadpanned.

His jest sent the entire room into paroxysms of laughter.

"Marine Corps Martial Arts Program," Johnson announced between breaths. "Starts at tan, then grey, green, brown and black."

"You wear this with a special gi or something?" one of the Brits asked.

"Nope, it's why we wear different colored rigger belts," Kramer explained, pointing to his own. "Cassidy and I beat each other up for long enough to get our green belts at our last unit, Tolliver has been to the instructor course, so he wears a tan tab on his green belt. Sergeant Johnson was assigned as permanent party at the school house at Quantico."

"I was supposed to be Motor-T support. Those nasty assholes hazed me until I finished passing the instructor-trainer course."

"That's why he gets to wear a red tab on his black belt," Tolliver clarified.

"Who's top man in the battalion?" Hondo asked curiously.

"First Sergeant Torrez has four red tabs to my three. And he is really good at beating that ass," Nealen admitted. "We went at it during the last battalion Staff NCO training session. There were lots of bruises. Doc Nasty prescribed Motrin and medicinal vodka to make the pain go away, then confined us to quarters for a day." Nealen looked Hondo up and down. "Which does not explain why you haven't moved up a belt in the last two years."

"There is a really good eskrima dojo in Kaneohe," Hondo replied cheerfully.

Nealend studied him, breathed in, breathed out very slowly. "Solo or doble?" he asked.

Hondo tilted his head to one side, a movement which reminded Natasha of her husband's hunting hound. "Both. After we get back, the guro wants me to start Espada y Daga."

"Remind me to go punch Guro Parajillo in the dick," Nealen declared. "I told him if any of you idiots showed up in his dojo he was to call me."

Nealen looked at the room, who were all staring at him, while Hondo tried and failed to hide the grin on his face.

"Somebody took up Filipino knife fighting while I wasn't looking," Nealen grumped.

"Buncha bloody damned ninjas," Munro interrupted.

"Nah. I knock that out of their heads pretty quick," Johnson replied. "Though Sergeant Cassidy has clearly agreed to be my assistant when teaching knife work."

"You're not really going to use knives are you?" Gallagher asked.

"Why not?" Johnson asked.

"What happens if somebody stabs their sparring partner?" she protested.

"Oh. Ma'am, I won't let anybody use live steel in the dojo. At this stage, it's just rubber training knives," Johnson assured.

"Oh thank goodness for small favors," Morgana breathed.

"Do you think you could work with my girls as well? We don't have anything quite like it, and frankly some of us could use lessons on how to throw a punch," Fitzsimmons asked.

"We'll need to order them mouth guards, but that's easy. How about we start tomorrow, before noon chow?" Johnson suggested.

"Sounds good to me," Fitzsimmons replied.

She looked to her notes, sighed, then looked at Nealen as she drummed her fingers on the tabletop. Nealen seemed to be waiting nonchalantly. By now Fitzsimmons was fairly certain Nealen could keep butter from melting in his mouth if the situation called for it.

"How long?" is the question Natasha decided as she stared at him.

Sigh.

It is not something which I have the patience to find out.

"Staff Sergeant Nealen, is it normal for Marines to swat flies with bricks?" Fitzsimmons asked.

The question, and how she'd stated it, did not have to be shouted to be heard in the quiet.

"Yes, ma'am," Nealen said without hesitation.

"Why?"

"Because it's really hard to be annoying when you're dead. It's also really hard to have problems if the problems are six feet under and missing their brains. Or they've been scattered across the landscape in very small pieces."

Fitzsimmons paused, hand dropping back to her side as whatever point she was about to make died before she could air it.

"I can't argue with that logic. I really can't."

"Ma'am?" Nealen asked.

"It's not that you're wrong. It's that the locals may not appreciate our methods. How many firefights have there been now?"

"Umm, since we arrived?"

"Yes."

Nealen began counting on his fingers. "Menez, Samuels at the gate that one time. The Wednesday over on Post Six. That one morning before chow —"

"Don't forget the middle of the Sunday double header," Kramer growled. "Pricks interrupted my baseball game on AFN."

"Oh yeah! That! Indecent gobshites, the lot of them! Couldn't wait till the seventh inning stretch at least!" Cassidy suggested.

"Focus!" Fitzsimmons demanded.

"Cassidy had that fun over on Post Three," Cherney volunteered.

"That little shindig at Post Three shouldn't even count," Cassidy snorted. "And Lyons clobbered most of them with the two-forty!"

"They went in your log, right Cass?" Nealen asked.

"Yes, Staff Sergeant."

"Good enough for government work." Nealen paused. "Twenty-two."

"And a half for the one fella we popped on post with the ell tee's help," Cassidy helpfully

Balcombe made a face from across the room at his expense.

"Good work," Nealen complimented. "Ma'am, if you call it a penny shy of two-dozen, you're probably right."

Fitzsimmons closed her eyes. Counted to ten. Opened them.

Nope, the merry, murderous bastards are still here.

"What do we have to show for it?" she asked.

"They've stopped shooting at the work crews putting in the airstrip," Cherney said helpfully.

"There is that."

"Several dozen dead Taliban," Johnson suggested.

"That many?" Gallagher asked in surprise.

"They're not fast learners," Nealen assured. "Otherwise they'd know the difference between goats and women."

"They really hate taking a Mark Nineteen to the chest?" Tolliver suggested.

"Nah that makes me happy," Samuels declared. "I'm looking forward to using them as Halloween decorations soon."

"Huh? What?" a British Sergeant asked.

"You mount the bodies on stakes outside the gate, stick a candle or a glow stick in their mouth just after sunset. Everybody else takes the hint and quits giving you trouble so they don't end up the same way." Samuels' nose wrinkled slightly. "Just gotta wait for the majority of the corpse to get eaten away by the birds and jackals. Then it stops stinking."

"Sweet Christ in Heaven! No!" Fitzsimmons shouted. She glared at Samuels. "What is wrong with you?"

"Diagnosed functioning sociopath with high loyalty quotients," Samuels replied calmly. "I keep a copy of the documentation on me in case people ask."

The assemblage stared at him, some horrified, others smirking.

"He's taking the piss ain't he?" Staff Munro asked.

"Here, take a look," Samuels held out a laminated card. "I even got it notarized."

"You're a psychopath," Munro said.

"At least I'm on a path, Staff Sergeant," Samuels replied.

Wincing at the byplay, Fitzsimmons pinched the bridge of her nose before she continued.

"Pistol, you Kipple, ever read *Fuzzy Wuzzy*?"

"Yes, ma'am."

"Recite it please," she ordered.

The boisterous Sergeant began to speak aloud from memory, eyes looking upwards in concentration as he went back through the words.

"We've fought with many men acrost the seas,
An' some of 'em was brave an' some was not:
The Paythan an' the Zulu an' Burmese;
But the Fuzzy was the finest o' the lot."

"That's the very one," Fitzsimmons confirmed. "We are not in Africa, and these are Pathans, but for our purposes, their name is Fuzzy Wuzzy. And we are surrounded by them. We need to exercise some tact and be slightly more circumspect with how we handle them."

"Would you like us to find a solution for that?" Nealen asked politely.

"I would greatly appreciate it, Staff Sergeant. We cannot kill everybody here. Though I will not deny your motivation at the effort. It is admirable, in a very, very dark way."

"Thank you ma'am," Nealen said.

"Secondly, we cannot afford to end up like the Black Watch, when it comes to Fuzzy Wuzzy or his mates," Fitzsimmons remarked.

She stomped out of the mess, leaving the Marines and soldiers to stare at each other. "Who-da-la what happened to the Black Watch?" Cherney asked, looking over at Pistol.

"Funny enough, I do know this story," Pistol admitted.

"What's that?" Cherney asked.

"So 'ere's to you, Fuzzy-Wuzzy, at your 'ome in the Soudan;

You're a pore benighted 'eathen but a first-class fightin' man;

An' 'ere's to you, Fuzzy-Wuzzy, with your 'ayrick 'ead of 'air --

You big black boundin' beggar — for you broke a British square!"

"That's nice, but it don't tell me nothing." Cherney complained.

"The Black Watch regiment was sent to Sudan in 1881 as part of an expedition," Pistol explained. "While marching they came under attack and formed square. Infantry on the outside, cav in the center and dismounted."

"Makes sense. That's how infantry roll, right?"

"Until machine guns became commonplace, yes. The Black Watch were ordered into a charge at a nearby enemy force forming for an assault. Bad communication meant that end of the square was not filled like it should have been. Fuzzy Wuzzy and company rushed the opening."

"Oh shit."

"Shit is right. They darn near broke the square. The troops held though, and wound up winning spectacularly."

"That's bad but at least they won."

"If that was all that happened, we wouldn't be talking about them," Cassidy warned. "The newspapers reported that the Highlanders broke and ran."

"But they didn't break!" Cherney protested.

"Dude, you think reporters being lying assholes is a new thing?" Hondo declared.

"Uhhhh..."

"Remind me to give your gun the lecture on William Randolph Hearst one of these days."

"Another history lecture?" Cherney gawked. "How many hours will it run this time?

"Only two. Plan to takes notes, there will be a quiz at the end," Hondo informed him.

"Is that why you don't have a girlfriend? You spend all of your time reading?"

"Last time I checked I've got bigger arms and legs than you do," Cassidy declared.

"Aside from the gym," Cherney snarked.

"Yes. I go to the base library. A lot. And bookstores. Hell, I'm waiting on more books from Amazon."

"So are we done discussing old battles?" Kramer asked.

"Almost," Pistol declared. "For decades after the battle at Tamai, one of the easiest ways to start a fight with a Highlander of the Black Watch was by loudly asking for a pint of broken-square in a pub. Common up through the end of World War One."

"It'll still catch a man a beating," Mayne assured from his seat. "Watched it happen when I was at Sennybridge one time. We were attached to a Black Watch unit for a month of maneuvers. After we finished, we went to the pub for a pint."

"As one does," Keating declared.

"This gypsy down at the end of the bar couldn't stop with the insults about soldiers. Usual bunch of bollocks and blarney. Worked himself right up into a lather he did. Then he saw their cap badge and declared that he was done. After all, what use did he have bothering to insult a buncha broken squares? I watched Colour Melvin throw back his pint march over and knock that stupid whoreson on his drunk pikey ass."

"Colour Melvin," Keating mused. "Do you mean the Scottish Division's Sergeant Major, Charles Melvin?"

"Aye. He was a brand new Colour then," Stirling assured.

"He's about as old fashioned Highlander as you can ask for and a proper man," Pistol added. "He was my RSM when I did a stint with that regiment. Follow him anywhere."

"He invited everybody in the bar not associated with those snot-nosed sheep stealers to clear out. He had a lesson in manners to teach," Stirling declared.

Stirling set down his empty tea cup, breathed in deeply at a memory. "The men of the Black Watch have never run from a fight. And we damn sure weren't about to start that night, even with half the bar against us." He smiled. "It was a very good night."

\#

Cassidy came out of the chow hall and looked around, enjoying the cool night air for a moment as he cracked open the can of Dr. Pepper. He tried to avoid junk food, but if a man had to have a vice, at least it was a quality one. Nearby in the smoke pit, Nealen stood smoking.

"Evening, Staff Sergeant."

"Evening bubba. What's happening?" Nealen asked.

"I think I got an idea, Staff Sergeant."

"About our problem?"

"Yes, Staff Sergeant."

"Well you got me here too, so you might as well spit it out," Mayne declared as he joined the duo. Pulling a cigar from its holder, the company sergeant major clipped one end with a sharp knife, accepted a light from Nealen and took a drag, then waved his hand airily at Cassidy to continue.

"Where we came from, Zaranj, we were in the market nearly every day. The vendors knew us by sight," Cassidy explained.

"You were spending money there, no surprise," Nealen replied.

"Yeah but that's just it. They liked seeing us because our money was good. And because we were there doing our thing without being pricks."

"True that."

"What if me, the terp, and the rest of Gun Five took a stroll down towards town tomorrow? We might be able to rustle up something."

Mayne's head leaned over to one side. "Eh, it could happen."

"Why wouldn't it, Sarn't Major?" Nealen asked.

"Captain won't like it. She figures the town is in on what's been happening to us."

"I'm not gonna say she's wrong, but I don't think she's entirely on target," Nealen countered.

"You've dealt with the locals before?"

"Afghan twice, Iraq four times before this," Nealen admitted. "More we spent money, more they liked us. Besides, it's not like we're going out drinking and carousing all night."

"Yeah that's an international incident waiting to happen," Mayne admitted, taking another drag on his cigar. "I just thought of something else."

Looking towards the medical tent, Mayne spied the person he needed. "Doc Gnem, a word," Mayne called out.

"Yes, Sarn't Major?" the medico asked as he came running.

"Sergeant Cassidy needs a shave chit."

"Sarn't Major?"

"If you would, write one up for him."

"Irritation and such from his helmet strap?"

"Very much so. I think 6 days should be about right."

"I'll get right on that, Sarn't Major. Be just a couple minutes."

"Good lad, thank you."

Cassidy waited until Gnem was back in his tent before he looked at Mayne. "I'm missing something."

"You ain't got a beard lad. In the Northwest Frontier, a man with no beard is no man at all," Mayne explained.

"Oh."

"I've seen you smoother than a baby's backside at breakfast, and by noon you look like an East End hobo. Give it five days, then go to town."

"Today's Sunday, so Saturday morning?"

"Sound about right to you, Nealen?"

"Yes, Sarn't Major."

"Good. Cassidy, take off after morning chow. But leave us something for dinner time in case you're delayed. Try to be sensible about what you do."

"Yes, Sarn't Major. I'll give Pilsen written instructions."

"Attaboy. Now git along. I've got to figure out how to explain this to the Captain when it all goes pear-shaped come Saturday."

\#

"Walls! Walls! Walls!"

The refrain had become familiar to the FOB's inhabitants. Nealen would, without warning make the call, with the expectation that his marines would drop everything and run to their assigned posts, preparatory to repelling an attack.

He really is a proper bastard about the matter, Balcombe decided as she watched Marines scurrying to their assigned posts. Even with the FOB as big as it was, he could reliably get a squad on the walls in the first forty-five seconds. Within two minutes, every marine not in FDC or named Jimenez would have their weapons aimed outward.

Just like when Stand To happens. And he doesn't care what anybody thinks about it. Rarely did any section make the same mistake twice. The first time a junior enlisted complained, it had been a swift punishment from his own corporal which silenced him.

Nor did it matter what was occurring. Nealen had triggered calls during meals with no warning.

I'll admit, I was kind of disappointed with that one, the Lieutenant remembered. She'd been so certain the men would bottleneck at the door, turning into a milling cluster of arms and legs and bodies crammed into the single doorway too tightly to exit properly.

On other platoons it would've been the case. Because normal men do not consider the most efficient means of exfiltration for such scenarios. Peter Nealen prized personal initiative in his subordinates however. The platoon's NCOs had seen the issue coming a mile away, then spoken amongst themselves about how to beat the problem and taken their sections through the problem individually, when they were sure he wouldn't notice.

Oh sure, the procedure had still been rough the first time. She and the girls had laughed at the sight of it all. But standing outside and timing it with him, in the Observation tower like she was right now brought the reality of the event home for.

"You really can do it, Staff," she breathed.

"Do what, ma'am?"

"Push men that hard. Without them breaking."

"Did you think they would?"

"Yes," Balcombe admitted.

He lit a cigarette, listening to the radio as each section announced their ready status, checking his stopwatch as he and the Lieutenant waited.

"Know what I did before this, ma'am?"

"I know you were a sniper."

"Yep. Force Recon."

"Why aren't you still doing that?"

"*Hogfather, this is Local Suck, we're up,*" Jimenez announced over the radio.

Nealen checked his watch.

"Minute fifty-five and a tenth. Good work. All sections, stand down and return to your daily tasks."

As men drifted back to whatever they'd been doing, Nealen put the radio away.

"Medical exam revealed serious knee issues. Even with surgery, there was no reasonable way I could expect to continue as I had been. Doc said if I wanted to stay in, I'd switch job fields."

He lit a new cigarette, held the pack out to her, and got it lit before he continued.

"Arty rides in trucks everywhere. Compared to being Recon, this is light years easier on the body."

"Not so much hiking and marching."

"Hell no. Mind you, I still run them the same way I ran a Recon platoon."

"Oh?"

"Think about it, ma'am. I've been to the very pinnacle of human performance. Delta, Seals, Green Berets, PJs, the whole alphabet soup of spec-ops badasses. I knew how to get the very best out of men before I changed jobs. More than that, they know that what I'm putting them through isn't about ego, or power trips. None of that stupid BS."

"They do?"

"My Marines trust me. They know the only reason we're doing this is because the alternate option is death or captivity by the Taliban."

"That's a dark outlook."

"But true," Nealen countered.

"Indeed." A highly unpleasant thought, as Camille Balcombe had no desire to find out what the Taliban's hospitality would mean for her.

"They can't stand the idea of those goatfucking child-molesters winning at anything," Nealen continued. "Thus 'I can do all things through Spite, which motivates me.'"

Balcombe finished her cigarette, stripped it, and dropped the remains into an ammo can.

"Staff Nealen, you lot are absolutely mad."

"Yes ma'am."

"I thought you were mad clear back to that sniper duel."

"I expected as much."

"But I'm damn glad you're here."

"Thank you, ma'am."

She left him to his thoughts as she tromped down the stairs, considering the nature of men who would willingly subject themselves to such punishment.

Why do they do it, she wondered. *What makes them do it? More than just spite. What makes them be this way?*

Chapter 16

Things Will be Great When You're Downtown

Hajji Jamal ben Badr walked into the center of the village where men with rifles waited. Had been waiting, apparently since before the Dhuhr call to prayer. They had spoken little, and threatened none, asking only to speak with the headman of the village, for which the Hajji felt no small amount of relief. As the only villager who had made the pilgrimage to sacred Mecca, he was called for. That he had firsthand knowledge of the West, and spoke English never mattered to his fellows.

At the center of the village, one man sat upon a low chair. Unlike his comrades, he wore neither helm over his head, nor dark glasses to cover his eyes. Instead, he wore a keffiyeh, dyed richly green, and there was good growth of beard on his face.

Ah, a proper man sent to speak with us, the Hajji surmised.

A blanket had been placed upon the ground before him. In the center, a square of cloth covered something.

With any luck, I am right about what that cloth covers.

"Salaam Alaikum," the seated man declared.

"Walaikum Salaam."

"You headman. You speak for village?"

His Pashto was rough, badly accented, but his tone was strong.

"I do."

"Good. I speak with you," he gestured toward the cloths. "Please. Sit. Partake."

ben Badr felt quite pleased he was correct in his estimation — the cloth covered a steel dish holding salt and bread. Fresh too, to judge by the taste and soft texture as he thoughtfully chewed through it.

Politely, he bowed his head, and a subordinate stepped forward at a word from the man, removing the items. The man in turn gestured to another who stepped forward. His beard was longer, shot through with gray, though he did not carry the look of the people. Yet he wore a turban proper, and at his waist, a beautifully set dagger rested comfortably.

"I speak on behalf of this man. A translator. His command of Pashto is limited. He does not wish to convey insult, even by accident."

ben Badr nodded his head politely. "I understand." His voice changed slightly. "However it is unnecessary" he continued in English long unused. "My father ensured I received a strong education while on the Hajj."

As he watched, yet another subordinate stepped forward, placing a tea service and small plate of what looked to be sweet meats on the ground before him. All of it smelled divine and he was impressed to see steam slowly rising from the tea pot. His eyes widened slightly as the American slowly filled both cups with a very steady hand, before nibbling on an item, sipping from his tea, then motioning for ben Badr to do the same.

"It is rare to be so received by an American."

"Thank you, I consider it a gift of traveling."

ben Badr felt a smile growing on his face as he looked at the younger man seated across from him.

"I should like to hear of your travels. It has been a long time since I journeyed far."

The young man smiled broadly. "And I would be happy to speak of it."

#

The whole of the chow hall was chattering that night, as soldiers and Marines sat together at tables, speaking amongst themselves as enlisted will do. The soldiers all wondered what Cassidy's sign meant. He'd left it hanging outside the door — "Gone to fight Seminoles." If the Marines knew, they'd said nothing, though there had been many grins shared at it.

Nealen and Mayne had supervised Pilsen finishing dinner, with the meal ready by eighteen-hundred, none of which alleviated the chatter. Rumors abounded, as enlisted are wont to do since man first marched away to war, but nobody who actually knew for certain was speaking. Yet.

"Least he made it easy for us," Mayne said calmly as he scooped the dense shepherd's pie onto plates.

"Aye, but I really am worried about him," Nealen admitted, ladling gravy from a massive pot.

"Considering we didn't tell the Captain, she's gonna be right pissed if he dies in the process."

"Nah, Pashtunwali is in effect," Nealen said. "The Taliban would be idiots to violate that."

Mayne grunted. "True, but that doesn't mean they won't try."

"I'd almost be insulted if they didn't," Nealen confessed.

"Look at all of you eating me outta house and home!" A voice bellowed from the door. Heads turned and Cassidy smiled as he saw the quizzical expressions on upturned faces.

"Report, Sergeant!" Nealen yelled from across the room.

"Green! Green! Up! Staff Sergeant," Cassidy replied, drawing near so he could speak without shouting.

"How much did it cost?" Mayne asked.

"One poncho liner, a tea set, and a quarter-ounce krugerrand." He grinned broadly. "I didn't have to use my stash of dollar bills.

"The hell were you bargaining for?" House asked, leaning in to hear the conversation. "And with what?

"Chow. I drew cash from the bank before we deployed. Two hundred dollars in ones," Hondo announced proudly.

"Who brings two hundred dollars in ones to Afghanistan? Johnson loudly demanded. "What kinda strip club did you think you were gonna find out here?"

This set the hall to laughing and even Cassidy grinned. "Well Johnson, I was hoping for a classy place. Not the kind where they give you a pity discount for having less teeth than the meth head stumbling around onstage!"

"Ohhhh!" the marines chanted. "What you got for that, Sergeant?"

"You walked into that one Johnson!" Nealen prodded. "But seriously, we good, Cass?"

"Oh yeah, we're good Staff Sergeant. We'll take delivery the day after tomorrow. At sunup."

"Why the delay in delivery?"

"I need the engineers to build me a temporary stock pen and chute, plus space to slaughter. It's gonna be an awful mess. We don't need it becoming a health hazard either."

"Good thinking," Mayne declared.

"You tell the captain yet?" Hondo asked.

"Nah. Better to beg forgiveness than to ask permission," Mayne explained.

"Oh goody." The grin on Cassidy's face belied how much he was looking forward to all of it. "That's my favorite way to do business!"

#

Lance Corporal Ostrovsky held the cigarette between his lips and took a slow drag before taking another sip of his coffee. The sun was up, the whole camp was bustling about, and he'd almost finished his breakfast. A flip of the wrist to check his watch and he nodded.

"What time is it?" Shiver asked.

"0853. Almost off post."

"Hell yeah. Be nice to shower and get clean."

"That sounds amazing," Ostrovsky said.

Moooooooooo!

"Hey did you hear that?" Shiver asked. "Sounded like a cow."

Moooooooooo!

"Yeah, I hear it. Where's it coming from?"

The cattle lowed a third time and then both men saw it come around the bend in the road. In the lead was a large bull, horns tossing about as he walked steadily down the road, driven by a youngster holding a rope in one hand and a switch in the other.

"Would ya lookit that?"

"Think we could get Scarbro to ride it?"

"Maybe. He says he can ride most anything with hair."

"Ya know, that might explain his ex-wife."

"Dude, nothing explains her. She was nuts before she cheated on him."

Behind the bull they saw more livestock, sheep and goats, pushed and prodded along by children who drew closer.

"COG this is Post Three, we got a —"

"Heck yeah, they showed up!"

It was Cassidy, with lengths of 550 paracord in hand as he moved the barbed wire aside.

"Uh, Sergeant?" Ostrovsky began.

"Post 3, this is COG, say again your last. Came in broken and unreadable."

"COG this is Post 3. Never mind. Five Actual has it taken care of."

"Well ain't that nice?" Samuels replied. *"COG out."*

"Relax Bubba, Staff Sergeant knows about this," Cassidy assured.

"That's a whole farm out there!" Shiver objected. "Who the hell is gonna play Old MacDonald to this?"

"Not for long," Cassidy replied.

In all, Cassidy thought he'd done spectacularly well. One head of cattle looked to be a steer, two goats, three sheep, and a lamb. Hajji ben Badr had offered a camel as well, but Cassidy declined, knowing he'd be hard pressed to butcher the steer alone, never mind the unfamiliar dromedary.

Running loops of braided 550 cord around each animal's head, Cassidy paid the children in packs of gummy bears and Coca-Cola, then began his walk back across the fire base toward his chow hall. The temperature had yet to get uncomfortable, and he could feel a light breeze rolling across his face.

"As I was out walking one morning for pleasure, I spied a young cowboy a-riding along. His hat was tipped back, and his spurs were a jingle, and as he went riding he was singing this song. Whoopie-tie-yie-yo —, git along ya little —"

"What in the name of Christ Almighty is all that?" Captain Fitzsimmons shouted from the doorway of the mechanics' shed.

Well, the Captain was bound to find out anyways he reminded himself.

"Good morning ma'am!" Cassidy cheerfully declared.

Captain Fitzsimmons stomped toward him, a confused glare written across her face.

"As to what this is, ma'am, it's a steer. Least it was the last time I checked," Cassidy said calmly.

"Why do you have animals inside my FOB?" she asked pointedly.

"You told us we needed to improve community relations, so I went and improved them."

"By stealing livestock? This is now an international incident!"

"No, ma'am. No rustling involved. Leastways nothing that'd get me a Texas necktie party."

It hadn't occurred to Cass that he was drawing a crowd. Indeed, most of the Marines were now gathered around them, as were a significant portion of the Brits.

"Well if you didn't steal them, what did you do?" Fitzsimmons demanded.

"Went into town and bargained with Mr. Hajji ben Badr for some livestock. Gave him one of your tea sets, a spare poncho liner and hard cash."

"What exactly are you going to do with all these animals? Start a farm yourself?" Gallagher asked in disbelief at what she was witnessing.

Cassidy tapped the steer on its rump. "This is several roasts plus tallow to make Yorkshires, at least a couple stews, brisket and I'm liable to throw half of it on a spit for some open air barbecue. That's why it's got a load of dried lumber on its back."

He moved on to the goats. "Cabrito chili. These are good for forty pounds apiece, so figure twenty gallons of chili per carcass, maybe a skosh more. Serve it over rice or pasta and that's two meals easy. Maybe four. What doesn't get eaten on the first go round can be thrown in the freezer and reheated every so often to break up the monotony."

Patting each of the sheep in turn, Cass smiled. "Americans ain't big on sheep, because we use beef a lot more. But we're Marines. We'll eat anything at least once. I can stuff these, roast 'em and they'll feed the whole base ma'am."

"You know how to butcher all of this?"

"Yes ma'am. Skin and gut today, then hang for twenty so the meat tenderizes. After that I can serve as necessary. It'll keep us in chow for days."

"Very well. Just be quick about it. I don't like to think about animals suffering."

"Oh but ma'am, they need torture!" Hondo declared.

"They need torture?" Fitzsimmons asked, shocked at his brazen attitude.

"It's how you make the meat taste better!"

"Even a lamb like that little one?" Gallagher pointed.

"That lamb is special ma'am. McSweeney, you like the girlfriend I brought you?"

The crowd roared in approval. Pistol's mustache danced as he belly-laughed, then clapped a hand on McSweeney's shoulder whilst the flustered lance corporal sputtered indignantly, turning bright red with embarrassment.

"But Sergeant, I —"

"Joke's on you, Little Miss Muffet!"

\#

He was bare to the waist, arms and hands covered in blood as he worked. Flecks of blood marred his face.Speed was of the utmost importance. They couldn't afford to have the animals be a hindrance more than a day. Cassidy had put produce on the edge of going bad in front of them to keep them sated and complacent.

After an early lunch, with several farm boys in the platoon who'd done slaughter work before, he and the working party set about skinning, gutting, and hanging each animal in turn. He settled into a rhythm as he worked, letting himself move to a song none but he could hear as his knives flashed.

"Hey, how's it going?" Sylvie asked, watching the steer carcass rotate in midair on the trapeze the engineers had rigged up for him. The working party weren't in sight then, but she kept the banter light.

"Doing alright. How's your day been?" he asked her, trying to stay casual as well.

"Not bad, thought I'd come see what was keeping you busy."

"Sergeant, we've got everything hung up like you ordered," a Marine announced as they rounded the corner.

"Good, I can handle this last one." Cassidy blinked away sweat. "Stand fast uglies. Just wait, right there." He looked to Sylvie. "Lyons, my body armor is right there by the door. See the green carabiner on it?"

"Uh huh."

"Round brass key on my carabiner opens Bluebeard's locker. Take 'em there, if you would please. They are authorized three cans, Monster, Red Bull, or Rockstar, and a bag of jerky apiece."

Jaws dropped. "You have all that, Sergeant?"

Cassidy grinned broadly. "I do."

"You're good," Santangelo said, awestruck.

"It's a gift. Now git."

"Yes, Sergeant!" the marines cheerfully chorused.

Minutes passed as he continued about his work, finishing the last strokes of his knife across the carcass before he wrapped it entirely in plastic sheeting. Sanitation mattered, even here. Perhaps especially here. Food poisoning, salmonella, anything that might make people sick was a genuine concern.

Reaching for zip ties on his work table, Cassidy secured the sheeting in place around the hooves. Only then did he lift the entire mass off its suspension and carry it into the reefer where the rest of the meat was hanging. It was cold work, making the hairs on his bare, wet skin stand up rigidly.

Part of why I hate this job. I still hate being cold after all these years. He reminisced. *I want somewhere warm when I retire.*

He'd thought about Camp Lejeune, down in the Carolinas, but returning to Southern humidity had been an unwelcome experience. Twentynine Palms, up in the High Desert plateau, was too hot. And dry. And not a lot of dating opportunities.

Kinda like this hellhole.

With a heave, Hondo put the hook on the bar overhead. He checked the writing on each one last time, to make sure he'd done it correctly, then stepped back out into the quickly dimming night.

Speaking of sunshine, Camp Pendleton was nice, but I'm not sold on Southern California. Or more of fricking Monica.

Throwing a padlock on the door, he stepped back, lips pursed as he considered his next move: Cleanup.

At least I don't have glassware to worry about.

Dishwashing had long been an undesirable task. It was part of why he preferred to cook. And part of why he kept his mouth shut about his talents around guys in the unit.

Hawaii's been good to me though. Yeah, it is starting to grow on me. Aside from the cost of living, I like it there.

Returning to his workspace, he began washing down the surfaces he'd used. *Sanitation to keep the flies and mosquitos away.* Grasping a shovel, he shifted bloody sand into the bucket of a Bobcat. Just like the rest of the waste, it would be disposed of properly.

Finally, the only thing left to clean was himself: his arms and chest were covered with gore. He could feel the splashes of viscera dotting his burnt copper face.

"I really hope you're not done yet."

Turning in surprise, Hondo saw Sylvie, sitting on a makeshift chair beneath the limited shade, sketchbook and pencils in hand.

"What are you doing?" he asked, curious as he toweled off, enjoying the clean feeling.

"After the lads finished getting their loot from Bluebeard's locker, I started drawing you."

"You what?"

"Aye. I think it's a rather nice likeness."

Standing, she moved closer so he could see.

"That is nice."

She wrinkled her nose as he examined the sketch. "Something is pungent," Sylvie said drolly.

"Starting to smell a little?" he asked.

"I wouldn't suggest that it was pleasant."

"There's that dry understatement again," he suggested as he moved in once more.

"Oh no you don't!" the brunette protested, trying to scoot back and maintain the hold on her precious cargo.

Cassidy waggled his eyebrows and Sylvie laughed.

"Go clean up in the showers. I'll have somebody take the Bobcat load down to the dump."

He frowned, as if questioning her intentions.

"I'll be waiting here for you to get back. Promise."

"Okay. Just make sure you have the backhoe scrape out a deep hole before you dump the load."

"Will do." She blew him a kiss and he smiled broadly, then grabbed his rifle and made tracks.

It was only the work of a few minutes to get the load handled before Sylvie could get back to work at her portrait, sketching with care as she worked to capture the essence of the man. It was in the moments when he was alone that she found him most inviting. The brooding nature slipped away, replaced by a thoughtful, kind man who was honest about his faults in the same way he was honest about his brilliance.

And he doesn't see when I'm watching him, wondering if he's playing me. If he's a grass running a fraud, he's damn sight better than any I've ever met before. Thank you for those lessons as well, Grandmere.

That brought another thought to mind — at some point he was going to hear about her grandfather. And wasn't that going to be a conversation?

Wonder what Granpapa will think when he meets him?

The idea was so shocking it stopped her, physically and mentally, in an instant.

Wait! Who said anything about taking Cassidy home to meet my family? Sylvie wondered.

Where did that thought come from? In what world could I get away with taking home a man such as this, to meet my very proud, very proper, English family? He's not landed, he's not titled, and he's definitely not English. With Grandmere, it was acceptable because she came from a titled French family. Patricia, Delphine, and Eloise would be furious at having to explain him to all their society friends. After all, he's just a common soldier.

Even as she completed the thought, a part of her railed angrily against the notion. Hondo demonstrated time and again so much that made him desirable. Even if he'd been partially homeschooled, his education and the depth of his raising was astounding! Heat rose in her cheeks at a recent memory.

He's also very good with his hands.

Of all the boys the Terrible Trio tried to trot past me when I was younger, who among them could've matched him in knowing poetry, or history? And still been entirely capable of not only slaughtering a steer but possessing the skills to cook all of it? Or win a firefight?

"Baby, what has got you so worked up?"

The voice came from behind her, spoken gently as his lips brushed her ears, then down the back of her neck whilst his arms encircled her.

"Unf," Sylvie grunted.

"I'll take that as a 'I'm not going to tell you right now' and 'go back to what you were doing because it feels good."

Sylvie chuckled, setting aside her pencils and paper once more. Leaning back into his arms, she enjoyed the sensation and smells of her wild, wonderful man. Far out on the horizon, the sun sank lower, throwing up bands of pink and purple in the western sky.

"Tell me, did you come to the Frontier looking for a woman?" she asked.

"No, I didn't. After — after the last one, I didn't want a woman in my life."

"And now?"

"I'm... debating it. A lot."

"You are?"

"Uh huh."

Parting his grip, she stood and strutted toward the partially open door. Cassidy watched her sashay, entranced by the sight of her hips swaying about. Everything about it enticed him and he felt his anticipation slowly rising.

Before he could say anything, she looked back at him in a manner so sultry his breath caught, even as she stretched against the door jam.

Not simply leaned either.

Posing he realized. *She's posing. For me.*

Sylvie arched backwards, showing off her still-concealed curves and causing his mouth to go dry.

Monica had done similar, but it was always to show off for the crowd around them. Never had there been anything just for him.

Not like this.

Even as he studied that lithe and fulsome form, he noticed she was now sauntering back toward him.

Staying in his seat, he drank in the sight of her.

A wonderful, calming, exciting dream.

Slowly she draped one languid arm around his neck, then the other.

"I… I don't… I…"

A finger placed across his lips silenced him.

"I like when you look at me that way. I like feeling wanted by a man who respects me."

"I didn't know," Hondo confessed.

"I want you to wrap me in your arms and not let go. Nothing more, nothing less. Can you do that?"

"Aye, milady, we'll do that very thing."

Chapter 17

Well it Looks like Another Tequila Sunrise

"Sergeant, I don't know why, but we have an entire MRE box full of — stuff," Pilsen confessed when he walked into the kitchen, aforementioned box in hand.

"Huh? Oh yeah. That one," Cassidy said absently.

"You know about this?"

"It's the rat box."

"Sergeant?"

Hondo sighed and looked up from his report. "Look, not everything in the Meals Rejected by Egyptians is all that tasty. Or desirable."

"I can see that," Pilsen said.

"Personal taste also comes into play. So guys throw everything they don't want in the rat box. Somebody else comes along and they want it, they take it."

"Okay, but why, if you like bread, is there so much in here?"

Cassidy looked at him curiously.

"Have you never tried MRE bread, son?"

"No, Sergeant."

"Huh, let's fix that."

Slicing open the package in front of him, Cassidy tore off a hunk of the bread and passed it over.

"Stuff is dense," Pilsen commented, popping it into his mouth. His face changed colors as he chewed, but he said nothing before he'd consumed a half-liter of water and swallowed emphatically, forcing the last chunks to go down.

"I get it now," Pilsen declared as he reached for another water bottle.

"Glad you do," Cassidy said, returning back to his own MRE.

In the privacy of the kitchen, Joseph Pilsen wondered, not for the first time if he hadn't come upon a major secret. They had loose supplies bouncing around, and nobody was using them.

What do I do with them? He asked himself.

Thinking back across the many delights he'd learned to make, the young private wondered if he couldn't conjure something out of these leftovers.

Maybe. But first I'll need to go see what all I have.

Much later, once again back in the cool and privacy of the kitchen, Pilsen examined what he'd found.

All three gun crews had a rat box. Some had two. As did Motor-T, Comm, and FDC. Some of the birds had started similar boxes and he'd found a box stashed in the mess after lunch. There were literally hundreds of fifty-seven gram packets labeled "White Wheat Snack Bread" spread across the countertop, not to mention dried cranberries, raisins, and other items.

Waste not, want not the Sergeant says. *If that's really the case you might just think I've lost my fecking marbles after this.*

Making notes from the lessons Grandma Abbie had taught him so long ago in the bakery, he began working his way through the contents of the foil-and-plastic wrapped packets one at a time.

\#

Hondo walked into the kitchen after his second lifting session of the day, wondering where Pilsen had gotten off to. It was very nearly dinner time, which meant the evening service should be almost finished.

"Afternoon Sergeant," Pilsen announced cheerfully.

Huh. That's a change. Wonder what's got him in a good mood?

"What've you been up to, bubba?"

"Baking, Sergeant."

"Tomorrow's bread?

"No sergeant, though that is also done."

"Oh?"

"I made dessert, sergeant," Pilsen declared.

"Dessert?"

"Yes."

"I gotta see this," Hondo said, trying to hide his skepticism.

Drawing back the lid from the small foil baking tray, Pilsen handed him a spoon, motioning for Cassidy to dig in.

"Uh uh. Tell me what I'm looking at first. Present it as if you were serving this to the Crown."

"This is a stuffed bread pudding, laden with raisins, cranberries and apples. It has been decorated with candied almonds."

"Nicely done. Now, to see how it tastes."

Digging in with the spoon, Cassidy sniffed it, enjoying at once the smell of brown sugar and cinnamon making everything so pleasant.

Looks good, smells good, let's see if it tastes good — Oh yeah, he nailed that one.

Cassidy finished chewing, took another bite. And another. Finally, he put the spoon down.

"Okay son, that was fan-freaking-tastic. But we ain't exactly loaded up on bread around here. So where'd you get the means to make that?"

"After we talked earlier, I went to every section and collected all of the Rat Boxes."

"This is made from MRE bread?" Cassidy said in disbelief.

"Yes, Sergeant."

"Wait, is that where all of the ingredients came from?"

"Yes, Sergeant," Pilsen repeated, nodding his head slowly.

"How much did you make? Just this pan?"

Turning, Pilsen opened the oven. "I had enough to make four hotel trays worth."

"Son, that's a lot of bread."

"We've been eating a lot of rations, sergeant."

Cassidy began to laugh. He did not stop till he had doubled over and his laughter turned to hiccups as tears ran out of his eyes.

"Sergeant, what's so funny?" Pilsen said worriedly.

"You —" Cassidy pointed, then doubled over. Finally he stood up, wiping away the tears.

"Do you know why bread pudding came to be?" Hondo asked.

"No."

"Housewives had to figure out how to make stale, old bread, usable. What works better than milk, eggs, and butter, soaked into the bread, then baked in an oven?"

"Nothing?"

"That's right! And for years, the answer of what to do with hundreds of MRE bread servings has been sitting right in front of me."

He settled down, then looked at Pilsen. "Well done. It tastes excellent. Now, walk me through the recipe. Show me your work."

By the time Pilsen finished, he knew two things: he'd done something very right, and he had gained the sergeant's approval.

"Frankly, nobody is going to believe this.And it just occurred to me, it's a real shame we forced you on the path to sobriety."

"Why's that, sergeant?"

"Because if you had a still full of good brandy, we could take some of the sweetened condensed milk we keep for tea, and make it into one helluva topping for this."

Do I tell him? I haven't drank any of it, so I might be fine. Oh well, in for a penny, in for a pound.

"Sergeant, would rum do the job?"

Cassidy stopped. Stared, his nostrils flaring as he inhaled then slowly exhaled.

"Yes, Private Pilsen. Yes, rum would absolutely work in a sauce. Not that you would have any rum on your person."

"Who? Me?" Pilsen feigned. "Sergeant, that's illegal. I absolutely don't have any rum on my person right now."

Cassidy waved a hand.

"Relax bubba, I believe you." He pursed his lips in a light smile. "But ya know, this country is haunted. Just as sure as the Irish have Leprechauns and Hawaiians have Menehune, the Arabs and their Pashtun cousins have the Djinn."

Pilsen crossed himself. "I believe you Sergeant. Grannie Abbie, the baker I worked for always said the wee folk and fae were forces to be reckoned with."

"Matter of fact, I think I'm gonna step out and address this very serious security risk with Corporal Jimenez right now at this instant," Hondo asserted.

"How, um, long, do you think you'll be, Sergeant?"

"How long do you think before mischief will occur, private?"

"With the wee folk, one can never tell, but I'd give 'em a good ten minutes. At most."

Cassidy checked his wrist watch. "We'll give 'em fifteen, see what they come up with in the margin." He waggled a finger under Pilsen's nose. "You keep a sharp eye out for them. I'd hate to think what would happen if they slipped in here and started causing shenanigans!"

"Aye aye sergeant! You can count on me," Pilsen promised.

Cassidy's face softened as he looked toward his charge from the door. "I know bubba, I know I can."

Then the door closed and he was gone.

In that silence, Joseph Pilsen felt himself standing that much taller.

As he stepped around the table to grab his notebook, he saw Chef's clean handwriting on the torn-out page.

300 mils milk

½ can sweetened condensed milk
Half stick butter
Pinch of white sugar
2 splashes of rum.
Combine milks, butter, and sugar in large pot. Whip together until smooth, over low heat. When all sugar dissolved, stir in rum. Drizzle over single pan. Increase proportion accordingly.

He had signed it with a smiley face sticking its tongue out at the reader.

It's like peeling layers off an onion, Pilsen told himself as he went to a back corner of the well-built mess building and began moving everything out of the way. His last still, full of spiced rum, should be doing nicely despite the awful Helmand weather.

"Corporal Jimenez, have you noticed anything out of the ordinary?" Cassidy asked as he walked into the Ops Bunker.

"Out of the ordinary? Like what?"

"I think we had a Menehune or two stow away in our gear when we left island."

"You do?"

"Aye. I think we should be on the watch for them."

"Did you say Menehune?" Nealen demanded loudly.

"Aye, Staff Sergeant!"

"Well hell, so long as they brought spam musubi, I won't mind that one bit."

"Spam musubi?" Lieutenant Balcombe said slowly from her desk.

"Yes, ma'am."

"What is that?"

"Think sushi, made with fried Spam then lightly glazed with good teriyaki sauce. It's a very Hawaiian sort of food," Nealen explained.

"Uh huh. Don't tell me you actually eat that," Balcombe demanded.

"Why wouldn't we? It's delicious!" Jimenez replied. "We throw those in our dump pouches before we go out to do field problems for the day.

"But it's Spam!"

"Ma'am you come from a nation where beef is often boiled without spices, taste, or good sense, and broilers are the mainstay," Hondo retorted.

Jimenez wrinkled his nose at the suggestion.

"Boiled beef?"

"Yeah," Cassidy said. "Not my favorite thing to eat when I lived there."

"The spirits of my ancestors would beat me if I did that," the stocky Latino declared. "Rise up and beat my ass like they did the Aztecs."

"You'd deserve it," Nealen agreed.

Cassidy looked down at his watch. "Look at the time, crap! I need to go check dinner right now!"

He left for the door at not-quite-a-run, leaving Nealen to stroke his chin.

What is my Sergeant up to now? Hmmmm... bet it has something to do with dinner.

\#

"Private Pilsen, did you make dinner?" Natasha asked after she put her spoon down.

"Yes ma'am. Chef reviewed the menu and I made it under his supervision."

"I don't recall seeing dessert on the menu."

"It was a last-minute addition," Pilsen confessed.

"What do you think of it, Sarn't Major?" Fitzsimmons asked.

"Just about to dig in, ma'am."

Pilsen waited, watched as Mayne's face seemed to move from its usual calm to a strangely quizzical look, only for whatever question he might've had on his lips to die unspoken, replaced by a serene smile.

"Private, this is fantastic. In fact this whole meal is excellent. Well done."

"Thank you, Sarn't Major," Pilsen replied, shocked to hear the praise coming from him.

"You're welcome lad. Go ahead and carry on with what you need to do."

"Aye, Sarn't Major."

"That was nice of you," Morgana said quietly.

"When I was a boy, we lived in Rhodesia and Mother made a bread pudding just like this. I loved coming home from school to find a tray worth cooling on the windowsill." He closed his eyes and exhaled slowly. "Happy memories."

There's rum in this, absolutely no doubt about it. I can taste every single bit of it in the sauce. Cassidy runs a tight ship, which means he knows this is in here, in violation of all the regulations. I really ought to ask Pilsen where he found spiced rum in Afghanistan, but after Cassidy came through the command post earlier, I know exactly what response I'm going to get.

As if it weren't already clear to him.

Wee folk. When in doubt, the wee folk did it.

Mayne waited until there were only a few people left in the mess to corner Cassidy and Pistol.

"Gentlemen," he said calmly.

"Sarn't Major, how can we help you?" Cassidy asked as the older man approached.

"I need a moment of your time. Both of you"

"For you, Sarn't Major, we always have time," Pistol promised.

"Oh good." Stepping into the corner, Stirling inclined his head toward the younger men.

"Sergeant Cassidy, don't you think it's about time Private Pilsen received his first chevron?"

"Yes, yes I do, Sarn't Major. He's shown positive attitude, outstanding work ethic, and solid turn around in discipline."

"He's PTing twice a day, and I expect he'll do very well in the Army boxing tryouts," Pistol added.

"Excellent. I assume then, seeing as he was entirely lacking in ambition or drive before he came here, that the private has none of the necessary rank insignia."

"Likely Sarn't Major," Pistol rubbed his chin.

"Would you two have any problem picking up the cost of some rank insignia for him?"

"Not at all. How many do you think we should order?"

"I was thinking four." The Sarn't Major paused. "Nah. Better add a fifth."

"A fifth?" Cassidy stated slowly.

"Yes, Sergeant. A fifth. Just for … Good measure," Mayne spoke carefully, annunciating his words in a precise manner.

"Sounds wise, Sarn't Major," Pistol agreed.

"I'd like to think that fifth will be kept in reserve and used sparingly."

"Absolutely," Cassidy agreed. "Wouldn't want to ruin a good thing."

"Right you are lads." Stirling clapped a hand on their shoulders. "I'll be off now, have a good night."

"Evening, Sarn't Major," they chorused as he left.

Pistol had the good graces to wait until the company sergeant major was fully out of the mess before he turned to Cassidy, who was casually leaning against a wall, stroking his chin.

"What did you do?" Pistol demanded.

"Me?" Hondo said innocently.

"Yes. You."

"Did you know that there are wee folk hiding around in the FOB?"

"Wee folk?" Pistol barked a laugh. "Hah. A likely story."

"Seriously, Wee Folk, because there's absolutely no other way possible for rum to have ended up in the cream sauce Pilsen made to go with dessert tonight."

"Yes, that would be quite difficult," Pistol admitted as he considered the situation.

"The good Sarn't Major was expressing to us the hope that we would not be rash when using such an ingredient in the future," Cassidy continued.

"Ah. A wise piece of council."

"Notice his deft way with words. He never asked me if we had any rum. But he suspects that I know it was used."

"Was it?"

"Indeed."

"And you know where it is?"

"Not at all."

"Who would?"

"The Wee Folk," Cassidy said as his eyes slowly glanced left toward the Private diligently sweeping the floor before he mopped it for the night."

"I see. I'll have to keep an eye out for them meself."

"You and me both. Never know what they'll do."

\#

Joseph Pilsen was promoted to Lance Corporal shortly thereafter, along with several other privates from either side. He was the only one in the formation, however, to have his rank pounded onto his chest by both an American and British Sergeant.

More than the rank, the acknowledgement he now received from his fellow soldiers made him feel he had finally turned a corner in his life.

The fifth month of the deployment had now begun for the engineers.

Chapter 18

Ain't No Cure for the Summertime Blues

"Ma'am have you checked in on the girls lately?" Mayne asked Fitzsimmons. Both were sitting in the command post, drinking water and avoiding the worst of the heat.

"I hadn't, no. Something I should be worried about?

"Probably not, though I will add that today is pugil sticks."

"What in the bloody hell is a pugil stick?"

Mayne laughed. "Ma'am, why don't you come with me?"

\#

"Come on Pilsen!"

"Take his head off!"

In and around the makeshift ring Johnson and the Marines had constructed for formal instruction, it was a madhouse. In the center, a marine and an engineer were swinging away at each other with short, blunted pole weapons as the crowd cheered them on.

"How's it going, Staff Sergeant?"

"Pretty well, ma'am! Your girls are taking to the material pretty well." Johnson was nearly shouting to be heard above the din. Tolliver, as a tabbed instructor, was refereeing the bout.

"What's next?"

"Well they've already tested out, so we'll be awarding them their belts here shortly. Had a buddy at Leatherneck print up certificates for us. Those will come out on the next supply convoy, in the mail."

The crowd roared as the Marine scored a particularly good hit and sent the scrawny cook staggering backwards.

"We live in an age of smart weapons and spy satellites. Why are we encouraging them to beat each other with sticks?" Fitzsimmons asked.

"Because computers don't shoot people in the face, ma'am, Marines do," Johnson said.

"It doesn't matter how much you blast something all to hell and gone, ma'am. If you can't put boots on it, you don't own shit," Stirling added.

"Oh. Very well." Fitzsimmons watched Pilsen, normally a passive young man, aggressively swing his pugil stick around to catch the marine in the ribs.

"Nice hit," Johnson noted.

"Just how far are you planning to go?" Fitzsimmons asked.

"Today was our first time mixing the boys and girls together. I wanted them to understand that the Gray Belt is more challenging. You can really hurt somebody doing this trash."

"Trash?"

"Yes, ma'am," Johnson assured.

"Isn't trash bad?" Fitzsimmons pressed.

"Not if it's good trash ma'am."

"Are you using it as a placeholder?"

"Yes ma'am, just like 'stuff.'"

"Sergeant Johnson, how did you lot come up with your own language? I keep hearing English spoken, but it's nothing like I was raised with."

"It's a gift ma'am." he smiled toothily. "You ain't even heard Kramer give a convoy briefing using all sixty-nine definitions of the future subjunctive tense of the verb 'to copulate.'"

"That does not sound like something the good sisters of Saint Marie would've taught." She sighed, breathed in. "Very well, this all sounds reasonable to me."

"Thank you ma'am. Oh and you might want to stick around, we're about to kick a class."

"Take your seats!" Keating ordered. The staff sergeant waited for compliance with his order before he began to speak.

"On the American side of this, they take the time to teach the history of their Marine Corps. Today though, we're teaching British Army lore. You get to learn why this FOB has its name."

"1876, South Africa is in the hands of our Empire and Frank Bourne is a twenty-three year old Colour Sergeant. Had been so for two years. He still holds the record for youngest NCO of that rank in the British Army. At the battle of Rorke's Drift he proved that he deserved to be such. He was the company Colour Sergeant when a force of approximately 4,000 Zulus charged the Rorke's drift mission, determined to kill the infantry and engineers stationed there. One-hundred sixty-five men stood their ground in that awful place. Nearly a tenth of those lads died there. All were wounded in some way. But they won."

"Eleven soldiers received the Victoria Cross in that place. Colour Bourne received the Distinguished Conduct Medal. That medal would later be replaced by the Conspicuous Gallantry Cross. Colour Bourne would go on to become a Leftenant-Colonel in the Army. Courage, lassies, knows neither gender, nor rank. Fear is inevitable. Fear happens. Courage is knowing that fear, and moving forward in spite of the damned thing. A determined stand, and a refusal to give in to fear can make an army, just as it can break the enemy."

Keating let them digest that information for a moment. Silence was good in that respect, Fitzsimmons thought as she surveyed the site.

Let them all chew on what courage means.

"Tonight, with evening chow, we'll be viewing the defense of Rorke's Drift through the movie *Zulu*. While it's a dramatic showing, I do hope you'll learn something from it."

#

The lower portion of Afghanistan is near-totally featureless, lacking much in the way of physical landmarks. Storms move rapidly across the landscape without any impediment to stall their movement. As he scanned the northern horizon, Brian Kramer felt an odd twinge.

"Hey Sergeant Cass!"

"Yo."

"What does that look like to you?"

Cass scrunched up his face, then spat out a sunflower seed as he glared at the spot Brian had indicated.

"Think we're about to have some company, hoss."

"What kind?"

"Think we're about to get rain."

"Oh good, cuz it's fricking hot out here."

When the downpour came, it was a welcome relief. Men ran about, checking on items of note as their chiefs gave orders.

"All stations, confirm your status," Nealen ordered over the radio.

"Comm is good.

"FDC is good."

"Gun Four up."

"Gun Five up."

"Gun Six, Morales is wrapping the last line right now."

"Outstanding. Tell your rock munchers if they play in the rain that's on them. Survey-Met says this storm will run till sunset. Otherwise, nothing changes."

"Solid copy on Five," Cassidy declared before dropping the phone back onto its cradle. "Now what do I do with my day?"

"Hey Sergeant, we're gonna go play in the rain for a while!" Beagle declared.

"Go play in the rain, nasties. All y'all smell awful," Hondo replied.

The Marines laughed and whooped as they spilled back out of the hooch and into driving rain, wearing only their running shoes and skivvy shorts.

"Closest they've been to a beach in months. Lord knows they need a break," Cassidy told himself with a smile. He still hadn't put his blouse back on, nor did he want to. What he'd felt so far was comforting coolness.

Hearing a whoop, he looked to see Tolliver leading a charge into the rapidly swelling puddles. Howls and laughter greeted Hondo's ears as several engineers came running to join the fun, similarly dressed in shorts and t-shirts. Crandall's much abused soccer ball returned and this time it was every man and woman for themselves as they dove into the mud and muck with glee.

"Guess this means I can add 'improved international relations with foreign allies' on my next fitness report," Cassidy jested to himself as he pulled a poncho from his rucksack and slipped it on. His stomach started to rumble. "Good thing I got dinner ready and in the oven."

He paused at the entrance to MarineLand enjoying the overhead cover as he studied the rain and the terrain. *Best way to get to chow hall and not get all muddy is —*

Something grabbed his hand, tugging at it with urgency. It was Sylvie, smiling as she looked at him, water dotting her face and sticking to her hair.

"Fancy going for a walk?" she asked.

"I could be amenable to that," Cassidy replied with a smile.

She grabbed at his hand again, slippery palm sliding down his wet fingers before the calloused pads found purchase on her slick skin.

"Follow me," she ordered.

"Where to?" he said loudly, trying to be heard above the rising noise of the storm.

"You'll see."

#

"Brother, today is a fortunate day!" Abdul al Mohammed bin Bahrawar declared as he made his way inside the house of his elder brother, Hajji ben Badr.

"Indeed, Allah smiles upon us. This will be well for our crops and herds. Please, sit."

Abdul sank onto the thick pile of rugs as one of Hajji's daughters brought in tea for both men. "I don't know how long it will last, but I am grateful for it still. My date palms were starting to look questionable."

Ben Badr stroked his beard thoughtfully. "It makes me wonder."

"Wonder what?"

"Think brother, when was the last time we had such rain?"

Abdul pondered on his brother's words. "I honestly don't know."

"I do. Five years ago, when the Americans had their base in operation, the first time. They purchased dates. And other items from us."

"So?" Abdul grunted, staring at his elder brother over his teacup.

"Before that, it was two years after I came home from Hajj. After the Americans called on us during their race to Lashkargah."

"You think —"

"I believe The Bestower is prone to whimsy. Certainly every time they have come and we displayed Pashtunwali, we have been blessed."

Abdul stroked his beard. "He is the Judge of us all. Heathen, infidel and believer alike."

"Indeed. And yet notice how these infidels honor us when they come amongst us. They bring bread, and salt. And they brought gold."

"They what?" Abdul sputtered.

"Enough gold for the entire village. More than we've seen in five generations. Tell me, when did the Taliban ever do such a thing for us?"

Abdul set his teacup down. "Brother. That is a dangerous thing to say right now."

"The blessings of The Most Generous speak loudest."

Abdul looked at the window as the rain continued to fall, a steady deluge. Outside, he could hear his children, shrieking and laughing as they played in the muddy road.

It is good to hear my sons laughing. I have missed that.

He turned back to ben Badr, and considered the mood of his brother. ben Badr had been a student at university once, before the Taliban rose to power. He had been away on Hajj then, and who knew what else, before returning to the village of their youth. With him came books, and hard lessons about farming. He kept one eye firmly centered on the traditions which bound their tribe and clan together.

But his other eye? Ha! That was tightly focused on making life better for them. Slowly, he had worked to develop their crops, their fields, and what they could produce. His time on Hajj had not been spent in simple idleness and pilgrimage. Not if Hajji ben Badr had anything to say about it. Even now, the nomads were making more stops in Dishu, and spreading word of the good quality of their wares.

All of which the Taliban threaten. They insist we grow heroin. That we send our sons to die for their cause.

Abdul looked to the window once more, spying his little boys as they scampered about.

Which of them must I send to die getting caught making roadside bombs? Which must I make wear a suicide vest and die in a most unmanlike fashion for a madman's lunacy?

He looked back, considering what manner of man spoke with him right then.

Not simply my brother, no. The elder brother who held my hand as I took my first steps. Who stood in the place of our father when the Beneficent One called him to Paradise. Who has done good for our land and our people. He upholds what we are as men. As Pashtuns. He is asking me to stand shoulder to shoulder with him.

Abdul ate and drank in quiet peace, allowing his elder brother to do the same. When both had finished their tea in the shiny new set gifted to them by the Americans, Abdul cleared his throat.

"I know not what course others may choose. My jezzail needs cleaning." He sipped more tea. "My long knife too."

"That is well. If I have one good man with me, I can stand against the world."

Hmmm. More rifles would be handy, where this matter is concerned.

"We should speak with our kinsman. Achmed bin Bashir will be of great assistance."

"Oh?"

"He acquired a knowledge of Soviet arms while you were away on Hajj. His collection is — extensive."

"Good. We shall visit him when the rain stops."

In the silence both brothers nodded in agreement, then turned to look back out the window at the falling rain.

For the ashes of our father, and the children of our sons Abdul told himself. *Such has always been the way of our people.*

#

Still holding her hand, Cassidy ran along behind Sylvie, through the deluge to a bunker he couldn't remember seeing before amongst the pile of prefabbed concrete, barriers, and timbers. The entrance yawned open as she led him inside and out of the rain.

"How'd you know about this place?" he asked, eyes blinking as they refocused, adjusting to the darkness.

"I built it with a forklift and some patience. We needed space to hold the more volatile welding supplies, I needed a place where I could be an introvert."

She flipped a switch, allowing the lights to kick on, and swirls of color filled his vision. From one end to the other, a series of tools had been laid out on a makeshift table against one wall. Material sat in various stages of completion.

"Afore you lot came along, this is how I tried to decompress when I was too awake to sleep."

"It's impressive" he admitted. "What is it?"

"It's what I did before Uni," she explained, more quietly. "Metalsmithing."

"When did you graduate?"

"Few years ago. I took a sabbatical after my boyfriend decided that whores were a good way to get what I wouldn't give him."

"His loss." Hondo's fingers traced the edge of the outline drawn in chalk on one section of concrete. "Is this so you don't lose track of your ideas?"

"It is. I like having a plan for art."

Her fingers slipped around his, holding them as he continued to examine her work.

"How will you get it home?"

"On camera."

The light sputtered, then died. Garish white light disappeared, leaving the bunker plunged into semi-darkness as rain dripped and drabbled at the edges of the open window and entrance into the bunker.

"Well that's a shame. I wasn't done looking," Hondo confessed. He shucked out of the poncho, hanging it on one shelf so it could dry off.

"You liked it?" she asked, a strange note in her voice he'd never heard before. As if she were scared.

Why? Why is she scared? He wondered.

"Yes. I'd pay for weapons decorated with these designs."

"Randall said I always had my head in the clouds about everything."

"That's his fault." Hondo stepped closer to her as he spoke. "Randall ain't here. I am."

"I know but —"

"I don't scare and I damn sure don't run."

"No, you don't," Sylvie agreed. She'd watched him too much to say otherwise.

"So let him go. Enjoy what you have right here."

"What's that?" Sylvie asked.

"Why don't you tell me?" He replied with genuine seriousness.

Slowly, she kissed him, an act which made him pause, and he looked at her with an innocence she couldn't help but wonder about.

"You're a very good boy. I like that about you," she admitted.

"You do?" Cassidy asked, stunned by the revelation.

"Yes. I want you to stay that way. Even though you-"

She bit her lip, trying to calm the butterflies roiling through her stomach at warp speed.

"You make me want to be a very bad girl."

"I'm sorry," he said quietly as he looked away from her.

"No! Don't be. "But I —"

"Stop."

A finger touched his lips. "My turn."

"Yes, ma'am."Look at me," she directed as she grabbed his chin. "Just because I feel that way doesn't mean it's bad or wrong. I'm a big girl too, remember?"

"Girl is not the word I would–"

"Hondo Darling," Sylvie interrupted.

"Yes dear?"

"Please hold me."

He opened his arms and she sat down on his lap, mindful of the thigh-holstered magazines on his left side, and the knives dangling from his belt.

"Tell me, how far have you ever gone with a woman?" Sylvie asked.

"I… uh… um… never have."

"Why do I want to believe you?" Sylvie asked, trying not to sound sarcastic or suspicious.

"Because I really never have. Only kissing. Ever."

"Wanna know a secret?"

"What's that?"

"I'm a virgin too."

"You are?"

"Did you think otherwise?"

"I wasn't sure what to think."

"Why?"

"Because the last time I loved a woman she hurt me. I don't want to hurt again."

It was an honest, earnest pain, innocent even, like a young boy in this moment.

She ran her fingers through his curly hair. "You poor, poor dear. What did she do?"

"Told me if I loved her, I would give up my Marine Corps."

"What an awful woman," Sylvie declared.

"If I had to walk away from this, I would be pathetically bored."

"Perish that thought," Sylvie teased. "Where is this ex at now?"

"New York City. Trying to become a star on Broadway. I took orders to Hawaii so I'd be far away from her."

"And look where it brought you," Sylvie chuckled softly. "Into my arms." She kissed him deeply.

"Thank you, Sylvie," he said quietly.

"I won't give myself to you. But we can share this much," Sylvie promised.

Her chest rested against his, and he very slowly drew in a breath.

"Thank you, Sylvie," he repeated.

Outside, the wind and rain drove aside all other considerations, washing away the pain of years in the process.

Chapter 19

Please Mister Postman, look and see

Breakfast the next morning was a subdued, relaxed affair. Morgana couldn't quite put her finger on it and studied the room.

What's the departure from baseline? Hmmm.

Eventually, she saw the pattern. The marines were no longer sitting in a block. They had dispersed themselves throughout the room, rather like sprinkles atop an ice cream cone.

Or they've paired off with some of my girls.

Her eyes narrowed as she did the math in her head.

They got here the beginning of September, it's now the second week of November. We haven't had anybody come up pregnant. Yet.

"Morgana, you're using that look again," Mayne said quietly as he sat down across from her.

"What look, Sarn't Major?"

"The one that says you're the opposite of chuffed and thinking about it quite a lot."

"Sarn't Major, look at the room."

Stirling scanned it, then went back to his coffee.

"Aye, what about it?"

"When have you ever seen the marines sit in anything besides a solid block?"

He scanned the room once more, counting and noting who was where.

"Hmmmm."

"You see it?"

"Aye." He applied Texas Pete hot sauce to his eggs before scooping up a large forkful with gusto.

"What do we do about it?" Gallagher demanded.

"What is 'it'?" Stirling asked innocently.

"This! You know they're screwing. Or at least started yesterday," she grumped.

"No, I don't. Nor do you," Stirling corrected.

"But —"

"We have no evidence," he interrupted.

Her jaw fell at his retort.

"Not one shred," Stirling continued. "We have ideas. We have suppositions. We can suspect our little darlings of banging harder than rabbits in heat. But evidence?" he snorted majestically. "Dear woman, we'd have more to go on if we took a shit in our hands and clapped."

Morgana mulled over the matter as she masticated a muffin.

"I hate when you're right," she finally admitted.

"At a guess, half our little fillies are sore after yesterday's activities. They'll be walking funny or trying hard to hide it. And you'll notice that the marines are positively beaming with joy today."

"They are?"

"Brighter than the Eddystone lighthouse on a moonless night."

Morgana glowered. "Of course they are." She spread jam across her toast. "It's not that I'm mad at them for being happy. But what happens if a girl gets pregnant?"

"Then we, you, me and Nealen need to have a chat with her, and if she's keeping the baby, a chat with the father."

"A chat?"

"A chat." He shoveled down another forkful. "You didn't hear this from me but Doc Gnem received a hefty package two weeks back."

"What was in it?"

"Rubbers."

"Good."

"And pre-natal vitamins."

"Why?"

"No reason for mother and baby to not be healthy."

"Fair enough." she paused. Looked at Stirling seriously. "I really hope nothing happens in the last month. We don't need the paperwork. They don't need the heartache."

"Your lips to God's ears."

"What —" she stopped. Lowered her voice. "What if it's not enough?"

"Then we'll have to solve things the old way, like good British soldiers."

\#

The rain disappeared overnight, clouds moving far beyond the horizon as easily as they had blown in. Four days after the storm, one would never have known it had come through. Just after breakfast, one of the guard posts called in a dust cloud on the horizon, and what looked like vehicles.

Soon enough, a route clearance team was winding its way into the motor pool, followed by three large up-armored semi-trucks towing forty-foot containers.

"Colonel DuBois! We weren't expecting you!" Fitzsimmons admitted, more than slightly shocked as the handsome man made his way from one of the up-armored vehicles to greet her.

"That was intentional on my part, Captain. Hard to call an inspection proper if everybody knows you're coming."

"Oh." Natasha's face fell slightly.

He leaned in closer, so only she could hear him.

"Relax, Natasha. You're doing fantastic out here."

A loud cheer from the marines interrupted them, and she saw a younger, taller man making his way toward them.

"Before I forget, may I introduce you to Mr. Harper? He's the platoon commander for the Marines."

"Lieutenant, welcome to FOB Bourne."

"Thank you, ma'am. I'm happy to be here," Harper declared.

"You are?"

"Those are my Marines, they are getting shot at, therefore I need to be with them," Harper said in a tone which brooked no argument on the matter as Natasha appraised him.

Taller than herself or DuBois, he was rapier lean, with a rolling gait one normally found on a horseman. His calm demeanor belied intelligent, thoughtful eyes and handsomely boyish features. Though Natasha did note the coarse calluses on his hands when they shook — he'd clearly spent serious time moving weights in a gym.

"Thank you Lieutenant, I'll expect to see you joining us at the officer's table during evening mess tonight."

"It'd be my pleasure. By your leave, I'll go see to my platoon."

"Of course."

He walked away purposefully, towards the raucous, hooting crowd streaming in from across the FOB toward the trucks.

"Good lad and popular with his men, though a tad… severe in how he handles certain matters," DuBois mused.

"You think he'll be a problem?"

"For you? No. The Taliban? That's another matter entirely. Would you believe he brought a sword here with him?"

"A what?"

"A sword. Apparently he gave his word to a brother officer that he'd bring it and continue his fencing practice."

Natasha pondered the matter. "If I hadn't spent the last two months dealing with his insane asylum of a platoon, I'd think you were talking stories."

Dubois gave a wry laugh. "Indeed. The lot of them are every bit what we need. And in the absence of Paras, Greenjackets, or a regular line company, they are the best we can do."

"Not that I'm not grateful, mind you sir. They're just a little odd."

"That they are. Now, while they all enjoy mail call, I'd like to walk the posts with you and hear your thoughts on how things are coming along here."

"Yes sir, right this way if you please."

#

Mail call was a happy affair, much as it had been for thousands of years in any martial formation. Letters, packages, oddly shaped bundles. It was all part of the little pleasures troops far from home enjoyed, a reminder of the normalcy which existed outside of southern Afghanistan.

"Which of you is Cassidy?" a private demanded impolitely. "Come get yer shit!"

Stomping straight at the mail clerk, Cassidy turned on his preferred snarl.

"There a problem, boy?"

"Oh… uh… uhm…" the Private stammered.

"How many chevrons you see on me?" Hondo demanded, bending over the miscreant Private to give him his full attention.

"Uhm… Three… Uhm… Sergeant."

"How is my package addressed?"

His eyes darted left, towards the container's bill of lading. "Uh… um… uh… 'Sergeant H.M. Cassidy'."

"So you knew my proper rank," Hondo accused.

Gulp. "Yes. Sergeant."

"What do you think you should do right now?"

"Push, Sergeant?"

"Move," Cassidy ordered.

The Private waited a long second, but a glare from his own Sergeant told him he would find no succor there.

"Don't look at me, Clanton. Pay the man," a sergeant named Connolly ordered.

Cassidy waited while the Private counted aloud, one of Cassidy's booted feet resting between the Private's shoulder blades as he read a letter from a high school friend. By the time he'd finished, and placed the letter back in its envelope, rivers of sweat poured across Clanton's flushed face, the private clearly not enjoying the situation in which he now found himself.

"Halt at the top, Clam Slam," Hondo said conversationally, loudly sipping water from a condensation-covered bottle.

"Aye aye, sergeant!" Clanton shouted.

"I hope you're enjoying this."

"Yes, sergeant!"

"Good. Your arms are shaking. Are you tired?"

"No — sergeant!" Clanton said through gritted teeth.

"Ya know, you look a trifle warm. Why is that?"

"Don't. Know. Sergeant!"

"Uh-huh. Kramer, toss me a bottle would you?"

"Sure thing, Sergeant!"

Taking the fresh water bottle in hand, Hondo took the cap off the neck with the draw slash from his facón.

"That Corporal knows my first name. I've spilt blood with him all over this province."

Hondo pushed Clanton's face into the dirt, then bent down low.

"He saved my life once," Hondo snarled. "He still uses my rank."

Upending the bottle, he poured it over the back of Clanton's head. A slurry formed beneath him, quickly turning to mud as the exhausted man gasped at the icy shock.

His facón returned to its sheath, Hondo smiled coldly.

"Know what you're going to do now, Clanton?"

"No, sergeant!" Clanton gasped.

"More's the pity," Hondo admitted.

"You know, he is enjoying that way too much," Stirling admitted as he smoked a cigar, fresh from its packaging.

"I dunno, Sarn't Major, he sounds awful restrained right now," Kramer declared.

"Why not Kramer?"

"He's still speaking English."

"What else would he use?"

"Brazilian Portuguese."

"Huh?"

"At that point, we all clear the blast zone," Kramer said.

"Ah."

After elucidating on Clanton's sins, and extolling at length the virtues of sound living, Hondo bade the mud-covered Private recover to the standing position.

"Now, what do you have for me?" he asked, far more conversationally, drinking water as he did so.

Turning to hide his burning, muddy face as he stood there, Clanton rapped his knuckles against a large container sitting on the LMTV's bed. "This is for you, Sergeant. We weren't sure what to make of it. We've never had a single package this big come in before."

Examining the bill of lading, Cassidy saw a familiar signature and paused.

I love you Mama Sophia, he smiled cheerfully. *In two weeks, you're getting more flowers from Mr. Reimer. As daddy said, know thy audience, and what their needs are.*

"How long to get it off-loaded?" Hondo demanded.

"Two minutes Sergeant. Show us where you want it," Clanton replied, desperately eager to please.

"Sergeant, is everything alright?" Lieutenant Balcombe asked as she approached, clearly concerned.

"Ma'am, do you remember how I asked to borrow the Iridium some weeks ago?" Hondo asked.

"Dimly, but yes."

"You wanna know why, ma'am?" he said, working hard to keep his demeanor calm.

\#

"Oh yeah!" Cassidy proclaimed ecstatically.

The container had been deposited near the chow hall but everybody had flocked towards it, curious at what had Cassidy so excited, or why he would receive such a large package. Nobody asked how he knew what the combination to the padlock was, simply that he spun the tumblers without hesitation, throwing open the doors for all to see within. He'd taken a moment then, to admire the handiwork before he began giving instructions for offloading. All Balcombe could do was stare in shock.

Within, the container was full, end to end. Barrels and boxes, each labeled according to their contents. Sugar. Flour. Salt. Different peppers. Varieties of pasta she'd never heard of. Dried produce by the barrel. Crates of kitchen tools so heavy they needed multiple men to shift them.

"What is all of this?" Balcombe demanded, slightly awestruck.

"Enough kitchen supplies to see us to the end of deployment," Cassidy replied.

A shrill shriek erupted from the back end of the container, two women stumbling out with a bulky, locked box between them. 'Brownies' the label read.

"Take it straight to the kitchen! If I don't see it when I walk in, I'll let Lyons have at you!" Cassidy bellowed.

"Yes, Sergeant! Nothing will happen to the brownies, Sergeant!"

"Is that really —" Balcombe began.

"If that's what Mama Sophia labeled it, I can guarantee that's what is in it," Hondo assured.

"Oh," Balcombe breathed. "Mama Sophia?"

"Sophia Marrick. My adopted mother."

"I can't begin to imagine the financial strain incurred by all of this," Balcombe admitted politely.

"Ma'am, her husband owns the resorts I worked at. The concern is appreciated but very unnecessary."

"Oh good. I take it that your family supports you being here."

"Yes, ma'am." He shrugged. "Leastways, Mr. Tom's daddy and granddaddy don't hold it against me any more."

"Whatever would they do that for?"

"They were Army officers."

"I see."

Hondo's thoughts drifted back to a simple red-bordered white flag which hung in the window of the Marrick Corporation's boardroom. Had hung in that window since 1918. Down the vertical centerline, gold stars and blue stars adorned its white field. Thomas Marrick had fully supported Cassidy enlisting into the service. Just as his great grandfather had sent his own sons, off to war. Service to their nation was something the Marrick family knew very well.

God bless you, Mister Marrick.

"What are you going to do with all of this?" Balcombe asked.

"Magic, ma'am. Magic."

#

Dinner that night was a splendid affair. Between the supplies from home, what DuBois had brought with him, and the local staples, Cassidy turned out enough chow for all of the soldiers, marines, and supply convoy elements to eat their fill.

"I don't know how you got all that work done when you're eating like this," DuBois admitted as he looked around the cheerful mess.

"Sergeant Cassidy is a wonder sir," Mayne declared.

"It also helps that Nealen's Marines understand the local patois sir," Fitzsimmons admitted.

"They do?" DuBois asked.

"Yes sir. 'Gun' is a universal statement. As is 'knife.'" Mayne said it cheerfully, and DuBois smiled at its simplicity.

"Indeed. Next month, assuming everything is going well, we'll run down the necessary equipment to stabilize the airstrip," he declared.

"That's wonderful news, sir," Fitzsimmons interjected.

"I'm not done, either. Sergeant Major Mayne, call the room to order," DuBois ordered.

"Aye sir. Company, atten-hut!"

DuBois waited until he was sure he had the attention of all the personnel present.

"You are here, performing your duty to our nation. You have not stepped back from that duty. Even at the cost of lives and bodies. That is a hard thing to ask of you. But you have done it, like so many generations before you."

"You are the first company in a new regiment, formed out of an attempt to utilize the best strengths of our Army's engineers. You did not know this when you left your barracks at Catterick. Just that you needed to be here. For that, I thank you. Captain Fitzsimmons, please come here."

"Sir."

The Colour Sergeant accompanying DuBois passed him an ash wood pole around which had been wrapped red and blue fabric. A quick flick of the wrist let the heavy silk flare out for all to see. Emblazoned in the center of the field stood a silver horse forcené and the Queen's Crown. The symbols were well-understood by the British soldiers, and though they did not understand all of it, the Americans held their peace for the moment.

"Until such time as we finish the formation of the regiment, its first company will be the repository of the regimental colours and honours. I pass these into your care, Captain Fitzsimmons."

"Sir."

"Do you have someone in mind for Colour Guard?" He asked as Natasha fought back hot tears of fierce pride.

"Sergeant Pistol!"

"Yes, ma'am!"

"You are hereby designated as Guard Sergeant of the Colours."

Taking the banner from DuBois, she passed it to Pistol, who reverently received them, then brought the staff up, rendering honours to Colonel DuBois. Exactly as a Sergeant ought to do.

A camera clicked away, snapping multiple frames as salutes were exchanged, and the room broke out in raucous applause. Through it all, a reporter watched and listened. That mattered when one was dealing with soldiers.

\#

Elyssa Castrum walked the length of FOB Bourne, surprised and pleased. A civilian correspondent for the BBC, she had been given a tip to go see how the current occupants at FOB Bourne were holding up.

It was rough-edged, something she expected to see after so many months covering war on the Northwest Frontier. Sandbag-covered buildings dotted the landscape like so many green and brown toadstools, full of surprises. Like those Americans.

Nobody told me that rowdy lot would be here she had fumed, annoyed at the lack of information. Then she had thought back to what the briefing officer had told her, and wondered — *what if that really was all he had known about? But why hide that an American unit was here?*

And so she had continued on her way, listening to conversations as she slipped from one building to another, using the micro-cassette recorder concealed on her belt in place of a notepad and paper. There would be time enough for those later. Now was the time for study, for observation.

Elyssa knew soldiers. She had been one before hip injuries saw her leave the Army on a medical discharge. Where simple questions couldn't pry out answers, she had Marlboros. Men desperate for a cigarette would talk.

What she had not expected was the sheer volume of cheer. The personnel she spoke to were *happy*. Even if it was one-on-one, they all had the same joyful disposition.

How? Why? To what end?

When Colonel DuBois's aide finally told her it was time to leave, she had more than enough for a story. She had material for two, possibly even three!

But where do I start? Why not the beginning? I suppose that doesn't hurt.

She remembered then, the fighting positions she had seen dug in at several locations on the FOB. The Marines had insisted on them for all personnel, she was told. They had scraped out their own positions by hand as a matter of pride, scoffing at suggestions they use excavators. Pulling out the new-fangled tablet her bosses had provided her as an alternative to larger and bulkier laptops, she began to type.

"In a hole in the ground there lived a hobbit."

Almost, she told herself with a smile. Deleting 'hobbit' she typed in 'soldier.'

That's more like it. Now let's get to work, why don't we?

#

Elsewhere, a man heard jackals howl, and shuddered. He was no fan of the wild dogs, never had been, never would be. Saeed al Musafazi much preferred cats. They at least could be counted on to clean up after themselves, and unlike dogs, felines were regal.

He was waiting for his subordinates to finish drawing up plans and what conclusions they had reached about the growing airbase near their position.

"Brigade Leader?"

"Yes?"

"We're ready if you are."

Stepping back into the well-hidden tent, Saeed was reminded of how much he truly despised American and British technology. Their satellites and drones made hiding even in the deep desert a risky proposition. In some ways, this was worse than trying to deal with Russians back in his native Chechnya.

I miss the cool mountains and the pleasant green valleys, he sighed.

Basayev heard that sigh, and could make an educated guess why he was hearing it.

I miss home too, boss. Yes, yes, I know Allah has called us here on jihad, but I really miss having cool rivers and green trees near us too. This heat sucks.

"What do you have for me?" Saeed inquired.

"We would like to continue probing their defenses. Especially near the areas where they are performing construction."

"Good. But to what end?"

"With what the emir is sending, we would like to do this —"

The conversation continued long into the night, as the men drank coffee and worked through their plans. At the end of it all, al Musafazi stood, nodding appreciatively. "All things are in His hands. May this be according to His will."

With the information provided by the believers inside the camp, we stand a chance of scoring a major coup, for ourselves and the Jihad.

"We will need the entirety of the brigade. As well as all the caches we can possibly access."

"Understood. We will make it so."

"May the Beneficent One guide your hands."

Chapter 20

Easy like Sunday Morning

Sylvie sat in her usual place at the small table in the corner of the kitchen, sipping chai tea and watching Cassidy get breakfast ready for the base. She treasured these moments. Early in the morning before everyone else was up, she would slip out of her tent and there he was, waiting just outside for her so that she didn't have to wake anyone up to go out with her. They'd go to the gym for a short workout, nothing super strenuous. Then she'd hang out with him in the kitchen until it was time for the day to start.

There was always fresh brewed coffee and tea ready by the time the soldiers and Marines got to the kitchen, which meant that he must have put it on just before meeting up with her. He would pour her a cup, and she would sit at the table in the corner. As far as she could remember, the table hadn't been there before the Americans had shown up. She wasn't even sure where it came from.

Best as she could guess, Cassidy had "acquired" it — and two chairs to go with it — once he had taken over mess duties. *I could be entirely wrong though,* she reminded herself. *Before the Americans came along I didn't have any reason to go into the kitchen.*

But now, here she sat, in the wee hours of the morning, keeping company with the hulking, angry, wonderful American. An interesting thing she had noted was that though he kept a sour demeanor most of the time, he wasn't angry around her. He would yell and bellow while chewing Pilsen or any of the others right out, but he was always kind to her. Happy, even.

Right then, he was quietly singing a tune, completely off key, but he was singing. She'd been around him enough now to pick up on some of his quirks. If he was silent he was either bone tired or brooding, 'Beware! Do not approach! Danger' flashed an invisible sign above his head.

If he was humming he was content. You could still get chewed out, but the chances were lower. If he was singing, like he was today, he was happy. On rare occasions there might even be a little hop to his step as he moved around the kitchen. That was Cassidy on cloud nine.

That meant that he had had a *very* good day and very little could spoil his mood. The chance of hearing an angry rant out of him in that mood was next to none, but the chance of hearing one of his passionate rants on obscure topics went way up. Literature and history were his favorite subjects to rant about, but he had strong opinions on a myriad number of topics and it was anyone's guess what he might choose to go off on next.

Some days she listened intently. Others, she tuned out and just stared at him, appreciating his intense gray eyes, the sharp features of his face, and his melodious baritone voice. It was interesting that his voice could be both so pleasant on the ears and not, depending on the situation.

When he sang? Oh it was terrible! The man couldn't carry a tune if his life depended on it. Kramer mentioned they had been thrown out of a karaoke bar in Japan, Kramer for drunkenness and Cassidy for ruining "Margaritaville" while stone sober.

Yet still, hearing him sing to himself while going about the kitchen calmed something deep within her and set her at peace, made her feel like she was home.

"Have you ever heard about European star forts?" Cassidy asked with his back to her.

Sylvie smiled and leaned forward in her seat. *This should be good.*

"A little, my degree centered around the Baroque period, right after it. Tell me more."

#

Morgana Gallagher was not, by nature, a morning person. Nor was she much of a camping enthusiast. The cots and sleeping bags provided by her Majesty's army left much to be desired. Especially when Morgana considered her plush, Super King-sized bed. A bed covered with satin sheets, buttressed by goose down pillows, and the devoted Spanish-Irish male that she had the joyous pleasure of calling "husband". But she was a loyal sort, and the British army had her loyalty through and through. By it she had earned her living, and secured her future. And so here she was, enduring the cots and the dirt and the early mornings, because she had a job to do, and she had people who depended on her to do her job.

One thing she could not endure, however, was a morning without tea. Not only would she not endure it, no one would be able to endure her. It was in the best interest of the FOB's occupants to make sure the woman had a cup of tea in her hand shortly after she managed to stumble out of her cot and blearily made her way to the Command post in the morning.

Morgana rubbed at her eyes, willing herself to mumble out a greeting to the Ops staff coming off night shift.

"Morning Gallagher," Mayne said brightly.

"You're awfully cheerful," she grumbled, squinting at him, "It's much too early for all that. I have had no caffeine. Need caffeine."

"Well let me be the first to say I've got a cure for what ails you."

Oh he is much too chipper for this early in the morning.

She could barely see through half-lidded eyes, but she could still smell just fine. And the scent wafting beneath her nose was heavenly.

"Is that breakfast tea?" she asked, breathing in deeply.

"With milk and sugar," Mayne confirmed, amusement twinkling in his eyes.

"God bless you, Sarn't Major."

He brings tea. We can deal with the day, she thought as she took the paper cup from him and brought it closer to her face.

"Thank Cassidy, he makes sure there's a fresh pot in the morning now. I figured I'd see you in here first and grabbed an extra cup."

"A saint among men, you are." The hot brew disappeared into her mouth as she drank greedily.

"Feeling a bit parched are we?"

"This morning in particular deserves more than just one cuppa. Please tell me there is more where that came from," she implored him.

From the moment the first drop had touched her tongue she could feel the revitalizing effects of the tea take effect.

Warm and wonderful, full of caffeine, and brewed to perfection, she thought far more happily than she had been minutes prior. *Cassidy has outdone himself.*

"Aye," he said with a slight nod and a smile, "but if you go in there for more you're likely to hear an earful from Cassidy about his latest obsession."

"Let me guess, some obscure battle that no one's interested in?"

"Lyons seemed pretty interested." Mayne said pointedly, taking a sip from his own cup.

She raised her eyebrow and placed her empty cup down on the table.

"Lyons you say?"

"Saw her in there when I went to grab tea, hanging on his every word as he ranted."

"Hm." She grabbed the cup again, intending to take another sip before remembering that it was empty. She glared at it before throwing it in the trash. "What was he ranting on about this time?"

"Renaissance engineering if ye can believe it. The lad could probably give you lectures on fortification building."

"That... actually sounds interesting." She considered this information, brain still groggy and waking up, before glaring at the empty cup in the trash can again, "I need more tea."

"Why don't we stroll over and see if he's still going strong? I only left a couple minutes ago and he had a full head of steam going."

"Sounds reasonable to me."

\#

The front door was still locked, but the back door opened easily at Mayne's sharp knock. "Morning Sarn't Major!" Cassidy didn't even blink when he saw the second visitor. "Colour Gallagher! Good morning, ma'am!"

"Sergeant, good morning. Do you have more tea on right now?" she asked politely.

"Yes Colour, care for some more?"

"I would, in fact."

As Cassidy filled her cup, Gallagher took a seat.

"So, what do you know about fortification construction?"

"Ma'am?"

"I heard you giving Lyons the lecture on star forts earlier," Mayne added. "I'd like you to give it to the Colour Sergeant."

"Oh. Very well. Let me get these trays from the oven. Then I can do that thing."

Morgana was used to hip pocket classes, both as an instructor, and being on the receiving end of them. There were many which bore no further thought once they were complete, the presenters had been that bad. Cassidy was not such a one however. He went to work with commendable efficiency, directing Lyons to grab various items as he built a diorama on the large countertop surface and pointed where necessary, referring to her when he asked questions. At length, he concluded, noting that it was almost time to begin serving breakfast.

"Well, you've certainly convinced me," she finally admitted. "Nicely done."

"Thank you, Colour."

"If you had time to prepare, could you give that as a lecture to my engineers?"

Cassidy paused, looking down at her in her seat. "Ma'am?"

"Seriously, can you do it?" Gallagher pressed.

"I could, but why the devil would they listen to me? I'm a cannon cocker! You know, pull-string, go-boom?"

"Son, you're not giving yourself credit," Stirling suggested. "You said it yourself — a man ought to know how to take down somebody he's matched against. I'm impressed you've taken it this far. We're engineers who build this stuff, we ought to know how to breach them as well."

"Like sappers?" Cassidy asked.

"Very much so. I'm rather partial to that work," Stirling admitted.

"Which is fine by me. You can have all of that filthy hullabaloo," the Colour declared firmly.

"Not a fan, Colour?" Hondo said lightly.

"I have zero interest in trying to clear mine belts or barbed wire," Morgana admitted without hesitation.

"But Bangalores are fun!" Stirling protested. "Just use the appropriate number of sapper lizards."

"Sapper lizards?" Sylvie asked, confused.

"Joys of a well-spent youth, young lady," Stirling assured her.

"To you, maybe. I prefer building things," Morgana declared. Her eyes returned to Cassidy, tapping her chin as she considered something.

"What are you thinking Gallagher?" Mayne asked.

"How long does it take you to prep dinner service?" she asked, directing her question to the American.

"I start it at noon-thirty and I'll need till about fifteen-hundred-ish."

"Plan a lesson, we'll host it in here, then have everybody walk around and look at what you've put together. Need anything for it?"

"Expo markers. I can use those to draw on the plastic tablecloths, and we have plenty more in stock for some reason," he said, voice trailing off.

"Good enough. Say tomorrow afternoon, before dinner?"

"Yes ma'am!"

"Good lad." She paused. "Lyons, while you have a reputation for being fairly well-behaved, I'll admit I still had my doubts. Thank you for proving me wrong."

"You're welcome, ma'am?" Sylvie said in confusion.

Gallagher exhaled through flared nostrils.

"Unlike *some* of your peers, you're not shagging random Americans after hours any chance you get."

She swore disgustedly under her breath, face twisted in an expression of resigned annoyance. Mayne studied her curiously.

"Oh? Were you made privy to the recent gossip?" He asked, amused at the woman's frustration.

"Oh, worse than that," she braced both hands on the table and stared off into the distance, reliving the terrible experience. "All I needed was a screwdriver. *Instead* I got Collier, answering the door, wearing a *Marine* poncho liner."

Cassidy and Lyons glanced sideways at each other. Cassidy was fighting a smile and Lyons' was unfazed.

Of course. Of course it was Sandra, Sylvie told herself. *The brazen hussy has regaled me with enough of her misadventures with the opposite sex that I can believe it.*

"Oh, so caught in the act? That's rather bold even for her. I presume the clothes she was supposed to be wearing were nowhere to be seen?" Mayne asked.

Whatever Mayne thought of the revelation he seemed unperturbed, as if he was expecting this.

"Oh they were in sight all right. Draped on boxes, on the floor, on the back of a chair. And not just her clothes mind you," She turned to glare at Cassidy, "Among the disaster were what looked to be one of your people's uniforms."

Cassidy put both of his hands up in a plea for innocence.

"Wasn't me, Colour, I swear."

"Oh I'm aware it wasn't you, Sergeant."

"I'm curious, Gallagher, what did the girl have to say for herself, being caught in such a state?" Mayne continued his casual inquiry.

"I asked her why it was her clothes seemed to be everywhere except *on* her. And all she had to say for herself was 'It's just a touch hot when I'm trying to sleep, Colour.'"

"That sounds reasonable," Mayne admitted.

"It was only eighteen-forty-two, and she was in the toolroom. I'm fairly certain that her cot is not kept in the toolroom."

At the memory of it all, Morgana pinched the bridge of her nose. She needed more tea. Cassidy bit his knuckle to try and stifle the laugh that threatened to escape him.

"Did you find out who it was she had hidden back there?" Sylvie asked, a grin on her face.

"Oh for fucks sake!" Morgana slammed her palm down on the table, "Like I want to know who she slept with?! That means paperwork! I need more paperwork like I need another dead soldier's family to write to."

"But you still know who it was," Mayne stated.

Gallagher stared at him, a certain deadness in her eyes, "I told her I was going to leave, and when I came back in fifteen minutes' time she better be dressed and whoever she had in the back better be gone."

Gallagher pitched her voice in a fairly good impression of the red headed corporal.

"Yes, Colour. Absolutely, Colour, nudity not tolerated, Colour."

Cassidy bit down harder on his lower lip and Lyons grinned widely. That was Sandra all right.

"Impertinent thing. So, who was she with?" Mayne's tone spoke disapproval, but his eyes still twinkled with amusement.

"Well I would never suggest that I hid nearby and timed them."

"No, of course not."

"And at the thirteen minute mark, there definitely was not a skinny black lad with glasses come a-whistlin his way on out. Like he was headed to the ice cream parlor."

"Skinny black lad, glasses..." Cassidy's voice trailed off. "Shockley?"

If looks could kill, Hondo Cassidy would have been rendered into a smoldering pile of ash from the glare Morgana gave   him.

"I did not hear that name, Sergeant Cassidy. And none of you know *anything* about this, am I clear?"

"Know anything about what, Colour? I know nutting. I hear nutting. I see nutting!" Cassidy asked with feigned innocence.

"Marine, why do I have the sneaking suspicion you've used that line before?" Stirling said lightly over the rim of his mug.

"I blame it on my charming personality, Sarn't Major. I am so very easily misunderstood. Care for another cuppa, Colour?"

"God, yes, please."

Mayne waited till she was most of the way finished before he spoke again.

"Gallagher, would you mind heading to the Command post and letting the Captain know chow is very nearly ready? Take a cuppa with you to her, please."

"Ya know, that sounds like a brilliant idea. Why didn't I think of it?" She nodded at Cassidy and Lyons before making her way out the door.

Mayne took a sip of his tea and waited a few seconds after the door was closed to speak up again.

"Cassidy. I look after my girls, such as they are in this ragtag outfit which has already seen the mission well and truly blown to hell. Tell me about Shockley."

"Oh you don't need to worry about Collier, sir. The girl can look after herself. Honestly, I'm a bit more worried about Shockley," Sylvie piped in.

"Be that as it may, it is still within my best interests to know more about the boy."

"Then you'd best start off changing your perspective on him, Sergeant Major. That one ain't a boy."

"Well then what is he?"

"He's the man who walked into Fallujah his first enlistment, got commended twice for bravery and shot once. He's goofy, to the point that he's almost incapable of being serious about anything."

"And they made him a Corporal?"

"Because when it comes to troop leading, he's solid. Even tempered, considerate, and he'll outwork farm boys twice his size just to prove who the big dog is."

"How is he still a Corporal?"

"Got out in 2008, knocked around for a while, decided to get back in. He's due for reenlistment about three months after we get back."

"How is he with women?"

"Doesn't have a regular girlfriend, mostly just goes to town and tries to be really charming. Which he can be. I go along as designated driver occasionally and I have no complaints about his behavior. He just never had one who'd stick around and give him a chance."

"You don't drink, Cassidy?"

"No, Sarn't Major. Not my thing."

"Why not?"

"Not my thing, and the last time I got intoxicated, I tried to burn the barracks down."

"We shall endeavor to keep you sober. Does Shockley drink?"

"He likes beer. Even if it's love-in-a-canoe beer."

"Sounds like the two of them were made for each other," Sylvie mumbled, arms crossed.

"If she doesn't mind Japanese anime and beer, she'll be fine. If she enjoys reading anime, and likes really good beer by the gallon, that is a very distinct possibility."

A grin split Hondo's face. "Which still doesn't account for what she thinks of the anaconda."

"I'm still traumatized by that," Sylvie said, "but listen, I bet you anything that's the whole reason they're involved with each other. I betcha it was Sandra who seduced him to begin with, knowing her."

Sylvie's face flushed a bright pink again as she recalled some of the more toe curling stories her best friend had regaled her with.

"I've heard some of the stories too, Lyons, and I'm inclined to agree with you," Mayne agreed. "Still. I like to make sure my people are going to come out of this without too much scarring," he took another sip of his tea.

"If you're worried that I'm going to do anything about it, don't. I noticed that she's been happier than I've seen her in a long time, and she's doing her job better too. I know when to stick my nose in things and when not to. And this is not one of those times."

A timer went off behind Cassidy and he went to attend to the business of getting breakfast out of the oven and all set up. Lyons looked at Mayne, a certain pride and gratitude welling up within her. Of all the people to work for, she was serving with some of the best. And knowing that he looked out for them, for each of them individually, put her at ease.

Mayne nodded to her and went out the back door of the kitchen, leaving her standing by the table alone with her thoughts.

#

"If there are no further questions, this concludes my period of instruction at this time." Cassidy loudly declared to the packed room. Lifting his cup up, he spat more seed hulls into it, pleased as he surveyed the room. The lecture seemed to have gone well enough, and he hadn't screwed up too badly.

"Colour, floor is yours."

"Thank you Sergeant. Listen up you lot." Gallagher ordered.

The engineers straightened up in their seats, wondering what she had planned.

"Myself, the XO, and Sarn't Major are all in agreement — our defensive setup needs work. Now that we've expanded outwards enough for the airstrip, we're going to improve our fixed defenses."

Motioning for a Private to prop up a wide plywood sheet, Gallagher directed their attention to it. "Corporal Jimenez drew up our entire perimeter in size large so that you understand how much we have to cover. Wellington, Garnet, Kitchener, Slim. Who remembers what those are?"

"Field Marshals in the Army," Pistol volunteered.

"Point to Sergeant Pistol. Kitchener to the North, Slim for South. Garnet for East. Wellington for West. Each platoon gets one wall. How you design it is entirely up to you. But whatever you design, you build and emplace. Hedgehogs, caltrops, tanglefoot, protective, tactical, and supplementary strands. Plan for two hundred to two hundred-fifty meters of depth. Staff Nealen, you're up."

"Beginning tomorrow morning, the Marines will push out a perimeter on Wellington. Advance Party rolls out before first light, clears the area on foot. No later than zero-five twenty, dozers will be following gun trucks to their assigned locations. Dozer drivers, you're making hasty fighting positions. Then you'll roll back to the job site. Weatherman says we're good for daylight until eighteen hundred. That's when we load up any unfinished work and go back inside the walls. Security platoon will follow. That's day one."

"Day one?" a voice asked from the back.

"Yep." Nealen looked through the crowd toward the speaker. "Each day, we're going to focus on a different wall. The Marines will be holding over a thousand meters of frontage on three sides for security."

Nealen's voice became harsh. "It's going to be hot, nasty work, especially if Tommy Taliban comes calling before we're finished. NCOs, do not be out there micromanaging how the boys and girls dig. Do make sure your people are staying hydrated. Cassidy will have a radio and a truck to run water out. Any questions?

"How many days are we going to be out there?"

"Four days. At a minimum."

"Minimum?"

"I will be inspecting the positions," Stirling announced. "So long as it meets standard, I won't make you redo the work."

"Gonna be a long week," a voice grumped.

"Long walk home, too," Pistol barked.

"Quite right," Mayne stepped forward. "Once all of the work is done, we're going to be taking a few days off. Light work and minimal duties. No need to kill ourselves. We've still got a couple months here till we go home in December. Anything else?" he demanded. "Going once. Going twice. Done."

Gallagher saw Cassidy throw her a high sign.

"Anything else we need to discuss can happen over dinner. Right now we're going to get moving before our chef tosses us out!"

Laughter greeted this pronouncement and bodies moved with alacrity to avoid their highly certain fate.

As Cassidy was ushering people out the doors, he heard a polite voice speak up.

"Chef, would you like me to take a look at that broken hardware, see what I can do to fix it for you?"

Cassidy turned, a smile drawn widely on his face. "Sergeant Lyons, your assistance would be much appreciated with my deep fryer."

Sandra smiled as she heard the by-play.

Those two are trying so hard to act like they're only talking business and work. As if.

"I'll head into the back and start giving it a once over," Sylvie declared.

"Thank you so much for your assistance Sergeant Lyons," Cassidy replied.

I wouldn't say nobody is fooled by you two, because I'm not gonna go around asking, but it's plain to see — you two are entirely smitten with each other. And I like it.

Slinging her rifle, Sandra made her way out of the mess and into the afternoon sunlight, humming as she did so. Had she paid any mind to it, the busty redhead would've realized she was humming "The Bride's March" as she walked.

Within, Cassidy finished locking the doors and double-checking them. He hated people walking into his domain while he was performing the preparations for a meal. Finally, assured that all was secure, he made his way into the kitchen.

"Hello, loverboy," a husky voice softly proclaimed as he stepped across the threshold, arms wrapping around him from behind as a lithe form melted into his. "Looking for me?"

"If you're the handywoman, yes."

"Oh, I can be very handy. Hands-on work is a specialty of mine." Teeth nipped at his earlobe and he shivered as the shocking sensation coursed through his body.

"A specialty, eh? Does it cost extra?" He asked.

"It does," she assured.

"How much does it cost?"

"More than you could possibly pay," she promised.

"That's a very hefty fee."

"Is it now?"

"Do you take alternative payments?" He asked.

"Like?"

"Nutella croissants."

"Oooo, that sounds intriguing."

"Could possibly throw in a foot massage or two."

"What if I told you I could use one of those right now?"

"I would be pleased to oblige you, dear lady."

Without waiting for further instruction, his hands wrapped around her waist as he lifted and turned, placing her on the brushed steel counter nearest them. Sure fingers quickly worked to undo the laces of her boots, sliding off one then another. The socks came next and with these he was slower, letting his fingers move up to mid-calf before slowly rolling the fabric down.

"I warn you, I —"

Her words disappeared as his thumbs identified a tight knot in her calf muscle and dug deeply into the tissue.

"Owowowow!" Sylvie yelped.

"Why Sergeant Lyons, one would think it's been a minute since you've had that attended to."

"Yes." she stated through gritted teeth. "Oh, that feels better."

"Indeed?"

"Yea, verily."

His fingers moved to the other calf and she leaned back, savoring the feeling.

"Randy hated the idea of touching feet. If my feet hurt after a night of standing around at boring dinner parties in stilettos looking fabulous for him, 'tough luck and keep a stiff upper lip, luv.'"

"Silly wanker. Even I know better than that," Cassidy spoke amicably as he continued working.

A particularly tough knot in the arch of her foot finally broke under his ministrations and she smiled at the sense of relief.

"Yes. Yes you do." Nice as it was, Sylvie still felt suspicious. "Tell me, where does a single man learn to do such excellent massages?"

"The massage therapists at our spa were willing to trade time in their chairs."

"For what?" Sylvie asked.

"I had free run of the kitchens before I became an official employee. So long as I stayed out of the way, nobody questioned a very hungry boy making meals of prodigious size. Even if those meals involved a couple dozen chocolate-filled patisserie."

"Ah. What a sensible notion, asking a teenaged boy what he's up to."

"Yeah, I suppose so. Just wish some folks wasn't so apt to be stupid when I'm around."

"Such as?"

Hondo fell silent.

"Hondo. You have the distressing habit of speaking countrified whenever things start getting rather, shall we say, rowdy."

"Well there was Chance's bachelor party. I don't know if Mrs. Llewellyn is still mad about us missing the rehearsal dinner."

"A stag party which got out of hand, color me surprised."

"If'n them Cunningham's ain't wanted any trouble, they shouldn't have gone rustling cattle!" Hondo exclaimed.

"Normally, young men go to clubs for a stag party."

"Ayup."

"Strippers, liquor, and an unholy performance of the most licentious behavior."

"Ayup."

"Instead, you went hunting cattle rustlers. What happened next, a shootout at the OK Corral?"

"No, although I did have to buy the Two Bit Saloon a new jukebox."

"Why?"

"Cuz shooting Cairo Cunningham in the face, in a room full of witnesses would've gotten me arrested. Even if he was a horse-thievin' jackass."

Sylvie gawked before her senses finally returned to her. "Do you go looking for trouble?"

"Me? No. Trouble just sorta happens."

Silence prevailed as he continued with his work, strong fingers slowly working their magic on her aching muscles.

"And there, all finished. Better?" he said.

"Yes, much."

Helping her off the counter, she regained her feet in time for him to take her into his arms, he closed his eyes and let the near-total quiet envelop them.

"Hmmm, this is nice," Sylvie murmured into his shoulder as they stood together.

"Long day?" he asked.

"Not so much that, as just having some time for the two of us."

"I can agree with that."

"You don't smell bad either."

"I'm glad to hear it. You smell better."

She looked down into his eyes. "Do I?"

"I can smell it in your hair. That citrus and jasmine shampoo you use." He breathed deeply. "Love smelling it."

She kissed him then, savoring the taste of him as their tongues darted back and forth and his hands danced across her back, searching for knots of pressure to release.

"Oooo you evil man, that feels so good."

"All for you, my dear," he cheerfully growled.

"How did you not get snatched up already by some American lass?" she asked finally. "Surely there's been somebody who caught your eye before?"

He grimaced. "That's a story all its own. Why don't we get the room prepped and I tell you?"

As they set the tables, he began to speak, in a very calm deliberate voice.

"I didn't do much courting in high school. I loved being in the kitchen with daddy, in the gym lifting, or running the skeet range on property with Mr. Leslie. He's a retired hunting guide. Girls didn't matter much to me."

"That's —"

"Weird, ya I know."

"You're not exactly a normal man."

"Never aimed to be."

"I couldn't have guessed."

"Anywho. Anastasia came along when I was twenty-two. I was at Lejeune and she lived in Charleston. Then I left for a sea deployment.

"She wasn't happy about that?"

Cassidy shook his head. "Not even slightly. My battery disembarked in Kuwait. Spent months running convoy security around Iraq. Anastasia was irate."

"What did you think?" Sylvie asked, already certain of the answer.

Cassidy snorted, then a slow smile spread across his face. "I was too happy to care. Middle of a running gunfight through Al-Anbar, I found happiness. I told her as much."

"She must've been thrilled for you."

"So thrilled she went out and married somebody else a week after I came home. Sent me a wedding announcement and everything. Included a hand-written note too."

"Oh?"

"I found better. To which I said 'big whoop.'"

The way he says that, is he trying to use bravado to cover up the pain? Or is he really over her? Sylvie wondered.

"I'm sorry."

"I'm not. Thanks to her I got really good at throwing knives."

"You used her picture, didn't you?" Sylvie asked.

"I can hit her in the ass from eleven meters away, either hand."

"The picture is still usable? For a target?"

Cassidy shrugged. "I had a hook up. They made me copies."

Oh yeah, he's moved on from her, Sylvie chuckled inwardly. *I wonder if Randall's grandmother does something similar with my picture since I dumped sweetling Randy all those years ago?*

"Evil. I like it. Any others?" Sylvie asked aloud.

"Monica. Met her after I had done a deployment with Three-Eleven, two years ago. She wanted a Marine husband." He made a face.

"I think I hear a 'but' in that statement," Sylvie said consciously.

"Monica wanted all of my time. Even if I was on duty."

"Did she think you worked banker's hours?"

"There was that. And she thought her rich parents would object to me."

"Huh?"

"She expected that her sophisticated family would not get along with a Marine enlisted man."

"So what happened?"

"I was late to a party one Saturday. She started yelling at me for it."

"You were late. So she started yelling." Sylvie made a face. "How does that make sense?"

"It was our engagement announcement party," he admitted.

"Oh. Yeah. I can see how that would be a problem."

"Me too. It wasn't like I tried to make a mess of things. First, we got a last minute request to go shoot artillery for grunts in the field that week. Still shouldn't have been a problem. Then I had to perform casualty evac on injured marines. I stumbled out of the hospital to my truck, and drove straight to meet Monica at her parent's house down in Rancho Santa Margarita."

"Hoo Lordy, you must've been a sight."

"I would've been fine even coming out of the field under normal circumstances. The hospital trip made me all kinds of late."

"You didn't think to call her?"

"Phone was dead. Took a chunk of shrapnel through the screen."

"How did you get so unlucky?"

"I don't know," he confessed. "But yeah, I walked into her parents' back yard, probably two hundred people watching me. I've still got my body armor on, blood all over me, hadn't seen a shower in a week. Or shaved in a day and a half."

"Exactly what the modern socialite loves to see at her soiree," Sylvie declared, catching a half smile from Cassidy.

"She didn't ask who's blood it was or what happened. Monica just came off a chair screaming," he continued.

Sylvie's face scrunched up as she considered the implications of such treatment. "I wouldn't be happy right then, if I was in your boots."

"I wasn't. Granted, I was late and I hadn't called. I can understand Monica being mad. But she crossed a line." He breathed in, reliving the moment. "She told me if I really loved her, I'd quit being a Marine."

"Given that you're standing here, I can guess what your answer was."

"Only partially."

"Huh?"

"I told her —" his eyes lifted upwards slightly at the memory. "That Crandall almost died in my arms while we ran him to the hospital. We ended up doing a direct transfusion from me to him so he wouldn't bleed out. And I would appreciate it if she tried greeting me with something more congenial than her present snit fit."

"What happened?"

"In the field, or with Monica?"

"Both."

"The gun suffered an in-bore explosion due to a faulty fuse. It was an ugly mess. Nobody died but it was a close-run thing."

"Ah. Still, I can't see why she wouldn't be reasonable about that."

"There was definitely a lack of reason. She grabbed a carving knife from the buffet and took a swing at me."

"Oh. Damn. Oh big damn."

"That was when her daddy decided he'd had enough. Craig is his name. Nice guy."

"While her mother and aunts hauled her off, I started to leave. Craig asked me to stay, eat, and relax."

"What?"

Cassidy shrugged. "Like I said, nice guy. We'd gotten along in the last six months, particularly because, as he explained the next morning 'you're not after my money, and you don't try to impress people with how you're about to make junior assistant partner at your daddy's firm.'"

"Ah. I know the type."

"I'm sorry," Hondo admitted.

"You seem to remember this really well," Sylvie admitted.

"It was only —" he counted the months out on his fingers. "Seventeen months ago? Yeah, seventeen."

"I hadn't realized it was that recent," Sylvie said.

"Life," he shrugged. "It happens."

"So you two talked, you and — Craig was it?"

"Yeah." Cassidy shifted a stack of plates onto the line and opened the box of plastic flatware.

"Craig didn't want us, his family and mine, to separate on bad terms. The man really cared about his self-image and doing right by others. He also felt it was high time little Miss Priss got a lesson on how to treat people. He asked me to make a trade."

"Why?"

"He owned a car dealership," Hondo said."

"He what?"

"Dealerships," Cassidy corrected. "He owns, the last time I checked, seven in LA and Orange County. Jaguar, Mini, BMW, Mercedes, Alfa Romeo. Man loves himself some foreign imports."

"Foreign cars are popular in America?"

"It's Los Angeles. Money is popular in Los Angeles. Mind you before then, I didn't know how he made his."

"How could you not?"

"Never asked."

"Why not?"

"It wasn't my business."

"What did you talk about?"

"Not much. Normally, we'd shoot pool. Sat with him on his back porch a time or two. Enjoyed the sunset."

Sylvie realized as she listened to him speak that she was sizing him up.

How would he fit in with Grandpapa and Brabham? What would he think of my family?

"Please don't tell me he gave you a car."

"Sort of. He asked me to trade in my old truck."

"Whatever for?"

"Craig had just gotten Monica a convertible as a graduation gift. Pretty little red thing. He was so ashamed of her behavior, he handed me the title and keys. Then gave Monica my busted ass truck."

Sylvie clapped a hand to her mouth. "Oh that is righteous!"

"It certainly felt so. 'Specially when he told me all I had to worry about was oil changes, and gas."

"Do you still have it?" She asked.

Hondo grinned broadly.

"Come to Hawaii. I'll take you for a drive around the island in it."

"Right. Uh huh," Sylvie said skeptically.

"What? You don't believe me?" he asked.

"Either you're the biggest story teller I know, or you miraculously stumble through trouble without dying a horrid death."

He shook his head lightly, grinning. "It's a gift. And driving in Hawaii is fun. Everybody drives slow there. I like it that way."

"What is slow?"

"Most of the island you're doing under fifty. Miles per hour that is."

"Which is how many kilometers?"

"Ummmm. Last time I checked it was right under… I wanna say eighty. Ish. I think."

"Huh. I wouldn't have guessed that."

"Most don't. That's Hawaii for you. Hell, unless I'm racing to get back to formation, I ain't real worried about getting anywhere in a hurry."

Sylvie stared at him in surprise. "Uh huh. And what are you doing while you drive?"

"Drinking something cold. Playing music. Enjoying that cool ocean breeze."

Sylvie pursed her lips. "Sure you are." she gestured around the room. "I'm trying to imagine you doing anything calmly. I can't."

"Again, come to Hawaii and you'll see it for yourself." He surveyed the room. "Tables are set, chow line is laid out, looks like we're all set for dinner. Ready to open the doors?"

"Sounds good to me."

He scooped her into his arms for a final hug. "Come around after movie time tomorrow night. I wanna show you something."

\#

At dinner that night, Cassidy had music playing through his speakers as the company ate, when he heard a debate start near the front of the room.

"And I'm telling you, there's no way in hell, I'd stay away from her!" a Marine said far louder than appropriate.

"What are you lot on about?" Pistol demanded sternly from one table over.

The rambunctious band fell silent beneath his glare.

"We... ummm... we..."

"Out with it!" Pistol barked.

"Tawny Kitaen, yes or no, Sarn't?"

Pistol's glare turned sour as he stared at them. "That's what's got your testiculars in a double half-hitch? Really?" He gestured at the wall behind them where the projector showed the woman in question busily dancing on the hood of a white Jaguar. "You have to ask?"

"There is absolutely no way on God's green earth I would keep that woman for more than a night," Corporal Ratliff declared loudly from the far end of the table, diverting attention away from the hapless privates and lances.

"Oh you wouldn't?" Keating demanded.

"No, Staff. I surely would not."

"And why is that? Taking up the cloth are ye?"

"Because if Davey fookin' Coverdale, Mr. Higher than Giraffe Pussy atop Big Ben on Cocaine, thinks yer too barmy to play with, you is fookin' Fruit Loops!" Ratliff exclaimed.

"You know, I can't find fault with that," Keating admitted.

"And if Chuck Finley couldn't deal with her while he was pumping steroids into his taint, then yeah, there's a problem," another marine added.

"Huh what?" a brit asked.

"Chuck Finley, her ex-husband after Coverdale? He was a baseball player, one of the major steroid users. Claimed she was committing domestic abuse and divorced her ass."

"Which is why the Musical Director for the Chicago White Sox played this song as Finley was warming up before a game," Hondo declared. "The musical director got fired for that little stunt."

"Okay, now that we're on the topic, can one of you please explain baseball? What is so fun about hitting a ball with a stick?" A British soldier asked.

"Hooo boy," Nealen said ruefully from his seat at the Staff and O table. "We best get moving now."

"Whatever for?" Stirling Mayne asked.

"Because, Sarn't Major, you see my boys over there?"

"I do."

"Yankees, Red Sox, Mets, Cubs, Braves, and four Chicanos from East LA who bleed Dodger freaking Blue."

Comprehension slowly dawned on the Sergeant Major's face.

"Oh. This is about to be a religious argument, isn't it?"

"Imagine the Thirty Years' War. But the pope's name is Babe Ruth."

Chapter 21

Take It On The Run Baby

"What was tonight's piece de resistance?" Sylvie asked as she walked into the mess.

Cassidy had been briskly working with a mop when she entered. He looked up brightly at her, smiling as he worked.

"The seminal classic of masterpiece theater, Coyote Ugly."

"I didn't know Marines watched chick flicks."

"We do when there's fire and beautiful women in hot leather pants involved."

"Touché."

Cassidy squeezed out the mop in its bucket, then disappeared into the back. Seconds later, he reappeared, pistol belt still around his waist.

"So, what's up?" Sylvie asked.

"Do you remember asking me how I met Monica?" Cassidy asked cautiously.

"Yes," Sylvie said carefully.

"We were at a dance."

"A dance?"

"Yeah."

"What kind of dancing?"

"Nothing that involved a pole," Cassidy promised.

"I should hope not!"

"Right then it was…" His voice trailed off as his mind drifted back across the years to a night still fresh in his memory. "…Salsa music and the guy she showed up with was tripping over his own feet."

"Oh well, we can't have that, can we?"

"She seemed to be in distress and I thought I could help."

"Of course you did. Certainly you had no ulterior motives in mind?"

"Who? Me?" Cassidy slapped a hand across his heart. "Be aggressive in demonstrating my fitness as a male to propagate my bloodline? Never."

Sylvie laughed at his temerity. "I expect to hear David Attenborough narrating that scene for the BBC."

"Allow me," Cassidy offered. "Here we have a wild hood rat. Once the hood rat reaches sexual maturity, she will begin a mating dance called 'twerking' in an effort to find a mate who will provide her with food and shelter."

Sylvie guffawed loudly, cheeks flushing with color as she laughed at his performance. "Rude creature, how dare you cast aspersions on the plight of the noble hood rat!"

"I do believe that is the first time I've heard 'noble' and 'hood rat' in the same sentence." He waggled his eyebrows at her. "Impressive."

"Smart ass. You should see some of the clubs I've been dragged through," Sylvie looked askance at him.

Cassidy shrugged. "I usually end up as designated driver. Hood rats, hoochies, and hoes from different area codes are not a surprise to me anymore."

"The man knows his Ludacris."

"I have a wide taste when it comes to music."

"Is that how you learned 'salsa' was it?"

"Kinda, yeah." He seemed bashful in the moment, demonstrating a near-childish quality she'd never seen in him before.

"What exactly did you want to show me?"

"Do you know how to two-step?"

"Two-step?"

"Try this."

Taking her hands one at a time, he placed them on his body in what seemed to be the right places, then reciprocated and began to direct her through the steps. As he did so, Sylvie noticed that his attitude and his mannerisms had changed. He became more gentle, more refined. Subtle even.

Like he thinks I'm delicate.

As they moved around the freshly swept and mopped floors, she noticed his movement becoming more graceful, instead of the usual brisk stern directness he normally displayed. He was also very quiet.

"Cat got your tongue?" she teased.

"No. I'm just feeling relaxed at this moment."

"You? Relaxed? Mr. Angry relaxes?"

He blushed again as he bit off whatever response was about to leap off his lips.

"Now that you've got the steps down, why don't we try it to music?"

"What kind of music? Sylvie asked playfully. "Raggaeton?"

"Country."

"You mean cowboy music?"

"Uh huh."

He played around with his iPod for a moment, then straightened up and took her hands as the sound of a keytar being strummed filled the empty space around them. He moved in time with the rhythm, guiding her around the floor in a fluid motion she hadn't thought him capable of.

Sylvie's mind thought back to when Grandmere had her taking ballet lessons. *'Learn to feel the music and move accordingly'* her tutor had ordered. Sylvie had felt alive in those moments, and wondered if she were one of the few who understood precisely what that meant.

Not anymore. I think Cassidy gets it, She told herself as he spun her around then dipped her, and gazed longingly into her eyes.

It was the first time Sylvie could remember seeing a man look at her that way. Not lust, either.

Love.

"We should have a staring contest," he murmured.

"Why?"

"So I can spend an afternoon looking into your eyes."

She blushed. "They're mismatched. The doctors call it heterochromia."

"Don't care what they call it," he replied. "Want to see more of them."

He kissed her eyelids then, in between one step and then the next.

Oh, you sly devil, you. I like that in a man.

It was then that Sylvie had another realization.

We're close enough for my field belt to rub up against the buckle of his rigger belt. Normally, I don't let men get this close, but I like him right there.

A warm heat started, low in her belly, and Sylvie bit down on her lower lip, trying to hide the shock.

What is he doing to me? How?

After two more songs, they found seats at a table, sitting across from each other on a bench, knees touching as they drank cold bottles of water covered in condensation.

"You're just full of surprises tonight, Cassidy," Sylvie admitted.

"I try," he shrugged.

Sylvie wondered then, if this was Cassidy being vulnerable with her. *He's certainly acting like it. Nothing gruff or crazy, just him. Maybe I should see how far inside he'll let me get.*

"What's your first name?" She asked, genuinely curious.

"Hondo."

"Hondo Cassidy. Sounds like a gunslinger from a cowboy movie."

"Aye it does, doesn't it?" He said. "I love the way your name rolls off my lips."

Sylvie stared back at him, curious.

"Sylvie." He said it slowly, cocked his head to one side as he studied her, a look she'd seen several times on her grandfather's hounds. "Sylvie."

Taking her left hand in his, he continued murmuring her name as he gently kissed her fingers, letting his lips dance along the palm of her hand to where the cuff of her uniform sleeves ended, just below the wrist. The heat in her belly intensified.

"So that I know, what's your middle name?" He asked finally.

"May," she stammered, trying to keep her heart from leaping out of her chest the way it was beating.

"As in 'Sylvie May I kiss your hand?'" he teased.

He didn't wait for her response to begin gently stroking her right hand the same way he had her left.

"First foot massages. Now this? One would think you enjoy touching me, Hondo." she gently chided.

"Oh I do," he promised. Placing a kiss on her forehead as he leaned forward, he smiled. "Another round of dancing milady Sylvie??

This time she didn't wait to get close, her arms encircling his waist as he stepped in. If it fazed him, he didn't let it show, gliding into the first steps as a new song began on his phone. Sylvie rested her head on his shoulder for a moment, before she felt the warm heat and her own thoughts starting to run wild.

Kiss his neck. See what happens. Maybe nibble on him a little. He might like that too!

She did so, letting her teeth softly nip his earlobe and felt, rather than heard, a groan start within his chest. Then he began doing similar things to her, with that same feather-light touch he'd used on her fingers. The contact sizzled, electric shocks running rampant across her skin as he did so. His hands got tangled in her bun, pulling it loose to cascade down across her back, a long brown waterfall across his fingers as they played with the strands. One of his hands, she wasn't quite sure which, teased her scalp as he began to kiss her cheeks, her face, her lips.

Oh God, she thought hungrily, *bring those right back here.*

In the quiet solitude of the dark desert, two very lonely people found more parts of their souls coming alive, becoming whole, as loneliness gave way to a joy neither of them had ever before experienced.

"Tell me," she asked at length when they had found their seats again. "Was Monica ever this good?"

"Truthfully?" Cassidy hesitated. "She was more graceful on her feet, but less confident." He looked down. "I blame the present lack of grace on the boots."

"What about the confidence?"

"Monica didn't know what she was about. You know. What she was made of."

Sylvie stared at him, puzzled.

"Remember the time you showed me spark testing in your shop when you were repairing my weight bar? How you knew what the metal was because you could prove what was in it?"

"Uh-huh."

"She'd never had that. Nothing like what we've been through."

"Sounds like she was super brittle and just needed a proper whack to fall apart."

"I know I'm a lot to deal with." Hondo shrugged. "The women in my life either love me or hate me. Ain't any middle ground"

"Well bloody good on her part. Look what she gave me!"

Cassidy smiled. "I am not complaining." His voice dropped. "Especially because you are that much better a kisser than her."

"Really —"

Her words choked off as Cassidy's mouth smothered hers. Hands scrambled, grabbing and stroking as he pulled her onto his lap, before they both broke for air.

"And why would I want Monica when I can have a Lioness?" He asked.

"And what would that make you? A very brave Devil Dog?"

"Woof woof, milady," Cassidy barked.

She pinched him as his hands began to play with her hair once more. "Cheeky bugger."

"It's a gift," he said, voice muffled as it was by her hair. And then he was silent.

"You alright?"

"You smell amazing. I love the feel of you. I love how you're all hard and harsh for everybody else. Then you come in here and melt into my arms." he sighed, still speaking in that slightly awestruck voice. "I could hold you for hours like this if you let me."

"Maybe I will," she said.

Another, smaller part of her spoke up then — *We go home in December, back to Chard Barracks and him to his island. This is just a summer fling and it's almost over already. What will you do then?*

Sylvie banished the thoughts in an instant. *I'll take what I can get and damn the heartache later.*

Outside a lone jackal howled into the night and the stars rose higher in the Helmand night sky.

Chapter 22

Where Is Your Boy Tonight?

"Sergeant, um, we have um, two o' yer blokes out here with a question."

Pilsen stood in the doorway as Cassidy looked over his inventory sheets. *It is not quite 0800. Somebody has already got a case of the ass. Meanwhile, I still don't know what I want for dinner. Originally, it was going to be lasagna. But that just doesn't sound good right now.*

He looked up from his brainstorming at the younger enlisted man.

"What did they want?"

"Something about ummm… tea, I think." Pilsen said mildly.

Cassidy pursed his lips. "I'll come see what they want in a minute," he announced loudly for the benefit of the marines waiting. His voice dropped. "In the meantime, that was three ums. Gimme thirty."

"Aye aye, Sergeant."

By the time Hondo passed from the kitchen into the mess, Pilsen had made it to his seventh four-count push-up, counting aloud so the sergeant could hear him pay what he owed. Two Marines, fresh off guard post to guess by their dusty attire and the lines of sweat on their uniforms, stood next to the tea service, staring at it.

"What's up guys?" Hondo asked.

"Sergeant," the first Marine drawled as he turned about. It was Shiver, a bespectacled and cheerful marine from southern Alabama. "Is there any chance we got some sweet tea hidin' aroun heaah?"

"Damn son, did nobody ever teach you how to pronounce yer 'rrrs'?" the second marine, John Scarbro demanded in the North Texas twang so many of the battery were accustomed to hearing.

"I cuhn say mah 'rrrs' just fine when I say 'Roll Tide'. Which is what we dun did last month. In y'all folks's house," Shiver countered.

The byplay was too much for Cassidy and he barked a laugh at the exchange while Shiver grinned impishly.

"I walked into that one," Scarbro admitted bashfully.

"Yeah you did," Cassidy agreed. "Now, if you're looking for southern style sweet iced tea, we might have the fixings for it. Shiver, how do you normally make yours?"

"Make the water nice and hot, add tea bags then let it boil for a minute. While it's still boiling, I stir in mah sugar."

"Uh huh. How much sugar you use?"

"Two cups o' cane sugar per gallon pitcher."

"You measure your sugar?" Scarbro asked.

"I don't wants it too sweet."

"And how much sugar do you use, Scarbro?"

"I kinda eyeball it."

Cassidy cocked an eyebrow. "I'm impressed people in Alabama who aren't tourists know how to count." He sighed. "Lemme see what I can find." His glance darted back to the lance corporal who held position in the front leaning rest. "Pilsen, recover and go find out how much sugar we have in stock."

"Aye aye, Sergeant!"

As he scrambled out of sight, Scarbro watched him leave, impressed. "You and Sergeant Pistol are really putting him through the wringer."

"We're trying to make a man outta him."

"Good luck," Shiver said.

"We'll succeed, if we don't kill him first."

"I found two cases of sacks like this one, Sergeant!" Pilsen announced as he walked back in, hoisting a familiar pink and white paper sack with blue lettering.

"Hmmmmm… Pilsen, hand me that," Cassidy ordered.

Hefting the sugar in one hand, he considered the implications of his actions.

Math. Almost Weaponized Math he told himself. *And the Brits'll think I've lost my damn mind.* Chuckle. *If they haven't already.*

Producing a grease pencil, he began talking aloud as he worked through the math, drawing a crowd of people to listen as he did so.

By the time he'd finished, the British soldiers in the room were staring at him in fascination. Cooper had a look of horror on her face.

"You're not going to add all of that to good tea, are you?" Cooper asked.

Cassidy smiled as he hefted the sugar in one hand, then set it on the table.

"Yes, I am, Cooper."

"Why?"

"Because I can. And then we're making ice to go with it."

"You're all fecking mental," the soldier declared.

"Shut up and watch how this works."

Looking back down at his handiwork, he felt satisfied with what he had put together.

"I like this very much. You three, go to the kitchen, drop your gear. We've work to do," he ordered the Marines and Pilsen.

"Aye aye Sergeant."

Grabbing up the plastic tablecloth, Cassidy followed his charges into the kitchen, securing the door behind them as he continued to give orders.

"I want all of the raw chicken out of the reefer right now. It's frozen so rinse it with cool water then leave it thawing on the countertop. Fetch eggs and flour. Then get the jugs of oil and set them beside the deep fryer. Shiver, Scarbro, wash your hands, then bring me the coffee urn, two drink cambros, and one of the tall pots.

"What're we making Sergeant?"

"Southern style dinner. Fried chicken, mashed potatoes with gravy, sweet iced tea and Pilsen, do you know how to make pasties?"

Pilsen stood up straightly, chest puffing out. "I damn well ought to, I'm from the home of 'em!"

"You're from Cornwall?" Cassidy said surprised at the sudden response.

"Fishing town called Newquay just outside of Cornwall, Sergeant."

"And you can make 'em proper?"

"I can."

"Scale the recipe enough we can make three per person. Hand sized."

"What'll we do for filling?"

"We've all those apples that need to be eaten. I'll take care of that. Cinnamon and spice and everything nice, that'll make the ladies happy."

"Oi, I expect it will, Sergeant," Pilsen said cheerfully.

Speaking of which, I need to tell Nealen whom I've borrowed for the next couple hours. And make sure their chiefs know they ain't gaffing off.

\#

"Has anybody seen Chef?" Sylvie asked as she strode into the mess.

Silence met her and she wondered why for a moment.

"He's in the kitchen, been there since just after breakfast," somebody said finally.

"Huh."

Wham Thump

"What was that?"

None of us know. We figure he's torturing Pilsen some more."

Wham Thump

"Oh come on, like he would do that?" Sylvie protested.

"He's an absolute shit to his own kind. Doesn't bear thinking what he'd do to one of us."

Sylvie sighed at the lunacy of the suggestion and grabbed an American MRE. *Chili mac, oh lovely.*

Looking around, she saw none of the usual hot sauce bottles available to diners in the mess.

Damn, we must be out. I'll have to go see if he has any in the back.

Sylvie could hear loud music playing. Not rock music, this was more twangy, but it was definitely that awful wailing country sound Cassidy enjoyed. Pushing against the doors, Sylvie found them locked. She hammered on the door, twice, but nothing happened.

That asshole. He's been avoiding me all day, locks me out, and there's no damn hot sauce. Fuck. This.

Tossing the unopened MRE back into the box, Sylvia stomped back out the door of the chow hall.

#

"Love, why are you on edge?" Sandra asked, pulling Sylvie's attention away from the length of pipe she'd been working on.

"What makes you say that?"

"You're being bitchy. And not in the cute way," Sandra informed her.

"I what?" Sylvie said, setting her safety glasses down on the worktable.

"You're snapping at everybody who comes into range, and you've been grinding the same pipe with a dull cutting wheel for a quarter-hour now."

"Nothing is wrong!" Sylvie snapped as she turned off the angle grinder, heaving it across the work bench.

"Yes, love. Of course." Sandra hopped onto the work bench. "You're tense."

"You think?"

"I think what you need is some time with your man," Sandra suggested slyly.

"My what?" Sylvie demurred.

"C'mon, don't play with me Sylv. I know you've been seeing someone. You're up early every morning, you're getting work done even faster than before. And when you're not in here, you're nowhere to be found."

"Ever think maybe I was in my workshop?"

"Out in the overflow stacks? I looked."

"Maybe I was sleeping," Sylvie suggested.

"You snore too loud for that."

"I do not!" Sylvie replied.

"Think we should ask him?"

"I have not taken him to bed!" Sylvie protested.

"Gotcha," Sandra said with a smile and Sylvie blushed hard.

"You — you —"

"So where have you taken him?" Sandra said idly.

"Nowhere, you fancifully minded trollop!"

"Trollop is it? Tsk. You really are on edge, love. You don't break out the five-pound words unless you're proper pissed. Tell me, has he been avoiding you today?"

"Yes," Sylvie snarled.

"Take twenty and go settle those frazzled nerves." Sandra looked at the worn pipe. "Otherwise, I don't think we have enough metal. Or grinder wheels, for whatever ails you."

"Fine, I'll go," Sylvie grumped.

"Not like that," Sandra grimaced, placing a hand on her friend's wrist.

"Like what?"

"Like you don't care about how you look."

"But I don't!" Sylvie protested.

"Not right now you don't. First off, redo that nasty bun."

"Okay fine."

Sandra rooted around in her pockets while Sylvie went through the steps of redoing her thick brunette hair, the length of which came down past her belt buckle.

"Good. Now while you do that, I'm gonna try a hit of this," Sandra said.

"Hit of what?" Sylvie asked.

The mascara which appeared was not expected, nor the eye liner pencil.

"I don't want to look tarted up!" Sylvie protested.

Sandra grabbed her by the jaw, applying the mascara to her lashes with care, following them up with eye liner.

"There's a difference between looking like an East End whore on holiday and looking like you're serious about a man," Sandra explained. "Hold this."

Sylvie took the mascara, eyes widening as a lipstick tube appeared. "How on earth do you —"

"Appearances, old girl. Must keep them up."

"Very well. What else?"

"Try smiling for a change," Sandra instructed.

"Smile?"

"You have a lovely one. Should put it to use."

"You really think so?"

"I'll bet he delights in every smile you send his way."

"Okay, fine," Sylvie surrendered.

"No mirror in here, otherwise you'd be able to see. This look suits you much better."

"What do I look like?"

"Fantastic. Gonna tell me his name?"

"Not yet."

"You will soon enough. Now, go knock 'im dead."

#

Slipping around to the back door of the chow hall, Sylvie tried the knob how Kramer had shown her. It turned easily and she opened the door to let herself in.

Pilsen, whom she spied first, stood near one wall pushing potatoes through an industrial-sized cutting machine. Fat chunks of potato fell into a bucket. At a counter, two marines were dipping chicken into flour and egg yolks, then laying them on trays.

"What are you lot doing?" she demanded.

"Making dinner, Sergeant," Scarbro declared.

"Where's Chef?"

"In the reefer."

"Good. Wash your hands. Take twenty. In fact," she checked her watch. "It's twelve-oh-seven. Be back at twelve forty-five to finish what you were assigned."

"Yes, ma'am," all three chorused as they scurried through the open door.

"Pilsen," Sylvie said.

"Yes, sergeant?"

"Lock the door behind you."

"Yes, sergeant."

\#

Outside in the sunlight, all three junior enlisted lit up cigarettes.

"I hope she chews him out right proper," Pilsen said. "He's an asshole."

"Believe me. We know," Shiver assured.

"Most of the time we think he just hates everybody." Scarbro drew on the cigarette. "Except Kramer."

"Well they's boys so no surprise they get along." Shiver said. "Oh and Ryan. Him and Ryan get along way too well."

"Ryan is a scary dude," Scarbro admitted.

"He's the big one ain't he?" Pilsen asked.

"Uh huh. But it ain't the fact that he's big that's scary."

"What is it then?" Pilsen pressed.

"He's not right in the head."

"None of you are! You're all fecking mental. Every day. It's like living in a house where every room is wired with explosives."

"Yeah. We kinda are."

"But we ain't boring."

"Okay I'll give you that one."

Pilsen looked at the butt of his now finished cigarette. "I should really stop these. I think they're going to kill me."

"Dude, we are in a desert full of people who want us dead. The camel spiders would like to kill us too."

"I'm more worried about the camel spiders," Shiver admitted.

"Me too," Scarbro declared. "Let's go get some lunch. Come on, Pilsen. You can sit with us."

"Thanks."

He gave a last look towards the rear door of the kitchen, wondering how badly Sergeant Lyons was laying into Sergeant Cassidy right then, before dutifully stripping his cigarette

"Did you see ol' girl when she stormed in?" Shiver said cheerfully as he and Scarbro slowed their walk to a crawling pace.

"You mean that lava red lipstick and the makeup?"

"Brother, that wasn't no makeup. That was warpaint. She gonna hurt somebody."

Both men looked toward the rear door thoughtfully as their new friend joined them.

\#

"Two hundred forty in the last two hours, should be able to get the rest finished well before…"

Hondo's voice trailed off as he walked into the kitchen. *I'm missing something. Somebody. Three somebodies.*

"Where the hell did they go?" he asked the empty room.

"I sent them to get lunch." Sylvie stalked toward him, furious in her countenance.

"Um. Hi," Hondo stuttered.

"Why have you been avoiding me?" Sylvie snarled.

"Huh?"

She was wearing lipstick. The kind he'd daydreamed about seeing her wear. The fact that her face was wreathed with fury didn't detract from the overall image.

She looks gorgeous when she's mad. Today is a good day to die.

"Well?" Sylvie demanded.

"I was busy."

"Too busy to say hi?"

"Ummmm —"

She pushed him into a chair. "Too busy to tell me what you were up to?"

"Not... necessarily."

And her eyelashes look very nice right now. Like I need to lay kisses on her eyes and tell her she's beautiful.

"Then what was it?" Sylvie demanded.

"I forgot."

"You forgot? About me?"

"I got kinda busy making dinner."

"What about dinner was so important?"

"Apple pasties."

"Pasties? You forgot me for pasties?"

"We're making nearly seven-hundred of them!" he protested.

Sylvie shook her head in frustration, loudly sighing.

"Hondo Cassidy, you don't know much about women, do you?"

"I stick to guns and knives for a reason," he admitted.

"Women need to hear certain things," Sylvie cautioned.

"Like what?"

"We need to be reassured that you love us. And miss us. And care about us."

"How do we do that?"

"Well you can start by saying that you missed me. And care about me."

Cassidy drew in a breath.

"Sylvie, I missed you this morning."

"Only this morning?"

"Hard to miss you when you're sitting on my lap," he said sincerely.

"I'll give you that one."

He started to lean into her and she held up a finger. "Ah ah."

"Sylvie, I care about you," Hondo admitted.

"How much?"

"A lot."

"Enough to forget a bunch of damn pasties?" She snarled.

"Yes."

She leaned in to him, lips brushing his cheek gently.

"Show me how much you missed me," she commanded.

He kissed her this time and she melted into him. When they both paused to catch their breath, she let her lips wander along the edge of his ear.

"Was that so hard?" Sylvie asked.

"It's not what I'm used to," he confessed.

"I couldn't tell."

"I think I need more practice," Hondo admitted.

"I agree. Oh, I should probably tell you."

"Tell me what?"

"You're my hostage."

"I'm what?"

"I'm not leaving. Until all this lipstick is gone."

"As you wish!"

For a long time there was only the sound of two people losing themselves in each other.

#

"You think they're finished yelling yet?" Shiver asked.

"I'm not going in there," Scarbro declared.

"Pilsen, go open the door," Shiver ordered.

"Why me?" Pilsen demanded.

"Because you're the junior lance. And we're senior to you," Scarbro chided.

"Fine."

Before he could lay a hand on the door, it swung open, nearly catching him in the face and knocking him backwards into the dirt.

Lyons stepped out, straightening her uniform and adjusting her headgear just so. There was a wisp of a smile on her face as she blinked and looked around the space.

"What are you doing in the dirt, Pilsen?"

"Waiting to get back in the kitchen ma'am."

"Fair enough." Her head jerked towards the door. "Git."

"Yes ma'am."

He scrambled through the door and she glanced over at the two marines who casually returned her gaze.

"I owe you money?" she demanded.

"No, ma'am," they replied.

"Then get where you need to be!" she barked.

"Yes, ma'am."

Both marines hustled through the door, closing it behind them.

Sylvie waited for it to click shut.

Men. Why must they be so difficult?

Her smile grew wider as she ran a finger along her lips.

Whatever else his faults, he does know how to kiss. And do it well. I am definitely going to have to do that again sometime. It's nice to be wanted.

She stepped off, not noticing that for all the scowl she strived to maintain, there was a certain bounce to her walk.

Within the kitchen, all three men went back to their stations, working as if they'd never left. Cassidy stood over the deep fryer station, patiently filling it with oil as they went about their tasks.

"Everything alright Sergeant?" Shiver asked.

"Yeah." He emptied the first jug, tossed it at the trash can, then lifted the second up.

"Miss Lyons just needed to discuss the menu with me."

Shiver shot Scarbro a glance but the lanky Texan said nothing as he worked.

Empty jug in hand, Cassidy made his way across the kitchen, a slightly bewildered expression on his face.

That was when Shiver saw it. There, on his neck, just above the collar of the green skivvy shirt: bright red lipstick.

Sergeant, you gonna make me a rich man, the Alabaman thought cheerfully as he went about his task.

#

That evening, there was much joy to be had in the mess. The Marines were grateful to see comfort food, and that it had been properly done. To their surprise, the brits dove into the food as well, though there were many questions regarding the wisdom (or lack thereof) of consuming iced and heavily sweetened tea.

"Meal like this reminds me of having lunch at my girlfriend's parents' house afore I left home," a marine named Sweetwood admitted.

"Where you from, Sweetwood?"

"Nocona, Missouri. Little not much of nothing town. Mostly farms."

"Ya know, that's what I can't figure out," Paternostro declared from an adjacent table.

"Whatcha mean, Patty?" Sweetwood said

"All of us in Jersey can take a girl across the river to New York City or run down to Atlantic City and the casinos."

"Can go to the beach on Coney," Parente added helpfully.

"Hell yeah! That too," Paternostro continued. "We got plenty of nice restaurants to eat at. Can catch a show on Broadway. What do farmers do for fun in the middle of nowhere? Go fishing?"

"Yeah? And? What's wrong with fishin'?" Scarbro asked. "We uns took a truckload of barrel racers down to the river one weekend, spent the whole time drinking beer and watching them fish."

"Barre– what? Scarbro, when are you gonna start speaking English?" Lance Corporal Lamb demanded, his Boston accent rapidly exploding with indignation.

"Ain't like you're any better, Lambchop," Shiver snapped. "And it's called barrel racing," he said slowly, emphasizing each syllable. "How bout them cowgirls?"

"Boy ain't they something?" Scarbro replied wistfully.

"Okay, you can take 'em fishing. What else is there to do?" Paternostro asked.

"Watch tweakers try to steal ammonia from storage tanks."

Every eye in the mess looked down the table toward Sergeant Johnson, the Motor-T sergeant who had just spoken.

"What weirdness are you on about, Yank?" Pistol demanded.

"I'm from small town, Oklahoma," Johnson explained. "Not too far west of Sweetwood's place come to think of it. We got big ol' storage tanks at the edge of town, full of ammonia. You pick a spot about a hundred, maybe a hundred and fifty yards away, turn off the lights, drink beer, eat snacks. Talk."

Laughter filled the room. Both groups knew what talking inevitably led to.

"2300, that's when the first ones would show up. They'll approach the fence, try to get over it, then up into the ammonia tanks so they could steal some."

"How long does that last?"

"They'll keep at it till almost sunrise the next morning when Sheriff Schmalenberger wakes up."

"What's a tweaker?" A Brit asked.

"Hardcore crystal meth users. Can't hold still for a damn thing," Hondo said seriously.

"What was so important about ammonia?" A marine asked.

"Major meth ingredient," Johnson explained. "They need it to get their next hit. Or pay for it. The ammonia plant owners know it too. Things got pretty entertaining once they started electrifying portions of the fence line. Nobody is ever sure which parts are live, so the tweakers hit it in waves trying to figure out."

"And you took women. To watch this insanity?" Leftenant Balcombe asked seriously.

"Hell yes, ma'am!" Johnson said happily. "Half the time it was liable to be a cousin of me or the gal I was with. Every third Friday, it was somebody from the reservation, and I'm kinfolk to a whole slew of them too."

"Nealen, please tell me you have more sense than what I'm hearing right now," Balcombe demanded as men and women laughed at Johnson's declaration.

"Yes ma'am, I do as a matter of fact. Met my wife at church during Bible Study," Nealen replied.

"My faith in humanity is slightly restored," Balcombe said resignedly.

"Why can't any of you be more like him?" Munro demanded.

"Well ma'am, there is no good story which ever began with the words 'I was at church reading my bible…,'" Cassidy opined.

Munro frowned. "That's fair, I suppose."

"Now on the other hand, I've got a fair few which involve the words 'I was at church and somebody needed a knife,'" he added.

"You go to church?" Gallagher interjected

"Yes, ma'am I do."

"He's Mormon," Paternostro said.

"He doesn't drink at all," Lance Corporal Lamb said.

"Ain't you got like eight wives back in Utah, Sergeant?" Paternostro said.

"Bubba, I can't get one good woman to stick around and love me. Hell makes you think I could find eight sober women willing to put up with my unprepossessing hind parts?"

"Ummm —"

"Furthermore, I'm from Wyoming, by way of Florida," Hondo said.

"Isn't Wyoming the same place as Utah?" Paternostro asked.

"Nope. Lot less people. I don't think we've got two hundred-thousand in the whole state."

"That's like half my neighborhood back in the Bronx!" Parente declared.

"Pretty much," Hondo admitted.

"Hey Sergeant Johnson, considering you convinced some gal to go watch tweakers be well, tweakers, you got any good ones?" Sweetwood asked.

"Good ones of what?" Johnson asked.

"Pickup lines, Sergeant. We're trying to figure out who's got the best around here," Ostrovsky chirped.

"He needs a girlfriend before I'll believe he's got a line that works," House derided.

"What makes you think I need a line, Tex?" Johnson countered.

"Why wouldn't you?" House demanded.

"I've got George Strait lyrics!" Johnson said cheerfully.

"Hell yeah!" Scarbro whooped. "God save the King!"

The Brits looked at each other in confusion, before staring at the Texan Marine with dubious frowns.

"Scarbro, I know you're going to find this hard to believe, but women can rule countries. The ruling monarch is a queen. Her name is Elizabeth II," Gallagher explained slowly.

"Well ma'am, that's nice and all, but if you listen to country music or you live in Texas, you know who the King is."

"You have a King in Texas?" Munro asked. "Since when?"

"His name is George Strait," Perez added. "I'm from Maine, which is almost motherfreaking Canada. We know who he is."

"Shoot, I've gotten more girls with his songs, at a bonfire, than I can remember," Scarbro declared.

"Right? Me and George and 'Marina Del Rey,' baby," Johnson pronounced.

"Who is George Strait?" Private Cooper asked, confused. "Is he like Barry White?"

Silence.

"Little girl, did you really just ask that?" Johnson said, bewildered.

"Yeah, she did," Lance Corporal Rodd confirmed.

"Ain't you people civilized over there?" Scarbro demanded angrily.

"Well yes," Cooper said testily.

Cassidy held up a hand. "Scarbro, I don't think they know what country music is."

"How can they not, sergeant? That's crazy talk!"

"I lived in England from oh-one to oh-three. They had one country music station for the whole United Kingdom," Cassidy explained.

"No wonder they got so many problems," Scarbro opined.

"I think I got a fix for that, bubba," Johnson declared.

"You do, sergeant?" Scarbro asked.

"I brought my copy of 'Pure Country,'" he assured.

"Yes! Yes! Thank you, sweet nine-pound ten-ounce baby Jesus, on a pogo stick. I was about to lose my mind," Scarbro said excitedly.

"Not tonight you ain't, friggin Aggie goofball," Johnson said with a smile as he made to leave for his tent

Returning to his work, Hondo began whistling a song he'd learned in boyhood about ocean front property in Arizona.

\#

Far later in the evening, only the NCOs from either service remained awake, chatting amicably in the mess.

"Nah, I'm just not a fan. They're not my thing," House declared when pressed on his preference.

"Dude, I am totally okay with that," Jimenez admitted. "Means more Asian girls for me."

"I'm still trying to figure out who would date you, Cassidy," Collier said loudly.

"None of y'all got to see Mónica," Kramer declared somberly.

"Monica?" Sergeant Johnson asked.

"No, no, no. Accent on the o, Johnson," Kramer corrected. "Moh-nee-cahhh."

"She one of those posh types?" Sandra asked.

"Mónica was smoking hot, with a side of crazy by way of her mother being a full-blooded Italian from Naples," Hondo said, crumpling up a water bottle before throwing it at the trash can.

"Nobody gets involved with an Italian woman because they're nice quiet women," Paternostro declared. "I love my mother and sisters. But I will swear before God and His Angels that they drive me friggin crazy."

"Is that why you're in Afghanistan?" an engineer named Sharples teased.

"Yes," Paternostro insisted.

"Then why do it?" Sharples said, curious.

"Do what?" Cassidy asked.

"Get with an Italian girl," Sharples said. "If they're so crazy, why bother?"

"The food," Johnson declared longingly.

"Kramer, you remember the time I brought —" Cassidy began.

"Shrimp and Lobster Tortello. With a big ol' side of tiramisu," Kramer groaned happily. "Best meal ever."

"Shrimp and what?" Paternostro demanded.

"With garlic sauce. Which is before we discuss all the times he showed up at Monday morning formation giving away chicken parm sandwiches," Hondo added.

"He what?"

"Literally strolled up to formation right before a field op carrying a picnic basket full of chicken parm for our Gun section."

"Jeez! Sergeant, why didn't you marry her?" Parente, further down the table demanded. "If she can make good chicken parm, you'd have the Bronx lined up to marry her."

"Guys, I don't know if anybody's ever told all y'all this secret, but I possess a serious allergy to catching knives with my ribs."

"She didn't —" Sandra said, dismayed.

"She tried really hard."

"Tried?"

"She shattered a carving knife on my side plate."

"That's ludicrous!" Sharples declared.

"That's life," Cassidy assured.

His statement settled down over the crowd with a heft and weight which made others feel ill at ease.

If she's not going to ask, I might as well, Sandra told herself. *C'mon Sylvie, quit playing dumb.*

"What would make you settle down?" Sandra asked.

"Me?" Hondo asked.

"Uh-huh. We know Sergeant Johnson needs a thrill-seeker. And Scarbro likes to go fishing, for some damned reason none of us understand yet. But what about you?"

"A blade. Not stuck in my ribs. Or my back."

"Something like your facón?" Kramer suggested innocently.

"Wouldn't hurt," Hondo admitted.

"What's that?" Sandra asked.

Reaching into the small of his back, Hondo produced a long blade with an s-shaped guard. Taking it by the fuller between his left thumb and forefinger, he held it up for the British soldiers to see. Light glinted off the brass rivets which held the simple stag handle slabs in place for a grip.

"Where on earth did you find that?" Sylvie asked, professionally curious as she examined the blade from her seat.

"Find nothing. I spent a long summer on a ranch in the Brazilian pampas, learning how to handle cattle from my mother's family. When I left, the gauchos presented me with this."

"What do you use that for?"

"Nearly anything," Sylvie opined. "Facóns are fighting knives. But a gaucho can use it for all the fieldcraft one expects to see in the wilderness."

"Wicked." Sandra examined it more closely, then sat back. "A year ago, if you told me people still killed with knives in war, I'd have sworn you were crazy."

"And now?" Shockley asked.

"Oh you're still crazy, but I know better," Sandra admitted.

"Good. It's the only way we're gonna survive out here," Shockley suggested.

"You really think we can?"

"Why not?" Shockley said.

"Ummm.."

"To piggyback off what he said," Hondo began to a chorus of groans. "It would behoove you —"

"Oh sweet crap, not a fricking 'behoove' and a 'piggyback.' Future Sergeant Major of the Marine Corps over here!" Tolliver teased.

Hondo ignored him as he continued to speak. "— to consider that the Taliban have yet to win any engagement above squad-level."

"They haven't?" Cherney asked, as this news surprised even him.

"I looked before we deployed. An individual fire team or engagement team might lose most of its people. But a squad? Nah, the Taliban ain't nearly that good."

"Wish to Christ we didn't have to be here, like this," Maresley grouched.

"What do you mean, Mare?" Sylvie asked.

"Remember all the speeches and stupid trash we did before we left?"

"Sort of. I kinda tuned it all out," Sharples admitted, several others nodding their heads in agreement.

"I listened. Painfully, but I listened."

"And?"

"We're supposed to be some sort of political statement about women in the services."

"That's why we're here?"

"Aye. We're supposed to prove what we can do without men getting in our way."

"All it's done is get our people killed."

"You know that. I know that. But do you think it matters to any of the toffs at Number Ten Downing Street?" Sharples lamented.

"So long as they get to argue who was the better Top Boy at their snobby school, likely not," Sylvie lamented.

"Shame there's no good beer in sight. This talk is making me all kinds of unhappy and I want a beer to wash it down," Sharples said.

"I could really use six right now," House admitted. The burly comm chief stood. "I'm out for the night. Sleep is a precious commodity. I recommend all y'all do the same."

Before sleep finally overcame her as she sank into her cot, Sylvie considered Hondo's words.

"A blade," he had said

What manner of blade would he find acceptable? The use dictates the edge profile and type. A dagger? A bowie? I'd say a wakizashi but he doesn't seem to be big on Japanese culture. Maybe a gladius? What manner of blade would that man desire?

Chapter 23

We are the Fiend Club

Shannon Dolan enjoyed being a Marine. At times, the job sucked all kinds of hairy goat wang, but that was bound to happen anywhere you worked. Hell it happened even at Disney World. His cousin Sandy had spent ten years there and over beers would freely recite stories of the insane and weird things she'd seen working in the busy theme park.

Still, Dolan enjoyed what he did — driving trucks. Uncle Sam paid him to drive, rain or shine. Didn't matter if it was ordnance, trailers, trash, howitzers, or the number of tires involved, Dolan could drive it. At present, the gregarious Irishman from upstate New York found himself moving equipment with a pair of British women. Miller and Larson were also Motor Transport, and the three had been working on moving crates and identifying supplies since lunchtime, out in this section of the base.

The fact that both women were pretty certainly helped, along with their willingness to get their hands dirty. That wasn't the lackanookie speaking either — they were genuinely pretty women.

Miller, the shorter of the two, was a feisty blonde with intense green eyes. Larson had dark brown hair shot through with red streaks and the amount of attention they were giving him, just for moving some gear, was unreal.

I'm no slouch at being charming, but where did this come from?

He almost lost his grip on the box staring at Miller's ass as she sashayed about.

Yep. That's got my attention.

She must've had eyes in the back of her head right then, for she looked over her shoulder at him as he struggled to adjust his grip and not drop the box, then winked at him.

"That should be the last one, Dolan," Miller announced coyly.

Dolan felt a soft mewling sound issuing from his mouth as he set the box where they needed it, trying to hide exactly how alert he felt right then.

"I'm glad you're helping us, moving all of this around on our own is a pain," Miller admitted.

"Glad I could help," he said politely as he took a seat and crossed his legs. *Still not the lackanookie speaking, I'm just trying to be polite. I'll catch my breath then walk back to the hooches. After they've left. Yep. Uh-huh. Sure thing.*

He closed his eyes, enjoying the shade of the camo netting overhead. Thus he was unprepared for Miller to climb on his lap and kiss him. At that point, his eyes shot open and he looked up to see her smiling face.

"You can be somewhat oblivious at times," she stated,

"You think?" Larson said as she sat down beside him.

"Who what?" he squeaked.

"Miller and I were betting on whether or not you'd notice her shimmying along," Larson said cheerfully.

"Ummm."

Miller had stepped in front of him, close enough he could make out the details of her freckles.

"We both think you're handsome, you've been super helpful, and we figured you might enjoy something relaxing," she explained.

"Um. Thanks."

"We don't mind sharing. So long as there's enough of you to go around," Larson added.

"We were planning to take showers after we got done today. Then you came along and we decided we might as well justify them," she teased. "Larson's gonna take a smoke break."

Miller waited until Larson had stepped outside to grab him by the shirtfront so she could pull him over to the pile of netting.

"You don't have a girl back home, right?" Miller demanded.

"Nope."

"Positive?"

"Mama Dolan's baby boy is very single, Miss Miller."

"Oh good, that makes this even easier," Miller admitted.

It was cool beneath the camouflage netting, and the way the boxes were arranged made for a private space. Somehow he hadn't noticed that till now.

And all that extra netting is piled high. Should be comfy to lay on.

Miller pulled off her uniform blouse. The undershirt came next. After that, there was no time for anything else..

That had been the first night. A day later, Miller had found him while he was walking to dinner and mentioned that Larson needed his help in the motor pool storage after dinner with shifting spare parts around. And while she lacked Miller's feisty nature, she had been an absolute joy to spend time with.

Loneliness was a part of his life. Shannon had dallied with women over the years, but the loneliness was still there. And in this place where a man was always on edge, he'd been secretly afraid to let his guard down. In that space though, Shannon Dolan found his mind and body at ease as the two lovely women kissed him, touched him, and loved on him. By degrees, his body relaxed, and for the first time in a long while, he felt whole again.

The second week of their dalliance Dolan realized that he had never thought camouflage could be attractive.

Combat lingerie, aisle three. Not what you'll see in Jordan Marsh back home.

The ache he'd felt was gone, replaced by satisfaction and a satiation he hadn't experienced in a long while. More than that, he enjoyed their company. Both women were sweet, thoughtful, and exactly what he'd always wanted.

"I apologize for leaving you ladies, but it's almost sunset. NCO call awaits me," he announced.

Olivia pouted and Hannah frowned. fought the coursing desire to stay there, with them.

Now it's Olivia and Hannah, not Miller and Larson. At least, in here, he reminded himself.

"We understand," Larson admitted. "And Shannon?"

"Yes, Hannah?"

"Motor-T supplies are always bulky, we'd appreciate it if you came by next week about this time."

"It would be my pleasure," he flashed her a winsome smile as he stepped off, wishing he hadn't needed to leave so soon.

One more time would leave me still wishing for one more time beyond that.

Setting his boonie cap just so, he took off at a quick walk, whistling as he went along.

He was only ten paces away when the mortars arced in, whistling as they slammed into the midst of the supplies where both women still stood.

\#

"I kinda wanna meet whoever is calling the shots on that mortar." Cassidy declared as he listened to the whistle-crump sound of incoming fire.

"Why would you wanna do that?"

"Aside from stabbing the bastard in the face, somebody should tell him he's doing a good job."

"Excuse you?"

"Sumbitch's nickname oughta be Davy Crockett. If he had something bigger he wouldn't be bouncing his shots off the bunkers."

"That's a good thing?"

"If you wanna kill us, yeah."

"Well thanks for that reassurance!" Sylvie protested.

"We'll need to get the LZ cleared for the helo," he said casually.

"Why?"

"Expect we're gonna have at least a couple casualties from this."

"Medic!" a voice called out.

"Corpsmen up!" another proclaimed.

"Told ya. Davy Crockett got 'em. Sumbitch is good."

A pregnant silence filled the air and his lips moved as he counted aloud. When he reached thirty, he looked left then right.

"Tommy Taliban's likely done for the day. They'll shift position to somewhere pre-marked. Likely also keeping an eye out for where the birds come from."

"Birds?"

"You know, dustoff? Helicopters?"

Rather than wait for a response, Hondo moved to the next task on his list. Sylvie stared at him, angry and confused.

"How can you be so calm right now?" she demanded.

"How can I not?"

"People are dying. Probably even dead."

"That's the price of our business."

"And how can you defend the attacks?"

He looked at her queerly, then went back to his work.

"I didn't," Hondo said, far more grumpy sounding now.

"Yes you did! You said he was good. How can you say that?"

"Because he is." Hondo shrugged. "Skill is skill. Don't matter who has it."

"He's our enemy!" she spat.

"So? Doesn't mean he's stupid!"

"Why are you defending him? Are you some kind of traitor!"

Cassidy stopped his movement. Set the knife down. Pointed at the door.

"Leave. Now."

That had been an order. In the sharpest, rudest manner she'd ever seen him display toward a woman. And he'd spoken that way to her.

"Excuse me?"

"You. Your attitude. And that tone of voice. I didn't ask for any of it," Cassidy declared.

"Yeah, well maybe you deserve it."

"Go to hell, Orphan Annie."

The use of the old nickname bestowed by her cruel cousins brought on feelings she hadn't experienced in years."

"You — you —"

She didn't have time to register that he was moving before he'd seized the container of dishwater and thrown it into her face. Anything she might have said disappeared in a wave of suds and dirty water.

"Get out. Before I throw you out," Cassidy ordered.

"You know what? Fuck you!" Sylvie screamed as she came to her feet.

Cassidy pointed at the door diffidently. He didn't look back after it slammed shut. Simply changed the song playing from his iPod. In the silence of the kitchen, new music began to play, a harsh, discordant tale of hate. Hate wrapped around a core of despair.

#

"The kids aren't alright, ma'am," Peter Nealen informed Morgana as they both drank water and considered the day's events in the quiet mess.

"No staff sergeant, no they are not," Morgana agreed.

"Think we could give them a chat?"

"With what?"

"We gotta bring them back down to earth, remind them that they're still mortal. We've been winning so long it's hard to remember what it's like to lose at anything."

"That is a strange thing to say. But I agree with it."

Nealen leaned back, face still pensive as he pondered the matter.

"You teach lore with the MCMAP lessons. Got anything that covers loss?"

Nealen's face lit up. "Oh, yeah. Yale and Haerter."

"Who? Never mind, doesn't matter. It's almost bedtime, what if we kick the class before breakfast?" Morgana stated.

"We'd certainly have a captive audience," Nealen said.

"Agreed. Make it so, Staff."

#

"The Americans and British took losses. The helicopter came and went and has not been back."

"It is not enough. We must push them harder!" a newcomer argued.

"Aye but if we rush the matter, what then? What if they bring reinforcements down here?"

"Who cares? We are the Chosen of the Supreme! Who can stand against us if He is with us?"

"Peace brothers. Peace," the brigade commander proclaimed. "Your words have merit. We will wait for word from our informants within the firebase, as well as word from the papers. Soon our brothers will be here in strength."

The group commanders nodded in agreement, considering his words.

"Tell me, what is our end goal?"

None spoke and he sipped at his tea before he continued his lecture.

"We need hostages. Live hostages are worth their weight in gold."

Understanding blossomed.

"If we draw too much attention, too soon, we risk the loss of our entire effort here. Let us be patient, content to harass and draw strength. When our brothers arrive, we will strike."

His group commanders nodded and he returned to his tea as they began to discuss the best means of knocking out the defensive positions.

Chapter 24

Six Seconds

"Sit, kneel, bend, all of you!" Nealen ordered, waiting for all of the British and American personnel to follow his instructions before continuing to speak.

"Been a shit day, ain't it?"

Nobody spoke. Clearly nobody wanted to. Finally, Samuels looked at him directly. "It hasn't been a good one, Staff Sergeant."

"No, Samuels, no it has not. That happens. Johnson, you were in Three-Five, weren't you?"

"Christmas of 2010. I was a brand new Sergeant, first deployment I didn't have to drive a Humvee."

"Rough times?"

"We lost a lot of good Marines."

"How bad was it?"

Johnson didn't hesitate to respond. "We lost twenty-five, KIA, and two hundred wounded across seven months."

"All in Sangin?"

"Uh huh. My best friend Tony Chan bought it there."

"I hear you," Nealen assured. "Loss happens. And it can happen quick. Learning to live with those losses and still function is where winning is made."

He let his gaze take in the audience before he continued. "General John Kelly gave this speech a few years ago, speaking about the deaths of Marines under his charge. When he gave this speech, he had just four days prior received news regarding the death of his eldest son, a Marine Lieutenant on his third combat tour. If there is anybody better fit to speak on such a loss, I ain't met him." Nealen looked to one side. "Sergeant House, you mind doing the honors?"

"Absolutely, Staff Sergeant."

Stepping forward, the barrel chested-Texan drew in a breath, mentally steeling himself as he began to speak, pitching his voice so as to be heard by all present.

"22 April, 2008, two Marine infantry battalions, One-Nine "The Walking Dead," and Two-Eight, were switching out in Ramadi. One battalion was in the closing days of its deployment, the other just starting its seven-month combat tour. Two Marines, Cpl. Jonathan Yale and Lance Cpl. Jordan Haerter, twenty-two and twenty respectively, one from each battalion, were assuming the watch at the entrance gate of an outpost that contained a makeshift barracks housing fifty Marines. The same ramshackle building was also home to hundred Iraqi police, our allies in the fight against terrorists in Ramadi — known at the time as the most dangerous city on earth, and owned by al-Qaeda.

Yale was a dirt-poor mixed-race kid from Virginia, with a wife, a mother and a sister, who all lived with him and he supported. He did this on a yearly salary of less than $23,000. Haerter, on the other hand, was a middle-class white kid from Long Island. They were from two completely different worlds. Had they not joined the Marines, they would never have met each other, or understood that multiple Americas exist simultaneously, depending on one's race, ethnicity, religious affiliation, education level, economic status, or where you might have been born. But they were Marines, combat Marines, forged in the same crucible, and because of this bond they were brothers as close — or closer — than if they were born of the same woman.

The mission orders they received from their sergeant squad leader, I'm sure, went something like this: "OK, take charge of this post and let no unauthorized personnel or vehicles pass. You clear?" I'm also sure Yale and Haerter rolled their eyes and said, in unison, something like, "Yes, sergeant," with just enough attitude that made the point, without saying the words, "No kidding, sweetheart. We know what we're doing." They then relieved two other Marines on watch and took up their post at the entry-control point of Joint Security Station Nasser, in the Sophia section of Ramadi, al Anbar, Iraq. A few minutes later, a large blue truck turned down the alleyway — perhaps sixty to seventy yards in length — and sped its way through the serpentine concrete Jersey walls. The truck stopped just short of where the two were posted and detonated, killing them both.

Twenty-four brick masonry houses were damaged or destroyed. A mosque one-hundred yards away collapsed. The truck's engine came to rest two-hundred yards away, knocking most of a house down before it stopped. Our explosive experts reckoned the blast was caused by two-thousand pounds of explosive. Because these two young infantrymen didn't have it in their DNA to run from danger, they saved one-hundred-fifty of their Iraqi and American brothers in arms."

"The General interviewed several Iraqi police who had been witnesses to the events of that day. One of them declared, tears in his eyes "Sir, in the name of God, no sane man would have stood there and done what they did. They saved us all."

House laughed wryly at this. "I suppose now is as good a time as any to remind you

that Marines are definitely not sane men."

"Oh come now, Sergeant Cassidy isn't entirely given to delusions of grandeur," Pilsen declared sotto voice.

"No, he just is," Munro muttered.

The dirty looks and proud grins House saw scattered through the crowd told the boisterous Texan they were listening. This too was a part of Marine Corps' tradition — the oral storyteller who passed on a lineage and history. A duty reserved for sergeants dating back to a tavern in Philadelphia.

"Normal men, normal women do not march toward the sound of gunfire, determined to fight. We, all of us, are not normal. Accept that, embrace it. And in the absence of orders move to the sound of the guns."

"What was not known at that time, was that a security camera on the post recorded some of the attack. It happened exactly as the Iraqis described it. It took exactly six seconds from when the truck entered the alley until it detonated. You can watch the last six seconds of their young lives just like I heard it," he said, voice catching for a moment as he fought tears.

"I suppose it took about a second for the two Marines to separately come to the same conclusion about what was going on once the truck came into their view at the far end of the alley. No time to talk it over, or call the sergeant to ask what they should do. Only enough time to take half an instant and think about what the sergeant told them to do only a few minutes before: 'Let no unauthorized personnel or vehicles pass.'

"It took maybe another two seconds for them to present their weapons, take aim, and open up. By this time, the truck was halfway through the barriers and gaining speed. Here the recording shows a number of Iraqi police, some of whom had fired their AKs, now scattering like the normal and rational men they were, some running right past the Marines, who had three seconds left to live. For about two seconds more, the recording shows the Marines firing their weapons nonstop. The truck's windshield explodes into shards of glass as their rounds take it apart and tear into the body of the son of a bitch trying to get past them to kill us, their brothers — American and Iraqi — bedded down in our barracks. We had no idea our lives depended entirely on two Marines standing their ground. Yale and Haerter never hesitated. By all reports and by the recording, they never stepped back. They never even shifted their weight. With their feet spread shoulder-width apart, they leaned into the danger, firing as fast as they could. They had only one second left to live, and I think they knew. The truck explodes. The camera goes blank. Two young men go to their God. Six seconds.

"Not enough time to think about their families, their country, their flag, or about their lives or their deaths, but more than enough time for two very brave young men to do their duty."

He could no longer hide the tears, and taking his glasses off, wiped his eyes as he looked out at his audience. House stood there, letting the wave of emotions pass over him, before he put the glasses back in place.

"Count it out with me," his voice rasped as he held up a finger. "One Mississippi. Two Mississippi."

The crowd joined his chant. The Brits had no idea what a "mississippi" could be, but it certainly didn't sound pleasant at the moment.

"Three Mississippi. Four Mississippi. Five Mississippi. Six Mississippi. Boom."

Silence engulfed the crowd, wind idly kicking up motes of dust in the cool morning.

Nealen stepped into the silent void. "For those who didn't know, the incoming battalion had a young Lance Corporal there to set up digital comms. His name was Matthew House. He was manning the security cameras when the attack occurred."

The assemblage looked to House with new respect as he stared back stiffly unyielding.

"Walking Dead," House declared.

"Oorah, One-Nine," Nealen replied. "Now, girls, how are we doing?"

"Still hurts, Staff Nealen," Sylvie said.

"It's going to. Death hurts, emotionally. But you cannot stay stuck on a friend's death," Nealen proclaimed. "Remember them. Honor them in your actions and deeds. But do not let them become a deadweight which keeps you from moving forward. Me, I say a prayer around the rosary for each Marine I've buried. Because somebody should remember them. Even if it's just me."

He caught a sign from the Sarn't Major and fell silent.

"We are almost done here. Once the airfield is constructed, a company of the Scots Dragoons will be deploying here as the garrison force while we rotate back to Herrick. You have all done exceptionally well, to get this far. I am proud of you, and the incredible work you've done. You've nothing to be ashamed of," Mayne announced.

"We've still had no word on any of our three wounded. We won't until tomorrow. When we do, I will relay that information personally, to every man and woman here. Are we clear?"

"Aye, Sarn't Major," several personnel replied.

The door behind him opened.

"Excuse me, Sarn't Major."

"Yes, Sergeant Cassidy."

"Breakfast is ready, sir."

"Very well then. Come along now, you all know the drill."

#

"Has there been any news regarding our attack?"

"Nothing yet."

"Surely you could call —"

"Absolutely not!" Basayev pointed skyward. "Remember that they are listening. As though Shaitan himself were whispering in their ears."

"That cannot be possible."

"It is how they caught Osama. Do you desire his fate?"

"What do you mean 'how they caught him?'"

Saeed sighed. "Friends in the Pakistani Ministry relayed to us that American spy satellites were watching and scanning for couriers using electronic communication."

"They can listen to our calls?"

Saeed nodded sagely. "Indeed. They even have the means to track a call back to where it came from."

He held up the clear plastic bags which held his cellphone and its battery, separated. "We do not use electronics except in the most extreme emergency, for this reason. If the Americans knew we were here, and soon we will be here in force, we would find ourselves the object of airstrikes without mercy."

All present grimaced.

"I really do not like getting strafed by jets."

"Nothing the Russians left us is good for shooting them down."

"Hence the caution. I know the call to be patient is hard. But our brothers are bringing more arms with them. And they will be here soon. At which point, we will engage the westerners, take the firebase and capture such prizes as has not been granted to the Faithful in many years. Allahu akbar."

"Allahu akbar," they intoned, and returned to planning for the coming venture.

#

The sergeants, as usual, left the mess. This time, they were followed by a shadow who kept his distance, waiting.

"Sergeant House," Joseph Pilsen asked at length.

"Hey, what's up, Pilsen?"

"Were you really there, that day?"

House paused, considered what he'd seen from his fellow sergeants as they worked to make a real soldier out of a formerly drunk young baby-faced boy too far from home.

"Yeah," he rumbled at last. "Yeah I was."

"Why did they do it?"

House sighed, stared off into the distance.

"Because that's what it takes to survive in places like this."

"Could they have made it to cover?"

"No. And if that bomb had made it inside the walls, we'd have all died."

"Does– do– do we all have to make that sacrifice?"

House shook his head. "No. No we don't. But if that day comes, you best be ready for it. And you best be man enough to do the right thing."

"Why?"

"Imagine if you had to live with yourself, knowing you failed the people who needed you most."

"I — I can't. I've never been any place where that's happened."

"I can," House replied. "I still kick myself for it."

"Oh," Joseph said slowly.

"Yeah. Big oh. It'll hurt worse than a knife in the ribs." He thumped his knuckles into the younger, smaller man's chest. "At the end of the day, there's only one person you have to live with. That's the man you see in the mirror. If you can't live with him, you're in trouble."

"I think I see what you mean."

"Good. Decide what kind of man you want to be. Now. Not tomorrow. Not the day after. By then it's too late."

"Yes, sergeant."

Joseph Pilsen turned back towards the kitchen, thinking all the while about what House had said. *What sort of man am I? Am I a good man? What would make me good? Does anybody think I'm a good man? How do I prove I'm a good man?*

The question refused to leave his mind till sleep overtook him as he drifted into a heavy slumber a long while later.

Chapter 25

What you gonna do when they come for you

The news that Miller and Larson had died on the helicopter back to Leatherneck broke during the afternoon message traffic, causing an ugly mood to settle into place. Several Marines were in the Mess, grabbing water before post when they heard the report.

"Those fuckers," a Marine hissed. "Why don't we have any guns with us?"

"Could we even hit them with Triple Sevens? I thought they were too close for anything, even at high angle?" Ochoa asked.

"Not if you get Brady the right target data," a voice suggested, causing heads to whip around.

Lieutenant Harper looked up from where he was busily refilling a thermos before he went to relieve Brady in the FDC. "All he needs is the data and we can drop the world on those bastards."

"What'd you hit 'em with, sir, X-cal?" a marine asked, referring to the expensive but highly useful GPS-guided Excalibur artillery round they had been trained on.

"Don't even need that. Get me a counter-battery radar. We can drop rounds on 'em before they know what we're up to," Harper explained.

"What's counter-battery radar?" Menchaca asked.

"It tracks the stuff people shoot at us, back to its point of origin."

"You know how to use that, sir?"

"No, but Huck does. It's what he did before he went FDC. He can run that, Brady does the numbers. Master Guns Guptill taught him how to do it with a slide rule faster than the frigging computer."

"Still doesn't get us any guns," Menchaca stated.

Harper glanced towards a husky Lance Corporal from FDC who was staring at him curiously.

"Thiess, get a message to whoever's on watch at Delaram via BFT. Tell 'em to get Lieutenant Vetter on the Iridium for me," Harper ordered.

"On it, sir." The husky Wisconsin farm boy was out the door and moving with speed.

Shortly, Thiess came back holding the sat phone as Harper finished mixing sugar and powdered creamer into his coffee. "Here sir, I got the Lieutenant on the other end."

"Good." Harper stepped into the kitchen, voice hushed. Minutes passed before he came back out, handing Thiess the device once more. He grabbed his thermos, free hand slowly flexing as he looked across the room.

"Cassidy," Harper said starkly.

"Yes, Sir?" The sergeant said.

"How quickly can you get three gun trucks prepped to roll?"

"Pretty damn quick. Sir."

"Good. Think you can make it to Delaram and back in eighteen hours?"

"Only way I won't is if I'm dead," Cassidy answered.

"Good enough."

"Leave at zero-seven?" Cassidy asked.

"Yeah. First Platoon will be waiting for you."

"What about Staff Sergeant Nealen?"

"Leave that to me." Harper tapped his matte black rank insignia. "A sergeant's duty is to teach marines how to fight. My duty is telling you where to fight. And where to die."

He surveyed the room, full of angry men focusing on a single purpose. "No more dead girls."

Growls met his words.

"Damn right, sir. No more dead girls," Kramer assured.

#

While Marines purposefully slipped through the FOB, attending to the tasks necessary for a convoy's departure, Harper went looking for Nealen. He found the Platoon Sergeant sitting on his cot, cleaning his rifle and pistol, clearly in a foul mood himself.

"Nealen, the boys are gonna make a supply run tomorrow."

Nealen looked up

"They are? Hadn't heard we were short on anything yet."

"Short on a few things."

"Like?"

"If we get caught, we're all going to Leavenworth."

"Huh. And why are they doing this?"

"No more dead girls."

Nealen shoved the takedown pins back into place, performing a functions check on his carbine before he put it back on the cot.

"Who all is going?"

"I was thinking of three gun trucks plus the LVSR and a scout vic."

"They'll need the fuel truck, too. They can refuel in motion that way."

"Works for me."

"What time did you tell them to leave by?" Nealen enquired.

"I told Cassidy we leave at zero-seven."

Nealen shook his head negatively. "Not good enough, sir. He'll need every cool minute possible. Zero four reveille, zero four-thirty departure. Should have some light by then."

"Makes sense."

"I really wish we didn't have to do this."

"We don't have a choice. It's this or death by a thousand cuts."

"Why not send Kramer? He's been a sergeant before, sir. Convoys are his bread and butter."

"I know, but Cassidy seems to be in a foul mood."

"More than usual?" Nealen asked, ears perking up.

"Over a woman, if you can believe the rumors. Helluva lot of betting going on over all of it."

"Oh. Goody," Nealen snarled.

"I know. I'm still processing it myself."

Nealen looked up stony faced at his Platoon commander. "Think he can really do it?"

"If we fail, it won't be because we didn't try."

"We?"

"I'm sending them into harms' way and the threat of court martial if they're caught. The hell makes you think I'm staying here?"

"I understand, sir."

In that void of silence, both men reviewed what they were doing, running through all of the options before them.

"Good luck, sir"

"We'll need it. That and a lot of prayer." Harper stepped back out of the tent, closing its door flap.

Left alone once more, Peter Nealen wondered what would happen next.

Because the reality is that if we fail here, we'll likely all be dead.

Reaching inside his shirt, Nealen produced the worn rosary his grandfather had gifted to him when he graduated boot camp over a decade prior.

"Lord, if you're listening, my boys could really use a hand right now."

\#

"Christian, I don't know how you folks do casualty stuff, but who's going to escort the girls' caskets home?" Mike asked. The two men were sitting in Mike's office, quietly drinking coffee and poking at the dinner their aides had grabbed for them.

"I hadn't made it that far yet," Christian admitted, idly pushing a french fry around the ketchup.

"But you do that, correct?" Mike pressed.

"Aye."

"If you'd like to borrow Corporal Dolan, I don't think he'd mind the duty."

Christian looked up. "You sure?"

"I just came from the hospital, he needs something to keep him occupied. Him and Crocetti."

"Crocetti. Isn't he one of the lads on your security detail?"

"He is. Crocetti was giving Larson CPR until Doc Gnem pronounced her dead. Gunny Pililaau had to haul him off her. He cried ugly tears. Now he thinks he's a failure as a Marine."

"Son of a bitch." DuBois shook his head in sad consolation. "If he couldn't save her, he couldn't save her. That's what happens in a soldier's game."

"You know that, I know that. He only got to the fleet in time to make the deployment roster. And he's due up for promotion in a couple days, but now?" Mike shook his head sadly. "I don't know what to do with him."

"Boys his age are still hooked on trying to save the pretty girl, not watch them die. Especially not like that.."

"I'm worried he's gonna risk himself pointlessly next time we take contact," Mike admitted.

"Can I have him as well?" Christian asked after a moment's deliberation.

"It'd probably be for the best. Get him someplace calm, let him come back down to Earth."

After a moment, DuBois nodded. "I understand. Jenkins!" he called out.

DuBois' aide poked his head into the office. "Sir?"

"Get with the J-1 shop. Cut orders for Corporal Dolan and —" Christian looked back toward Mike. "You said Crocetti is picking up on the first of December?"

"Yeah."

"Lance Corporal Crocetti to escort Lance Corporals Miller and Larson home. Mike, what uniform do your lads wear for funeral details?"

"Bravos," Mike declared, then corrected himself. The British soldiers would have no idea what he was referring to with the short-hand slang Marines used. "Blue Dress Bravos. Ribbons and shooting badges. Dress white cover."

"Understand, Jenkins?" DuBois asked.

"Sir? What's going on?" the aide asked.

"You heard that two of our people came in yesterday, KIA, escorted by Marines?"

"Yes, sir."

"Those Marines were with them when they died. Colonel Roach witnessed those Marines trying to assist our soldiers during the medevac out of Dishu. And when that failed, they escorted their bodies to the hospital, from the airfield. Dolan still had shrapnel in his leg." DuBois swallowed. "Crocetti was performing CPR on Larson when she passed."

Jenkins stared, surprised at the report he was receiving.

"This is a matter of the honor of the Army, Jenkins. Let us not be found wanting," DuBois declared.

"Yes, sir! USMC Blue Dress Bravos with ribbons and shooting badges, plus a change or two of civilian attire. Emergency reserve fund all right for this sir?"

"I don't care if we have to overnight it over from DC. Hell, I don't care if I have to use my Barclay's card. Certainly better than anything my wife's used it for at Harrod's in the last three years."

"Understood, sir."

"That'll be all, Jenkins."

The door closed as the aide withdrew and Mike stared curiously at his fellow Colonel.

"Nobody made them do what they did, Mike. The lads just did it because it was the right thing to do," DuBois explained.

"Thank you," Mike said quietly.

"No. Thank you."

\#

Well before the sun presumed to knock upon Twilight's door, six trucks fired up in the motor pool. As their engines turned over and air tanks refilled, Kramer led the convoy briefing. All the Marines present were drinking strong black coffee Cassidy had brewed to clear their sleep-addled minds.

"Listen up assholes," Kramer announced. "We're driving to Garmsir, hooking up with a route clearance team, then driving to Delaram. Guns are right where we left them. We roll in, pass the trucks to First Platoon. They'll take care of loading up the SL3 gear, guns, and any spare ammo they could grab. They are also grabbing a counter-battery radar for us. Jepson, Kenyon, Thompson, you are driver, VC, and gunner for that. While First Platoon is getting us refueled and loaded, I expect all of you to grab chow, then catch an hour or two of sleep. Formation on the trucks at fourteen-fifty. We leave Delaram at fifteen-hundred and drive straight back here."

"What's the order of march?" Corporal Domine asked.

From behind Kramer, Cassidy spoke up for the first time that morning.

"I'll be in front with Logan and Ma Deuce in the Scout Vic. Fuel truck between Four and Five, wrecker between Five and Six. Don't worry about what's ahead. Just watch my flanks."

"Roger that, Sergeant."

"Dispersion will be one-hundred fifty meters. Comm should have everything set up by now," Kramer said calmly. "Anything to add, sir?" He asked, looking toward Lieutenant Harper.

"Understand that I do not give a damn about speed limits. Those craven cowards from Base Safety aren't out there. The Taliban are. Logan, I want land speed records in that scout vic," Harper declared from where he leaned back against the fender of an Oshkosh truck. "If I suspect for even a heartbeat that you're not trying to win the Daytona Five Hundred out there, Sergeant Cassidy is under orders to donkey punch you."

"Sir?" Logan said worriedly.

"He will continue to do so till you drive faster or your kidneys have nothing left to bleed," Harper stated flatly.

"Yes, sir," Logan said, more than slightly aghast.

"We are not stopping for anything," Harper continued. "If your truck breaks down, throw everything and everybody on the next vehicle in line and keep moving. We can acquire new trucks at Delaram. This base is exposed and in danger without us here. The less time we're away, the better off they are. Understood?"

"You're coming along, sir?" Hondo asked.

"What kind of man would I be if I didn't?" Harper challenged.

"A worthless one, sir," Tolliver suggested.

"Damn right. All yours, sergeant."

"Roger that, sir." Hondo spat seed hulls into an empty spit bottle, eyes daring any man present to challenge him as he checked his watch.

"No more dead girls," he snarled. "Kramer, final inspection in four minutes. I'm gonna go get my fifty ready."

In the back of the crowd, men took note of his surly attitude as he stomped away, more rancidly harsh than normal. Loud music began to play from a speaker high up on a turret at the front of the convoy as he single-handedly manhandled a Ma Deuce up and into position on the turret's ring mount.

"I don't know what he's playing but it ain't good, Corporal," Perez told Tolliver.

"Whatcha mean?" Tolliver asked.

"The sergeant's music. It sounds like the narcocorridas I heard growing up in Nuevo Laredo."

"What're they saying?"

"It's not Spanish. Might be Portuguese. But uh —" Perez blanched at a line. "Nothing good. Nada. Nunca."

"No es un problemo chico," Samuels suggested. "El Sargento necesita luchar contra un hijo de puta."

"You speak Spanish, Corporal?" Perez gasped.

Samuels grinned weirdly in the half-lit morning. "Me esposa es un cubana peliroja."

"Odale." Perez looked him up and down. "Un cubana?"

"Si chico."

"Suddenly there is so much about you which makes sense," Perez glibly declared.

"Any questions?" Kramer loudly asked from up in front

"What happens if we get caught, Corporal?" Ostrovsky asked.

Cherney sighed unhappily. "Kramer, who could they send to stop us?"

"Probably MPs," Kramer admitted.

"That's it? Them?" Ostrovsky stated disdainfully.

"Yeah, that's it."

Ostrovsky lit a cigarette and took a long drag. "By the time they get here we'll either be heroes or we'll be dead. Screw it, let's go!"

\#

They came out of the deep desert, vehicles moving rapidly, as the turret gunners scanned for any sign of threats. Twice, they had seen shepherds tending to flocks, but nothing more than that.

Rather than leave a junior marine in the turret scanning for trouble, Cassidy had assigned Shiver to handle the radio and maps while he took the turret. He needed to see the land, to feel the wind rushing against his face in the early morning light. He needed to feel alive again. Just as he needed to sate that primal urge which always demanded he stand. Stand and fight.

Something moved far ahead, prompting him to reach for the high-powered binoculars resting in their case. He examined the land, then keyed his radio's throat mic."

"Bama, this is Gun Five Actual."

"Send it."

"Think I just saw somebody drop down out of sight, are we coming up on any wadis?"

"Map show's a bunch of 'em through here."

Changing the frequency on his radio, Cassidy keyed the mic.

"All stations, prepare for imminent contact."

That woke men up from any dregs of lethargy which they might have settled into. Rounding the bend in the road, the Cougar began to chug up the hill, sky lining itself against the morning sun.

Cassidy heard Shockley calling out the report over his radio. *"Contact right, four o'clock!"*

Cassidy had time to see a man wearing a djelba and dishdasha take aim with a Russian-made RPG when he heard the sound of automatic weapons fire.

THUNK THUNK THUNK.

Shockley, sitting on the Mark Nineteen in Vic Two, laughed as his high explosive grenade rounds caused a sympathetic detonation of the warhead. The nameless rocketeer disappeared in the blast. When the smoke cleared, nothing remained.

"Scratch one tango," Cassidy announced.

"Think his buddies will take the hint?" Shockley asked over the radio net.

"I hope not," Hondo growled into the radio.

"Is it true he's mad at one of the girls?" Cherney's driver, Swanger, asked once he was certain Cherney had taken his hand off his radio.

"That's what people have been saying," Cherney asked. "Which one did you hear it was?"

"I think it's that smoking hot brunette, the Sergeant," Swanger replied.

"Lyons?"

"Yeah."

"What makes you say that?"

"When we were having a rain day, I thought I saw them disappearing into the supply yard together."

"Huh."

"I've heard she's an ice queen," Swanger added.

"Dude, if you looked like her, you'd have every dickhead imaginable trying to get in your pants," Cherney explained.

"Oh. Yeah. Huh."

"Be like trying to walk down a hallway getting shot in the face with hot dogs every step of the way."

"Thanks, I'll pass." Swanger spat a stream of brackish brown liquid into his spit bottle. "If he's busy chasing her, he ain't busting our balls like a sonofabitch."

Spit.

"Somebody get that man laid so he calms down, please."

#

Cassidy's desire for a fight would be realized over the next several hours. Thrice more along the route, they found themselves engaged. The Marines expected it. That did not mean they had to tolerate such trespasses. Fanaticism alone is not enough to counter the employment of automatic weapons. It makes for equally horrible cover and concealment against high explosive warheads and copper-jacketed steel-core ammunition.

By the time they arrived in Delaram, it was just after noon. Staff Sergeant Hakim had Marines from First Platoon there to meet them. Second Platoon swung down off their trucks to make room for First, who quickly disappeared into the base with their vehicles.

"Remember," Kramer chided. "We meet here at fourteen-fifty. Fifteen-hundred we roll out. This should put us back into Dishu by twenty-two. Everybody understand?"

"Oorah!"

"Move uglies!"

Chapter 26

The Revenue Man Wanted Grandaddy Bad

Private Abigail Clarke shut the book she was reading and checked her watch. *2227. Oh I'm gonna pay for this one in the morning.* She shoved a makeshift bookmark between the pages and tucked it away under her cot. On instinct she reached for her grandmother's rosary and felt a small spike of panic when she found it missing from her neck. She looked hastily around her cot before remembering that she had left it at her workstation in the electrician's workshop.

Shit. The workshop was on the other side of the FOB. Her face twisted in a silent snarl as she examined her choices. She could wait until the morning to get the rosary, or she could wake someone up to appease that rocks-for-brains American Corporal who had instituted the two by two rule.

The rosary had been given to her by Grandma Buckner just before she passed away. The smooth sandalwood beads were Abigail's only tangible gift she had left of that loving old Cornwall woman. Well made and well worn, it was a physical reminder that someone loved her, and that there was a world that existed outside this hell of a desert. Additionally, going through the prayers was a ritual and an anchor that she relied upon to help get her through each day and fall asleep each night. Waiting until morning wasn't an option. She looked around at the sleeping girls. Waking them up wasn't an option either, not for a necklace that only held importance to her.

Option number three it is. She thought resignedly to herself.

She swung her legs out of the cot and into her boots, lacing them up halfway over her bare feet before tucking the remaining length of laces around her ankles. She wasn't going to be going far, and she wasn't going to be gone for long. There was no need to gear up.

She snuck out as quietly as possible and made her way through the tents, across the motor pool and towards the workshops, half walking, half jogging. In the darkness she did not see the three Afghan Police loitering around the freshwater point when she passed it. She did not see them when they took an extreme interest in her, a woman, walking alone at night, wearing only shorts and a tee shirt instead of the usual uniform and armor.

Abigail reached the electrician's workshop and grabbed the extra key from where it was hidden, slipping inside after a bit of fumbling with the lock. For some reason, that copy of the key didn't like to work very well. *Probably why it's the spare key, no one wants to have to tote this one around.* She flipped on the lights and made her way to the back corner of the room where her workstation sat. And there it was, the rosary, right where she had left it, hung on the wall out of view. She let out a sigh of relief and pulled it down, pressing it to her lips and saying a small prayer of thanks to her God.

The door slammed shut.

A gut instinct started sending up alarms in the back of her head. The door should have shut behind her immediately, not several seconds later. She turned towards the room's only exit and felt the adrenaline shoot through her veins like cold fire. There were three men standing between her and the door, three Afghan Police in their dirty blue uniforms: one by the door and two advancing on her.

"Hey! You can't be in here!" she barked at them, trying to muster as much authority as she could manage. A horrible smile broke out on the face of the older man advancing on her.

He had the longest of their unkempt beards, peppered with grey hairs, and his smile showed yellowed teeth with gaps between them. He muttered something to his companion, hungry eyes fixed on Abigail, and the other man barked out a laugh. This one was younger, his skin wasn't as leathery although it was darker, and his beard was greasy and black.

The one standing by the door, guarding it she realized with a sinking feeling, was the youngest of them yet it would seem, and only had a few scraggly whiskers marking his expressionless face.

In milliseconds Clarke examined the situation. No one knew she was here, hell, she wasn't even *supposed* to be here. It was the middle of the night, no one was going to walk in on them. It was three against one, worse even three men against one woman. She didn't have a gun. Like an idiot she had been so preoccupied with hating the stringent rules put down by that arrogant American that she had completely forgotten why they were put in place, and like an idiot had completely disregarded them. She scanned the room, looking for something, anything that she could use as a weapon. She found nothing.

All of the tools were locked up tight, and the only materials within reach were the spools of wires that required a forklift to move, fat chance of her being able to use them for anything. All she had were her fists and the rosary clutched in her hand. They carried no weapons either, and where she could have had a chance if it was one against one, or even one against two, one against three was going to be impossible. Diplomacy was out, there was no chance she could talk them into retreating, the hunger in their black eyes reminded her of predators that were hunting down their first real meal in months. Hyenas. Jackals. Terrifying. The only two options laid out before her were fight or don't. And as God was her witness, there was no chance in hell that she was going to roll over and submit. If these goat humpers wanted to take this pound of flesh they were going to have to pay for it.

She bent down slightly to keep her knees from locking and balled her fists, trying to remember everything she had been trained. She was in a corner.

Get out of the corner.

Too late.

Greasy Beard charged at her, going for her wrists or arms. She ducked down and to the side, trying to get out into the open. It didn't work. Where she had managed to miss greasy beard's charge, old guy had moved quickly behind his companion and slammed her hard up against a tool chest, ramming her head hard against it, stunning her and knocking the wind out of her. The metal handles from the tool chest dug sharply into her arm and back, sending intense sharp pains shooting out from it.

She struggled to clear her head and regain complete control of her limbs, but before she could she found herself pulled hard onto the ground by her hair and dragged more into the middle part of the room. She tried to grab at the pair of hands above her head, tried to loosen their hold on her hair, but only loosely managed to claw at them before being swatted away.

#

Joseph Pilsen shook the cigarettes to pack the tobacco in tighter before he pulled one of his few remaining sticks out, thrusting it between his lips and fishing around in his pocket for his lighter.

"Screw me sideways twice over. I'm ready for this shit to be done."

The day had been unusually long, nothing seemed to work right, and there had been no word regarding the convoy. For all he knew, they could be broke down somewhere, ambushed and all dead, or abducted by aliens and taken to the nether regions of the galaxy.

"Aliens would at least make sense," he grumbled. "Nothing else about this godforsaken place does."

"What was that Pilsen?" an unwelcome voice asked.

He steeled himself, refraining from using the immediate phrase which came to mind, at least where Sergeant Lyons was concerned. She was still a Sergeant, he was still a Lance Corporal.

And while Chef might be mad at her, that doesn't mean Pistol won't kick my ass for being insolent.

"Just talking to meself, Sergeant. Really don't like this desert. Don't like it much at all."

"I don't think any of us do. Too hot, too dry. No good places to get a pint or fish and chips."

Pilsen did not want to be talking with her right then. He had come to respect Sergeant Cassidy in his time here. Sergeant Lyons, whatever she had said or done, hurt him. Oh sure, the man tried to hide it. And he was magnificent about the matter.

But Joseph Pilsen knew a thing or two about women and the injuries they could bring to bear. He'd lived through enough heartbreak for one lifetime already. Right then, Pilsen despised Lyons.

Jumped up goody-two-shoes with her nose in the air. No wonder she's still single and nobody wants her around.

"No, ma'am, there really isn't."

Just say what you want to then leave me alone, dammit he raged.

"Have a good night, Pilsen."

"You too, ma'am."

She left, and he went back to considering the changes which had occurred in his life as he enjoyed the view overhead.

Finally, as the last of his cigarette burned away, he considered going to bed.

Think I'll lock up and hit the rack he told himself.

Before he could step back inside the kitchen, Pilsen heard a noise that sounded oddly like somebody was crashing around in one of the shops.

"Why would be anybody working this late? It's nearly twenty-two thirty."

Following the sound, he went looking. There were definitely lights on. And he could hear what had to be fighting.

Why is somebody throwing down in a shop when we've got a MCMAP pit?

Kicking the door open, he stepped through. Clarke, and what looked to be two ANP were grappling about.

"Oi! Get off her!" He shouted as he moved across the space in four swift steps, hooking the buttstock of his rifle around in a horizontal slash just like Sergeant Johnson had taught him, taking the first man in the ribs. Pivot step, keeping his boots clear of Clarke's feet, the barrel jabbed forward, catching the other man in his cheek. Blood flowed out of the gash, the man falling backwards from the force of the blow.

Switching hands, Pilsen, reached down to help Clarke up.

"What's going on girly —"

He never saw the pipe wrench which hit him in the small of his back. On a more developed man, it would've been a glancing blow. Pilsen was still building muscle though, and it laid him out, knocking him down in a clatter.

All three policemen forgot about their original victim as they stared at the much younger man for a moment, collectively drawing breath and trying to collect themselves. That was when they set about stomping.

#

"Jimenez, how goes night watch?" Nealen asked in the dimly-lit darkness near the Command Post as he lit up a final cigarette for the night.

"So far Staff Sergeant, we're doing okay. Be better when Sergeant Cassidy and the rest of the guns get back."

"Yeah we will. Staff Sergeant Hakim says they left at fifteen-hundred on the dot," Nealen added.

"Good. We need it."

Shots rang out in the night, causing both men to spin in place as they started scanning for threats.

"Who fired that?" Jimenez shouted into his radio.

"Sounds like it came from one of the shops!"

A woman's shrill scream sounded, galvanizing both men to move at a sprint, Nealen in the lead.

"QRF to the shops! QRF to the shops! Stand to!" Jimenez barked into his radio.

They had gone over the possibility of infiltrators, Nealen and the dutiful Corporal. In the event of such an occurrence, the only smart solution was to put the FOB on full alert immediately. Nealen had even practiced it, timing the Marines to see how quickly they could get into position.

"Help! Somebody help!"

Nealen saw Private Clarke come tearing out of a shop, tears in her eyes and clothing askew.

"Get a doc! They hurt Pilsen!"

Beyond, through the open door, Nealen saw a pair of boots on the ground, unmoving and his heart sank.

Christ preserve us.

\#

The convoy moved through the desert at a leisurely pace. Just fast enough to keep air moving through the open windows, slow enough not to draw attention from any American patrols. Younger men had shaved their still-growing beards to look more like young boys, going so far as to dress down to the appropriate age. Some of the more slight figures even sported black burqas and chadors. If stopped at a roadblock, they wouldn't look out of place. Given the cargo they held, it was best for all if they looked the part of innocent nomads.

Each of the six trucks in the convoy carried broken down parts to tubes, rockets, and their control systems. One would've had to strip the vehicles down to bare frames to find all the parts, if they had no foreknowledge of what they were looking at or for. Which was exactly how the commander of the Deshu Brigade of the Army of the Faithful wanted it.

#

Within the dwelling's space, lines had been drawn across the sand. Rocks marked particular points.

"Our sources inside the compound said that the marines have increased security, but they have not seen additional weapons or personnel arriving and staying for any length of time."

"They have barracks in a row here, with workshops and storage spaces next to it. Those will need to be cleared out. No grenades, if we can help it. Dead hostages are no use to us."

"What about the Marines?"

"Keep a few alive. Kill the rest. It will make handling the houris easier."

"How do we get inside?"

"The rest of the brigade is bringing what rockets and heavy mortars they can grab from caches. Additionally, we're waiting on this" He threw a newspaper onto the low table. "The ministers who pushed for this collection of houris to be formed are coming to investigate the base."

"Ministers," several men said at once. "That would give us leverage."

"Indeed."

"They will not want to come out here via truck," Ahmed announced.

"What do you mean Achmed?" Saeed asked.

"Remember I have spent time working on American bases. The air conditioning in vehicles is often the first thing to go."

"Decadent westerners, so weak. So frail," another man, a muj from the mountains declared.

"Ministers like their comforts. They will not want to spend hours in a truck, sweating," Ahmed hastened to add.

"What would they do then? Fly in?"

"Why not? It is much faster for their purposes," Ahmed suggested

Saeed stroked his beard.

"Aviation gas is volatile. If we hit it with rockets, it should combust nicely."

Looking over the layout, he gestured. "If you had to fly here, how would you do it?"

"Two helicopters, possibly three. One for the VIPs, one for the staff, and they will likely run down extra supplies. Staff and cargo go on the air strip."

He stabbed at the map. "Plan for the VIPs to be around here."

"Why?"

"They'll want to make an entrance."

"To remind all that they're in charge."

"Yes."

"Then we'll plan for rockets on that target, and mortars elsewhere."

"Sahib, what word on the sapper charges?"

"It should be here shortly," Saeed assured.

Chapter 27

He Never Come Back From Copperhead Road

They came up out of the darkness, a seething roar in the night, diesel powered sharks bursting through a sandy tide. New bullet scars showed on the armored hides, but the men and their precious cargo were very much intact.

Cassidy, for his part, felt that much better. He'd added tallies to his logbook, more men for his honor guard on *that* day.

Ancestors, see these, and know that I have not wasted your name, nor mired it in cowardice.

It was perhaps a slice of pagan mysticism leftover after his family had converted to Christianity. But it endured. And he refused to let go of the strange comfort it gave his soul.

Some part of him missed her. Missed her company, missed the calm of her presence. He'd heard repeatedly that she was a cold and distant woman, almost to the point of anti-social. But he'd never seen that from her.

Warmth. And that smile. Gah, I miss that too. It made my whole day better. Even losing Monica didn't hurt this much. I had planned to marry Monica and it didn't hurt nearly this badly!

Fighting makes me happy. Just wish it hadn't been with her.

He fiddled with the strap on the pistol holster, wishing once again for an apology he knew with certainty she'd never give.

Here I go again he told himself, repeating the refrain of a song he had used several times in his life. *Here I go again.*

A familiar landmark hove into view and Hondo breathed a sigh of relief. *Nearly home.*

"FDC, FDC this is Five Actual. How copy?"

"Five Actual, this is FDC, we read you loud and clear," Joanna Bellmore declared from her seat at the radio.

"Roger that, we are six klicks out and approaching fast."

"Six klicks out and approaching fast. Solid copy." She paused. *"Theiss has you on GBOSS."*

As the towed guns came through the gate, headlights flickered on, halogen-light beams splitting through the darkness. Hondo knew that Nealen wouldn't be interested in tactical shenanigans.

Thou art not paid for thy methods Nealen had preached. *Thou art paid for thy results.*

And results, in this case, was getting three howitzers fire-capped, preparatory to laying down The Hate.

As the gun trucks moved into their respective positions, men boiled out of the back, shouting commands in the darkness, heaving and pulling the multiple tons of steel about. Pintles slammed shut, free of their loads. Commands went up to the ground guides. Men sprinted, leading their trucks out of the way.

Barrels swung about as the gunners called out corrections to the men gathered around their respective muzzles, shoving and pulling to find the correct azimuth of fire. Each of the three guns would be established to cover a different arc of fire. Six was pointed northward. Five would be aimed southwest, while Four had been set for southeast.

Heavy bases set down lightly, followed by the remainder of the system, to retain their lay on the azimuth of fire. Shovels smashed into the earth, picks rising, only to fall with enthusiasm. Dust filled the air, choking and blinding men as they dashed about.

"It's a wonder they don't lose their heads," Fitzsimmons admitted as she watched the madness in motion, listening to the shouted orders and thrown curses.

"Give 'em time, you might be right," Stirling suggested.

"Not tonight, not my Marines," Harper assured as he stomped up to join them.

"Welcome back, leftenant, enjoy your drive through the country?" Mayne asked.

Harper spat a wad of spent chew into the dirt. "Always a pleasure to count the varying shades of brown and camel shit one encounters in the Northwest Frontier, Sarn't Major."

"You even said that with a straight face," Stirling remarked. "We'll make an Englishman out of you yet, young man."

"Sorry, Sarn't Major, but "God Save the Queen just isn't as pretty as "Kelly, the Boy from Killane" or "Roddy McCorley.""

Stirling smiled at the jibe. "That's why we kept the best part of Ireland for ourselves."

"If you say so, Sarn't Major, though it does make me question your taste in whisky."

"Nothing wrong with Bushmills."

"Aside from all the dirt."

"Hush up you two, yer as bad as schoolboys on holiday," Natasha commanded.

"Yes, ma'am!" they chirped.

If she noticed Harper begin humming a particular tune, she said nothing. Not even when Stirling began to join him for the second verse of "Little Armalite."

Already men were running up from the ammo bunker, green shells in their arms as they ran with the heavy burdens, slamming them onto ready boards and spinning fuzes around in the noses.

"Ready on Five!" The radio Harper had on his belt squawked.

"Five is Ready!" FDC intoned.

"Ready on Six!"

"Ready on Four!"

"Four is ready, the battery is ready."

Harper held up his radio. "Gunline! To the rear of piece! Fall in!"

"What are you going to do, have them start shooting?" Fitzsimmons asked.

"No, ma'am. Staff Sergeant, you ready to inspect Guns Platoon?" Harper asked in a tone far too cheerful for the tableau.

"Absolutely, sir," Nealen said with equal enthusiasm.

"Ma'am, Sarn't Major, care to join me?" Harper invited.

"Are you sure?" Fitzsimmons asked.

"It'll please the boys, ma'am," Nealen assured.

"I understand, lead on."

"Yes, ma'am."

Around them, Sgt House and his wire dogs were busy running reels of wire, stringing up the guns appropriately. Two lines per gun. The first was for the field phones each gun possessed. The second ran to a computer terminal mounted directly on the howitzer, to pass and receive fire mission data, all run back to a spider box, and thence to the FDC.

Lance Corporal Hankins came behind all of these, ready to hook up the generators he'd positioned earlier in the day. These would provide power to the guns' electronic suites. Fitzsimmons didn't quite understand how or why a cannon needed electronics.

Just that it was.

What they had said before they left rang in her ears with profound fury. "No more dead girls."

God bless the vicious bastards. Jesus knows you can't take half of them home to meet some girls' parents, but by God they're exactly the heartbreakers and lifetakers I need right now, Fitzsimmons told herself as she walked past them, wondering what would become of their rashness.

Nealen explained what he and Harper were looking for as they examined each gun, to verify their status as fire-capped.

"We'll check Five last," Harper declared at length.

"Weren't they first?" she asked, curious at his declaration.

"Yes ma'am, but they're my adjusting piece," Harper said as if that explained everything.

"Your show, carry on Marine."

Four had two rounds improperly fused, and Six forgot their swab bucket. These items were corrected even before the inspecting party had fully stepped off either gun and the Marines returned to where they could be easily seen.

"Now for Five," Nealen declared.

"What is the adjusting piece?" Fitzsimmons asked. "I did familiarization with supporting fires in officer training, but that was ages ago."

"Everybody has a point of reference," Nealen explained. "In the artillery and mortars, an adjusting piece does that. FDC will adjust everybody else's position based off the individual guns' relation to the relative position of the adjusting piece and its fall of shot. The adjusting piece is expected to be the fastest, most accurate piece in the platoon or battery."

"Ah. And how does one get that way?"

"Knock-knock Gun Five," Harper called out as he held up a hand.

"Enter and be recognized!" Cassidy replied.

Careful to step over the slit trenches each wire dog was now back filling, Harper looked toward the Captain, a devilish smile on his dirt-covered features.

"In Sergeant Cassidy's case, ma'am, he and Kramer run gun drills with a ruthlessness I find admirable."

"Thank you, sir. Appreciate the compliment," Cassidy drawled out.

Looking over the gun, Fitzsimmons saw nothing out of the ordinary. It was only when Mayne elbowed her that she noticed something different.

"Look ma'am, the spades are already run all the way in."

Thinking back she remembered how on the other two guns, the heavy spades were barely biting into the stiff red earth. Here the spades were so far back they had fully depressed the shock absorber mechanism each possessed in the base of the trails. The blades were also completely backfilled.

"Cassidy, why did you do this?" she asked.

"Locks the gun into place, just like if you were tucking a rifle into your shoulder ma'am."

"Won't that stress the recoil mechanism harder?"

"Not enough to notice, ma'am."

"But what if it breaks? What will you do then?" she pressed.

"Before then, we'll have had the barrel swapped and the ordnance officer will let us know if the gun is still good to shoot."

"That's a dangerous game, Marine."

"Not as dangerous as losing, ma'am," he declared with certainty.

"Leftenant Harper, I think that finally explains it," Fitzsimmons declared.

"Explains what, ma'am?" Harper asked curiously.

"You Marines are so cavalier about everything. Especially when it comes to dying."

"Yes ma'am."

"You care more about winning the fight, than anything else."

"Yes ma'am."

"Do you really think you can win every fight you get into?"

"Sir, didn't we have a conversation like this back in Zaranj?" Nealen asked.

"Do believe we did, Staff Sergeant," Harper assured.

"Would you mind explaining it to the captain, sir? You say it so well."

"Of course, Staff Sergeant, that's what I get paid the big bucks for," Harper said cheerfully as he looked on proudly at his Marines. "Ma'am. Soldiers in the Army are part of a martial organization, likewise the US Navy. The Air Force vacillates between a country club and a corporation. Sure their winter uniforms make them resemble the Waffen-SS, but have you ever seen them in the summer? They look like a Good Humor Ice Cream Man convention."

"Not if it's Air Force women, sir!" Kramer added.

"Praise be unto Chesty Puller for Air Force women. Truly they are divine, sir!" Cassidy said helpfully.

"Amen," the Marines intoned as one.

"Just when I think I've got you lads straight you come up with some new crap I hadn't considered yet," Fitzsimmons observed.

"It's a feature. May I continue?" Harper said.

"Please. I'm enjoying this."

"Our Marine Corps really is a cult. Likely the last true war cult in existence. These are the worshippers," he gestured proudly at his Marines. "My NCOs are the shamans. They teach the marines how to march and shoot and fight."

"Which makes you what?" Natasha asked.

"I am their war chief. I show them where to die."

"Is that why you're so reckless?" she persisted.

"It only looks reckless. We weigh the odds then throw ourselves into what we do, ma'am. Because if we win, what danger remains? Every action we take in the name of our Corps is what we shall be judged by, both the old men who've gone before us and the next generation of boots who come after us. If we're hard on the privates and lances, it's because we want them to be every bit as angry, motivated, and capable."

"Give him one!" Nealen barked.

"Oorah!" the Marines shouted.

"Guns, bring it in on me! Sit, kneel, bend," Harper ordered.

They scrambled to obey and he counted heads. Satisfied, he smiled.

"Beginning tomorrow morning, when we go "Stand To" every Guns Marine runs straight here. The walls will be manned by everybody else. I want you all ready to drop steel on target, understood?"

"Errr!"

"Gun chiefs, you will commence gun drills on your own time and determination. Train to standard. Time on deck is twenty-two fifty. Rack out and get some sleep. Cassidy, Doc Knighton says we need to have a chat in the med tent."

\#

Hondo looked down at the battered body of his assistant, slowly flexing his hands as he struggled to remain calm.

"Who. Did. This," he stated flatly.

"It was Afghans, Sergeant," Clarke declared. "Three of them. Pilsen heard them attacking me and came running."

"Why didn't he shoot them?" Harper asked politely.

"They were right on top of me. One of 'em he had his, his —" Abigail struggled for words and Harper gently waved a hand.

"Say no more, I understand," Harper replied.

"Urrrrrr," Pilsen groaned, stirring on the cot.

"He's alive!" Abigail screamed, rushing to wrap her arms around her rescuer.

"Why. Shouting. Too. Bright." Pilsen wheezed.

"Easy bubba, you got thrown for one," Cassidy said, holding a water bottle to his lips.

"Ribs. Hurt." The smaller man winced as the female private released him from her tight hug.

"They're going to. Doc's got something for the pain," Hondo said proudly.

"Who attacked you?" Harper asked.

"A. N. P." His eyes squeezed shut. "Shit. Hurts. To talk." His eyes flashed back open. "Clarke! Where's Clarke?" he demanded, trying to rise from the cot. "Can't let. Hurt her. Too nice. Bird."

"I'm right here, Pilsen," Clarke assured soothingly.

At the sound of her voice, he sank back into the cot.

"They hurt. You, love?"

"No. Thanks to you." She squeezed his hand, "You saved me."

"Doc, you gonna keep 'em overnight in here?" Mayne asked from the back of the tent.

"That's what we'd planned," Knighton admitted. "He's not showing any signs of concussion, but it keeps him close by just in case."

"Good man. If it's alright with you, I'd like Private Clarke to remain here as well, just for the night."

"Sounds fantastic, you good with that,Doc Gnem?" Knighton asked.

"Fine by me."

"I'll have their bedding brought over here," Mayne declared. He moved toward the door, stopped.

"Leftenant Harper, sir, would you care to join me in the mess?"

"I'll be along in a few."

"Understood, sir."

"Chef?" Pilsen coughed as the others trooped out of the infirmary.

"Aye bubba, I'm still here."

"Sorry. I. Lost. I'll. Do. Better. Next. Time."

"You did just fine bubba. You did enough to make the difference. Ain't nothing more I could ask of you."

Reaching over he gently tousled the boy's hair and tucked him. Standing, he moved out of the medical tent, trying to contain his emotions.

Hondo thought he could hear something howling far off in the darkness. A cry which repeated itself. A predator's clarion hunting call.

"Yeah." He growled. "You and me both."

Without looking toward the medical bunker, Hondo lengthened his stride as he went looking for something to cut the road dust from his mouth.

This gets resolved tonight.

One absent hand brushed the hilt of his facón, tucked into the small of his back like he'd learned ages ago down in the Brazilian Pampas.

Just like back home.

A shotgun-blasted memory spoke from years past and he smiled, fondly remembering the smell of gunpowder whilst he had handled a man's business in the old way.

\#

"Pistol, my friend, what ails you?" Hondo asked as he stepped inside the mess and began making up a batch of hot chocolate for himself. He was thirsty and warm chocolate seemed like a good idea right then.

"Many things, Cassidy my friend," Pistol replied. "Right now, Leftenant Balcombe is explaining why we ought to call the redcaps. Have 'em haul off the accused in irons and sort it out that way."

"You disagree?"

"You know how they treat the word of a woman around here," Pistol snarled. "I'm not keen on putting Clarke in the crosshairs of an Afghani court over this."

"Aye. There is that," Cassidy conceded, looking toward where the Staff and O were holding a highly animated meeting.

I know how far I'd go for one of mine. I also know the measure of the man standing by me Hondo ruminated as he began swallowing hard, consuming his drink before looking back to his fellow sergeant.

"Pistol, why don't we go for a walk?" Cassidy suggested.

"Where shall we walk, my fine American friend?" Pistol asked.

"I believe we should take our stroll around the corner, my fine British friend. The night is dark, and we ought to do as Sergeants must, ensuring that every guard is properly manning their respective posts in a proper military manner."

"And if we find any man lacking?" Pistol asked.

"Then we shall punish them in accordance with the law," Cassidy declared.

"I find myself entirely in agreement," Pistol replied sonorously.

If the gathered Staff and Officers noticed either man leaving the mess, they said nothing.

Harper, however, noticed. He'd gone for a walk through the scene of the crime. He had known from the get-go there would only be one way to rectify this matter. That he had not gone further into the mess than the doorway yet was due to his own patience.

He saw Cassidy exit, followed by Pistol, to be joined by two more figures, also in Marine Desert Marpat. All four of whom were checking weapons as he approached.

"Evening, sir," Samuels declared.

Kramer fiddled with a sling strap while Cassidy withdrew his long knife from its customary sheath in the small of his back, making a show out of checking the edge.

"Evening gents, going for a tour of the posts?" Harper asked.

"Yes, sir. Figure we should do that to help out Corporal Jimenez," Hondo explained.

"Splendid. I'm going to join you," Harper declared.

"You don't have to do that, sir," Kramer said politely.

"There's a lot in life I don't have to do," Harper admitted. "Some things though, I do for the spite of it all."

"Sounds like something an Irishman would say, beggin' your pardon, sir," Pistol said politely.

"None taken, I'm from a little town called Philadelphia. If the family history is to be believed, a mad Irishman got on a fast boat to America steps ahead of questions about a burnt-down tax office," Harper admitted.

"Ah," Pistol said.

"While there are many officers I would not wish to walk with, Pistol, this officer is worth having around," Cassidy admitted.

"Does he Kipple?"

Harper cleared his throat.

"Now this is the Law of the Jungle — as old and as true as the sky;

And the Wolf that shall keep it may prosper, but the Wolf that shall break it must die.

As the creeper that girdles the tree-trunk the Law runneth forward and back —

For the strength of the Pack is the Wolf, and the strength of the Wolf is the Pack.

"There's two of you lot that are civilized!" Pistol said in admiration.

"I resent that implication," Cassidy waved deprecatingly.

Jerking his head toward the ANP compound, the Marines took Hondo's cue and slowly began drifting in that direction, Kramer in the lead, the former combat engineer scanning for any sign of booby traps.

That the drift so happened to look like an infantry wedge, with sergeants holding down the flanks, James Harper chalked up purely to coincidence.

"Now, how will we know which of the miscreant lads is our ne'er-do-well?" Pistol asked, addressing the task at hand once the shadows had totally enveloped them.

"There was blood all over the shop where the attack took place. Based on their injuries, little of it belonged to our people," Harper interjected. "How many ANP do we have on hand right now."

"Patrol went out before we left. Those guys usually leave a small fire watch. Patrol should be back tomorrow, unless they came back early."

"Not a chance," Pistol said. "Inshallah time is in effect." He looked to Harper. "You went looking at Clarke's shop, sir?"

"Irishmen becoming cops is a tradition in America," Harper explained. "I have three uncles who are homicide detectives, and a brace of cousins in various departments. A man learns a lot when business gets discussed over drinks and cigars after dinner."

"Very well."

Kramer held up a hand, pausing them in their movement. Samuels started to speak, then paused, sniffing the air.

"You smell it, Samuels?" Kramer asked.

"Aye. Cassidy, take a big ol' whiff of that and tell me what you think that is," Pistol interjected before the brooding man could speak.

Cassidy breathed in. Closed his eyes. Unconsciously flexed his hands as he reached for the pistol holstered on his leg, smoothly drawing it before he reached down to his left hip, drawing the facon he kept there. In the semi-lit evening gloom, little of the blackened blade could be seen save its keen edge.

"It smells like somebody over there is busy chasing the dragon," he admitted as he worked through his emotions.

"So it's not just me?" Kramer asked.

"Not at all," Cassidy growled. "I can understand weed, and hash to some degree. But I've never understood heroin."

"Neither have I," Pistol confessed.

"Horse. Smack. Dirty Dragon. It's all the same — utter poison." Cassidy's scowl deepened as he looked towards the ANP's camp. "I got used to smelling it on my mother. Sir."

"How long has it been, devil dog?" Harper asked politely.

"Almost twenty-three years."

"Well, let's go see what we find. Possession and use of heroin is a violation of not only Afghan national law, but General Order Number One. And we are in a combat zone. Which means such actions are punishable by a commissioned officer acting in accordance with the laws of war and military discipline."

Four feral grins, eyes blazing in the starlit darkness, met his, then turned to present their weapons as they advanced towards the compound where music played and lazy smoke drifted out through a window.

\#

"Tolliver, you seen the LT? I could've sworn he was supposed to come join us," Nealen asked.

"No, staff sergeant, I got no idea," Tolliver replied.

"Looking for me, Nealen?" Harper asked from the doorway. He stepped through, flanked by Cassidy, and Pistol.

Nealen frowned.

There's no way. No, no he did not. Absolutely no way.

"Yes, sir, I was," Nealen said.

"Well, here I am. Got anything for me?" Harper asked.

"Not really, sir."

"Understood. In that case, I'm gonna go rack out. It's late and I imagine we all need some sleep."

"Yes, sir."

Harper clapped a hand on his shoulder as he passed by and spoke quietly. "Don't worry about taking out the trash, tonight at least. I found a couple NCOs to help me carry it to the burn pit."

I'll bet you did, Nealen mentally scowled.

There was no need for the man to get that involved with an issue easily handled at levels so much lower! It infuriated him immensely.

Shut up another part of his head declared. *You're just jealous you didn't get to mete out justice with him. Besides, who else could you have trusted to handle this matter correctly, Jacob Hudson? Don't kid yourself.*

"Oh, very well, sir," Nealen said politely.

"When the ANP get back, escort their platoon commander over. I want a word with him," Harper directed.

"Yes, sir. Also, we'll want his driver too," Nealen said.

"Voice of experience, Staff Sergeant?" Harper added. "Thank you, I appreciate it. You've done fantastic work here, and you need to know that the entire chain of command, up to division is singing your praises."

"Thank you, sir."

"You're welcome, you've earned it."

"Sir, is everything all right?" Stirling asked from several feet away.

"Absolutely, Sarn't Major. Myself and two sergeants took it upon ourselves to walk the posts and make sure all is in good order. I would be remiss in my duties if I did not ensure the good order and discipline of all my men."

Stirling bowed his head politely. "I understand. Tell the truth I've been a bit remiss in that. Thank you, sir."

"Of course, Sarn't Major, we're all in this together."

"Hey Pistol, you ever heard a song called *Copperhead Road*?" Cassidy asked in a mood Nealen found almost frighteningly cheerful after the last week of churlish surliness.

"Can't say as I have. What's it about?"

"Running moonshine, a general disregard for the law, and the idea that tax men don't need to come back from wherever they go. I think you'll like it," Kramer suggested as Cassidy hit 'play.' A chorus of bagpipes filled the room for a moment, then gave way to pounding drums and Cassidy began to sing, followed by the voices of several other Marines who knew the lyrics.

#

Sylvie walked into the chow hall, thirsty and hungry in the early AM. She'd had a late night settling the birds back down, had to be back up early, and didn't want to deal with people much. To her surprise, Cassidy was not in the chow hall, but Sarn't Major was, bustling about with getting the coffee and tea service going.

"Good morning to you, Lyons. Sleep well?"

"Nothing that can't be cured by sleep in a proper bed. What are you doing up this early, Sarn't Major?"

"I told Chef to take it easy this morning, and Sergeants generally do what I tell them to. Besides, it's breakfast rats this week, something simple enough even I can do it."

"If you say so, Sarn't Major."

"I do."

She paused, wondering how to proceed.

"What are we going to do about Clarke and Pilsen?" Sylvie asked.

"Beyond proper trauma care and counseling, nothing." He sipped from his styrofoam cup. "No need for us to do anything."

"Why?"

"Think back to when they showed up."

"I was on post then."

"Getting an eyeful of American diplomacy?"

"Something like that."

"When they first arrived, Nealen promised he'd bury any of his men who laid a hand on you girls."

"Oh."

"The Captain and I were there for it. 'It's a big damn desert and you won't be missed.' Colder than Brecon in winter, that one." Mayne set his mug down.

"Now, if he's willing to do that with his own troops, to enforce good order and discipline, what do you think he'll do with foreign troops who do such a thing?"

Sylvie contemplated this, then looked at Mayne. "He's likely to enforce the rules the same amongst them."

"Aye. And what man would do that, or allow it, if he didn't have his troops and officer backing him?"

"Yeah. Huh. What makes you so sure the matter's closed?" Lyons asked.

"You should've listened to the song Cassidy started playing last night after he came back from 'walking the posts' with Pistol and Harper. It started with bagpipes and moved on to talking about getting chased by the police for the sale of all sorts of contraband. Quite lovely, really. Right before it though, Harper told Nealen that he'd found some NCOs to help him take out the trash."

"Oh." Sylvie blinked. "Why are you turning a blind eye to it?"

"Who says I am?" Stirling asked mildly.

"But what if we get investigated?" Sylvie pressed.

Mayne shrugged. "Option One: I heard two Sergeants took an evening walk around the interior perimeter, performing the customary duties of a Sergeant of the Guard. Records indicate that Sergeant Pistol was in fact Sergeant of the Guard last night. I heard a Platoon Commander joining them, ostensibly to check his personnel on post and ensure that the NCOs are maintaining standards."

"And Option Two?"

"There was a grave violation of criminal law, which will require a court trial sure to become an international scandal, and Private Clarke will get dragged in front of cameras and posed questions by poncy barristers who want to humiliate her."

Sylvia pondered this. "What happens to Clarke, now?"

"A female Private was injured in an accident. That she is getting counseling on the side for it, in a non-reporting status, is entirely her choice."

His mouth quirked for a moment, shaking his red-silver mustache about.

"Afghan courts are notoriously troublesome. And a good chunk of those ANP lads come from a culture that doesn't recognize courts they can't shovel baksheesh at."

"Won't anybody ask questions?" Sylvie persisted.

"The ANP Platoon Sergeant is likely to tell his Lieutenant to shut up and soldier on. Smart money is that they're from the same tribe. In return, the Lieutenant and the Sergeant will pocket the extra pay for the missing men, with some shared to the platoon mates for their silence. After some time, the Lieutenant will report that the missing men in question have deserted, replacements will be sent down from Kabul and everybody moves along."

"That's very —"

"The hard side of reality, dear girl. Army's full of secrets. We, the non-commissioned officers, are the keepers of the secrets. It's our responsibility to do so with an eye towards preservation of good order and discipline. If I didn't let your lad and Pistol handle business, do you think anybody in our company would be happy with it?"

"No."

"You're right. Which fosters resentment and lack of discipline. The boys would be even more likely to lash out on their own. Can't have the lads being sloppy about such things. And with the Afghanis' disregard for courts or laws, we only have one option to effectively maintain discipline. All armies run on discipline, metaphorically speaking."

"We do?"

"Aye, an army without discipline is just a bloody great mob. Being a professional soldier means being more than a mob."

Mayne stood. "Your lad's young. Impetuous. Stiff-necked as an ox. He needs a mite bit more refining, but by God he'll do. He'll do just fine."

"We're not... That is, we... Um. Yeah."

"Suffer a breakdown in diplomacy?" Mayne asked politely.

"Kind of."

"Ah. I see. And trying to explain this to yet another male is painful."

"Yes."

His eyes were steady at her over the rim of his mug before he set it on the tabletop.

"Never mind trying to go to one's female peers for sympathy, which means explaining how a prime stud is now back on the market. And all the fillies prancing about, God bless their pea-picking little hearts, have no qualms about scoring the king of the herd."

Sylvie grimaced. "Something like that."

"Not that rumors have been running rampant for the last week." He leveled his gaze at her. "Unless you consider throwing a bucket of water at somebody to be tactful and polite."

"I don't know that the Marines have ever heard of tact."

His mustache bounced as he considered her statement. "If I didn't know Nealen or Harper, I'd say that was likely. Which does not change the fact that good communication is an important part of healthy relationships. Take the Colour —"

"Who's taking me where?" Gallagher announced as she stomped in, canteen cup in hand.

"Morning Morgana, I was just imparting some wisdom to the Sergeant here," Mayne nodded.

"Oh good. I've been meaning to do the same," Gallagher declared as she began making a fresh cup of tea. "I don't suppose you could use your influence on a certain man to quit making everything so damnably hot!"

"It has gotten a tad warm of late," Mayne declared drolly.

"Men should be spicy, not meat," Morgana snarled. "If I wanted my tongue seared off, I'd ask you to break out a torch and go to work!"

"About that..." Sylvie hesitated.

"We may have a problem, Morgana," Stirling declared.

Her eyes did not leave Sylvie as she spoke calmly. "The rumors are true, Stirling?"

"Without knowing which rumors you're speaking of, I can neither confirm nor deny, old girl. You know how that goes."

"That somebody stomped out of the mess last Tuesday, soaked head to toe in wash water. And hasn't been seen in the mess since."

"It appears so."

"And that nobody has been able to pry out of either party what happened, or why. Except that Cassidy has reclaimed his position as King Asshole the First. And a certain Sergeant has reverted to being the frosty bitch we saw when she first came to the unit."

"That too."

"Anything you'd care to add, Sergeant?" Morgana acidly asked.

"I don't understand men. Much less that damn Marine!" Sylvie swore.

"Well, in that case, let's all sit down and have a chat. Stirling, would you be dear and lock the doors, please?"

"Be happy to."

As he did so, Morgana made an additional cup of tea. Then, grabbing both, sat down at a table and indicated for Sylvie to do the same.

"Let's start at the beginning. Tell me how you and that damn Marine got together. Don't forget the juicy bits." She smiled at the surprise on Sylvie's face. "What? I enjoy good drama now and then. I'm old after all, not celibate."

Slowly, Sylvie rehearsed the story of their meeting, all the times Cassidy had cooked for her, building the gym and lifting together. The morning chats and walks together to deliver chow to the guard posts. Through it all, Morgana continued to listen and Mayne refilled their tea cups.

"Now that we're both mad at each other, it seems like a complete waste," Sylvie admitted.

"You're right. And wrong. All at once."

Sylvie's face screwed up as she stared at Gallagher.

"Huh? How?"

"He jumped to the extreme response. Not smart, kind of not acceptable. But not surprising. Think about it — the Marines truly believe that everything out here is going to try killing them. They also believe they can win if they respond hard enough and quick enough to kill that thing first."

"If you think she's kidding, I watched Leftenant Harper tell the Captain how they are the last true war cult."

Morgana chewed on this information. "Ya know, he's probably right."

"I was afraid you'd say that," Sylvie admitted.

Morgan shrugged. "I'm not inclined to say they're wrong. Some of them really live it too. Tolliver. Cassidy. Nealen. Pretty certain Harper does too."

"I am starting to think Cassidy suffers from delusions of grandeur," Stirling admitted.

"He is a delusion of grandeur," Sylvie declared sourly.

Morgana pointed out the window toward the Marine's space in the FOB. "Tommy Taliban thought shooting mortars at us was a smart idea. We have cannons now. If they're stupid enough to keep shooting, our lads are going to rip their world apart."

Stirling chuckled at this.

"Something funny, Stirling?"

"Just remembering the last time I saw artillery in action. Iraq. Brand new Corporal on my second hitch. Hell it was my second deployment. Evil bastards were sitting in buildings all around us, had our convoy pinned down and no way to say boo." He set his mug on the table.

"It's a nasty experience being under heavy machine gun fire. I don't miss Dishkas at all. This American voice pops up on the radio, ask for the coordinates of the surrounding buildings, and our position. Then he tells us to wait. As if we're about to dash off for high tea with her Majesty right then!"

"Good God that sounds just like them," Morgana declared.

"Doesn't it? Anywho, we're taking it in the teeth when there's this roaring sound like a freight train tearing through the sky. Next thing I remember is explosions, all around us. When the dust settled a while later, four buildings were gone. The Americans dropped enough ordnance on those buildings they were blasted down to the foundations. We gathered up our wounded, and nobody bothered us again the entire way home." He sipped his mug. "Matter of fact, nobody bothered us again for a month."

"They can be a little excessive," Sylvie admitted.

"They have a baseline which starts at 'fight with everybody' and runs straight to 'The Almighty knows His own.'"

"Eh," Sylvie winced. "Yeah."

"That isn't necessarily healthy. Especially in the long-term."

"I can see that," Sylvie said.

"Now, how long have they been here, on our base?" Gallagher asked.

"I don't know," Sylvie confessed.

"Just shy of three months. That's quite a bit of time to learn about a man and what will set him off." Gallagher glanced at Stirling. "Don't you dare say it."

"I hear nothing," Stirling chirped.

"Sure. Right." She looked back to Sylvie. "Now, you may not know this, but those Marines are always looking at everybody else and how they fight. They do it analytically."

"I hadn't."

"Remember the night we watched '300'? The screaming and chest thumping?"

"I can't forget it."

"Good — that's how they view themselves. They expect others to fight them. The Marines are always analyzing how people do stuff, especially as it pertains to fighting. Cassidy recognizes that the bastard son of a donkey running those mortars is good. If Cassidy wants to win that fight, he's got to be at least that much better than them."

"Oh."

"In our profession, this is known as having a healthy respect for your enemy."

"Huh."

"Now that we've gotten through all that, consider what you called him," Stirling reminded. "Traitor, was it?"

"Yes."

"If you were a man, you'd have caught a right hook for saying that. And a left or three if that didn't do the job."

"I'd say you were crazy, but the last three months have shown otherwise."

"You're learning. Good," Morgana declared.

"Remember when him and Pistol first met?" Gallagher asked.

"Uh-huh."

"Just before that, McSweeney had decided to run his mouth."

"Oh my God. McSweeney's a twig!" Sylvie declared.

"If he'd kept running his mouth, we'd probably have gotten to watch Cassidy break him like a damn twig. That fool owes Pistol his life."

"It would almost have been worth it," Sylvie said deliberately.

"Some men take themselves seriously," Stirling continued. "Think about it — what does that man read? Kipling, Cornwell. Old westerns. Hell he brought copies of biographies on William Marshal and El Cid."

"Did he really?" Gallagher asked.

"Knights. Paladins. Flawed as he is, it's what he desires to be," Mayne said.

"I spit on all of that," Sylvie said, with mounting realization.

"Yeah. You did," Gallagher declared.

"More than that, have you asked about his family at all?"

"Beyond what he's said about living with his uncle, no."

"I jogged Nealen and Kramer one night about it, while you two were canoodling in the kitchen," Gallagher admitted, causing Sylvie to blush. "Don't tell me you weren't doing otherwise girly. I saw him giving you the foot massage. I know very good and well where your head was at by the time he got done."

"How?"

"He forgot to block off one of the windows completely."

"Oh," Sylvie admitted with a blush.

"'Oh' is right." Morgana held thumb and forefinger wide apart. "I was slightly jealous of you right then."

"It was a really, really good foot massage," Sylvie admitted.

"Your masseuse's mother was a habitual drug user who turned to prostitution and trafficking heroin."

"Bloody Hell," Sylvie swore.

"Yes. Hell is a good way to describe growing up in that environment. When he was seven, she got arrested after killing two customers. One of the witnesses was an undercover copper. The other was Hondo."

Sylvie's mouth fell open. "Oh my God."

"He watched it all happen. The judge sent her up for twenty five, no possibility of parole."

"So she's still in?."

"Aye. He hasn't seen her since."

"Christ in Heaven, what an awful mess."

"His uncle, the one who sent us that container?"

"Uh huh."

"That uncle took him in. Cassidy's childhood is ugly. He doesn't let people in without good reason."

"People like Kramer."

"Exactly. Those two have deployment time and more years besides together. Kramer is the closest thing he has to a brother."

"So him being King Asshole is a survival mechanism?"

"More or less. His every waking moment is spent proving to all creation that he is more than simply the son of a drug-dealing whore. I'll bet he's halfway to a degree already," Stirling explained.

"If somebody gave him the right push, he'd make a decent officer," Morgana suggested.

"I hear a 'but' to that," Sylvie added.

"Think bigger. Five, six centuries ago, that's a man who carves a kingdom out for himself with a good sword and a bunch of loyal retainers following his banners," Stirling said.

"I never thought of him that way," Sylvie confessed.

"It gets easier when you've the benefit of years of hindsight, like myself or the Colour. You have to learn to read people in this profession, or you'll never make it out alive."

"He needs polish," Morgana added. "Polish and good craftsmanship cover a multitude of sins."

"You think I can do that?" Sylvie said slowly.

"It's a possibility," Stirling admitted gently.

Morgana cleared her throat. "Returning to the original topic, you need to understand that he let you in. He made himself vulnerable to you."

"And I used that to hurt him."

"Uh-huh. To be clear, that does not absolve him of overreacting or being stupid. You both need to sit down and apologize to each other."

Sylvie made a face.

"Look girly, I'm not saying drop to your knees and give him a blowie!" Morgana declared.

"Thank God. I don't know how," Sylvie confessed.

"Collier could teach you," Stirling suggested.

Gallagher choked on her tea.

"Really?" she demanded when she could regain her composure.

Stirling shrugged dismissively. "She keeps Shockley happy. Could probably make a bad country song like your lad and his mates are always listening to, about it."

"Dicked down in Dishu," Sylvie suggested wittily.

This time, Morgana Gallagher had her mouth full of tea when Sylvie's comment registered. She snorted tea across the table in a violent explosion and Stirling fell out of his seat laughing.

"You people are all going to be the death of me!" Gallagher moaned, rubbing her face with a napkin. "Seriously, black tea hurts going out your nose."

"At least I haven't had to explain my family to him," Sylvie grumbled.

"You mean your grandfather, the Earl Lyons of Broseley?" Stirling asked innocently.

"Him." Sylvie's brow furrowed. "Wait. How do you know about him?"

"How could we not?" Stirling asked. "It was a concern for a while that you'd use your familial connections as some will, to get out of work."

"Fortunately Colour Baker over at Hobart speaks very highly of you. Told me I'd be a damned idiot if I didn't help you get your third stripe," Morgana said cheerfully.

"Good man, Colour Baker. Army needs more like him," Stirling agreed. "Now, as to the matter at hand — you and Cassidy do need to at least have a proper sit down."

"Okay," Sylvie admitted. "I can do that."

"Just wait till after I've gotten ahold of him, with Nealen. He needs to know he screwed up too," Stirling explained.

"I can wait. And about my family?"

"What about them?"

"Do I have to tell him?"

"If the relationship survives, it's probably a good idea to explain that your family is worth a healthy amount," Morgana said carefully.

Sylvie put her head in her hands. "Shoot me now," she groaned.

"What's the matter, aside from the money?" Stirling asked.

"My aunts," Sylvie snarled. "The darlings of the society pages."

"We all have our cross to bear. Yours are named 'Patricia,' 'Delphine,' and 'Eloise,' as found in the society pages," Gallagher teased.

"The nice thing about being here is not listening to them prattle on about what they're going to do once they inherit the title," Sylvie admitted.

"You aren't the inheritor?"

"Nope."

"Is that why you're in the Army?"

Sylvie shook her head negatively. "I wanted to prove I could make it on my own, without the money. Without being somebody's bimbo. Whether I retire from the Army or go into private business for myself, it'll be because I chose it."

"That's fair. And well done on your part."

"Thank you."

"Now, let's get where we need to be. There's a mite of work still to be done," Gallagher directed.

Chapter 28

Look What The Cat Dragged In!

"Chef," Gnem acknowledged when Cassidy stepped into the medical tent.

"How's he doing, Doc?" Cassidy asked Gnem.

Gnem shook his head side to side as he glanced at his charge.

"Still weak. They really worked his ribs over."

"Sounds about right for that pack of animals," Cassidy growled.

"Yeah. He'll be slow going for a long minute."

Sitting down on the sandbag bench, Cassidy began to drink from a water bottle he'd shoved previously into his thigh pocket.

"Everything alright? Pistol asked as he finished drawing on his cigarette and threw the butt into an empty powder canister.

"Sort of," Cassidy admitted. "Right now, all I want is five more hours of sleep."

"I hear you. Let me know if you need hands in the kitchen."

"Will do."

"And Hondo?"

"Yeah, Hugh?"

"Thanks for taking a walk with me earlier."

"That's what friends do for each other."

"Aye, so it is. My glory was I had such friends."

#

"Commander, our source within the compound missed their check in."

"They may not be available," Saeed suggested.

"Perhaps, still better that we should keep an eye on such irregularities."

"Yes it is."

Given all that had been forwarded to them by allies in various locales, along with the fighters who had managed to evade American efforts and make it here, Saeed Musafazi felt much better about the odds he faced.

"How soon will we be ready to strike?" he asked his subordinates.

"Within a week, no more than that, Inshallah."

"The Emir gives us news which bodes well for our operations here."

"News from the Emir?" Shamil asked his chief.

"Indeed, Shamil. It seems the Americans and their British lackeys have grossly underestimated the perversity of their politicians."

Shamil smiled.

"How fortunate for us."

"Yes, now get moving. We have work to do."

\#

Elsewhere, a young police lieutenant and his sergeant were sitting in their vehicle, considering their options.

"The Americans are not happy, Uncle," Lieutenant Nasozai stated.

"No kidding. Really? What gave it away?" Sergeant Nasozai replied.

"Wouldn't have been the man playing with a sword in his lap," the younger man declared sardonically.

"Nope. Not at all,"

"So what do we do now?"

"For at least the next month, we do nothing. Except pocket the pay of those four worthless swine."

"I like this." the lieutenant said even as he bitterly punched the dash of his dusty patrol vehicle.

"What ails you, nephew?"

"I'd like a turn with one of the British houris —"

"So say we all."

"I don't blame the men for doing so either. Though I severely doubt even a British houri would so much as glance at those unwashed and uneducated morons."

"Also true."

"But have the sense to do it from a position of strength, Allah dammit! Not like rats hiding in the shadows. This is easy duty! Just be patient, take your time, and make the best use of this posting. Why do the handless swine not understand this?"

"That, I cannot say," his Uncle mused. "Though you are correct."

"I suspect we should stay on patrol at least for the next few weeks," Lieutenante Nasozai sighed as he relented. "It would keep those trigger-happy Americans from taking aim at us with everything they have available. Including those damn cannons they seem to have acquired."

"I like the sound of that a great deal, oh nephew mine."

"I thought you would say that."

"Your concern is noted. And appreciated."

The lieutenant drank tepid water from a bottle he'd grabbed whilst passing through the Western portion of the FOB. "Let's go tell the men how their comrades decided to return home."

"Indeed. And to leave the westerners alone."

\#

"What's gone wrong now?" Nealen asked as he and his section chiefs stepped inside the CP. The room was already full with every other NCO in the company.

"No idea," Harper replied. "Sergeant Major says the Captain got a call on the sat phone and only came out of the privacy booth to hand him a note calling for us before she went back inside and finished her conversation."

"Well. Damn."

The Marines took seats against a wall as Cassidy ambled in.

"Cassidy, if you ever decide combat arms is too exciting, I'll bet we could get you hooked up to become an Aide for a General," Harper offered.

"Thanks sir, but I like fighting too much to stay away. Besides, Generals do boring trash, and I ain't found a reason to slow down yet."

"What've you got there, the menu for tonight's dinner?"

"Yes sir. It's already sitting in the reefer. Goes in the ovens at fifteen-hundred and by seventeen we're golden."

"What's for dessert?"

"I used up our last load of apples making apple cake. Should go over well with this crowd."

"I like it," Harper said approvingly.

"Lads, lasses, everything has gone to shit," Fitzsimmons announced from the front of the room.

The whole room stared at her unhappy expression, wondering why the pronouncement.

"We were supposed to do this all on our own. No men, no outside help. Just us." Her jaw flexed.

"Now, thanks to those articles in the Times and our two new KIA, the people that sent us here are coming down to investigate us. They'll be here in two weeks. For a full dog and pony show."

"Damned indecent of them," a voice muttered sotto voce.

"I agree. But it's the hand we've been dealt. Take the time today, start looking for what they'd be critical of." Fitzsimmons glanced at Harper and Nealen. "I'm not even going to bother asking you to take down your flag poles."

"Good. Because my Marines can justify it five hundred fifty six ways to hell and gone," Harper assured.

Fitzsimmons' mouth made an expression, almost like she wanted to smile. "I imagine you could. Fragging politicians is still considered bad form though."

"Desert is deep ma'am," Nealen reminded her. "My boys are handy with shovels."

"Excavators? We don't need no stinking excavators," Samuels mockingly stated.

"I believe that's called a war crime," Gallagher suggested gently.

"Not if it's the first time," Harper replied.

"Ma'am, loathe as I am to admit an officer is actually correct, I must confess, I find the Leftenant's logic highly irrefutable," Keating declared.

"You've been hanging out with the Marines way too much, Staff," Balcombe replied.

"Yes, ma'am, it's a vice of mine. Will likely happen again."

"Do we know how many people to expect, ma'am?" Cassidy asked, pencil and notebook at the ready.

"Beyond three MPs?

"Military Policemen?" Nealen asked.

"Oh no, Lord no. Sorry, Ministers of Parliament."

"Politicians. Joy."

"I have no idea if they're bringing aides or reporters or anything else with them. No clue at all."

"So you probably don't know how long they'll be here either, do you?"

"Not at all. Colonel DuBois will be getting back to me about that. They're flying out to speak with him next week."

"We will need that data ma'am, figures into my planning for meals properly. We may need to requisition more supplies."

Fitzsimmons looked toward the hefty Marine. "Let me think on that."

"Yes, ma'am."

There was something in the way he said those words that made Natasha Fitzsimmons extremely cautious.

Because God above knows I need another case of "the leprechauns did it" around here.

\#

There was no music playing in the mess. Nor did Nealen see any sign of his trusty sergeant in the gym. Wandering around surreptitiously, Peter Nealen and Stirling Mayne pondered where he could be.

"Why not just ask for him over the radio?" Stirling suggested.

"Honestly hadn't occurred to me, Sarn't Major," Nealen admitted.

"Five Actual, this is Hogfather. What is your location?"

Seconds trickled by.

"Hogfather, this is Five Actual. I'm in the MCMAP pit."

"Roger that, enroute to your position."

They found him there, on his back, head resting comfortably on a sandbag. He wore only skivvy shorts and PT shoes, his rifle resting nearby.

"Cassidy, what are you doing?" Nealen asked as he sat down nearby, swiftly followed by Mayne.

"Wishing the Taliban didn't suck at fighting, Staff Sergeant," Hondo said absently.

"Why?"

"Easier to die that way."

"Young man, what the hell is going on in your head?" Mayne asked worriedly.

Hondo sat up. "My first battalion, we had three KIA the whole deployment. Three, in nine months."

"Damn."

"Nah, damn is the fact that we've been home almost six years and had eight suicides from that same group of Marines."

Nealen stared at him, considering how to proceed. The Sarn't Major saved him the trouble.

"Cassidy, lad, you're getting stuck inside your head. That's a dangerous place to be," Stirling declared.

"It is, Sarn't Major, I agree. But I just don't care anymore."

"Noted." Stirling looked to Nealen, who nodded in agreement.

"I get the feeling, young man, that you need a chat, without rank," Stirling continued.

Hondo sighed. "It would be appreciated, cuz right now I got no clue what to do."

"Then for the purposes of this moment, he's Peter, I'm Stirling, and you're Hondo. We're three blokes having a talk and I'm going to enjoy a choice cigar while we sit here," Stirling explained.

The Marines waited for him to finish his routine. When he'd lit and taken the first solid inhale, he held the cigar up, basking in the pleasant aroma as the cherry burned merrily.

"At a guess, it's girl trouble," Stirling declared.

Hondo sighed. "Is it obvious?"

"Not really, but I have practice at this thing," Stirling admitted.

"Plus there isn't a good place to handle serious talk of women in barracks," Nealen added.

"I'd have better luck asking the Taliban how to bugger sheep," Hondo admitted.

"True. You'll get the best advice for that from a Welshman," Stirling suggested.

"What do you call a Welshman with a sheep under one arm and a goat under the other?" Hondo asked.

"What?" Nealen replied.

"Bisexual," Hondo deadpanned.

Stirling cracked a smile. "I should leave you, Pistol, Kramer, and a few others in a bar full of gypsies. I could retire off the winnings."

"What do you think of her?" Nealen asked, cautiously trying to get back on track.

"Sylvie?" Hondo said tentatively.

"No you clown, a Playboy centerfold!"

"I've met a bunch, they were all sweethearts."

Nealen pursed his lips and Stirling snickered. "Can't tell if he's taking the piss are ye?"

"With this one, strange things have a way of being true," Nealen sighed.

"Daddy and I were doing an audit of our SoCal location when Hefner asked if we would host a private party, because the Mansion was undergoing renovations right then. I convinced Daddy to let me make the dessert course." Hondo smiled. "The ladies couldn't believe a fifteen year-old knew how to make Black Forest Cake with Italian meringue. They spent the whole night trying to coax the recipe out of me."

"That sounds like a teenage boy's dream come true."

"The ladies were all very nice," Hondo admitted. "I still write to some of them."

"I'm sure," Nealen said drolly. "You have the weirdest luck, Hondo."

Hondo grimaced and Stirling snickered.

"Back to my question, what do you think of Sylvie, Hondo?" Nealen asked.

"I — I feel peace when she's around. Not like when we're in a firefight and my blood's up. I don't feel the need to go punch people in the throat when she's with me. I like having her with me." He made a face. "Least I did until she pissed me off."

"You're on a hair trigger. All the time. Everybody can see that. Much as I hate to say it, I think the stress was getting to you. Just like everybody else here."

"You feel stressed?" Hondo said in shock. "You're normally all icy and business."

"Uh-huh, I just process it differently."

"Oh." He sat back, considering those implications.

"I talked with her," Stirling declared. "Me and Gallagher, together. She didn't realize what she said, when she said it."

"Umm…"

"Nor did she know much about your upbringing." Stirling held up a hand. "Which I understand. But know this lad, couples have to talk about those things. Otherwise it rots the whole relationship."

"I second this, otherwise my wife wouldn't have put up with me deploying all these years," Nealen added.

"Dammit. I loathe talking about her," Hondo spat. "Only good thing she ever did was give birth to me, and even then, I'm amazed she didn't screw that up."

"She still alive?"

"Unfortunately."

"You go visit her or something?" Nealen asked.

"No. I check the prison's website once a month."

"You ever going to visit her?"

Hondo did not respond.

"I see," Stirling said gently. "Heroin trade is a nasty business. Surprised you made it out of there."

"I got lucky that night," Hondo confessed. "Didn't help when I had to testify against her in court."

Both men looked at him dubiously. "You were how old?"

"Seven when she was arrested. Nine when it finally went to court."

"How did she take that?"

Hondo looked far away. "First time? She called me a liar when she took the stand."

"What about the second time?"

"I was ten when she was sentenced. She called me a traitor."

The guilt and personal pain on his face was plain, even in the darkness.

"I've never lost a minute of sleep over dropping some evil raghead dirtbag son of a bitch. Every time they show up in my dreams, I laugh at them. But I still hear her, screaming at me as the bailiffs hauled her away."

"I know stuff like that ain't easy. But you're gonna have to talk about her with Sylvie at some point. That's how you demonstrate trust to a woman. You have to let them inside. You can't keep walls up all the time," Peter said.

"Why?" Hondo asked.

"She'll never truly know you. Or trust you," Peter said patiently.

Hondo sighed, looked around as if hoping some spark of divine intervention would spare him further discussion on that matter.

"But she's so perfect and nice and sweet and– and– and she doesn't deserve my drama."

"She has her own drama too lad." Stirling contemplated his next words carefully. "It's not my place to say all of it, but there's a reason she's so guarded. More than just the idiot from her last unit that tried to groom her." He saw the look on Hondo's face and held up a hand. "Nothing bad. But there's a reason for her manners. Her family's name means something."

Hondo breathed in. "I see."

"Good," Nealen said. "Now see this — you blowing up on her was not the right thing to do. Yeah, in those moments you want to explode on people."

"Uh-huh."

"You can not," Nealen cautioned. "In a committed relationship where two people with different backgrounds are coming together, they have to spend a lot of time learning how to communicate."

"I thought we were," Hondo said quizzically.

"You are, but how long have you been here?" Nealen countered.

"I dunno. Hadn't thought about it," Hondo shrugged.

"Less than a hundred days. Not even four months. You've only scratched the surface of that woman. Granted, that's further than any man prior, but it's still only the surface," Stirling informed him.

"I really screwed up, didn't I?" Hondo asked as the older man's words made it through his depressive funk.

"Yeah. You did."

Hondo buried his head in his hands.

"Hey Hondo, don't beat yourself up too badly," Stirling said politely. "Remember, I talked with her before I came and found you. She feels just as awful about all of this."

"Now I really hate myself," Hondo declared.

"No kidding. So you screwed up. This is the part where you apologize and move on."

Hondo looked up at his platoon sergeant. "How do I do that?"

"That I'm gonna leave to you."

"Dang it. I was hoping you could give me a cheat code for it."

Nealen chuckled. "If only it were that easy. Wouldn't be so many divorces in the world. Tell me something."

"Yes, Staff — Peter?"

"Could you see having a future with her?"

Hondo's shoulders slumped. "If she gave me a chance, yes."

"I wouldn't waste any time if I was in your shoes. We're not gonna be here for much longer."

"I understand."

"Good. Stirling, anything you want to add?" Nealen asked.

"I told her, and I'm telling you. You've got the makings to be a good officer, rough edges and all. Whether or not you make it there is all dependent on you and the choices you make in the next couple years. One of which needs to be real counseling."

Hondo grimaced. "I didn't enjoy the last one."

"So keep trying until you find one you can respect," Stirling declared.

"Do I have to?" Hondo pleaded.

Nealen looked over at his subordinate. "Bubba, we've all got loose screws upstairs. You. Me. My wife. Sylvie. The Captain. Every freaking body. Yours are so far outta tolerance though, that it's making you a danger to yourself more than the enemy."

Hondo frowned. "I don't like that. I like my enemies dead."

"Then I suggest you think real hard about counseling," Stirling told him.

"Yes, Stirling. I will."

"Good lad. I know you'll handle matters appropriately. Just like when you took the trash out the other night." A gleam split the night as Stirling Mayne smiled.

"I wouldn't know anything about that," Hondo calmly declared. "I was simply handling matters as a Sergeant of Marines ought to. That Sergeant Pistol chose to accompany me in the performance of our strict duties simply highlights the extremely positive nature of Anglo-American affairs at this time on Forward Operating Base Bourne."

"Indeed."

"Hondo, I will file a message with the Battalion Medical Officer that you'd like family trauma counseling when we get back. Doc Lizardo should be good about helping with that," Peter said.

"Thank you, Peter,"

"Not a problem, it's my job."

The Sarn't Major stood, dusting himself free of cigar ash. "Excellent. Now, let's be off about it, Staff Nealen. Time to finish walking the posts," Stirling commanded.

"Aye, aye, Sarn't Major."

As both men disappeared into the starlit darkness, Hondo wondered how the hell it had all come to this.

Chapter 29

Could Smell The Whiskey Burning

"How long they been in there?" House asked as he stared at the closed doors of the mess.

"About three hours now," Sergeant Johnson remarked from his seat in the shade.

"Really? Anybody come out?" House asked.

"Once in a while, we'll see a bird come out to hit the head, otherwise, not much. Right now, I'm just keeping an eye on things like Staff Sergeant told us to."

"Think Hondo will really do it?" House asked as he threw a skoal dip into his lip.

"Do what?" Johnson asked.

"Hold the first FOB Bourne chili dog-eating competition."

"Chili dog-eating?" Johnson said excitedly.

"Yeah baby. Said he needed to use up his supply of fresh peppers before they went bad and a proper trailride chili made with fresh goat seemed like the best option."

"Shoot, I ain't had cabrito in a long time," Johnson admitted.

"Right? Sounds delicious to me. Like home."

Both men sighed, wondering about home.

"We're so close I can taste the trip to Whataburger," House declared.

"You mean Braum's?" Johnson suggested, igniting an argument which both men relished.

Seated nearby, where neither Marine could see him, James Harper looked toward the mess, wondering how on earth he'd gotten into this disaster.

Oh, that's right. USMC. U Signed the Motherfracking Contract.

Harper paused to take a drink from his water bottle, then considered the nature of the matter.

They had assumed two helicopters, loaded with journos, security agents, and a photographer or two.

That assumption had been incorrect.

Two Ministers of Parliament, each of whom had brought their chief of staff, plus aides. And a BBC news crew!

"Staff Sergeant, why are them folks wearing suits?" House had asked.

"I dunno."

"Staff Sergeant, why do they have so much luggage?" Johnson asked.

"I dun — what do you mean?" Nealen asked, head twisting sharply toward where Johnson was pointing. Behind the guests, the air crew were busily moving luggage out of the hold of the Lynx helicopters.

"Oh goody. Guys, I think it's time we activate our GOTH plan," Nealen announced.

"GOTH, Staff Sergeant?" House asked.

"Go To Hell. Something me and the LT cooked up between ourselves. Pass the word, without radio, every section but Gun Six is to meet me at the gate in two minutes. Six is to make ready on the gunline."

"Aye, aye, Staff Sergeant," they chirped, quickly moving to obey. Whatever was about to happen, they wanted no part of it.

#

It took eleven minutes for Natasha Fitzsimmons to learn what Nealen had planned. By then, it was far too late for anything she could say to countermand the matter. She was also far too busy.

"Where are they?" a maroon-haired woman demanded loudly as she stormed into the Command Post.

"Who is 'they?' You need to be rather precise, given that we have a large number of personnel here at FOB Bourne," Natasha said languidly from her seat.

"The rest of the Americans. You brought them here for fetch and carry, didn't you?" another, older woman with gray hair and a serious mien demanded.

Balcombe studied the abrasive guests calmly. "I beg your pardon," she said finally. "What gave you that impression?"

"It's all in here," Maroon Hair declared, waving a copy of the London Times around.

"And you are?" Balcombe asked.

"Listero, Minister Smyther's Chief of Staff," the purple-haired woman announced.

"Well, Listero, Minister Smyther's Chief of Staff, why don't we try making introductions like civilized people, why don't we?" Natasha suggested.

The semi-sarcastic nature of her tone caused the Ministers to look at Natasha, who stood and stared down her guests.

"Well?" she said finally. "Or do you think I can read your minds?"

"Shahi Siddiq, minister for Hampstead, and Anne-Marie Smythers, minister for Reigate, this is Captain Natasha Fitzsimmons, a professional engineer and the commander of the company here," DuBois said politely. "These," he waved towards the women in pant-suits, carrying briefcases. "Are Simona F. Listero and Chandra Beebee, chiefs of staff respectively."

"So you're the one to blame for disgracing our project like this?" Smythers demanded, cutting off DuBois as she tried to stare down the captain in front of her.

"If by 'disgraced' you mean 'done my level best to get an airfield built' then yes, that's me," Natasha said calmly.

"That's not what the paper says," Listero said, waving it about.

"Really? May I?" Balcombe held out her hand.

Taking the paper in hand, she skimmed the article before turning her attention back to Listero.

"I'm not seeing what you're speaking of. Why don't we ask a third party?"

"By all means," Listero sneered.

"Mr. Harper, you're an educated man. You make sense of this," Balcombe said.

"It would be my pleasure, Ms. Balcombe," Harper declared, rising to his feet from where he'd been seated in one corner of the room, unnoticed before now.

"You're an American," Listero intoned, trying not to gawk at how he towered over her.

Harper ignored her as he read aloud those parts Listero had highlighted on the page. "I see nothing to support the accusations made, ma'am."

"It clearly says you're here to support Number One Support company. What else is there to do besides fetch and carry? You're not in any danger here," She retorted.

"Well that's certainly a novel interpretation of the matter," Harper said cheerfully.

Listero's glare slid off his cheerful countenance as he placed the newspaper in her hands.

"However, my Marines are either out on patrol, standing posts, or standing ready to provide immediate fire support, and they are thus unable to assist you at this time." Harper announced as he went back to sitting in a corner of the room.

Beside him, Nealen casually read from a book and listened to the reports coming in from the patrols.

"A likely story," Smythers grumped.

"You're certainly welcome to test any theories you believe in at your earliest convenience."

Listero stared at him, disbelieving that she had heard such arrogance. Wasn't the man aware of what her political connections could do for his career?

"Besides, you're a strong, independent woman. What could you possibly need a man for?" Nealen chirped from his seat.

"Oh," somebody breathed.

"Sergeant Brady, how many Marines are in the Platoon?" Nealen asked.

"Seventy-eight plus one Navy Corpsman, yourself and the platoon commander, Staff Sergeant. One Marine on funeral duties."

"Of those eighty one men present, where are they right now?"

Brady checked his board. "Each of our nine guard posts has a Marine on duty, plus the SOG and Local Security Chief. One section is on reaction duty. We have fifty-four men outside the wire."

"Where is Chef?"

"Prepping dinner and waiting to provide fire support as necessary."

"Thank you."

Harper turned back to the assemblage crowding the space. He'd had long conversations with both Mayne, Nealen, Fitzsimmons, and Balcombe about how best to handle the interlopers. Now he was enjoying taking the heat off Fitzsimmons.

"You have a chef?" one of the aides said disbelievingly.

"What? You don't?" Harper said politely.

Butter might've melted in his mouth then, even as he saw the maroon-haired pitbull become flustered.

"Prove it," Listero demanded.

"Five Actual, this is Fox Two Actual. How copy?"

"This is Five Actual, send it."

"Are you in the mess right now?"

"Affirmative."

"What's for dinner?"

"Chili con Cabrito, and Pilsen is putting the finishing touches on flatbread. I'm about to go rack out."

"Roger that. Carry on."

"Errah. Five Actual out."

"Why are you interfering with British army operations?" Listero hissed.

Harper coolly regarded her, but said nothing save cocking an eyebrow.

"I don't remember needing to answer any questions you might put forward to me."

The woman was even less amused when he put his radio back on his belt. Nor was she finished with her interrogation.

"This is a British base. Who gave you permission to put up an American flag?"

"Captain Fitzsimmons, ma'am, do you remember which of my Marines asked?" Harper said.

"Now that you mention it, I don't recall," Natasha admitted.

"Well ain't that a shame," Nealen said.

"Which really sums up my feelings," Harper declared.

"Oh?" Balcombe chirped.

Harper shrugged. "It may come as a shock, Ms. Balcombe, but I do not feel the need to apologize for the men under my command."

"Why is that flag still up?" Listero challenged.

Harper sighed, closed his eyes, knowing that Nealen was doing the same.

He knew how this conversation was going to end, roughly. Part of him wanted to avoid that event, but the mean, calculating part of him, the man forged in the crucible of war to best serve the country he loved, would not, could not back down. Not when it came to this matter.

"Why don't we skip forward a whole bunch," Harper declared. "I know what you're thinking. I am going to very strongly suggest you leave that flag alone."

"No. That symbol of oppression and colonization and barbarian behavior is coming down right now!" A second aide, one with green-streaked hair announced.

Green Hair stomped out of the room, followed by Listero and the other aides. Harper shook his head and looked to Nealen, who shrugged.

"You tried sir," the dutiful platoon sergeant said with a sigh as he pulled the radio off his belt

"Well aren't you going to stop them?" Balcombe demanded as she looked from one Marine to the other.

"Why?" Harper asked.

"But they're your colors!" Keating retorted.

"QRF, this is Hogfather," Nealen declared, thumbing his radio mike.

"*Jawohl,*" a voice declared, sounding for all the world as if they were trying on a bad German accent.

"Prepare to repel boarders," Nealen directed.

"*Jawohl! Mein teufelhunden! Blitzkrieg! Schnell! Schnell!*" the radio squawked, then went silent.

"Who was that?" Munro asked, confused.

"That was Samuels. He must be having an episode, again," Harper said calmly. "Staff Sergeant, please make a note to have Samuels speak with the medical section at Leatherneck about getting his meds adjusted again before we return to garrison in Hawaii."

"What is that psycho doing," Munro realized, face going grave as she digested Harper's words.

"Sociopath. He's a sociopath," Harper corrected.

"He's loony!" Munro said.

"At least he's on a path," Nealen added.

"Not helping, Nealen," Munro declared.

"I know, but a man should have goals," Nealen remarked, working hard to keep a straight face.

"The man is built like an Aryan recruiting poster," Harper replied. "Which is hilarious because he hates white supremacists as passionately as he loves Latin women. His wife is a five foot nothing Cubana."

"He's married?" Munro said in dismay.

"Quite happily. Slavishly devoted family man too. But to answer your question, he loves mocking the 'master race' idiots. When we see him in the gun park wearing a German pickelhaube and practicing his goose step, we know his meds need to be adjusted."

"Fecking weird," Munro proclaimed.

"He does a really good impression of Colonel Klink from Hogan's Heroes," Brady added.

"I'll say it again, this time with enthusiasm. Fecking weird," Munro restated.

"Cassidy is there too," Harper admitted. "He's still angry, you know."

"It's been two weeks! Surely he'd have calmed down by now," Munro suggested politely, ignoring the stares and confusion on the faces of their visitors.

Brady started laughing from his seat at the FDC center.

"You expect him to do what? Haha oh that's good!" Brady slapped his knee then pulled out a can of Copenhagen and began filling his cheek as he spoke.

"That man is always angry. Giving him a reason to be righteously mad? Well, it just feeds the fire."

"Oh." Munro frowned.

"The sight of these self-important bullies and their white-knights, trying to tear down our flag pole is going to go over very well with them boys," Brady assured. "Nealen told y'all how we like to scrap. He ain't funnin'."

Spit.

"In the field, when we go cold-tube, first thing that happens after we clean the howitzers is everybody drops their body armor, goes to the center of the gun line."

"Why?"

"We kick the ever-loving hell out of each other."

"Why on earth would you do such a thing?"

"Because we can. Because who's going to stop us?"

"Where are your officers?"

"What about me?" Harper asked. "My job is to ensure that traditions live on. Even if that tradition is kicking the hell out of some snot-nosed punks in suits who think they rate."

"That's what it's come to, fighting over a flag?" Minister Siddiq demanded.

Harper stood very silently, staring at her as his jaw hardened before he ground out an answer. "Yes."

"It matters that much to you?"

Screaming was heard, dying abruptly.

"What are you standing there for? Go do something!" Siddiq demanded.

"No," Nealen refused, answering for the Lieutenant.

"But —"

"We'll kill for that flag and what it represents," Harper declared softly.

"If you don't —"

"If I don't what?" Harper snapped.

Siddiq shrank back before him.

"What do I do for a living?" Harper demanded.

She looked around the room, finding no help in the offing. DuBois made a point of sipping tea from a cup which had magically appeared in his hands.

"I. Kill. People. At range and up close. Nealen has killed people. Will likely kill many more. My boys out there? They kill people," Harper curtly reminded her.

"Well —" Minister Smythers started.

"You came here and gave the insult. Insults have a price. You're about to see what that price is," Nealen said.

"It's just a flag," Smythers protested.

"Fourth Marine Regiment was on Corregidor when Wainwright surrendered to the Japanese Army. They burned their colors to prevent capture. Then they hid the American flag, and risked death for three years in a Japanese prison camp, keeping it safe. My grandfather liberated that camp and helped them run it up." Harper's voice went cold. "Do not presume to assume you understand how we feel or to what end we will go for the sake of those colors."

Both Marines stayed on their feet, sipping at lukewarm water in the near-totally silent Command Post. All three squads on patrol reported in, the FDC Marines moving their icons on the map display.

"Staff Sergeant, Sir, you got a minute?" Cherney called from outside.

Jumping to their feet, both Marines went out the door, followed by several Brits.

Please don't have let me down. Please don't have screwed this up, Harper prayed.

The collection of aides and interns had left looking tidy and neat. Now they were dirty, escorted at bayonet point. Or in Cassidy's case, tied up and marched back.

"We caught trespassers trying to come through our hooches, sir," Cherney proclaimed.

"You did?"

"Uh huh. Some of 'em were stealing from rucksacks."

"Well, we can't have that," Harper declared.

"We walked 'em back over here. Figured we'd leave you all to handle the matter. After all, what do we know? We're just dumb colonials," Cherney declared sardonically

"Understood."

Ordering their Marines to stand fast, Harper and Nealen walked over to the sergeant who was glaring at the person he'd restrained. This worthy, with his hands secured behind his back, was bent over at an awkward angle. Hondo's left arm had snaked under the bound wrists and up to the head, elevating the arms to a painful height and bending the man over. Hondo's left hand had wrapped around the bun in the younger man's hair, and the sergeant was clearly practicing his grip exercises as he stood there.

"Unhand him!" Listero ordered. Hondo pointedly ignored her as he looked to his leadership.

"Sergeant, what seems to be the matter?" Harper asked.

"Sir, this —" Hondo spat, sunflower seeds landing on the man's cheek in a gob of spittle. "Person was trying to force his way into the kitchen areas, without authorization."

"Didn't you hear me?" Listero screamed. "I said unhand — !"

Her words died in her mouth. Hondo's free hand held a knife, point of the tip resting comfortably between her eyes against the bridge of her nose.

"You are not in my chain of command."

Hands used to bearing weights around easily held the facón steady.

"You... You... wouldn't —" Listero stuttered.

"I am in an active combat zone full of people trying to kill me. Your money? Does not matter. Who Mommy and Daddy sucked off to get you a ministry seat? Does not matter. Whatever tabloid journalists you've got in your pocket?" His teeth flashed as he snarled at Listero. "Does. Not. Matter."

A puddle formed at Listero's feet as reality hit home. Hesitantly, she moved backwards, one slow step at a time, until she was standing near Smythers in the doorway of the CP. Hondo's long facón returned to its sheath in the small of his back.

"Where were we before that untimely interruption?" Harper asked nonchalantly.

"Are there authorization notices posted properly, Sergeant?" Stirling demanded.

"On every door, Sarn't Major," Hondo assured. "Furthermore, when I confronted him, he told me to go engage in carnal copulation with myself and did I know who his daddy was?"

"Tsk tsk. How unprofessional. Wouldn't you agree, Staff Sergeant Nealen?" Stirling continued.

"Absolutely, Sarn't Major. Though I do believe we should commend Sergeant Cassidy for his restraint, and demonstration of proper pain compliance techniques."

"Did you remember to search him?" Harper asked.

Smythers goggled. "You want to what?"

"I didn't sir, couldn't without a cover man," Hondo announced.

"Ah, allow me to help you rectify that," Nealen declared. His rifle came up, safety loudly clicking over to FIRE as he moved to a new position such that he would not be compromised in the matter.

"Now see here!" Smythers demanded. "This is highly irregular!"

"Actually, it's Standard Procedure, ma'am," Stirling informed her. "Until we can verify who somebody is, we can and will hold them after having searched them to ensure the safety of all our personnel."

"Just wait until the MOD hears about this!" Smythers snarled.

"Sergeant Cassidy, are you trained on how to properly search and handle Enemy Prisoners of War?" Harper asked suddenly.

"Yes, sir, I am. Gun Four, sit, kneel, bend!" Hondo barked.

Cherney's Marines moved with alacrity to obey, for which Stirling smiled behind his mustache as he pulled a cigar from its tube in his pocket.

"My name is Sergeant Cassidy and this is my period of instruction on EPW procedures!" Hondo barked. "Under normal circumstances, I would call my demonstrator in such matters a gentleman and give you their name. You've got to be a man before you're a gentleman though. He fails on both counts."

Even if I had a camera to record the last five months, nobody would believe me. Note to self, must get a copy of all the GBOSS footage. I'll never need to pay for a round of drinks ever again Stirling told himself.

The sergeant gave a thorough class, down to turning the man's pockets out as he stripped him down. The aide protested several times, but with his mouth covered by duct tape, there was nothing he could do to prevent a total examination of his person. Hondo even went the length of performing credit card swipes across his buttocks and inner thighs to check for hidden contraband. Through it all, Smythers seethed, while Listero stood, shaking.

Keating and Munro approached in the midst of it all, making a beeline for Stirling.

"Sarn't Major?" they said quietly.

"Yes?"

"Should we do anything?"

"Not while the sergeant is engaged in a lecture. Would be quite rude to interrupt."

"Oh. Well then," Keating said.

"Feel free to watch. I'm finding this highly educational."

"What about the ministers?" Munro said tentatively.

"What about them?" Stirlign replied.

Keating smiled, Munro goggled.

"What about them indeed," Keating declared, lighting a Marlboro cigarette.

When Hondo finished, Nealen rated his demonstration, corrected an error, and dismissed him.

"Sergeant, please feel free to leave this person with us. We'll see to them now."

"Understood, sir. Gentlemen, by your leave."

"Carry on, Sergeant Cassidy," Harper declared.

"Aye, aye, sir."

"Gun Four, you are dismissed. Return to quarters and prepare for guard mount," Harper ordered.

"Aye aye, sir!" Samuels replied. "Fall in nasties, time to gear up."

"Oorah!"

Samuels marched them back, heads up, boots striking the earth as he goose stepped, calling the cadence in German. Balcombe frowned and Harper smiled.

God bless my boys, Harper thought cheerfully. *I love my vicious pack of heartbreakers and life takers.*

Natasha and the ministers had watched all of it from within the Command Post. When Samuels had struck up a cadence as they marched she turned to face her guests.

"Let's go for a walk, shall we?" She suggested.

Outside, in the cool December air, Natasha watched as the ministers spoke with their personnel, before returning to Natasha's side.

"What is the meaning of this?" Smythers demanded.

"As the great warrior-poet Ice Cube once stated 'Don't start none, won't be none,'" Harper cautioned. "Manners count for a lot around here. I suggest you and your people learn them."

"You — animals," Siddiq snarled.

"You can send us to die on a lonely hilltop somewhere, and we will do it." Nealen casually stripped his cigarette, eyes never leaving hers as he did so. "But if you would do us injury, ensure that you do so such that you need never fear our reprisal."

Harper threw a wad of chewing tobacco in, tongue working the dense ball around till it had settled just so in his cheek.

"Now, what was that about handling some luggage?" Harper asked the assemblage at length.

They collectively gaped at him. Looked toward the flagpoles once again, then back to him.

"An' it's Tommy this, an' Tommy that, an' anything you please;

"An' Tommy ain't a bloomin' fool — you bet that Tommy sees!" Harper declared, voice cold as he spoke loud enough for all nearby to hear.

The line of poetry caught the ministers and their staff off-guard, while Stirling smiled behind his mustache once more.

God bless you my son, that was lovely.

Leaving the furious guests to ponder upon the imparted wisdom, both Marines turned about face, casually walking back to their hooches with wide smiles.

"Thank goodness the Battalion Commander encourages us to educate our NCOs, sir. Hate to think how we'd be doing without good sergeants and corporals," Nealen said when they were far enough away that neither could easily be heard.

"Indeed Staff Sergeant. Lieutenant Colonel Goedecke is a treasure," Harper replied.

Thereafter, the ministers, their staff, the Captain, and as much of the base's female personnel as could be spared were engaged in serious discussions in the mess. None of the Marines were interested in being nearby, and with the variety of patrols ongoing, nobody bothered to spare the women any pressing concern. Nealen had detailed two sergeants to keep an eye on things, and carried on with business as usual. How long the state of affairs could last was anybody's guess.

That night, the goat chili was a hit, at least amongst the base's uniformed personnel.

"Don't you have any vegan options? Meat is murder!" complained Listero.

A tan package flew through the air, landing the table and knocking her tray into her lap.

"Why did you do that?" she shrieked.

"Vegan Spicy Penne Pasta, good for what ails you!" Hondo announced. "You will take it outside, as the MRE and its attendant heater unit represent a significant fire hazard."

"But… but…" Listero stood, gesturing toward her wet clothing smeared with the remains of the chili.

"Yes?" Hondo said with a smile.

"I'm a mess! And there's no chairs or tables outside."

Hondo's smile grew wider. "Every man and woman here has used sandbags to make furniture. Don't tell me you're too good for sandbags?"

Listero wilted under his gaze. "No," she eked out.

"Oh good. I'd hate to think you considered yourself privileged. On your feet, and out the door. No fire hazards allowed in the mess."

He stayed in that space, smiling down at her as she had exited the mess. Looking down the table at her fellow aides and chief of staff, he smiled beatifically. "Is there anybody else looking for a vegan option?"

"Nope."

"No."

"We're good."

The gaggle of civilians swiftly declared their contentment, several of them digging in with renewed determination. That their foreheads were covered with rivulets of sweat running down across their faces as they struggled through their servings of rice and chili was total happenstance. After all, a responsible Mess Sergeant would never earmark a singular vessel of chili for important guests, much less one heavily laden with the finest king cobra chilis to be found in Northern India. *A responsible Mess Sergeant—*

\#

"Brigade commander, the helicopters left, but our observers tracked them to Leatherneck," Basayev reported.

"Then we wait for them to return."

"We will make it so. Allahu akbar."

"Inshallah, my son," Saeed blessed. "Inshallah."

The command passed quickly, and changes were immediate. Tonight would be a time for difficult tasks worthy of a Holy warrior in the service of the one true God.

Chapter 30

I'm A Rolling Thunder, Pouring Rain

Hondo Cassidy stood in the dark motor pool, wondering what to do right then.

I can go to bed, He thought, looking towards the hooch where his cot awaited. *Or I can go talk with her.* She was in her studio, hard at work, given how he could see slivers of light leaking out.

She said she's sorry, Mayne and them said it was so. But that was still a helluva thing to say to me. He ground his boot toe into the sand. *Besides, I don't know how to forgive a woman.*

It was the truth, he never had. Not since the night his mother let herself be taken away. He hadn't wanted to leave her, hadn't wanted to let go of her. She had promised she'd come back for him. And never had. She had left him, so he'd later been told, after she relapsed in jail, gotten high as a kite one morning and killed another inmate. He'd never seen his mother again.

If a man can't forgive his mother, why bother with a girlfriend?

It was the question he'd argued over ever since his conversation with Peter and Stirling. He still didn't know what to make of it. Or how to respond. For the first time in his life, Hondo Cassidy was at a complete loss for words.

\#

"Brigade leader, messengers report helicopters inbound. All assault elements have made it to their positions."

"In the name of the Prophet and the Most Holy whom he comes before, attack! Allahu akbar!"

The cry rang out repeatedly as the fire command went out across all circuits. Outside the hidden bunker, smoke billowed as rockets leapt from the multi-tube launchers which they had resided in for hours as their gunners awaited orders.

The Dishu Brigade had learned painful lessons across the last five months, and prepared accordingly. Eleven six-barreled launchers spewed forth fire and smoke, warheads ripping through the night in a searing slash, well outside what the Brigade commander and his officers believed was the maximum effective range of the American's indirect fire weapons.

One group, more enterprising than many of their fellows, had recently stumbled across a stash of stolen British arms dating back decades. When the call went out for fighters to assemble in Dishu, the Group commander had ordered his men to pack their jealously guarded treasure and bring it with them. As all three tubes were loaded by their crews and sighted in, the group commander rejoiced at his foresight.

"Remember, we only have enough ammunition for five salvos, we must make sure every shot counts," he advised.

"Inshallah, it will be enough," a one-eyed gunner replied with a toothy smile. Moving from one piece to another, he sighted in each as best he could on the far target nearly a thousand meters away. Returning to his sights, he aligned as best he could in the dark and let loose the first shot from the hefty hundred-twenty millimeter recoilless rifle. The second and third rifles followed suit.

And may Allah grant we make it out of here alive if we fail, the gunner told himself.

\#

"We have incoming!" Huck shouted as alarms began to wail and tracks could be seen onscreen."Multiple incoming!"

"Oh shit, what about the helicopters?" Brady demanded.

Already explosions could be heard. The ever dutiful Private Bellmore was repeating the emergency warning across all frequencies, as sirens began to wail.

#

Many projectiles missed their intended targets. The rockets had been crudely sighted in, but given the circumstances it was the best their operators could hope for. Several overshot the FOB, landing all around it in a cascade of explosions, throwing dirt and stones into the air alongside casing shrapnel.

Many is not, however, *all*.

None of the three helicopters had time to maneuver, ballistic projectiles ripping apart their relatively thin fuselages with contemptuous ease. Even at twenty meters' altitude, the crash of the choppers was monstrous. The lead chopper fell down between the engineers' material storage and the motor pool, aviation fuel igniting fire as it splashed out and around the site, erupting into roaring flames. Rockets also hit the number two and three helicopters as they hovered over the runway, dropping them out of the sky. Parts and chunks flew across the FOB. Half a rotor blade from one of the Lynx's became lodged in the wall.

Post Seven disintegrated under the combined blast of three HESH rounds from the one-twenty millimeter recoilless rifles striking in rapid succession. The Marines standing watch didn't have time to do more than blink before they were bodily thrown from their post, killed by the concussive blast emanating from eighty-five pounds of high explosive detonating simultaneously.

#

Sylvie stared at her current project, trying to shake the mental malaise she'd been stricken with.

"Why can't I concentrate?" she complained aloud. "The hell is wrong with me?"

It had been like this ever since her fight with Hondo.

Is he ready to apologize? She wondered, not for the first time. *Am I ready to try that either?*

A rumble of distant thunder was heard.

She looked up, then back toward her project. *What if I –*

The world shook, throwing her off her feet and across the small hut.

\#

"Bellmore, pass word, we need all hands fighting the fires, otherwise we'll be in a lot of trouble," Brady said as he tried to process the information coming in.

"Belay that," Mayne announced from where he stood in the doorway. "Anybody can throw dirt on a fire with a shovel or a front loader. Theiss, is the GBOSS working?"

Theiss tapped commands on his keyboard, and after a moment spoke up.

"Yes, Sarn't Major"

"Scan on thermal, outside the perimeter," Mayne instructed."Something's off. It's not a coincidence that they hit the helis by chance. That was too precise for the Inshallah School of Marksmanship."

Blobs began to appear on the monitor. Man-shaped blobs, which seemed to be waiting in the darkness.

"Range is fifteen hundred meters, sergeant."

"That's what I was afraid of," Mayne admitted.

"Afraid of what, Sergeant Major?" Harper asked as he ran into the Command Post.

"We have unwanted company outside, sir."

"Do tell."

"There's a pissload of ordnance in the air, and you'll notice these fellows are standing around. Waiting."

"They must mean to storm us," Harper said flatly. "But charging underneath your supporting fires is not something they can practice, so they'll need to wait till the last salvo launches, at which point, the real fun begins.

"I have a sneaking suspicion you're correct, sir."

"Theiss, keep an eye on them. Let us know if that changes. Sarn't Major, Marines to the walls, First Platoon on the fire in the material yard, Second Platoon to the runway, then immediately return to bunkers," Harper ordered.

"What about Third, sir?"

"Them and the BBC folks are in Number Three, right?"

"Yes sir."

"They can stay there."

"Aye, sir. Bellmore, you heard the man."

"Yes, Sarn't Major,"

\#

"Brothers, see how it burns, already we have struck them hard! The whole rotten mess needs only to be kicked and it shall disintegrate beneath our righteous cause. Advance and allahu akbar!"

"Allahu akbar!" men shouted in rejoinder.

To breach the walls, they had made the effort of building satchel charges and training assault teams in their use. Now these surged forward, moving through the darkness as they hoped and prayed that what they had done for preparation would be enough.

\#

Hondo ran towards the smoldering remains of the guard post, heedless of the fires burning around or behind him.

Those are my Marines on post. They are all that matters.

"Dallas!" Cassidy called out.

Nothing.

"Dallas!" he repeated.

Still nothing.

The firelit darkness made night-vision gear useless, and so he continued searching, praying for a miracle which seemed more and more unlikely with each minute.

Hondo found Baltierra first, head partially severed and his body charred, thrown from the guard tower by the blast. The only items still recognizable were the morale patch on the front of his ballistic vest and those goofy red gloves he wore.

"Damnit Baltierra, you deserved better than this. We'll come back and give you a proper burial soon enough." Cassidy let his gloved palm slide across the Marine's face, closing his eyes for the final time. "Sleep well till we return, brother. Now, where's Barranco?"

Stepping further into the debris, Cassidy looked, a sinking feeling rising as he continued to repeat the running challenge.

"Come on Barranco, where are you?"

He almost missed the body in the gloom, but for the helmet which fell off to roll around the ground at his feet.

"Barran — oh dammit!" Cassidy snarled.

The marine had been cut in half, upper torso separated from his legs by a giant something. He had bled out too rapidly to recognize what had happened.

Must've been whatever we got hit with.

Casting his eyes about, he tried his radio. "Any station, this is Five Actual. How copy?"

In the darkness he never noticed the chunk of shrapnel which had pierced the radio fall to the ground, tearing apart its sensitive electronics as it went. Hondo Cassidy was alone and nobody knew it.

#

"Most of the fires are out, but we've still got that big one where the VIP's bird went down, sir," Nealen reported when he stomped into the Command Post. "Got burning wreckage and avgas all over the material yard."

"Good work staff sergeant. Theiss, any more data from the computers?"

"Says the rockets are Type 63s, whatever that is," Theiss declared. "We also have mortars, and something else, but it stopped firing and hasn't popped back up again."

"Type 63 is a Chinese knock off of a Russian design. Real popular over here," Nealen added.

"Great. What are the posts saying?" Harper demanded.

"We're taking contact all over the place," Jimenez announced. "They tried to rush the walls after the rockets but we caught them in the open, stuck on our defenses."

"All posts reporting in?" Harper demanded.

"All except for Post Seven."

"What happened there?"

"Don't know, lot of smoke and debris in the air over there. Fires all over the walls on that side. Avgas musta splashed in to the supply yard and across the walls. House says they're trying to put out the avgas fire from the helo so they can clear the helo wreckage and get to the wall."

"Good. Keep it up."

A clatter came from the door as Colonel DuBois staggered in, Captain Fitzsimmons in his arms, followed by both ministers.

"She's taken shrapnel. In her legs," DuBois declared. "We put tourniquets on, but she needs more."

"Doc Knighton. You're up," Nealen commanded.

"Aye, staff sergeant."

Lowering the captain into a chair, they cut away her pant legs and went to work as Natasha fought back tears and pain through gritted teeth.

"Where's Leftenant Balcombe?" Natasha demanded.

"Balcombe and Munro are with First Platoon, ma'am. She'll be along when things quiet down," Mayne informed her.

Natasha looked at Harper as Knighton began speaking through his diagnosis.

"Ma'am, I strongly urge you to consider some morphine," Knighton urged.

"I won't be functional then," Natasha protested.

"You won't be functional if you're screaming in pain either."

What about Harper? She asked.

The boyish lieutenant knew his job, knew how to do a lot of things. But was he enough to save the situation? *I don't have a choice, and at some point, he's gotta learn to cross a river under fire.*

"Mr. Harper."

"Ma'am."

"You have command of the defense."

"Yes, ma'am." Harper mulled over a decision. "Sergeant Brady, my orders to all stations: Fox Two is in command. There will be no withdrawal without written orders. Those orders shall never be given."

"Oorah!"

"Nealen, take the reaction squad, a dozer and a half-dozen engineers to Post Seven," Harper ordered. He stabbed the map for emphasis. "If you need backup, call it in. Jimenez, you're doing a good job, keep it up."

"Aye, aye, sir," both Marines acknowledged as they went about executing the orders given.

"Brady, you got a drone running yet?" Harper demanded.

"Shores needs one more minute, sir."

"Start trying to figure out where these schmucks came from. When a group retreats, follow them back as far as you can and make note of it on the maps. They've got rally points and staging areas, just like we do."

"We can hit those with the guns," Theiss realized aloud.

"Exactly," Harper said.

"On it, sir!" Theiss yelled as he spun around in his chair, attention now focused on his screens.

"Jimenez, where's the QRF?" Harper demanded.

"Getting a working dozer right now," Jimenez called out.

"Good man, keep an ear out for any other issues. So long as they don't make it inside, we're fine."

"On it, sir!"

Natasha Fitzsimmons did the only thing she could do in that moment — sit back in her chair and watch whilst gritting her teeth. Knighton slipped a second syringe into her, and after the initial pinch, a cool flood of morphine rolled through her veins to take the edge off her pain.

"Excellent choice, ma'am," Stirling told her quietly.

"Sarn't Major?"

"The secret to winning a great muthering battle like this ma'am, is to not lose your nerve."

"Huh?"

"Ms. Balcombe is seeing to First Platoon. DiResta has Second Platoon in hand with Keating, Third is in their bunker, and Harper's clearly got his chaps taking care of seeing the wogs off."

"Which leaves me sitting on my fat arse doing nothing with a busted pair of legs and an absolutely shite headache." Natasha groused.

"No, ma'am," Mayne corrected. "Not doing 'nothing.' You're sitting there calmly, letting your people do their jobs and not losing your cool."

"How does that matter?"

"You think Brady would be able to concentrate on managing the flow of information to Jimenez or Harper if you were running around tearing out your hair and screaming like a wee mad banshee?"

Natasha laughed at the mental image.

"No, probably not," she said between giggles.

"Exactly. Now in a few minutes, you're going to announce that I need to visit the medics and see if they need help with casualties. You, of course, will stay here and hold the minister's hands while they piss themselves."

"You think we'll have casualties?"

"Ma'am, take a look outside. There's a lot of screaming hairy wogs outside. Somebody's going to get hurt."

"Don't let our guests hear that, Sarn't Major. They'll call you culturally insensitive."

Mayne sniffed grandly as he fixed the Captain with a look of utter nonplussed detachment. "I have spent more time in the service of her Britannic Majesty Elizabeth II, than those self-important dilettantes have spent diddling themselves. Cumulatively. What in the world makes anybody think that I care what they say?"

"Touché."

"And besides, in nineteen months I'll hit thirty years. At which point I'll be fishing in Malta."

"Cheers to that."

"Aye ma'am."

\#

Joseph Pilsen slowly made his way toward Bunker Number Three, trying to make light of the ordnance flying all around and overhead. His ribs still ached, but his ankle and hands had healed sufficiently. Doc Knighton assured him the head injury would clear up in time, but to take it easy till then.

I hate being this useless, Pilsen admitted. *By rights I should be happy to be off kitchen duty. But even Sergeant Cassidy is telling me to take it easy.*

He struggled to find the words for how he felt right now. It was a strange thing, to be so—

Appreciated.

That was the word he needed. Appreciated.

For the first time in his life, Joseph Pilsen felt appreciated. And it wasn't just because of what he could do, but what he had done.

Also helps that I had two good Sergeants giving me the beasting of a lifetime.

He looked down at the single inverted chevron of a Lance Corporal and smiled.

Thank God they pulled their punches, because those hurt like the dickens. But I earned them.

"Is that our favorite baker?" Clarke's voice called out from the far end of the reinforced hooch they used for a bunker.

That cheered him immensely. She'd stolen kisses from him after Doc Knighton had turned out the lights their second night in the medical tent, something which shocked him. That she'd continued to kiss him every night thereafter and hold her hand as he lay there recovering was perhaps a greater shock.

Abigail's a very nice girl Pilsen told himself, *a proper sort of lady a man would want to keep around. If she'll have me.*

A camera crew was set up and swung around to capture him walking into the hooch.

"It is," he replied.

I'll blame the Sergeants for that one too. With Chef's assistance, his baked goods had become a much-loved staple of the FOB's existence. And Sergeant Pistol kept him working out constantly. The muscle he'd put on since that seemingly long ago day gave him a sure strength as he went about his daily tasks and he no longer felt embarrassed to work without a shirt on, much like Cassidy or Pistol did.

"Sinful carbs," Leftenant Balcombe had declared with a smile and a wink when she sampled the night's fare not long ago. "At the rate you're going Lance Corporal, you're going to make some lady quite happy when you settle down."

He'd fought the rising blush in his cheeks at her compliments, basking in the adoration of his comrades. It felt good to be appreciated.

"What are you doing away from Medical?" Cooper asked in the half-lit gloom.

"Somebody get this man a seat!" another yelled.

A spot was made for him with startling quickness and he sat down heavily, placing his rifle on his lap.

"As to your question, Cooper, I figured Medical didn't need me in the way," Pilsen said. "Thought I'd come over here and enjoy some proper company."

"But what about the rockets?" another soldier asked, he wasn't sure who.

"What about 'em? If it's my time to go, then I'll go. Against Fate, even the Gods do not fight."

"You've been spending a lot of time with Sergeant Pistol and Sergeant Cassidy," Clarke declared.

"Sergeant Pistol swears he can make me the lightweight boxing champ of the Army."

"Really?" Cooper asked.

"Indeed. Says I'm not fast like most of them, but he can fix my lack of muscle."

"He's done a great job so far," Clarke admitted.

"I'm sorry," the BBC man declared. "I hate to interrupt, but this is all horribly fascinating. What's your name? What do you do here?"

"He's Lance Corporal Pilsen," Cooper declared. "He's our Baker."

"Which is different from Chef."

"You have a chef here?" the interviewer asked, surprised.

"One of the Americans, Sergeant Cassidy, is a trained chef. He runs our mess," Cooper explained.

"And he does a fantastic job of it!" another woman added.

"That he does," a third soldier declared. "Never imagined I'd have a professional feeding us quality bits at the arse-end of nowhere."

"The Sergeant is right, you know — incoming fire is easy to ignore when you've got a good meal in front of you," Pilsen jested.

The room tittered and the reporter smiled jocularly. "If you don't mind, may I ask you a few questions?" he asked, sticking out his hand. "James Cochrane, BBC News."

"I recognize you. Before I joined the army, I used to listen to you on the morning show while I got the day's work ready to go at a bakeshop in Cornwall."

"Thank you. How long have you been in the army now, Pilsen?" he asked as his cameraman swiveled round on the tripod to take in their newest interviewee.

"Since 2010. My enlistment is up after we go home. If I get out."

"Do you like being a soldier?" James asked.

Do I want to leave the army? No, no I really don't. I finally know where I belong.

Pilsen chuckled dryly. "It's miserable work. When Sergeant Pistol isn't trying to make a boxer out of me, I've got the angriest American you've ever seen running me around. I have to be up every day by zero-four to start the next batch of bread, and I work till nineteen or later making sure the next day's food is ready to cook. I do it all for sixty-three pounds a day before taxes. It's the best job I've ever had and I wouldn't trade it for anything."

He didn't know quite how or why that answer came from his mouth, just that he had said it as frankly as if he were discussing bread prices with a customer.

"I wish you all could try the bread pudding he makes. I don't suppose you brought any of that with you?" Clarke asked, batting her eyelashes at him as she did so.

And doesn't she look pretty like that? Pilsen told himself. *I never realized before that she has hazel eyes.*

"Not this time, love, I can't overwork my ribs after —" he caught himself, "— since my fall." He paused. "Sergeant Cassidy and Sergeant Pistol have been keeping my duties to a minimum."

"Why?"

"Don't want me hurting myself while I heal."

"Could you teach it?" Clarke persisted.

"I —" *had never thought of doing so.* He looked around the room full of good-natured and very lovely faces, all smiling at him in a way he'd never seen before. "I can do that. I think we've still got enough supplies on hand to make it again."

The near door banged open, overhead lights silhouetting a figure in a thawb. The room paused, as all eyes moved to the new occupant, even the camera on its tripod. Framed against the yellow light, stood a Taliban fighter with a rifle in his right hand.

Joseph Pilsen had never described himself as a fast-moving man on his best day. He had, however, spent every waking hour for months now, bouncing between a pair of men determined to make him a professional soldier.

Knowing he couldn't transition his rifle from his lap to his shoulder in time, he threw himself toward his target, swinging his left fist in a superman punch Sergeant Pistol would absolutely have beasted the bollocks off him for throwing.

The flying left connected with the man's stomach, knocking the wind from his lungs. His AK fell to the ground in a clatter as Pilsen's right fist looped around to catch him in the ribs.

Letting his head fall backwards, Pilsen drove it forward, the crown of his forehead delivering a Liverpool Kiss, blood exploding from a broken nose where it made contact.

Even blood showered onto him, he hooked his left ankle behind the Taliban fighter's foot and threw his right palm into the other man's left shoulder.

The dirty, broken-nosed man's head bounced off the metal door frame and he collapsed to the ground, dazed.

"It worked," Pilsen breathed. "It really worked.

KLUNK.

He saw the small, cast iron orb rolling along the floor from the Taliban fighter's limp right hand.

One

There was no cotter pin in place. Even in the weak light he could see the safety ring was gone.

Two

"Grenade!" He shouted.

Three

They were behind him. A whole bunker full of women he cared about.

Four

I cannot run, he told himself. *I cannot abandon my sisters.*

Five

His blood had frozen but not his body, and he drove forward to smother the deadly sphere.

Six.

He felt weightless.

Chapter 31

I'm Coming On, Like a Hurricane

Sylvie staggered upright, head swimming as she fought to control her nausea. One of the makeshift windows had been blown away, as had part of a wall, collapsing it inwards. Where Post Seven should have stood was a mounded hump of earth, blasted backwards into the FOB.

Out beyond the wall, she could hear shouting, despite the ringing in her ears. More than a little of the noise sounded distinctly like the cries of wounded men. Closing her eyes, she shook her head back and forth, trying vainly to reset everything scrambled inside her head. Vertigo threatened to drop her and she stopped the movement, struggling to breathe and settle her heart rate.

Flares soared into the sky above, bathing the area in strange light.

Those are red, she considered as she sought to grab her rifle.

Her fingers found the magazine, scrambling along the familiar stock as she pulled the weapon toward herself and leaned against a table.

Red is the same color we used to line the bottom of the ditch.

The thought hung in her head for a moment, spinning freely before neurons fired through synapses. *The same color we used to line the bottom of the ditch.*

"Oh merde!"

Performing a brass check, Sylvie sighted in on the gap,

Those same voices grew louder. Angry voices unhappy with running the gauntlet of razor wire, tanglefoot, caltrops and the like. Sylvie smiled despite the situation and took aim as the first man came through that she could clearly see.

Four shots lanced through his body, taking him down in a sodden heap. Just like the second man, and a third.

One man, smarter than his fellows, hooked a grenade around the corner, more a distraction than anything. Shrapnel bounced all around the area and then he was bouncing through. He clearly hadn't seen Sylvie's position though, nor considered that she might be behind cover. Her shots caught him in the shoulder, spinning him around before he dropped.

Her rifle felt lighter, and Sylvie hazarded a guess that her mag was low. Checking for her ballistic vest, she felt a pang of fear — it was across the room buried underneath an oxy-acetylene tank.

Oh you have got to be kidding me.

\#

Hondo was arranging the Marines' bodies and gathering their gear together when he heard the shots.

Looking towards their source, he saw it then. A hole had been blasted through the berm where Post Seven once stood. Not a large one, but big enough for at least two men to come through it.

And into the fire base, he realized with a chill.

Dead men in smoldering robes decorated the entrance, and as he watched, more fire poured out of a position, through the gap.

"I hate this damn country!" a woman screamed.

That's Sylvie, some part of his head realized even as he settled the gear into place.

She's chewing through ammo. Trying to convince them to stay away. If she's not careful, she'll use up all of her ammo real quick. God, now would be a great time for a sign.

His boot struck something metal and he looked down to see a familiar sight.

Huh. How 'bout that?

Fuck fuck fuck what do I do? The bastards are coming through and I don't have any way to stop them! Cold fear reached down into the pit of her stomach as Sylvie fought to keep her bile down.

What a shitty way to go.

She checked her magazine again, down to the one backup mag she kept on her person at all times.

Maybe ten rounds at best. Just gotta keep one for myself.

BAM BAM BAM BAM BAM BAM BAM

A machine gun opened up in front of her, green tracer fire traversing left to right across her vision, tearing through the breech with violent precision.

Overhead, trip-wired flares bathed the FOB and its environs with a variety of colors. Sylvie didn't acknowledge the rave-like flashes, engrossed as she was in watching Satan's buzzsaw slash through bodies clothed only in dishdashas and Soviet-era web gear. The source of that buzzsaw moved closer in rhythmic steps.

"Come on you sons of bitches! Aren't you dying to get in to heaven!?" a coarse voice bellowed out into the night.

There was an unfettered fury in that roar as the machine gunner swept his fire across either side of the breach in the berm. Men twisted where bullets impacted, flopping about in a grotesque ballet before they struck the ground, staying down.

The light above grew dimmer as the flares sank earthward, but the machine gunner wasn't finished. Advancing forward, he stood in the breech, ammo belts hanging off one arm as he brought the heavy weapon up to his shoulder in the classic rifleman's pose, shifting his aim ever so slightly with every squeeze of the trigger.

Whoever he was firing at seemed wholly incapable of touching him. She could see sparks and puffs of dirt where the AK rounds bounced off the ground at his feet. Still he continued firing, laughing with a wide-eyed smile she knew he'd have plastered across that dark, severe face.

Finally, satisfied (and likely the entirety of his belt expended), he stepped back from the breech, slowly moving backwards so his eyes never left the engagement zone. Elsewhere on the base, she could hear machine guns chattering and rifles barking still, but for the moment, this sector was clear. When he finally turned towards her, she felt her heart leap within her chest.

"Hey sweetheart. I brought you candlelight," Hondo Cassidy announced.

Sylvie choked out a laugh. "Is that what you call interrupting me in the middle of a good time?"

"I couldn't let you have all the fun."

He set the machine gun down, muzzle pointed toward the breech. The warmth in his voice and the joy she saw written on that familiar face made the knot in her stomach unwind.

"You are a sight for very sore eyes!" Moisture appeared at the corners and she fought back the rising urge to cry.

"Glad to know I could help."

Throwing her arms around him she sobbed in relief. Taken aback, he stumbled, then reciprocated, wrapping those arms she'd missed around her, hands slowly stroking her back.

"Hey now, it's okay. They're gone for the moment. You didn't get hit did you?" He asked.

"No! But they came so close!"

"Aye. Never said they lacked for courage. They're just too stupid to know how to chase women. Or what to do with 'em when they catch 'em."

Sylvie felt a laugh bubbling up. Some things about the man never changed.

"So what do we do now?" she asked.

"Post Seven is a loss. Haven't finished going through it though."

"What about —"

"Dead," he shrugged. "Think it was rockets. Got both of 'em."

Something that sounded like a growl escaped Sylvie's throat as her hands grabbed tighter onto Cassidy.

"Pieces of *shit*."

"Bastards likely thought with the tower out they'd be in the clear," He positively beamed. Even in the dark she could see that smile of his. "They didn't count on you. That held them up."

"I had some help."

"Yeah but you made it a lot easier. Well done."

"Thanks."

"I don't know how you're fixed for ammo, but I didn't have time to strip Baltierra or Barranco."

"Think their ammo is still good?"

"Likely. You've got time to look."

Sylvie cocked an eyebrow at him. "I don't think your fancy rifle is gonna be much use right now."

"Not hardly. I got night vision on this bad boy," Hondo slapped the rifle's stock cheerfully. He ambled toward the gap then brought the rifle up and began studying the terrain before snapping off a shot. A boom sounded, further out.

"That's another one," Hondo declared.

"Really?"

"He was stuck in the wire, trying to throw a satchel charge. Now we'll need a search party to find his testicles."

Sylvie made a face, then laughed at the insanity of the moment. "Should I leave you alone?"

"Don't worry, I'll be here when you get back," Hondo assured.

"But what about —" Sylvie asked.

"Today is a good day to die. But it is not my day," Hondo interrupted.

"Well okay then."

Cassidy listened to the sound of machine guns and rifles chattering all around them as he patiently waited for Sylvie to return. Tanglefoot, such as it was, seemed to be providing the greatest difficulty. He'd caught a further three men, tripping over the shin high barbed wire.

Tracers arced overhead. Behind his position the helicopter burned, a wall of flame cutting him off from the rest of the base. Until that was contained, there was no hope of reinforcements.

But I am not alone. Yea though I walk through the valley of the shadow of death, I shall fear no evil: for thou art with me; thy rod and thy staff they comfort me.

Catching sight of a thawb flapping as if being yanked, Hondo brought the rifle up to his shoulder, scanning quickly. Sights aligned, he gently squeezed his trigger backwards.

BAM.

Make that a fourth man since she left.

Precious seconds continued their passage with all the strain of hours, and then he heard footsteps.

"Dallas!" a familiar voice shouted from the darkness behind him.

"Cowboys!" he replied, then stepped back toward Sylvie's position.

She flopped down beside him, hands moving feverishly as she emptied her dump pouch of the heavily laden magazines, before passing him a small green orb, which he tucked into a pouch on his tactical vest.

"You've likely got a better throwing arm than me," she declared.

Shrugging, she dropped the machine gun belts wrapped over her shoulders to his waiting hands. "You were right. About the bodies. I got nine more mags," she informed him as he went about reloading the machine gun.

"Outstanding," he replied, laying the belts out just so.

"Think they'll be back?" Sylvie asked, settling in behind cover.

"Right now they're down there, licking their wounds. But yeah, I think they will."

"How long?"

"Anybody's guess. Inshallah time is kinda imprecise on this sorta thing." He squatted down, fiddling with something she couldn't see. Glowsticks cracked, light spilling all around them as he thrust them into half-filled water bottles and dropped them into the dark gap.

"You always know how to cheer a girl up, you know," Sylvie replied drolly.

"It's a gift." He lovingly patted the machine gun's upper receiver. "Stay on the 240 behind cover." He breathed in deeply. "It'll be like our first date all over again."

"Our first — How can you call that a date? There were no candles! No chocolate! No roses! How is that a date?"

"I had you baby, that was all I needed."

The response was a boost to her pride she hadn't known she would need.

"Ever played talking guns before?" Cassidy asked.

"What's that?"

"When they come through the gap, I want you to light them up. By the ditty. You'll fire a burst, then wait for me to do the same."

"With a rifle?"

"Yeah. It'll work a treat."

"You've done this before?"

"A few times. Ask Kramer, he was there for it."

"When was thi—"

A cry ululated from beyond the wall as a red flare arced upwards Cassidy prepped the grenade as whatever question Sylvie had on hand disappeared while she sighted down the length of the L7A2's still-warm barrel. Then she saw faces, bearded and hook-nosed, as they came through the gap, holding their AKs and moving cautiously.

Time slowed before she lit up the world with green tracer fire as Hondo Cassidy stood up just to her left, letting fly with the grenade held in his hand.

It flew through the air, detonating just beyond the breach's entrance. Men screamed in agony moments later and she smiled within herself. *That'll be a few less of them to deal with. Good.*

Above her, Cassidy began to fire with his rifle as targets presented themselves. Hot brass fell on her helmet, her back, bounced up into her hair. The scent of burnt gunpowder filled her nostrils and high above, a new illum round bathed the area in its unyielding white light.

#

Pililaau was already in the command post, following the ebb and flow of reports when Mike Roach ran in.

"Prael filled me in with what he knew on the way here," Mike explained. "What else do we know?"

"Not much, sir. They have multiple wounded, requesting casevac, and it's a hot LZ."

"Intel, any satellite imagery?"

"Online in seven."

The stark hellscape was shocking. All around Bourne's exterior, figures moved about.

"They look like they got hung up on something."

"Engineers must've decided to run up more defenses?" Pililaau suggested.

"Do we have any birds up?"

Prael shook his head. "We will shortly, sir. There is a problem though."

"Not enough fuel?" Roach asked.

"Worse, Meteorological says we've a massive storm coming through. Air ops will be suspended after midnight," Prael declared.

"Dammit." Mike scowled at the map. "Wait, Prael, we can take Pililaau and as much of his Marines with us on the birds headed there."

The Gunny held a hand up. "Sir, who's going to get the relief force moving if you're flying there with me."

"Umm…"

"I can take the boys and go reinforce Bourne, sir. You're the one we need to come get our asses out of the crack we'll be stuck in."

The logic was unassailable, forcing Mike Roach to surrender to the pragmatic sense his fellow Marine was making.

"I can do that."

Setting aside a fire team from Pililaau's platoon, both men made their way towards the helipad, where ground side personnel from the air wing were prepping a Super Stallion for departure.

"I can be there in eight hours by way of Garmsir. Seven if the storm swings north," Mike assured.

"Do what you can, just don't stop moving, sir," Pililaau told him. "Otherwise, this is gonna be a one-way trip."

"Platoon, how we doing?" Mike asked aloud.

"Ready to go bust some heads, sir," one of the Corporals shouted confidently.

"Good. I'm sending you to do exactly that. Gunnery Sergeant!"

"Sir."

"Your orders are to take your platoon plus ammo to FOB Bourne. You will report to Lieutenant Harper. Last report has him in command of the FOB right now."

"That one tall haole boy?"

"That's the one. Can you buy me eight hours?"

The gunny grinned. "Security platoon, you think we can buy the Colonel eight hours?"

Growls and barks greeted Mike's ears as rotors began to spin on the tarmac. Crew chiefs appeared at the top of their respective ramps, waving with flashlights for attention.

"Looks like it's show time!" Pililaau announced to cheers. "Platoon, column, move out!"

Mike did not wait for them to leave, Prael had arrived with a pickup truck carrying the fire team of Marines and Mike's kit.

"Sir, we've got places to be right now."

Climbing inside the cab Mike couldn't agree more. Prael threw it into gear and they were rolling across Leatherneck.

#

"Kathy, do you know any more than what we heard in the briefing?" Tamara asked.

"Nope."

"Crap."

"Yeah. Tell me about it."

As the Super Stallion helicopter rose into the night sky, Tamara Long checked her instruments.

"Come right two degrees and straight on."

"Roger that," Kathy Bathlicek replied. "How do they expect us to handle a hot LZ? We've only got our door gunners and Ries on the rear fifty."

"Think Gunny Pililaau will let us hang his Marines from a SPIE rig?" Tamara suggested innocently.

"The pinata jokes would never end," Kathy replied with a giggle.

"Komodo Eleven, this is Scarface Four," their radios crackled.

"Scarface? Tammy, you remember any Scarface callsigns around here?"

"No, I don't."

"Scarface Four, where you at?" Kathy asked.

"Port side high at your eleven o'clock."

Dark shapes moved past the Super Stallion in blurs and she dimly caught the outline.

"Those are the new Cobras," Tammy breathed. "Zulus."

"They move fast," Kathy said.

"Scarface, I know Cobra pilots are good but I don't think the two of you are gonna be able to clear all of that space for us on your own," Kathy declared over the radio.

A snort came over the airway. *"Who said there's only two of us?"*

"Kathy, I see more birds coming fast at our six!" the crew chief announced over the helmet comm.

"Belay my last. Our apologies, Scarface."

"No offense taken, Komodo. You worry about getting the devil pups back here with a quickness, we'll make sure your LZ is clear."

"Roger that." Kathy paused. "Scarface Four, this is Komodo Eleven. Do you guys really weld bayonets onto the front of your birds?"

"Of course not."

"See?" Tammy hissed. "I told you they didn't!"

"Komodo Eleven, why mount a bayonet when you can use an E-tool?"

Tammy stared forward, indignant as Kathy laughed at her.

#

"Medic to Bunker Three! Medic to Bunker Three!" JoAnna Bellmore's radio shouted.

"That's where we parked the First Platoon and the BBC folks!" Stirling declared.

"Christ, did they get hit by a rocket?" Munro asked aloud. "I hope not."

The mental images of his girls, broken and twisted by explosive blasts, had to be forcibly pushed aside as Stirling followed Doc Knighton and Doc Gnem, with Colonel DuBois on his heels.

The entryway dripped blood.

No, Stirling corrected himself, blood was freely sluicing out underneath the edges and through cracks. Stirling felt his heart sink as he ripped the door open, expecting the worst.

Within, a body greeted him. Only one. That it had been a man was almost impossible to tell. Gashes and punctures covered the body, gaping holes which punched through the extremities and even parts of the torso. Where once a face had existed, it was now little more than mangled gore, much like the rest of his body.

Around the room, he saw his soldiers, covered with hot blood on their bodies, but Stirling knew what blood spray looked like. Right then he'd bet the Crown Jewels that none of the blood he saw belonged to the women wearing it.

Espying a ring of those women, weeping around a body, Doc Knighton raised his voice.

"Make a hole!"

Even in their grief, some part of their minds recognized the command and the crowd parted before him, revealing a sharp face with a cornsilk shock of blond hair. The torso had been covered with a poncho and Knighton slowly lifted it, then turned his head aside and let the poncho fall back into place.

"What happened here?" Stirling said, trying to be calm.

"Taliban came through the door," Cooper declared.

"Chucked a grenade," another said.

"Pilsen threw himself on it," a third said.

"We couldn't let that awful goat fucker live another minute," Abigal Clarke said slowly, refusing to let go of the dead soldier's hand.

You gave Pilsen the revenge he deserved, Stirling told himself.

Letting his eyes track back towards the dead man wrapped in a shredded thawb, Stirling understood how those great wounds had appeared.

You didn't count on our girls having their own knives handy to mete out vengeance.

"My God."

Munro said the words slowly as she surveyed the room.

The BBC reporter, James Cochrane, stood up from where he'd been puking into a trash can, wiping his mouth before he started fumbling with a water bottle. Hands shaking so badly one of the girls had to help him, he managed to rinse his mouth out and spit.

"That's the truth of it," Cochrane announced, finally able to speak once more. "I'll swear to it before God and the Queen Herself."

"I caught it on my camera," Covington admitted.

"How much?" Munro demanded.

"All of it. Hope to God I never see such a sight again," Covington said.

"There's nothing we can do for him, Sarn't Major," Doc Gnem pronounced. "He took the whole blast."

"God, what a brave man," Phil Bishop, the producer, proclaimed.

"Six seconds," one of the girls breathed.

"Six seconds and on to eternity."

Thusly, a legend is born. And I will be damned if I don't give him what he deserves, Stirling promised himself.

"What'll we do with him now?" Clarke asked

"Staff Munro, I need a hasty stretcher constructed," Stirling instructed. "We'll carry him to the medico station."

Munro's eyes traversed the room and she indignantly fought back tears as she considered what had happened. "Let's be about it ladies, Lance Corporal Pilsen deserves our best, one last time."

"What do we do about the goat fucker?" Clarke asked.

"Bring a dozer over. He can go to the trash. It's where he belongs," Murno pronounced.

The baleful, red-rimmed eyes which met hers agreed perfectly.

Chapter 32

White Lightning's Flashing

"Dallas?" Nealen called out as they drew near the breach. He could see bodies stacked up in the gap, so many bloody windrows across the dirt.

"Staff Sergeant, I really hate this damn country. Just like I hate punching cattle for a livin'."

Hearing Hondo Cassidy's voice made Nealen relax. *I haven't lost my strong right hand.*

"That's what I like to hear. Who's with you?" Nealen asked.

"Just me and Lyons."

"Oh good, one less missing person for me to find," Nealen said.

Stepping around the scattered construction material, Peter Nealen grimaced. He'd brought a mixed squad with him, Marines and some of the girls, to see what they could salvage from the situation over here.

"How're things?" Nealen asked.

Cassidy lay propped up against a chunk of concrete, breathing slowly. He had his pistol out, pointed in the general direction of the enemy. Lyons lay prone just ahead of him, resting on the 240 with her Enfield at hand.

"It got a little hot in here," Cassidy replied slowly.

Nealen surveyed the bodies. "A little?"

"Yeah." He winced. "One of the bastards burned me with a shot."

"Son, that is not a smart way to live for a long time. We passed Post Seven on our way here. That where the 240 came from?"

"Aye. We ran out of ammo for it. Lyons is down to two mags for her Enfield, and I've got maybe a mag left in my Beretta."

"Tangoes all dead?"

"Insurance is paid in full, Staff Sergeant. No booby traps neither."

"Good man. Get a reload from Courtney and get checked out over at the aid station. Both of you probably got concussions from whatever it was that they blew a hole in the berm with."

"Sounds like a plan, Staff Sergeant."

Cassidy struggled to his feet, then reached out a hand to Sylvie. "Let's go for a walk Sergeant Lyons."

"I agree, Sergeant Cassidy, let's."

They slowly made their way into the night side by side. Nealen wasn't sure if they were holding hands as they walked, but it was dark still and maybe his eyes were just playing tricks on him.

Nice to see they've made up.

"What do you want us to do, Staff?" one of the engineers asked Nealen, trying not to gawk at the hellish sight while Nealen's Marines formed a perimeter at the edge of the breach.

"Remember Cassidy's lecture on fortifications?"

"Yes, Staff."

"I want a redan here, 240 in the tip with rifles on either flank. Make sure to include overhead cover, in case they have more mortars in the offing."

"Roger that, what about the bodies?" an engineer asked, pointing at the corpses piled about.

"Stack the bodies in front of the redan. We can call an Imam later for burial."

"Hell, Staff Sergeant, I bet Cassidy knows the rites. Probably got it in a book somewhere," Shiver jested.

"Ya know Shiver, I might just put money on that," Nealen confessed.

A retching sound was heard and Nealen looked to see two of the girls violently vomiting.

"You musta missed the part where Cassidy said he paid the insurance," Nealen said dryly.

"Had. No. *Retttch.* Idea."

Shiver spat, leaving Beechnut splattered on a dead assailant's face.

"Isn't that illegal?" another engineer, visibly pale, asked.

"Nope. That's called *rendered hors de combat,*" Nealen explained carefully. "God bless him for being so thorough."

"We've had you lot here nearly four months. I still don't fully understand you blokes," one of the engineers admitted.

"Well now you're a little closer," Nealen replied. "Let's get working."

#

There were bodies lined up outside the medical bunker, clearly dead, covered with tarps or ponchos. Atop the torso, the distinctive helmet marked who it was. Sylvie and Cassidy were surprised to see a British helmet amongst the casualties.

"Who was it?" he asked curiously.

"Lance Corporal Pilsen —"

Cassidy dropped to his knees beside the dead Lance Corporal's silent corpse, hearing nothing else Mayne might've said. Reaching down, he pulled back the cloth covering Pilsen's face and stopped.

She wasn't sure what she expected of him at that moment, if only because seeing him be vulnerable was not an action Hondo allowed others. He was far too guarded for that.

He began stroking Pilsen's cheeks, tousling the cornsilk blond hair like a big brother might do. Or a father.

"Come on bubba, you can't do this. You ain't done yet. You got so much still to do."

"Hondo, darling?" Sylvie said quietly.

She had squatted down in front of Hondo, looking deep into his eyes. For a moment, he was a wounded boy with a broken heart all over again.

"I failed him," Hondo whispered. "Just like I failed you."

This was the fractured emotional part of his head speaking, Sylvie realized. The part which yawned open and threatened to devour his soul when his walls collapsed.

The last several hours have taken their toll on him, Sylvie said silently. *He needs me here, helping him the same way I needed him with a machine gun.*

"Hondo, darling," Sylvie admitted. "You didn't hear Sarn't Major, did you?"

"Hear what?" He rasped hoarsely.

"One of those blighty goat buggers got inside the perimeter. Tried to capture a bunker full of girls from Third Platoon. Pilsen took him down with his fists, then dove on the grenade the sick bastard tried to use."

"You're kidding me."

"Not at all, darling. He proved himself a man before God, Queen and Country," Sylvie declared somberly.

Hondo was silent.

"You helped him learn to be courageous when he had nothing else. Nor anybody else. You and Pistol."

Hondo stared into Sylvie's eyes before he finally drew a ragged breath.

"I just... wish... it hadn't been" he glanced at the body. "Like this."

"I know. But he died well." She leaned her forehead against his. "If that's what it took to save the lives of my girls, who's to say you were any less than a success?"

Hondo's eyes closed as he processed through the roiling emotions. Sylvie felt his hands tighten then loosen their grip on hers, his breathing slowly returning to normal.

He smoothed the tousled hair, and together they pulled the poncho back into place before they stood and faced the Sarn't Major.

"Have a bit of a spot over there?" Mayne asked, breaking the silence as he looked the Marine and his soldier over, carefully ignoring the clasped hands.

"Only a mite, Sarn't Major," Sylvie said.

"Are you two doing better?"

"I think so," Sylvie said as she looked at Cassidy affectionately. "Hard to be mad at a man who can romance ya with a machine gun in hand."

"I know plenty of Irish women on me mother's side who'd agree with yuh, lassie," Stirling assured.

"Nealen wants us to get checked out at medical, then reload and get to our sections."

"Sounds good. Be off with yuh then."

"Aye aye, Sarn't Major."

They disappeared through the open door of the medical bunker, Mayne watching carefully before he lit up another cigar and resumed his vigil over the bodies of the slain.

They'll do just fine. They'll do just fine indeed.

Taking a puff on his cigar, he watched the cherry burn with fascination.

Must speak to the Chaplain about those two.

\#

"Platoon, fire mission! Special instructions, at my command!"

The cannon was not an unknown weapon in the Northwest frontier. The Mughals, the British, the Russians, all had used such firepower at one time or another in their dealing with the tribesmen of Afghanistan. But those stories were decades, even centuries out of date.

As green-painted barrels swiftly rose in the night sky, Peter Nealen smiled. It was not a warm smile, full of the mirth and good humor for which he was known. No, this was a cold smile of a man who knew what it meant to reach out and touch the enemy with death's kiss when they thought they were safe.

He was on the gunline watching his Marines go through the steps of the profession which defined their lives and justified their existence.

Brass rang against steel as projectiles were rammed into breeches.

"Stand by!"

Number One Men went taut, taking up the slack in their cotton lanyard lines.

"Fire!"

BOOM BOOM BOOM

Breeches flew open as swabs dipped then rose. The dance had begun.

Back in the FDC, Matthew Brady watched the GBOSS screens with interest. Theiss had tracked three separate groups making their way toward, then away from Bourne as the attacks were repulsed. His observations were confirmed by the reports from the counter-battery radar. Corporal Jimenez had gone up into the overwatch position to observe the fall of shot, further confirming the data.

Now, each gun crew and their respective piece were aimed at a different target. Battery Three.

Brilliant flashes lit the dark screens for a moment as the massive high explosive rounds burst midair, covering the sand with a sleet of white-hot steel. Men fell, scythed down as so much wheat before the reaping blade.

"Ready on Five!"

"Ready on Four!"

"Ready on Six."

"Six is ready. The platoon is ready. Standby, fire!" Shores ordered over the radio.

BOOM BOOM BOOM.

"Ready on Five!"

"Ready on Six!"

"Ready on Four."

"Four is ready. The platoon is ready. Standby, fire!" Shores spoke into his handset for a third time.

In the darkness, the earth shook as the massive barrels recoiled, spade dampers taking up the load and biting deeper into the hard reddish-brown desert dirt.

Out in the night, men watched and waited, slowly counting as they watched from the guard posts. Dirt flew upwards then an orange blast briefly filled the western horizon.

"FDC, this is Spaniard. I've got secondaries on Target Braves. How copy?"

"Secondaries are confirmed on Braves. Anything from Red Sox or Mets?"

Jimenez shook his head. "Nothing, yet."

"Solid copy. Stand fast while we recompute."

"So we go back to waiting. Come on, pendejos. Help me send you all to hell where you belong.

Quietly he hummed a song. It was an old piece, known before its use by the Mexican Army outside a mission in San Antonio. In the bullet-riddled night, Jimenez could hear ghostly bugles wailing across the darkness.

It is a good day to die, he told himself as he scanned for targets.

\#

"Sergeant Lyons, where have you been?" Corporal Maresley demanded when Sylvie walked into her assigned bunker.

"I was in my shop when the Taliban blew a hole in the berm. Which sucked almost as badly as them trying to come through the hole right afterward."

"How the blazes did you make it out of that?" another woman demanded.

"Somebody gave Cassidy a machine gun," Sylvie said simply.

"Who would do that?" another soldier protested.

"Well this time it was the Taliban."

"Aren't they so lucky?"

"Blessed, blessed I say. As God is my witness, that Yank has excellent timing," Lyons admitted.

"Well, good to hear. It's been a rough night over here so far."

Sylvie surveyed the semi-lit gloom, recognizing many of the faces present. In the center sat what had to be a gaggle of aides, if their civilian attire was anything to go by.

At least with all the rockets and gunfire we don't have to hear another damn lecture she told herself. *I might just slap a bitch if that happens.*

"How many of us are in here?" Sylvie asked.

"All of second. Staff and the Lieutenant went to speak with the captain."

Which leaves me to wonder —

"Why?" Sylvie asked aloud.

"Why what, Sergeant?"

"Why are we in here, sitting on our bums?" Sylvie demanded loudly.

"Not like we can help man the posts, the Marines wouldn't let us take that risk," Corporal Maresley declared

"Gotta be something we can do," Sylvie responded.

"What?"

"What about taking them supplies?" Sylvie held up the carabiner full of keys Cassidy had left on her flak jacket.

"That's perfect!" A soldier quickly agreed.

"Maresley, take your section of three to the aid shelter, tell them we need the stretchers. Meet me at the chow hall." Sylvie quickly scanned the room. "Sharples, take your squad to the other bunkers, grab everybody Sergeant and below."

"After that?"

"Meet me at the chow hall," Sylvie directed.

"What about the rest of us?" Listero demanded. "You can't just leave us here!"

If Sylvie heard the unhappy woman, she said nothing as she continued to give orders.

"Collins, grab your section and follow me." Sylvie spared a snarl for the gaggle of aides. "You lot. On your feet and follow me."

"Why?" Listero demanded.

"Because I said so," Sylvie told her.

The aide crossed her arms. "What are you gonna do, shoot me if I disobey?"

The backhand Sylvie threw caught Listero's mouth, making her head snap back, as much from the shock of the assault as the force Sylvie had imparted. Listero was still recovering as Sylvie passed her rifle into Collins' waiting hands. Stalking forward, Sylvie snatched the aide up by her rainbow mohawk to deliver three rapid jabs, pulping Listero's lips where the hardened plastic knuckle guard of her worn gloves made contact.

Whap

Another slap, this time on the ear. "You listening, now?"

Slap

The second backhand drew blood from a cut on the cheek. "I said, are you listening now —"

Sylvie's left hand balled into a fist and she rotated her hips into the strike, driving deep into Listero's hefty gut with the blow.

"— Fat Bitch!"

Listero retched violently, twisting and falling to her knees amidst the detritus of her vomit.

"Ugh!" The now-terrified aide gasped as she tried to drop to the ground, held up only by the strong hand clenched around her hair.

"About time! I thought I'd have to use all the other strikes the Americans have taught us!"

Sylvie yanked the aide's head around so she could look up at her tormentor.

"In this room, right here, right now, nobody outranks me," Sylvie declared. "Insofar as you are concerned, I am the fucking Duchess of Hell. Do you understand that, Fat Bitch?"

"Yessss," Listero moaned.

Sylvie threw Listero down and took back her rifle.

"In Bourne, everybody pulls their damn weight! Doesn't matter if you've got a cock or a twat, you work! Right now our boys are out there fighting and dying to protect us. If we live through this night without getting raped to death by those evil Taliban cockheads, it'll be because of some hard ass American men."

"But... but..." Listero started to say.

"But nothing! We love those crazy, loud, dirty, rude American men. You harpies have done nothing but insult them. And whine at them."

"They're men!"

"They're our men," Maresley declared angrily.

"You don't need them," Listero countered weakly.

"Don't you get it?" Sylvie demanded.

"Get what?"

"Without them we'd all be dead already. Or getting gang-raped."

"They wouldn't. The... couldn't... why would the Taliban do that?"

"Because they're animals! It's what they do."

Listero said nothing as Sylvie jabbed a forefinger in her chest.

"You can hate them all you want. Hell they'd probably encourage it just for fun. But our men are out there dying to keep anything bad from happening to us. And you will respect that."

Sylvie scanned the room, seeing the resolution on the face of her fellow NCO. "Collins, put the aides in the middle."

"Easy enough, Sergeant," Collins said smoothly. Her squad stepped into their places and Sylvie caught a nod from her.

"Move out," Sylvie ordered sternly. Somewhere, a machine gun rattled and Sylvie wondered how long it would be until she saw her man again. *God keep him safe, please. I don't want to live without him.*

#

Maresely met them at the chow hall, arriving after Sharples, Halvetti, and Grierson. "Sorry we're behind. Had to run to the Gunline. Doc told me they had stretchers over there."

"Understood. How many does that give us?"

"Seven total."

"Good to go." Sylvie ran the numbers in her head once more. "We're going to move two stretchers per section. One is loaded with ammo, the other has water and caffeine."

"Caffeine?"

Sylvie jangled the keys. "Bluebeard's locker is full of surprises."

"Ooooooo," Collins said excitedly. "They're going to think we're better looking than Page Three models with cold beer!"

"First time in me life these A's of mine can stand a chance against Lucy Pinder's cannons," Evans said with a smile, giving them all a good laugh.

"Grierson, you'll take posts One through Four. Drop water and caffeine. Let me know over the radio how many wounded you're carrying to the aid station. Once you've done all of that, come straight back here."

"Got it," Grierson assured as a chain of women began stacking and moving cases of water on the stretchers.

"All of you make sure to get a headcount on how many lads are on the walls and which posts have what crew serves. It could be anything from L7s to the Mark Nineteens or the fifties. When you make the second trip, you'll be passing them machine gun ammo and speed-loading empty mags. Leave a second bandolier with every man. They're gonna spend bullets like water tonight."

"I hear you."

"Good. Halvetti, same thing but you've got posts Five through Nine, and check where Nealen set up that plug for the breach in the wall. I think he was building a bunker of some kind when I left."

"On it."

"Collins, you're going to MarineLand and FDC. You've got three guns to check. Don't forget to ask permission to step on. That's a damned hot place right now."

"Roger that, Sergeant."

"As for the rest of you, stack your rifles against the wall," Sylvie motioned toward the kitchen. "Let's put together an assembly line. We've got sandwiches to make!"

#

"Ohmygod what was that?" Listero screamed shrilly, dropping to the floor in panic as thunder split the night once again in a triphammer burst.

"I believe that's my boyfriend. Telling the Taliban what he thinks of them," Sylvie voiced aloud.

The kitchen went still in an instant. Up and down the line, women stared at Sylvie, some in admiration, some in horror.

"Sergeant, you mean the rumors about you and one of the Yanks —" Maresley started.

"Is real?" Collins finished.

"It is, Mare," Sylvie said as she cut cheese from a block with a food slicer.

"Is it Chef?" a Private asked.

"Yes."

"Is he a good kisser?"

"He's a damn good kisser when he's not busy stabbing people in the face and getting his damn ass shot the hell off like a damn fool!" Sylvie yelled, striking the tabletop with the maille-glove covered hand.

She glared in frustration at the people around her.

"Damn his hide for being a crazy fool to do what he does! Not enough to stay in cover and shoot at 'em with a rifle. No! That's not macho enough! The pig-ignorant bullheaded sonofabitch just had to go out with a knife and start busting heads while I was trying to clear a stoppage! Like to scare the hell out of me till kingdom come!"

"Well. Damn."

The kitchen rocked again as the gunline launched another furious barrage and the women tittered cheerfully.

"Ladies, I do believe Hell has frozen over," Maresley announced.

"This still doesn't settle the pool," Sandra announced from her end of the line.

"What're you talking about, Collier?" a Private snapped.

"Lyons, you take the stud stallion for a ride?" Sandra challenged.

"No ring! No ride!" Sylvie held up her bare left hand for all to see. "That's the rule."

Shocked silence greeted her ears before she heard Sandra whoop fiercely.

"Attagirl! I knew you'd win me the pot!"

"What?" Sylvie demanded.

"Everybody else bet on him taking you to bed with a quickness." She smiled broadly. "I'm the only one who bet against them."

"You bet on me?"

"I've known you how long? If you didn't take pretty boy Parduhn to bed, there's no reason you'd settle for Cassidy, who is nowhere near as good-looking."

"Settle? Hah, settle nothing!" Sylvie laughed, surprised at her own openness. "That man? Puh-lease. Need I remind you of his brownies?"

"Oh God, that man and chocolate are a danger to married women," another soldier moaned. "I don't know how I'm going to convince Reggie to make those for me. I love him, God bless him my Reggie is a sweetheart. But dearest Reggie burns water."

"Maybe we should kidnap Cassidy, bring him back with us to Catterick," a woman suggested.

"Yeah, no. I'll pass on that," Donal retorted. "I had to clean up the mess he made with Lyons over in the breach. I like living."

"Yeah, what did happen over there, Lyons?"

Sylvie sighed. *I need to get them back on track, but we'll never get there unless I satisfy the gossipy lot of magpies.*

"I was walking the perimeter when the rockets started dropping on us. Post Seven went down. The assholes used charges to blow a gap in the wall. I caught them coming in, which stopped them for a moment. All I had was my backup mag and just as I'm thinking 'this is it' Cassidy comes along with the L7 from the post like he's Rambo."

"Crikey."

"He stood in the gap, ripped 'em to shreds, then helped me build a position. The wogs came back around, so we gave 'em what for."

"Good show," a voice breathed.

"Now, if we're finished discussing my love life, I'd like to get back to making sandwiches with a quickness, understood?"

"Yes, Sergeant!" the room shouted, laughing as they went back to their work.

#

In the Camp Leatherneck Motor Pool, Mike Roach felt his temper growing shorter at the rapid rate. Much of it had to do with the pampered ponce standing in front of him, questioning his orders.

"Sir, it's several hours to Bourne, what if we don't get there in time?" Lieutenant Colonel Duff-McQueeg said fearfully. He might've been called patrician save for the sallow-faced complexion which graced his features.

Around him, the officers and men of his squadron watched, wondering why in God's name they had been awakened at this unholy hour.

"Lieutenant Colonel, what do you see on my collar?" Roach asked politely.

"Eagles."

"Which makes me what?"

"A Colonel."

"When a Colonel gives a Lieutenant Colonel an order, what should the Lieutenant Colonel do?"

"Follow orders?" Duff-McQueeg said hesitantly.

"Do you know how to follow orders, Lieutenant Colonel?"

"Sir?"

"Understand this — It is a long road to FOB Bourne. They have already been holding out for six long months. You lot got to sit up here, fat, happy and cozy, while a bunch of girl engineers took it in the teeth and the only help they got came from a platoon of American Marines. Colonel DuBois is trapped down there, waiting for us to bring a relief column. He needs men!" Mike pitched his voice to be heard across the motor pool.

"He told me to grab Scots Dragoons because he thought they were the men who knew how to soldier. Maybe he was wrong. Maybe I should go find those Fusiliers who just showed up, see if they know what duty and honor mean!"

Growls reached his ears as he saw Duff-McQueeg's face turn white.

"But — but — but —"

At that moment, Mike Roach prayed fervently. He did not want to relieve the man, for diplomatic and personal reasons. A report for cowardice like this would destroy the man's career, and likely the man too. But those were his boys out there dying, his Marines!

I need a miracle right now. C'mon, who's it gonna be?

Another officer stepped forward, a wiry, compact man with deep blue eyes and sandy blond hair. He put a hand on Duff-McQueeg's back.

"Sarn't Major McNamara."

"Suh!"

"Please see the commander to the Squadron Doctor! He looks shell-shocked."

"Right away suh."

Duff-McQueeg was hustled away, still half-dressed and highly confused. The officer, a Major from what Mike could see of his rank patch in the half-lit darkness, began barking orders to the Squadron. Finally, the man turned to face Mike.

"Apologies sir, he looked like he's had a bad go of things."

"It happens…"

"Major Patrick Hennessy, Squadron XO."

"Thank you, Major."

"Not a problem sir. We'll be mounted and ready to move out in ten minutes. Will you be riding with us, or in your own vehicle?"

"My own, this is your show. I don't care how you do it, just get us there —" Mike checked his watch. "By oh-eight-hundred. If we get there, and none of our people are alive, you will give the Taliban the peace of Genghis Khan."

"Make it a desert and call it peace?" Hennessy asked.

"Precisely," Roach confirmed resolutely.

Patrick nodded his head, then turned about face toward the Squadron. "Any man scared to earn his pay, step back and stay out of my way. The rest of you, mount your tracks and follow me!"

Chapter 33

Across the Sky

"Spaniard, this is Blackie-Seven. How copy?"

"Loud and clear," Jimenez declared into his radio.

"Bringing in five-zero-zero pound JDAMs, north to south."

"Target is enemy rocket position. Marking with illum."

"Understood."

"FDC, glowstick."

"FDC copies."

Somewhere on the gunline, a howitzer howled, dispensing another round into the air to fiery acclaim. The illumination round sailed along, disgorging its contents as it went. Instantly, three million candlepower worth of light turned the distant grid square from night to brilliant day with mind-boggling intensity.

Below the burning magnesium light, men squirmed, trying to sink into the sand, as if that would make them disappear from the Hornet fighter-bomber's camera suite. Those who did not squirm gawked, surprised both at the sound of cannon fire, and that such a light could exist in this place.

"Spaniard, this is Blackie-Seven. Eyes on target. Tallyho!"

"Cover your ears people, we're about to make some noise!" Jimenez warned across the company-wide net.

The Hornets dropped out of the sky in line astern, engine exhaust illuminating where they'd been for the brief instant before they discharged their lethal cargo on the now-illuminated and panicking men dashing about in confusion.

Jimenez watched as the pilots hauled back on the sticks, applying afterburner to their efforts. Rising on twin pillars of fire, they roared into the night sky as explosions ripped apart the night.

"Jesus, Mary and Joseph, thank you for letting me be born an American. I love my country," he declared as he crossed himself, awestruck at the fireworks on display.

"Spaniard, say again your last?" his radio chirped.

Belatedly, Jimenez realized that his thumb had been on the transmit button still.

"FDC you catching all this on GBOSS?"

"Yeah we are. This shouldn't be real."

"But it is," he said cheerfully, then released his hand from the radio.

#

"Sarn't Major, make a note," Natasha ordered as she watched the action from her seat.

"Yes ma'am?"

"At some future date, we need to send a case of the good stuff over to that squadron as a polite appreciation for the lovely show of force," Fitzsimmons declared.

Yes, they were just doing their duty. But it never hurts to remind the flyboys that they're appreciated, she told herself. *Manners cost a lady nothing.*

"Yes, ma'am."

"Why can't we just fly away on one of the choppers?" an aide suggested.

"Yes, Captain, if you don't mind, why can't we do that?" Siddiq asked.

"We have several factors working against us ma'am."

"Such as?"

"Do you mind the long explanation?"

"Well I do have a pressing engagement in Leeds tomorrow, need to be there for a charity cricket test."

Both women smiled wanly, recognizing and acknowledging how very deeply in trouble they were right then.

"There is only so much of any given asset, in a particular theater, at any one time. If you have say forty heli's in Afghanistan, you might only see half of them in operation at any time, the rest are down for maintenance."

"Is that normal?" Siddiq interrupted.

"I'd have to check with my cousin in Army Aviation, but it wouldn't surprise me. Flying is very hard on airframes, ma'am."

"Noted."

"That pool of twenty remaining heli's gets divided up between attack and transport. At best, there are ten available transport helicopters. You flew out on three." Natasha tried, and failed not to glance in the direction of the burning wreckage.

Siddiq and Barleycorn looked respectively abashed and shocked as the information processed for them

"What about the other seven?" Barleycorn asked.

"Could be anywhere. We have literally hundreds of operations and missions ongoing at every hour," Natasha said.

"The annual budget fights make so much more sense now," Siddiq said sadly.

"Yes ma'am, they do." Natasha shifted in her seat, trying to work out stiffness without disturbing Doc Knighton's handiwork on her stitched, taped, and glued legs.

"What else is there to consider," Siddiq asked.

"My next salient point on this matter is that we are in the midst of a very nasty and very hot landing zone. We can only receive and send off what heli's we have at great risk to the aircrews onboard."

"Who here is coordinating this? Surely you aren't hiding an air traffic controller nearby."

"That's what Corporal Jimenez is doing up top with one of Sergeant House's comm Marines," Natasha explained. "He's a twenty-three year old JTAC."

"Twenty-three? He's little more than a child!" Smythers exclaimed.

"No, ma'am, he surely ain't. He might be a Yankee from the Bronx, but he ain't no child." Brady proclaimed. "He's been doing a man's work since he was twelve, and a Marine since he was seventeen. Way we reckon it, he's all man, and all Marine."

Natasha looked significantly toward the FDC Chief. "Sergeant Brady, just how busy is Corporal Jimenez?"

"He's coordinated five air strikes, set up the first chopper insertion, and we've got another chopper on the way for more."

"I am suddenly reminded of the last time I went to the ballet for a show, when I was struck by how tired the conductor seemed to be."

"Why don't we hop onboard the American's heli's? Surely they have space," Listero chirped.

Natasha's smile turned into a glacial snarl. "The only people those are carrying right now, are wounded personnel. Insofar as I'm concerned, your pompous, pampered, spoiled ass can sit here and wait till hell freezes over all I care."

"How dare you —"

"I'd shut the hell up if'n I was y'all," Matthew Brady loudly announced from his seat in front of the FDC displays. He fixed them with a glare.

Listero tried to return the look, but Brady was unmoved. "I owe you money?"

The question caught her off-guard.

"Huh?"

"Do. I. Owe. You. Money?" Brady said slowly.

"No. But —"

"You think you got the balls to fight me?"

"No. But —"

"You talked an awful lotta shit earlier for someone who ain't worth much," Brady declared. "Your fancy degree, your bank account, ain't none of it means a pissant thing out here."

"Why are you —"

"I've never been one to hit a woman, but if'n you wanna fight, we can go right here, right now."

He removed his pistol belt, handing it over to Theiss.

"I'll make it easy for you," he declared, then waited, watching the normally aggressive woman as she realized how thoroughly outmatched she was.

"Go put yer nose in the corner, mind your manners, and I won't pull you over my knee for the ass beating yo meemaw forgot to give you."

The humiliation of being ordered around burned across her cheeks, but she did as told.

Brady waited until she had followed his orders before he turned back to his displays. He heard an electronic click and turned to see Shores concealing a camera.

"Whatcha doin' bubba?" Brady asked softly.

"Hoping to get famous on World Star," Shores admitted.

Brady chuckled. "Keep that safe. We may need it later."

"Will do."

"Sergeant Brady, what's the word on that first heli?" Fitzsimmons asked politely in the silence.

"Theiss?" Brady said.

"One-tree minutes out and closing. They've got corpsmen on board for the wounded," Theiss reported

#

"IR Illum on the way!"

Rifled guns made their presence known once more in the darkness, gouts of flame bathing the night in shades of orange and yellow as the big guns hammered away. Elsewhere, men in dirty robes heard that ominous thunder and cringed, wondering where the rounds would strike next.

Unlike the white light illumination rounds which had gone out before, these did nothing the unaided eye could observe. They were a special munition, designed only to emit light in the infrared spectrum. One could put the illumination round directly on the target to mark for air, without obstructing their view of the target, or rendering thermal sensors useless. The infrared light would serve to keep the grid square lit for quite a while, with the enemy none the wiser.

"Spaniard, this is Scarface Four, I have one impact to the north of Bourne. Taking it now."

"Solid copy. FDC, this is Spaniard, go cold tube. Air mobile friendlies in the area," Jimenez declared.

"FDC Copies all."

Jimenez watched in fascination as rockets streaked away from the Cobra's wing struts. Far out to the east, he saw red tracers slashing through the air with righteous fury. It was a sight which he'd seen before, but still drew joy from.

"Adiós pendejos. Tu pinche culeros."

His radio crackled.

"Spaniard this is Komodo Eleven, how copy?"

"Loud and clear. We have six casualties ready for immediate evac. Look for the purple buzz saw."

"Roger that, Spaniard. Be advised we are also landing reinforcements."

"Tell them to clear right when they exit the bird, we'll send casualties on the left."

#

High above, Kathy Bathlicek cast her eyes about in the darkness, before a spinning purple circle appeared from the semi-lit darkness. Coming down quickly, she kept the rotors turning as the gunny and his marines cleared out and to the right while stretcher bearers ran forward to meet the medics coming off of her helicopter. The time on the ground seemed to last hours as the injured were placed aboard, and the medics went to work performing what they could to save those lives.

"We up?" Kathy shouted over the intercom.

A hatch slammed shut on the fuselage.

"We are now!" Ries announced over his headset.

"Dee dee mau!" Tammy ordered the pilot.

Taking the collective in hand, the Super Stallion quickly rose, nose dropping as Kathy stepped on the gas pedal and powered forward.

The Cobras took their spots around her, an aerial shield against any further harm.

\#

"I'm looking for Lieutenant Harper," Pililaau announced as he strode into the Command Post. "The Colonel sends his regards."

"Ah, the redoubtable Gunny Pililaau has arrived," DuBois declared.

"Good to see you too, sir."

"Where is Colonel Roach, if I may?"

"He was headed to build a relief column. Told me I needed to buy him some time, sir."

"Excellent. As to the lieutenant, he should be back down in a moment from conferring with our Local Security Chief about how to best use you."

"I'm here, sir. Gunny," Harper said as he appeared in the stairway. "Whatcha got for me?"

"Two full squads and a short squad. Colonel kept a fire team for his own security."

"Hold that thought. I have an idea."

"Yes, sir."

"Thanks, Gunny."

"What's your report, Mr. Harper?" Natasha asked.

"Ma'am, Sarn't Major, we have the fires put out for now, and the enemy appears to be licking their wounds for the nonce," Harper reported.

"Casualties?" Fitzsimmons asked.

"Some ma'am, mostly amongst my Marines," Harper said.

"Understood."

Harper checked his watch "It's just after zero-one, ma'am. We've been at this for nearly three hours now. I recommend we move to seventy-five percent stand down, myself and the NCOs to take the first watch, Staff and remaining officers to take the second."

"Stand down to what?"

"Sleep, ma'am."

"You can think of sleep right now?" Fitzsimmons asked incredulously.

"Yes ma'am,' Harper assured. "Even if it's just two hours, it gives our people a chance to recover and recharge."

Fitzsimmons sighed, unsure of how to proceed. The notion went against her every instinct.

"It's a risk," she admitted.

"Aye, but what fights better, a man who's had sleep in his system or a man too exhausted to run his machine gun?" Harper argued. "Fox Company, Seventh Marines held Toktong Pass against a Chinese regiment, in part because Captain Barber ensured proper rest as much as he could for his men."

"How do you organize something like that?" Balcombe asked.

"Already done." Harper tore a page from his notebook. "Gunny, if you can put your people on the posts, we should be good to go."

"Can do sir."

"Spaniard, Fox Two," Harper called over his radio.

"Send it."

"We're going with option A. Echo Seven Papa needs you to walk his people to the post. Everybody else is to rack out in their IDF holes."

"Aye aye, sir," Jimenez replied. From above, they could hear him stomping down the stairs, likely snapping out orders on his radio as he moved.

"Survey Met, when is sunrise?" Harper snapped.

"Looking at zero-seven sir."

"Good, we'll split the difference. Brady, you'll take the second watch on the GBOSS," Harper directed. "I'll take first watch. We'll wake you at zero-four fifteen."

"Understood, sir," Brady said.

"You really think we can win," Fitzsimmons said. It was not a question, but a statement. A challenge. The captain's normally calm mask was slipping.

Not that I'm surprised. She's got to be thinking about what happens if she and the girls are captured alive. Harper sighed.

"We're in a siege ma'am," he explained. "The great and important secret is to not lose our nerve. We know help is on the way. We can see it on the Blue Force Tracker screen."

"But what if the Taliban have a trap set for him as well?" Balcombe objected.

"The Colonel has never let us down before. He ain't about to start now. So long as we stay calm, those bastards outside the walls don't stand a chance."

"And you really think we can hold till he arrives?" Balcombe demanded.

Harper held up his radio.

"Marines! What is our profession?

The snarls which answered in reply through the tinny speaker became a chant filling the silence of the night across the FOB. All those present could hear the eerie sound, an angry, predatory creature stalking the empty desert in search of its quarry.

"These are American Marines," Harper declared firmly. "Men like them held Belleau Wood against the Imperial German Army, took Iwo Jima, beat the Chinese at Chosin, and slaughtered the VC at Khe Sanh."

Harper's scowl became a righteous sneer.

"Baghdad. Wasn't shit. Fallujah. Wasn't shit."

He pointed at the monitor screen where his men bellowed their defiance into the night, pounding gloved fists against armored chests, and in at least three cases Fitzsimmons could see, violently head butting each other, helmets colliding and men falling to the ground on impact. Laughing as they fell, and rose again, still laughing. Exulting in their august status.

"Soon enough," Harper solemnly promised, "you're going to see why holding FOB Bourne wasn't shit neither."

Chapter 34

You're Only Young...

"Brigade commander, we've taken casualties all over!"

"Brigade commander, we lost dozens of men! How did nobody know about the obstacles?"

"I need bandages, where are the Allah be-damned bandages?"

The cacophony of voices was becoming too much as Saeed tried to process the information.

"Did we gain a foothold anywhere?" someone demanded.

"We ripped open a hole in the one wall, but nobody's made it back yet."

"And nobody will, another voice declared.

Turning, the several heads of the Dishu Brigade saw Shamil shamble into the bunker, bloody and spent.

"I sent an assault team in, right on the heels of my recoilless rifles. They never called back."

"Did you send a follow-on attack?"

"Yes," Shamil ground out. "One of the older men was instructed to wait in the darkness and report back what he saw."

"And?"

"They have covered the base in defensive trickery. Barbed wire everywhere, at ankle and shin height. There is a great ditch near the base of the walls, all the way around. Anybody attempting to charge the walls will find razor wire and spike traps."

"What became of the second assault team?" another asked impatiently.

"Cut down to a man. The fires are mostly under control now. They also managed to fly in helicopters during the air attacks."

"They what?"

"Achmed sighted them. He says they likely flew out all of their injured personnel."

"Did they take any new personnel in?"

"He is unsure, but it would not surprise him."

"Then we have only one viable option," Saeed declared.

"Brigade commander?"

"Aziz, how much rocket ammunition do we have?" Saeed asked, ignoring the question.

"Perhaps a dozen rounds, no more. The air attacks have been vicious," Aziz spat.

"Gather all of our remaining heavy munitions here," he gestured, pointing at a spot on the map. "Let's see, Basayev, bring me all the men you can find before dawn, to the same spot. Leave our pickets where they are, in case the Americans try to send a relief column."

"Are you sure they'd try something while the storm rages to the north?"

"If they were so easily pushed aside, we would have ejected them from here and Iraq a decade ago. We must make the best use of the haboob, else we lose this great opportunity."

"It will be as you say, Brigade commander."

\#

The Dragoons had made it to Garmsir by oh-four-hundred, rolling through the gates with their lights on when Mike caught sight of the tanks. Or, rather, caught sight of the tank barrels casually aimed in his direction.

"Colonel, do you owe somebody money?" his driver asked.

"No. Why?"

"Because it's been a long minute since I've stared down a tank barrel. I had forgotten how big they are."

Mike Roach looked out the window of his tactical vehicle.

"Huh, how about?"

His Cougar came to a halt and he cracked open the door, enjoying the quick rush of fresh, cool air into the too-warm cab.

The barrel had not moved from where it was pointed and Mike waved at it.

Range is maybe twenty meters. If we were trying to ambush them or play something sneaky, we'd be dead. Nice to see they're paying attention to their security.

"Evening. Surprised to see company after dark," a man announced as he stomped up in a khaki coverall. For having been awoken in the dead of night, he was surprisingly alert, possibly even cheerful.

"It's been a long night —" Mike paused, unsure of the Marine's name or rank.

"Major Kaag, sir, Charlie company, First Tanks."

"We still have Abrams in-theater? I could've sworn you all went home."

Kaag smiled thinly.

"Almost sir, we're due for rotation stateside in another month. Along with our tracks."

Kaag affectionately patted the steel behemoth the same way he might have a favorite horse.

A British lieutenant ran up. "Sir, Major Hennessy's apologies, but it's going to be at least ten minutes till we can leave. Refueling is, however, proceeding as quickly as we can make it."

"My compliments to the major, I understand," Mike pronounced.

"By your leave, sir."

Kaag noticed the by-play as more Dragoon officers joined them, admiring the tank up close.

"Sorry we couldn't get you home in time for Christmas," Mike admitted.

"It happens. Where you headed in such a hurry, Colonel, sir?" Kaag asked,

"Got a buncha girl engineers and cannon cockers from Twelfth Marines catching hell right now, down in Dishu."

"Riding to their relief?"

"Yeah."

"Mind if we tag along?" The major asked.

"If you've no pressing engagements, it would be appreciated," Mike said.

"You think those ungainly beasts can stay with our tracks?" a Dragoon officer demanded.

Kaag fixed the Dragoon with a gimlet eye as he turned his head slightly.

"First Sergeant Kay!"

An entirely too-cheerful smooth Cajun voice responded from atop the truck nearby.

"Yes, suh?"

"Sound boots and saddles! Officers and NCOs at my track, we ride in five!"

"Happily suh!"

Bugles sounded from speakers, causing men to appear, heads popping up out of track hatches like so many prairie dogs before they ducked back inside. Strange howls filled the air as the tanks powered up their turbine engines.

Kaag skewered his critic with an entirely too cheerful grin. "The question, little crunchy, is can you keep up with us?"

#

"Phil, who do you think we could score an interview with next?" James Cochrane asked, much to the dismay of his crew.

"Good bloody morning to you too. I haven't had my tea yet." Phil Bishop checked his watch. "It's almost six bloody am. You think somebody is coherent enough for questions already?"

"Why not Nealen?" Phil suggested.

"That has potential."

"I'd say the American lieutenant, Harper, but he looks like a Boy Scout. Nobody would believe he was in charge last night."

"True, true. Let's go talk to the captain and see what she can do."

"Where do you think we should set up, Tim?" James asked.

"How about the motorpool, by one of the trucks."

"With the burnt heli in the background?"

"Aye. Be a good look for how serious the night's been," Tim explained.

"As if we didn't have enough of that already," James admitted. "God knows folks back home are having kittens right now. When was the last time we got live footage from a firefight?"

"I honestly can't think of anything since the Iraq invasion," Timothy admitted.

"Same here," Phil declared.

"Will we be live?" James asked.

"No, let's tape it. We'll save the effort in case something major comes up, you know how the network can be," Phil reminded them.

"I dig it."

#

"Brigade commander, the vehicle is ready," Aziz declared.

"Basayev, are the men in place?"

"We wait only for your command."

"Good man. Aziz, send word that the gates of Paradise await the faithful who die in the service of the Jihad."

Aziz bowed his head. "It shall be so, Commander."

#

Shahi Siddiq was taking in an education she had never expected after she graduated Uni with her Masters' degree. She was surrounded by soldiers who were teaching her about their lives, their craft, and what made things so difficult for them. Shahi had long been engaged in budget fights (armies were outrageously expensive after all) but for the first time, she was understanding why they were so expensive. Nor was she trying to memorize all that they said. Her aide, Beebee, was busily writing in shorthand as if they were back in Professor Stern's chemistry class together.

"Now, you said that you go out training how often?" she asked, looking at the Marines.

"Two to three weeks every month."

"Shooting artillery?"

"Not always. Hawaii is limited on impact areas. We'll mostly practice running the guns, plus the parts and pieces."

"But that costs fuel, and it wears things down."

"Yes ma'am, I reckon so," Kramer admitted. "But I got a question for you?"

"Go ahead."

"What's the cost of losing?"

Shahi paused, her aide looking toward Kramer as well.

"Losing a war, or losing a battle?" he said.

"How about losing a battle, like this one?" he said.

"What happens to your soldiers here?" House added.

"I — I don't know."

"Jessica Lynch, that's what," Kramer grumped.

"Who?"

"Lynch was an American soldier captured by the iraqis during the invasion after her convoy was wiped out," Kramer explained

"It wasn't good for her. My cousin was an Air Force comms officer, and what information came through had to be kept close-held for several years," House added.

"Why?"

"Because if it became known that an American woman had been mistreated by Iraqi soldiers, the odds that we'd have let any Iraqi prisoners live is real low," Kramer declared.

Siddiq's mouth made an "O" but she said nothing.

"Don't get him wrong, we ain't saints," Johnson admitted. "But we have standards. We have a code we hold ourselves to. Somebody hurts womenfolk around us, a beating is the easy thing they'll catch."

House held up a book from his bag. "Sergeant Cassidy loaned me this, figured I could use it for some light reading."

Flipping it open, House began to read details of the capture and imprisonment of British nurses by the Japanese Army during World War Two. It was clearly painful for him to do so, and when he finished, the rage written on his face was palpable.

"I'd kill a whole lot of men to ensure these girls never got that treatment," House said with finality.

Siddiq stared at them, her dusky face pale as House's words bounced around in her head.

"Pilsen understood that," Clarke declared.

"Pilsen?" Siddiq asked.

"One of the Taliban made it over the wall and into our bunker while the BBC crew were interviewing us. Taliban tried to use a grenade on us. Pilsen dived on the grenade. He died for us," Clarke continued.

The room went silent.

"Anybody tell Sergeant Cassidy or Sergeant Pistol?" House asked. "They put a lot of work into him."

"Sarn't Major did," Johnson stated. "They're handling it about how you'd expect."

"Oh boy."

"Like the Okie said, we uns ain't angels, ma'am. Tin soldiers ain't no plaster saints. But we ain't thugs neither," House persisted. He looked to his British comrades. "How much time did y'all get on the range or in the field before you came here?"

"Maybe two weeks. Total," Sharples said.

"What were you doing in the meantime?" Shahi demanded.

"We had speeches," Maresley said bitterly. "Days upon days of speeches about women's lib."

"And it did fuck all nothing, Corporal," Clarke spat as she looked toward Shahi. "Ma'am, those speeches didn't do a damn thing. Not a thing at all." She jerked a thumb toward Johnson.

"The Captain asked Sergeant Johnson to teach us how to fight hand to hand. Like the Marines do."

"Whatever for?" Shahi asked.

"Because that's what we're good for, killing people and breaking things," Johnson declared. "Clarke worked awful hard to pass off two belts. Just like her fellow soldiers."

"We should've had it before deployment," Clarke declared.

"Or first aid training," another soldier said bitterly. "Didn't get near enough of that. I still think about how Corporal Lee died in my arms."

"But somebody made sure we sat through all those speeches," Maresley said disgustedly.

"What do you mean died in your arms?" Shahi Siddiq said in dismay.

"Corporal Lee took a round while he was out surveying for the airstrip, our first week here," Sharples said. "She was with him."

"I didn't know enough first aid to save him. He bled all over me. I kept trying to plug the bullet hole with my fingers but they weren't big enough!"

The young girl was crying now, angry tears. Maresely moved to hold the young private, wrapping her up in a hug as she sobbed. "I still hear him, breath rattling as he died, because I wasn't good enough!"

Her statements ran circles within the young Minister's head, and for the first time, the real cost of what she had committed through legislation was real for her. It had a human cost she couldn't have considered before. Looking toward her aide, Shahi realized the other woman was crying as well.

"We failed them," Beebee sobbed quietly. "What do we do now, Shahi?"

For the first time in a political career marked solely by success, Shahi Siddiq was at a loss for words.

What do I say? What do I do? Would she accept my apology? Is it enough?

An explosion tore apart the morning, throwing everybody standing within the bunker to the floor and removing any immediate need for the Minister for Hampstead to worry about her next political move.

Chapter 35

...But You're Gonna Die

They wound up with the Boy Scout anyway, much to Phil's chagrin. Captain Fitzsimmons declared that the only interviews they could give right then would be with the two lieutenants. Balcombe had found the means to clean up and even apply a little makeup. Like a rose shining forth at dawn, she looked perfect. Harper, somehow, was smiling. Irrepressibly. As if he weren't in the middle of a great muthering battle and thousands of miles from home in the Northwest Frontier.

"Good morning from southern Afghanistan, my name is James Cochrane. I'm here on FOB Bourne, with Lieutenant Camille Balcombe of the British Army's Engineers. Ms Balcombe could you explain what happened last night for our viewers at home?"

"Absolutely," she said, shooting the camera with a dazzling smile. "We came under attack from a very large force, which we believe is part of the Taliban's Dishu Brigade. They started with a rocket attack and tried to storm the walls."

Camille turned to look at James significantly. "Fortunately we've had wonderful assistance from Lieutenant Harper and his Marines."

"How are you doing this morning, Lieutenant Harper?" James asked.

"My Marines and I are doing outstanding."

"Really? Why is that?"

"Because this is what Marines do — we fight."

"But we've been surrounded and under siege since ten o'clock last night!" James protested.

Harper shrugged. "So?" He sniffed regally. "They have us surrounded, we can shoot in any direction and hit them."

"That right there sums up my feelings of the last several months we've hosted them here at FOB Bourne. It has been a pleasure to have them," Camille declared.

"I'll add that Ms. Balcombe has been a wonderfully gracious hostess. My Marines appreciate the work your gals have been doing. Last night they were truly magnificent in helping the wounded get prompt medical treatment."

The base's warning siren began to wail.

"Somebody must be shooting rockets again. Looks like we'll need to continue this inside a bunker," Camille Balcombe suggested.

Something made the hair on James' neck stand on end. Before he could say anything however, an unfamiliar voice made itself known over the radio.

"Local Suck, we got a car approaching the front gate at high speed," Harper's radio squawked.

James didn't wait for permission, he threw Camille onto his shoulder, running behind a 7-ton truck for cover in a manner any sensible person would've found disturbing. Not wanting to be left behind, the news crew came with. They had learned in the last twelve hours that when a Marine began running in a particular direction, it was in their best interest to follow.

"James! Put me down!" She shrieked. "This is undignified!"

Rather than listen, James dumped her on her back, then flattened himself across her.

The rockets struck, throwing up shrapnel and debris into the air. Several landed within the ANA compound, flattening it entirely.

A bomb detonated, drowning out any further indignation.

\#

Herbert Pililaau had just come out of the latrine when the shockwave bodily picked the large Hawaiian up and threw him backwards.

Rising back to his feet, head shaking like a punch drunk bull, he stared at the spot where the front gate had been. It, and a significant portion of the front wall of FOB Bourne were gone.

The radio on his vest was screaming, multiple voices trying to communicate all at once. All the gunnery sergeant could see right then were the Marines he'd put on post there. His Marines. His boys. He began to run, flipping his radio over to the channels he knew his squads used.

Come on boys, this can't be it. Not like this he prayed.

#

James came off his feet, moving at a sprint toward the Command Post. Something was going on here. The Taliban couldn't have thrown all that ordnance at them without trying for a greater reward. Insofar as he knew, he still commanded the defense of the FOB.

"Fox-Two to Charlie Papa, front gate is gone!" Harper yelled into his radio.

"Good to hear your voice sir, where are you?" Nealen's voice declared from the radio speaker.

"Headed for the CP. Get to the motor pool and make sure you rally our boys."

"Hogfather copies all!"

Slaloming into the Command Post for the second time in less than a day, James Harper was confronted with a scene of chaos.

"Sir, we got infantry heading our way!" Brady declared, pointing at the GBOSS screen.

"Range?" Harper snapped.

"Over a klick. "

"How many?"

"Gotta be at least two companies' worth."

The gate's down, anybody on that wall is likely dead or unable to respond Harper considered.

"Five Actual, this is Fox-Two."

"Send it Fox-Two!"

"Emergency relocation to the motor pool! Azimuth is due north. All hands to assist!" Harper ordered.

"Emergency relocation to the motor pool, Azimuth is due north all hands to assist, aye sir!"

The radio went silent as the Command Post's inhabitants stared at Harper.

"What are you doing, Leftenant?" Natasha asked.

"How fast can you run half a mile, ma'am?"

"A couple minutes, why?"

"You're in good shape. Last time you ran a half mile, you did it in PT shorts and shoes," Harper surmised.

"Aye."

He gestured toward the sight of his Marines hastily pumping a howitzer up onto its suspension as more men began grabbing ammunition and powder charges.

"I'm gambling our lives that my tired, dirty, hang-dog nasty buncha hellraisers can move and shoot faster than Tommy Taliban can run a kilometer in Jerusalem cruisers and man-dresses."

He nodded at the topmost of Brady's screen, the GBOSS camera fixed on a mass of men, all of them armed as they came on, headed straight for the gaping entrance.

"Harper, what is the radius on a one-five-five round?" Fitzsimmons said far too calmly for it to be solely the morphine speaking.

"Kill radius is fifty meters, ma'am."

"Oh. Good. Not terribly far then."

"Brady, how far away are the taliban?" Smythers asked hesitantly.

"Nine hundred meters. By the time Cassidy gets Gun Five moved and fire-capped, it'll likely be closer to five or six."

The room relaxed a fraction, waiting.

A hand touched his shoulder. James Harper looked back to see Camille Balcombe standing there, concerned.

"James, how big is the shrapnel radius on a one-five-five?" Balcombe said quietly.

Harper peered at his rifle, checking the chamber to ensure he had a live round loaded, tapped the forward assist and closed the dust flap, then stared back at her just as calmly.

"Over five hundred meters, Camille."

"You don't have to do this."

"Yes, I do. Because we don't have the rifles to stop them."

"Even with our reinforcements?"

"Even then. And I couldn't ask the captain to give that order."

"No. You couldn't." She gave his shoulder a squeeze for comfort, leaving it there as she watched the screens and prayed.

\#

Near ten-thousand pounds of steel and titanium heaved as men threw themselves and their load forward across the sand. Bad enough they'd had to pump up the wheels on the damn gun, but to move them by hand?

"What the fuck is happening?" Bath screamed

"Do I look like I fucking know?" Rodd shouted back.

"Move bitch, get out the way bitch, get out the way!" Kramer bellowed, trying to keep his feet moving in cadence.

He was at the front end of Five, heaving on the third wheel and tow mount, both of which were keeping the gun's muzzle weighted down enough that it was moving with surprising speed. Beside him was Hondo, face lit with a manic grin. Three more Marines hung onto the barrel. Behind them came two powder monkeys with powder tubes on their backs, followed by three Marines carrying tall HE rounds. More men were on either side of the heaving gun, muscles straining under the load.

"What the fuck is wrong with you?" Cherney shouted as he pushed from behind a spade arm.

"Those fuckheads in front are having too much fucking fun!" Ostrovsky observed.

"Shut up before I shoot you and do this myself!" Hondo barked as they heaved the gun about.

Nealen was waiting for them, pointing toward the remnants of the front gate.

"Five on me!" Nealen ordered. He waited for the gun to orient itself, then drop down into place as Hondo snapped orders to the men around him.

#

"Timothy, are you catching all of this?"

"I am and I can't believe I'm seeing this."

"Bishop, old boy, how is our uplink to London right now?"

"We can go live if you want."

Cochrane checked his watch. *It'll be after midnight in London, but prime news slots from coast to coast in the US and the Tokyo business crowd will be just waking up.*

"Tell London we're going live. Give me a three second count. Hurry!"

Turning back to face the camera, James Cochrane relaxed his facial muscles, watching as his two assistants went about their work. Tim's left hand went up, three fingers extended. James' face took on a broad smile, despite the dirt and dust and grime. He watched Phil scratch out MOLLY on a dirty white board.

So Molly McNulty will be gracing us with her photogenic presence on the BBC night shift, eh? Jolly good.

"Good morning from Southern Afghanistan, my name is James Cochrane, and I am coming live from what has been an epic siege in southern Afghanistan…"

\#

"FDC, Gunline."

"Send it," Nealen replied.

"Range to target is dropping below six hundred meters."

"Cassidy, adjust range to five-hundred meters!" Nealen ordered the crew.

Brady's smooth Texas drawl came back. *"Be aware you are inside shrapnel radius for one-five-five."*

"If we live we can worry about that," Nealen snapped. His finger came off the radio."

"Target, enemy infantry in the open!" Hondo snapped.

Around him, the gun crew repeated the command.

"Shell HE! Charge two. Fuze Time! One-point-fife seconds!"

Brass rang against steel as the long body of an M795 HE round snugly fit into place.

Gunfire snapped around their position, one Taliban fighter more fleet of foot than his comrades, trying to lay down fire on the cannon with an RPK.

PFC Rodd went down, a round punching into and through his left arm. Blood sprayed across the howitzer as he fell. Next to him, Ostrovsky went down as well, wounded.

Nealen's rifle came up, slamming out a hammer pair to drop the machine gunner where he stood.

Two men lifted Rodd, moving him out of the way so McCrae could take his place.

The breech block clanged shut, Number Two man twisting out of the way. Beagle stood at the Gunner's sight, Kramer just behind him, hands on his belt and flak jacket.

"Lead zero. Range five hundred! Fire at will!" Hondo commanded.

The distance was short, the instructions easy. Every man on the gun had been keyed up for hours on adrenaline, hate, their own fear, and now courage.

Natasha Fitzsimmons saw the shapes on the camera, moving quickly now that their impediments had been blown away. Her fingers gripped the table, knuckles white as she waited.

Thunder erupted.

It was the only way she knew to explain what she heard. A clap of thunder erupting from the gates of Hell.

Onscreen the running figures disappeared, knocked onto their backs when the first round detonated.

Men fell.

But not nearly all of them.

BOOM

Better than half the running figures were down now. Victims of an insatiable dragon who loomed ahead of them in the half-lit twilight.

BOOM

White hot steel sleeted across the ground, scything holes through the ranks of men.

\#

"Behind us, as you've just heard, is one of the cannons brought down by a group of American Marines, sent here to Dishu to assist Number One Engineer Company of the newly-formed Support Division, in a great show of international spirit and goodwill," James explained for those watching.

"Timothy, why is that cannon firing?" Molly's voice asked in James' earbud, well back in the UK.

"Since last night, we've been under attack by what I am told is likely elements of Taliban militia and Al-Qaeda."

"You called this a siege earlier, didn't you?"

"Yes, yes it's all terribly exciting stuff! First was a rocket barrage, followed by mortars and a general attack all over."

"When did this start?" Molly asked.

"Near ten pm local time."

"What time is it now?"

"Minutes before six," James assured. "I hadn't seen tracers flying like that since I covered the battles in Ramadi two years ago."

"Did something happen before you came on the air?"

"Yes, Molly. Just before the cannon went off, we were hit with rockets and a vehicle borne explosive device, which blew down our front gate. Happened while I was interviewing two officers about the night's happenings if you can believe it."

#

James Harper felt his mouth going dry as he watched the carnage unfold on camera.

"Brady, my orders to Gun Five: repeat."

"Aye, sir."

The hammer blows fell. Men did not drop where they stood. They ceased to exist, torn apart in a high explosive blast which sundered creation with unremitting fury.

"We hurt 'em bad, sir," Brady announced as the dust cleared and he studied what remained of the Taliban foot soldiers.

"Good," Harper said flatly.

But not good enough he realized as he looked to an upper portion of the screen. He could see figures slowly beginning to wend their way forward once more. Some had sought protection in the wadis or behind small hummocks of earth. These were the survivors, men who'd been smart enough to get down and stay down as the guns fired.

"You can shell it, bomb it, blast it till the Kingdom's Come. Until you park a man with a rifle on it, you don't own a damn thing," Harper said quietly.

"A worthy sentiment Lieutenant. Are you truly prepared to go that far?" DuBois asked just as quietly. "Are you ready to pay that butcher's bill?"

Harper looked to DuBois, nodded his head even as his mouth tasted bile. "Brady, what's my wind call?"

"Seven miles per hour, sir. Blowing straight over our backs to the north."

"My order to gunline: two rounds smoke."

"Aye, sir. Run it, Theiss," Brady ordered.

"Yes, sergeant!"

"Anything else sir?" Brady asked.

Harper licked his cracked lips, trying to moisten them.

"Sergeant Brady, take your section and report to Nealen. He's to stand fast after they fire that smoke," Harper ordered.

"FDC on me!" Brady ordered.

Standing, the good-natured Texan moved toward the door, followed by his Marines, last of all Shores who was counting out the newest volley of fire.

"Brady!" Harper snapped, bringing the Marines up short.

"Sir?"

"You forgot our guidon," Harper admonished.

Brady smiled apologetically. "Guess I did sir. My bad."

"No worries," Harper assured.

Grasping the guidon stick, Brady pulled it from the stand then withdrew from the Command Post.

"Colonel, sir, I need to make a detour, but would you care to join me for a walk?" Harper asked.

"It would be my pleasure, Leftenant Harper. Where shall we meet?"

"In the motor pool. I've ordered Sergeant Cassidy to provide us with a chef's course of classic heavy metal."

"Excellent choice. Company Sergeant Major," DuBois said, using the man's full rank deliberately. "I have need of a good British soldier or two."

"I know where we can find them, sir," Stirling assured.

"Have them meet me in the motor pool. At the double," DuBois commanded.

Turning sharply, Harper and DuBois left the Command Post, faces set in matching grim mien.

"Bellmore, pass the Colonel's orders to all stations: every soldier who can walk and carry a rifle, report to the motor pool," Mayne declared. "Then get yourself out there, too."

"On it, Sarn't Major."

Stirling Mayne started to check his pistol, then thought better of it. Reaching for an Enfield on the rack, he checked the chamber from force of habit. Gleaming brass met his view and he let the bolt slam home before shouldering it and checking the sights one time.

"What are they doing?" Minister Siddiq said, slowly rising from her seat in the corner out of concern. "Where are they all going?"

Still watching the screen, Natasha Fitzsimmons heard the wise Sergeant Major speak for her as he made for the door.

"Then up comes the Regiment, and shoves the heathens out."

#

In the motor pool, Nealen had assembled his platoon, plus their reinforcements, weapons pointing towards the gaping hell-gate torn out of reality with a pitiless god's own fury. There were less of his Marines present than James Harper wanted as he approached. Some of those men lay on stretchers, Corpsmen tending to their wounds while Cassidy and Nealen searched with their rifles for any more threats who might take potshots at the Company as it formed.

Some detached part of James Harper's heart wept, knowing their ranks were depleted not only by those who stood guard in the towers but from on high.

Enough the Lieutenant commanded his thoughts. *There will be time to mourn our dead later. My duty is to the living.*

He checked the Sam Browne belt once again, trying to ensure his scabbard hadn't shifted too far out of place.

I still can't believe I brought this damn thing. After all, why would an officer need a sword for anything besides manual of drill in the twenty-first century?

Nearby, Mayne was reporting to DuBois, "Sir, Number One Company formed per your orders."

Still not enough, but we have no more we can add, Harper chided.

"What we doing, sir?" Gunny Pililaau asked DuBois, his leiomano hanging leisurely from a leather cord around his left wrist. Behind him, most of a platoon stood ready, faces grim.

"The Leftenant is running this show, Gunnery Sergeant," DuBois assured. "I'm here for moral support."

"Understood, sir," Pililaau rumbled.

Is it enough? Harper asked himself as he scanned his troops, noticing how the girls looked scared. Determined, but still scared.

"Corporal Tolliver!"

"Here, sir," the redoubtable Corporal declared.

If he was scared, Tolliver's face did not show it, his blue eyes bright in the early morning twilight amidst the layers of dirt and filth which covered every inch. His broad hands gripped the guidon tightly.

"Sir."

Harper turned to see Sergeant Pistol beside him, holding the regimental colours DuBois had brought down for the engineers.

"Sergeant," Harper acknowledged.

"Mind if I join you, sir?" Pistol asked.

"Not at all. I'd prefer the company."

"Thank you, sir."

Mayne had passed his sidearm to the sergeant, who confidently held it in his right hand, but was still studying the lieutenant curiously.

"You brought a sword, sir?"

"On a challenge from a brother officer, Sergeant. To bring it and find honest use for it."

"Beggin' the lieutenant's pardon, but sir, do you even know how to use a sword?"

"Stick the pointy end in the bad guys. Seems real simple to me."

Nearby, James Cochrane watched the young American as he ran through decisions. James had covered conflict for nearly twenty years, and what he saw in this moment reminded him of a line he'd heard once, from a late-night re-run.

"I saw a whole army, ready to run. Then a major of the 78th took a step forward and steadied the line," James told himself. *Time for a brave man to steady the line.*

"Tim, tell me the satcom uplink is still working," he snapped suddenly.

"London reads us loud and clear," Tim assured after a moment.

"Tell them if they cut back to us, I'll make us the most watched channel on earth. We go live in ten seconds, with or without them."

Tim spoke into his headset, then tossed James a thumbs up. "London copies all, we're up in five. Game faces."

James cleared his throat as Tim's fingers flashed down. *Three. Two One.* The Red Light signaling *live feed* came on.

"This is James Cochrane, BBC News, live from FOB Bourne in Helmand, Afghanistan. We've been under attack since just before midnight, when we were hit with rockets and mortars. In the hours since then, myself, my cameraman Timothy Covington, and producer Phil Bishop, have watched acts of courage and bravery which define the very best traditions of the British Army."

Out to one side, he caught the stretcher team moving with a marine who'd been shot as he worked to set up the howitzer. Rodd was still alive, of this he was sure. Cochrane swallowed.

"And the many American Marines whom are here with us."

He paused, working hard to maintain his composure as a second stretcher passed by. Hopefully Ostrovsky was still alive as well.

"A few minutes ago, Lieutenant Harper, the senior American officer, responded with artillery fire and momentarily stopped the Taliban attack. They've fired that great mothering cannon behind me eight times. While it appears to have temporarily stopped the Taliban, Lieutenant Harper does not believe they're finished."

James Harper, to his credit, was running through what he wanted to say, completely ignorant of the camera trained on him. He knew the rough form, but it was the wording that would matter. Something that mattered to them.

Screw it, we go with Mickey. Because Philly.

"Eyes on me!" He ordered as he stepped out to where everybody could see him.

Those gaunt faces gazed back at him, from a place unnamed and unspoken.

"I know you're tired. I know you're hurt. We all are." His tone deepened. "But we ain't dead yet, are we?"

Glances exchanged between the enlisted men and women. Silence.

He took his helmet off, screwing a finger into his ear for a moment. "I'm sorry, I can't hear you after Sergeant Cassidy laid down all that hate. Are we dead yet?"

"No," voices replied, many still muted.

"Y'all sound weak. Like hairdressers! Are. You. Dead?"

"We ain't dead, sir!" Gunny Pililaau barked. "They never stood a chance."

"Samuels, did you hear a bell?"

"Nein!"

"Jimenez, how 'bout you?"

"Hell no, sir! Los pinche culeros no esto tan buena!"

"Cooper, did you hear a bell ring?"

"No sir!" she shouted shrilly.

"Did Pilsen hear a bell ring?"

"Hell no!" Several shrieked at once.

"You're damn right!" Keating yelled.

Harper had their gaze, hot, angry, even stifling, as they glared at him, faces rimed in salt and dirt. Painted by rage.

A sweeping glare, left to right.

"You want heaven? You gotta pass through Hell first," Harper declared.

"Sir, we're just engineers!" Munro protested.

Harper rounded on the shaken Staff Sergeant, teeth bared. "Not today, Staff. Not today."

Fingers rose on his left hand, held where Munro could see them.

"Four times."

Waggling his fingers, he made eye contact with the girls nearest him. "Four times they came at us. Did it work?"

"No sir," Sylvie said, despite her guts roiling as her voice made strange sounds.

"You have shot them, stabbed them and blasted them! Despite everything they did, they could not break you."

Grins met his words as the import of what he said took root.

"I'm an Irishman from Philadelphia, I know exactly what a bell sounds like. And I ain't heard one, not till now."

Roots grew.

"I hear belles, mes chers. Mes madamoiselles. I hear you, my British belles. I hear all of you."

Roots began to drink.

"You are Hell's Belles!"

From wells of courage not previously tapped they drank deeply.

"You have beaten them time and again. By all rights we should all be dead but here we are!"

Seeds blossomed.

"There is only one thing left to do, to ensure they cannot come back. I must ask you to follow me, and ring out, one last time. Once more unto the breach, for God, England, and Sir Harry."

A pause, his eyes alighting on the blood-spattered howitzer where more of his men had fallen. Curls of heat lazily twisted up from the still-smoking breech.

The Marines looked toward that gaping wound in the wall, the curtain of smoke carried on by the swift-moving wind, then back to the man who had led them this far. He looked ready to lead them a little further.

"My Teufel Hunden, what is our profession?"

A guttural snarl reverberated across Bourne's broken landscape. No need for chest thumping now. They, and he, knew what he needed them to do.

"Marines! Do you want to live forever?" he demanded.

"Hell no!" they bellowed.

Harper took a final breath to steel his nerves. There was no way to guess how this would end. Simply that it needed to happen.

Here and now.

Harper turned his head to one side so his voice would be heard by all near him as he fingered the hilt of a sword he'd brought along solely on a drunken dare.

Because who would bring a sword to a gunfight? Joshua Chamberlain, that's who.

"Gunnery Sergeant Pililaau, platoon echelon left! Staff Sergeant Nealen, platoon echelon right! Company Sergeant Major Mayne, form wedge!"

Orders snapped even as the squads moved of their own accord.

"Sir, the company is formed!" Mayne declared seconds later.

"Sergeant Cassidy, three rounds HE! Tell those worthless dogs who's coming to drag them down to Shaitan!" Harper snapped.

Hondo's gun roared, fire blooming from the muzzle as the world watched a Sergeant of Marines manipulate his cannon the same way an artist handled their brush, painting the world in brushstrokes of fire and thunder.

BOOM

BOOM

BOOM

Twelve seconds' rapid fire work which deafened all nearby.

Just as quickly, Hondo's gun crew ran to take their places, rifles in their fists, or in his case, a pistol and Ka-Bar knife.

Death and hell awaited them outside these walls.

Time to dance with the Devil.

Harper drew his sword, letting the blade hiss as it slid from the scabbard, exactly the way well-cared for steel ought to, bringing the spine up against his shoulder, then extended his arm, aiming with the blade.

"Bayonets!"

Blades rattled out of sheaths, clipping into place just below the muzzle as they should. Banners rose in strong hands.

"Present! Arms!"

Rifles leveled at the enemy, held hip high.

"HAH!"

The Guidons flashed downward, spade-shaped steel pike heads gleaming as the strong hands which gripped their wooden shafts held them steady.

Death and hell awaited outside those blasted walls.

Death.

Hell.

And victory.

"Charge!"

\#

From where she sat, legs elevated and riding the morphine-induced calm, Natasha could only watch as her soldiers moved forward at a steady walk, accelerating to a trot once they cleared the front gate. Behind them, the BBC news crew followed, broadcasting as they went. Her shrapnel wounds ached dully despite the morphine, but she had enough control of her faculties to speak, despite the best efforts of the painkillers. Reaching out, Fitzsimmons changed the large overview screen to show the feed from the GBOSS.

"Sure, we missed the first wave of rockets. But most of our people were under cover."

"And," she emphasized the word "we tracked the second wave back to their launchers with our counter-battery radar. After that it was a matter of plotting. Sergeant Brady assures me he could have shot it with a brisket sandwich and a bottle of bourbon."

As Natasha spoke, she zoomed the camera in so the ministers could see what she was talking about. Grainy scenes resolved and Siddiq realized with a start the moonscape was not — each of those craters had been scooped out of the earth by the smoking cannon outside. Then the camera zoomed back, panning to a new spot.

"As for those filth at the front gate, well —" Natasha spat venomously. "I'll give them high marks for trying."

The camera zoomed in.

"But they get a failing grade for how badly they screwed this up."

She rechecked the screen, now on regular vision rather than thermal as the civilians around her realized that the people they'd been shooting at were now chunked. Shredded bodies decorated the road. Bodies torn apart —

As if they ran through a meat grinder.

Gorge unwillingly rose in tightly clenched throats.

"I expect my ladies will need to break out two of the dozers and dig a pit to collect the bodies. What's left of them." She smiled thinly. "They better hurry though. Those Marines are liable to start using a loose head for a pickup game."

"They wouldn't —" Smythers began

"They believe themselves to be the last war cult. They want the world to know that. Including all of the Pashtuns near us. Who by, the way, invented a version of polo involving a goat carcass full of sand, and horsewhips. American Marines playing footie with a loose head would be the greatest joke since Genghis damned Khan rode through. The locals out there covering our flank would adopt them into the tribe for it. And likely make Harper their first king in centuries."

That did the trick. Smythers emptied her guts into the trash can, heaving repeatedly before finally looking up, tears in her eyes.

"Water?" Natasha asked as she held out a bottle and paper towel.

"How? How can people live like this?" Smythers demanded through tears.

"This is a hard land, ma'am. It makes for hardy folks. The soldiers who can stand against them are every bit as hard."

Chapter 36

See My White Light Flashing As I Split The Night

FOB Bourne had rocked the earth all night long, blasting and roaring out of the fire-lit darkness time and again. Five times the Taliban had tried to take the walls, only to be repulsed with vindictive fury.

What the defenders lacked was a means to permanently end the threat. They could not run to ground the enemy who assailed them. Even with Harper's desperate charge, it was not enough to finish off the Dishu Brigade of the Taliban.

Not that they were alone in the fight. Theiss had caught muzzle flashes coming from the village. When he zoomed in on particular buildings, Fitzsimmons caught sight of the village men shooting at the Taliban as they retreated or came too close to the village.

Instead, the final act of revenge fell to the Dragoons who crested a hill and saw the scene set before them.

"Sir, looks like the FOB is still intact," Hennessy's gunner announced.

"Bourne Actual, this is Dragoon Actual. How copy?"

Static-filled silence greeted their ears.

"Bourne Actual, this is Dragoon Actual. How copy?"

"Dragoon Actual, Bourne still stands."

"Huzzah," a trooper breathed.

"We've marked what we think are their base camp locations. Also, the village is friendly territory. They've fought to keep the Taliban away from us during the night."

"Leave the village alone and targets marked on BFT. Understood."

Checking the tracker screen, Patrick noted how each of the three targets was marked with an arabic numeral

One, Two, and Three. How convenient.

Switching to the unit frequency, Patrick spoke into the radio handset with a fiery determination his men knew well.

"All Troops fall out by target number and hammer 'em. First Troop on me. Up and at 'em Dragoons!"

#

Shamil cringed at the memory, remembering the silence as Basayev led nearly four hundred brave men to charge forward in the morning twilight. Surely the moment was theirs for the taking!

A roar had sounded, twice and even a third time. He had known then that the cost of securing victory for the jihad was going to be much greater. But surely Allah had not forgotten His most faithful servants!

Even with smoke covering the objective, they could not fail, and Basayev had looked back towards the bunker where the Brigade's commanders waited with bated breath for news of victory, as if to say "come follow me, we can do this."

Then had come a roar, a primeval thing driven forward from the very halls of Iblis. Three rounds of high explosive violence, followed by a terrible screaming. Even from over a kilometer away, he had heard the screams and known then that their attack had failed. Less five dozen men returned, having survived more by accident than planning, describing the rain of steel which slashed through their numbers, white hot metal bouncing across the sand, through men, cutting them down seemingly at will.

Worse still, they brought word that the British and Americans had charged the remnants of that attack, using bayonets to cut down their assailants. Long blades wet red with mujahideen blood.

They sent their women after us. With blades.

He shivered in terror at the thought that weak, western women could possibly match the proud mujahideen fighters in combat.

Now, around Saeed were gathered the remnants of the Dishu Brigade. The once proud ranks had spent a night shot at, shelled, even helicopters and air strikes.

We are good for one more drive. Just one more and we conquer or we will be destroyed. Shamil mused.

"*Vehicles!*" a lookout shouted through his radio. "*Many armored vehicles!*"

Heads whipped around as smoke erupted from where the lookouts had been posted.

\#

"*RPGs! Three o'clock!*"

Kaag heard his lead tank's commander shout across the company frequency.

Twin contrails emerged over the lead tank's turret, exploding harmlessly well above their intended target.

"Fuck those crunchies!" the driver snarled, stamping on the accelerator. Seventy tons of American steel and ceramic plate slammed forward, into the RPG gunners, reducing them to red smears across the ochre sand.

"Tanks! Execute! Dig 'em out panzers!" Kaag ordered.

The steel behemoths were terrifying in their own right. Nothing so large should've been able to move so quickly, nor exist with such unabashed impunity.

Cannons roared, belching flame with a roar the Taliban knew far too well.

Men disappeared in flashes, high explosive ordnance turning flesh into steaming gobbets of rapidly expanding gore-filled balloons.

The Dishu Brigade knew they could not stand.

Hadn't been able to when the cannons roared just after sunrise, turning their charge into a shameful rout. Now, with cannons advancing into their positions and unable to effectively counter the heavy American armor or the lighter British counterpart, only a single option remained for the exhausted, devastated, thirsty and hungry Taliban fighters.

Flight.

Into the desert which had long been their means of safety.

Today though, a painful consequence emerged — they could not outrun modern bullets. Nor modern cavalry.

Men *ran.*

Men died.

Many out of breath and soaking their robes in their own feces as they were cut down, gripped by fear.

Some few, still carrying RPGs, tried to resist. These were struck by machine gun fire from infantry in the Jackal vehicles following close behind the Scimitars.

On this day, the silent ghosts of Elphinstone's long lost retreat from Kabul cheered as a mechanized fist of the modern British Army avenged their phantom forms. The steel hammer of light armor and heavy panzers smashed through the brittle glass which had been the Dishu Brigade after a night and a morning spent in a cauldron of hell.

Men dropped their weapons, raising their hands and falling to their faces in token of surrender, praying to a God they had only barely acknowledged before now with increasing fervor.

"Infantry, dismount and sweep for POWs. Terrance, call HQ and tell them we have a massive prisoner haul," Patrick ordered.

"On it sir," the Comm Sergeant replied from where he sat in the command track.

"Kaag, how are your tanks?"

"Green, green up. All tracks forming on the walls by platoons."

"Good man."

Peter Nealen stopped. He considered himself old as many staff NCOs do. That did not mean he was dead. The crafty sniper had finally seen the same thing his Lieutenant had. Hands, reaching under the table tops to clasp hands for comfort, in a way that boys and girls had done for years beyond his reckoning. Not just the now-happily engaged couple, but many of those present. Peter knew his Marines, knew they needed to let off steam, the Theater Commander's General Order Number One be damned. And he knew he could give no orders to these men otherwise, for they'd simply ignore it.

Never give an order you can't enforce. Leadership 101.

"Sir," Nealen said.

"Yes, Staff Sergeant?" Harper replied.

"These crazy bastards may yet be the death of us."

"God bless 'em aren't they awesome?" Harper said merrily.

"Best job I ever had."

To be continued.

Author's note:

This whole project started as a half-baked dream four years ago. I couldn't explain then why I did it, beyond the driving need to write. Then the events of 19 June, 2020 happened. A good man was murdered whilst doing the right thing. Because he could do no less when it counted. A month later, off San Clemente island, an amtrac went down with all the Marines onboard lost. It was training, nothing in a combat zone, but the loss hit just as hard.

I realized something because of those two incidents- I, as a writer, could give my brothers and sisters in arms immortality. To that end, several of the names of the Marines used are those from that fateful day. Likewise, many of the names for the British soldiers used herein are based on the names of recipients of the Victoria Cross, who's inscription reads "For Gallantry."

Herbert Pililaau was a young Hawaiian drafted into the US Army who posthumously received the Medal of Honor covering his unit's withdrawal from Heartbreak Ridge on a September day in 1951.

At some point, I used names derived from brother Marines I served with. Flawed men, but good men when you needed to stand and fight. Michael Roach is a prince among men.

Lastly, for those who knew her, and those who know of her, Captain Tamara Long, USAF, the real Komodo Eleven.

These names are written here, so that they shall not be forgotten.
They shall grow not old, as we that are left grow old;
Age shall not weary them, nor the years condemn.
At the going down of the sun and in the morning
We will remember them.

~Laurence Binyon, *Ode to the Fallen*

Acknowledgments:

To the friends who stood with me through it all, encouraging me and cheering me on when I didn't deserve the love or support: Emily, Tom, Sarah, Larry, Brad, Tank, Amanda, Dorothy, Patrick, and my big sister KC;

To the friends who kept reading and suggesting, when I didn't know how else to make the story come to life: Alyssa, Sarah, and Rebecca;

The technical assistance without which this would not have been so precise in certain regards: J L Curtis, Mr. Law Dog, Peter Grant, Manni Ratliff, Uncle David, Staff Sergeant Matthew Brady, Staff Sergeant Sara Christian, Sergeant Brian Kramer;

And to the many Marines who've mentored me over the years: Major Baumer, Lieutenant Colonel Anness, Captain Donnerstag, First Sergeant Potting, First Sergeant Torrez, Master Sergeant Moore, Gunny Tolliver, Staff Sergeant Huerta, Tony Samuelson, Clinton Ed;

Thank you, all of you.

SFMF

Glossary:

Private:
The very bottommost rank in any western-based military. When fecal matter rolls downhill, it stops at Private Shmuckatelli. You are worthless in the eyes of your seniors and NCOs. Pay Grade of E-1. Powered by caffeine and nicotine.

PFC (Private First Class)
Perfect For Cleaning. Yes, really. The pay is slightly better at E-2, but not by much. You are still equally worthless in the eyes of your seniors and NCOs. Known to marry exotic dancers of a dubious nature. Powered by caffeine and nicotine.

Lance Corporal
E-3 Workhorse of the USMC. Can lead a fire team or a squad, and handles the execution of daily tasks. Powered by caffeine, nicotine, and alcohol.

Senior Lance Corporal
Will have one, possibly two deployments under their belt, have likely even been corporals before getting busted down in rank and are just waiting to pick up again. Is an unofficial rank in the USMC. Certain officers will deny their existence. Those people are lying to themselves. Powered by caffeine, nicotine, alcohol, and hate.

Corporal
Experienced, generally calmer, more educated and thoughtful than lance corporals. Expected to be a squad leader, and in the absence of a sergeant, assumes the belief that they are supreme in their world. Powered by caffeine, nicotine, alcohol, and hate.

Sergeant

E-5. Noncommissioned Officer, often with 6-8 years of experience. Trying to pick up Sergeant can be a challenge in ground combat arms, unlike other MOS fields, where you achieve rank by dint of breathing and not smelling of booze. Powered by caffeine, nicotine, alcohol, hate, and likely a divorce.

Staff Sergeant

Usually an E-6, and in the USMC, nominally the senior enlisted man in a platoon. Normally over 10 years' time in service. Mixed bag of quality, likely to find nuts, much like when dating in Thailand.

Sergeant Major

In the American military, an enlisted man or woman with the paygrade of E-9. Some are good, some are bad. Paul Davis was a great Sergeant Major who took it upon himself to personally educate me about the necessity of good NCOs and what he expected of me as a brand new corporal. Thank you for that, Sergeant Major.

Colonel

Usually in command of a regiment. Usually busy trying to undo the damage caused to local environs by their junior enlisted. Some are good. Some are bad. Michael Roach was a prince amongst men and I would've followed him into Hell.

General

Wear shiny silver stars. Nobody knows what they do day-to-day.

Howitzer

Cannons, which in this age can perform direct fire, indirect fire, and high-angle indirect fire. The US Army runs tubes as light as 105mm, while all howitzers currently in use by the USMC are 155mm.

Mortar
High angle delivery system of shrapnel, smoke, high explosive, and hate. Useful for reaching behind a barrier via the parabolic arc of flight.

Battery/Company- a tactical element made up of multiple platoons. "Battery" is the term used by artillerymen. "Company" is the term used by everybody else. Except Aviation (Squadrons) and Cavalry. Nobody knows what the Cavalry are doing.

Engineers
Born out of a menage-a-trois between Bob the Builder, Al Capone, and your angriest high school chemistry teacher, these folks can build nearly anything, run heavy equipment, lay wire, and possibly even plumbing. If they are your friends, they'll help you blow up anything. If they are your enemies, expect them to destroy all that you hold dear with high explosives, det cord, and hate.

Jon LaForce

Born in southern Arizona, Jonathan LaForce spent his formative years in northern Los Angeles County before moving to Texas at the age of 19. Two years later, he enlisted in the USMC and found himself stationed in Hawaii. Had it not been so expensive, he'd have stayed in Hawaii at the end of his enlistment. Instead he moved to Utah and got his bachelors' degree in English.

Returning to the glorious state of Texas, he is quite happy living there. He enjoys making good barbecue, drinking Dr. Pepper, writing stories, and cases of hardball .45 ACP as gifts for all occasions- his birthday, Jesus's birthday, and Marine Corps' birthday.

Follow him here on Amazon!

☆ ☆ ☆ ☆ ☆

Rate this book

You can find this book and many more like it at our website:

www.cannonpublishing.us

"Because of the assault charges?" Nealen asked.

"CENTCOM's senior legal officer informally reviewed the matter as a personal favor to me. Absent the assault charges, there would be no issue with Sergeant Cassidy receiving the Cross. Instead, Sergeant, you can expect to receive the Silver Star Medal for exceptional valor in the face of the enemy."

"Thank you, sir," Hondo said, humbled.

"Regardless of the political decision, it's what you earned. Nobody can take that from you."

"Aye aye, sir."

"Thank you, Sergeant Cassidy, for being the right man when it counted."

Mike checked his watch, noted the time.

"I am deeply proud of all of you. I could not have asked for better men to handle this. You are a credit to your families, your units, and our Marine Corps."

"Thank you, sir," the room responded.

"You're welcome." Roach stood, followed by his men. "Now let's get out the door to mess night. It's bad manners to keep ladies waiting."

"Oorah!"

#

The hollow grinds had taken the most time. She'd done what she could to hammer them in with dies, making the rough forms. Grinder belts had carefully removed the remaining metal with the utmost precision possible.

Hiding a blade this size had been difficult. And her own desperation had nearly been the instrument of her undoing.

But it was hardened, tempered, sharpened, then sheathed in the cowhide Cassidy had been tanning at her request, before she wrapped it to disguise the shape.

"Good afternoon, Padre," Sylvie declared quietly.

"Good afternoon Sergeant Lyons. You'll be happy to know that your priest back in Catterick was ecstatic at your good fortune when I broke the news to him. Are we still on track?"

"We are," she beamed. "I'm nervous, but I think he'll like it."

She pulled back the wrap, watching as his eyes widened in surprise, before a smile appeared on his face.

"Well it is a little dated, given our people stopped using this method ages ago. But for your lad? This'll do. Oh this'll do, lass. Follow me, please."

Roach and Sergeant Major Orlando had almost made it inside the chow hall when Orlando saw DuBois wave for their attention.

"Colonel, sir, looks like the gentleman needs us."

"What's up Christian?" Mike asked as the Brit drew near followed by people he did not recognize.

"Mike, this is Sergeant Lyons and Padre Pascoe."

"Padre, nice to meet you in person."

"Likewise sir."

"Lyons, Lyons," Mike muttered. "Wait. You were the one who held the breach in the wall at Dishu."

She blushed. "I had some help from one of your Marines, sir," Sylvie demured.

"Shoulders out to here, bull necked and bull headed? Goes by the name Cassidy?" Roach asked.

"Yes, sir. He's a handy fellow for such moments."

"Isn't he? Good man when you're in a fight. Even if he's always angry about something," Roach admitted.

"He'd say it's a gift, sir," Sylvie admitted.

"Yes, he would," Roach added. "Anyway, what's going on?"

"It seems our Sergeant Lyons found herself falling for one of your Marines," DuBois declared.

"She what?" Orlando said, quite unable to believe what he was hearing.

"Himself is prone to whimsy," Pascoe assured.

"Who? Wait." Mike held up a hand. "Let me guess: Shoulders out to here? Bull necked? Bull headed?"

"Man with a bit of a temper on him, sir?" Sylvie added helpfully.

"It had to be. He couldn't do anything by a half-measure, could he?" Roach mused.

"No, sir. I don't think he knows how to," Sylvie admitted.

"You're willing to bless this union?" Orlando asked Pascoe incredulously.

"I verified this with the Company Sarn't Major. He and I go back," Pascoe assured.

"And?" DuBois pressed.

"It's real. They've been courting since the Marines got to Dishu, sir. The sergeants have been courting for several months now."

"That is… highly impressive."

"The Sergeant also asked me to speak with her parish priest back in Catterick about handling a certain matter, so that things are in proper order," Pascoe persisted.

"Putting the cart before the ox, aren't we father?" DuBois grumbled.

Sylvie batted her eyelashes innocently. "A lady has to learn how to gamble sometime, sir."

"Huh?" Mike asked, lost in the conversation.

"I'll explain it later, Mike," DuBois explained.

"Well then," Mike began to laugh, and he closed his eyes, taking a deep breath. "Oh yeah, this is gonna be fun to watch. I know that Marine quite well."

"You do sir?" Sylvie asked.

"I pinned him a Sergeant," Mike explained.

"Oh. I had no idea," she admitted.

"Anything else, Miss Lyons?" DuBois asked.

"What's his full name, sir?" She asked

"Prael," Mike declared.

"On it, sir." The aide declared, quickly making tracks toward the nearby headquarters building.

"Good aides are a treasure for helping you do your job correctly at this level," Mike declared. "Oh and Miss Lyons?"

"Yes, sir?"

"I expect an invitation to the wedding. Barring the needs of the service, I do plan to be in attendance."

"Of course, sir."

"Good, now let's get inside."

#

Within, the chow hall was brilliantly decorated for the holiday on the morrow, just like the other six such facilities at Leatherneck. Tonight though, Roach had decreed that its only occupants would be a mixed company of Brits and Americans who had spent a long while under the hammer together. They filed in, taking seats together.

Nealen, watching near the door, drew himself up, as Roach stepped into the room.

"Attention on deck!"

Boots crashed against concrete as the Marines shot to their feet, followed quickly by the British soldiers.

Ride a Tiger long enough and you start to grow stripes yourself, Nealen observed wryly.

"At ease, you may be seated," Mike ordered. Taking his place at the head of the room, where all could see him, he smiled.

"We remembered our dead earlier this morning. Tonight, in private, we remember the living. In conversation with the Chaplains, Captain Fitzsimmons and Lieutenant Harper, as well as the review of camera footage by my staff, we feel it appropriate that you are all recipients of the Combat Action Ribbon. It will be awarded to all present, including our British comrades. Even if you cannot wear it in uniform, please keep it in good health and remember us well. The appropriate paperwork is being mailed to Chard Barracks right now."

"Give him one!" Tolliver ordered.

"ERRR!" the whole room shouted.

For the first time since they'd arrived, Roach felt himself smiling.

"My staff has been taking care of several personal awards. Again, Lieutenant Harper, and Captain Fitzsimmons have been busy writing up the reports for each of them. My staff is handling this because in the Marine Corps we move on a mother freaking ocean of paperwork, and I did not want the sacrifices made here to be cheapened because of slow-moving desk jockeys."

"First among these will be Lance Corporal Joseph Pilsen. I cannot speak to what will happen when his case is presented, but I want it understood that Colonel DuBois and myself have put him in for the highest possible decoration of valor available to a British soldier. The sworn testimonies of the inhabitants at Bunker Number Three, along with the video footage provided by the BBC make his case for him."

"Additionally, tonight I am told that we have a series of promotions to handle. Corporal Kramer, Corporal Cherney, Corporal Samuels, Corporal Tolliver, front and center!"

This caused many strange looks, not because of the list, but because it wasn't the first of the month, when promotions were supposed to be handled.

"In accordance with the statements received from both Staff NCOs and Officers, it is felt that these persons are deserving of combat meritorious promotion to the rank of Sergeant, dated the twenty-fourth of December."

The promotion warrant was read aloud, Nealen and Mayne pinning each man properly. Nealen took the time to hammer one of the rank tabs into place with a closed fist, starting with Kramer. He then motioned for Mayne to do likewise with the second tab, to which the Sergeant Major happily assisted.

Tradition and orders complete, the promotees were dismissed to sit down amongst their friends once again. Awards were made, while Prael slipped into the back of the room to hand Pascoe a small note. The priest read it, then quietly passed the note to Sylvie when she came near him after receiving the Military Cross for her defense of the breach. She took the note, read it, smiled and mouthed a 'thank you' to him before taking her seat once more.

Mike had been stalling for time, hoping Prael could find what they needed quickly enough. His eyes settled on the bespectacled aide, who threw him a high sign in return. Leaning over, he spoke softly.

"Sergeant Major Orlando, please call Sergeant Cassidy up here."

"How well do you really know that Marine, sir?" Orlando asked as he sized up the wide-shouldered man sitting several meters away from them.

"Remind me when we get our hands on some quality Irish whisky, to tell you a story involving cowboy boots, a kilt made of fruit-by-the-foot, and a coon skin hat."

"If the Colonel is buying, I will happily drink his money."

"I expect no less, Sergeant Major."

Louis Orlando spoke out in the sonorous bass by which all the Marines under his charge knew him.

"Sergeant Cassidy, report to your Commanding Officer!"

"Aye aye, Sergeant Major!"

Cassidy ran around the tables and up to the front of the room.

"Good evening gentlemen! Sergeant Cassidy reporting as ordered!"

"At ease," Roach smiled. "I have been informed by impeccable sources, Sergeant, that you somehow found romance in this godforsaken slice of Satan's ass."

"Yes, sir!"

"Good. You know why that's important?"

"No, sir."

"Where else are we supposed to get the next generation of our Marine Corps? Devil pups come from somewhere."

"Understood, sir."

"Somebody needs to ask you a question. About face, son."

Turning about, Cassidy realized that Sylvie was standing there. She looked particularly pensive.

Why is she nervous? He wondered.

"Hondo McLintock Cassidy, you are without a doubt, the most spectacularly frustrating, annoying, difficult, well-mannered barbarian on the planet," Sylvie began.

"He's named for John Wayne movies?" Mayne asked Harper, with a voice just as surprised as the look on Hondo's face that somebody knew his whole name.

"Seems like it." Harper said.

"All of a sudden, there is so much about him that makes sense," Mayne declared.

"Doesn't it?"

Forward of where they sat, Sylvie continued to speak.

"The fact that you can make Nutella cheesecake with chocolate ganache, in Marine-sized portions makes it even worse when I think about the number of times I wanted to shoot you for being so damned insufferable! My waistline has suffered almost as much as the rest of me!"

"She's not wrong," Fitzsimmons muttered to Gallagher as laughter rippled around the room.

"Only time I've gained weight on a deployment. I swear to God it all went straight to my ass!" Gallagher hissed.

"I'm sure Angelo will be so heartbroken," Fitzsimmons muttered.

Gallagher choked down outrage at her Captain's sly jest, as Fitzsimmons turned her attention back to the front of the room.

"Hondo, I have something for you to keep. From me," Sylvie declared.

What she handed him came wrapped in cowhide. A brown and white spotted oxhide, cured under the Afghan sun for days. Grasping the edge of the hide, he drew it back. What he saw made him stop. The room wondered what the item was when he finished the motion and his hand came up holding a sheathed blade.

"Go ahead, pull it out," Sylvie instructed him.

"That's not what she said," Nealen muttered. Stirling kicked him under the table, biting back his own laughter at the same time as the sound of well-oiled steel sliding across leather rang out in the room.

What astounded Cassidy, as it did every other person in that room, was the sheer beauty of that nearly meter-long blade. Half a handspan wide, it was double-edged, with hollow grinds on each edge, a stout fuller running down the center line. The polished brass fittings and blade gleamed beneath the fluorescent light as he tested its heft, enjoying the feel of its balance.

"How? Where did you get this?" he asked in surprise.

"I made it. Forge welded an AK barrel together with the RPK of that asshole who shot you, and the pieces of your facón. The handle is wood from the RPK and AK stocks. The guard is cast brass cartridges from our firefight."

Too stunned to speak, he admired the blade, drinking in its lines as he studied every inch of it.

"Thank you, Sylvie. Why?" he asked.

"Hondo, I could spend the rest of my life wondering what I did wrong. Could spend it regretting my missed chances. I don't want that."

She looked at him, her brown and blue locked on his bright gray with an intensity he'd not seen even in the heat of battle.

"Hondo McLintock Cassidy, will you swear yourself to me, not as a servant or a slave, but an equal. To love me, to cherish me, even in old age, to be the joy of my years and the certainty of my future, the father of my children and the last man to ever take possession of my heart? Will you give yourself to me, and no other, and let me be the same for you, with the promise that we'll spend the rest of our lives making what we have work, because I don't want to have go all around the world and back, and get shot at again, or spend a night shooting Taliban so I can live to see the dawn, just to find another man half as good as you are. Will you marry me and make me your wife for as long as we both live?"

Cassidy felt his jaw starting to drop for the deck before he clamped it firmly shut.

Holyhellfireanddamnation.

He was dimly aware of Sergeant Major Orlando taking the sword from him before he could drop it, as his mind raced through what Sylvie had said to him.

But he already knew.

Down to the very essence of his soul, he knew.

"Yes, I'll be damned if I can say anything more than that but by God Almighty, yes!"

He kissed her then, stepping into the movement and dipping Sylvie backward, just the same as he, and so many other American boys, had seen a sailor do in Times Square. His world, and hers, collided in a screaming kaleidoscope of color and sights and sounds he could not have imagined. For a single moment, everything felt right and so he gave himself to her, his passion and his fury, all at once. As she deserved. The sureness of all his feelings for her made real.

When they came up for air, he realized that the whole room was on its feet, screaming their names and pounding the tabletops as they cheered.

It was at this moment Cassidy remembered a lecture from his drill instructors on public displays of affection while in uniform. An offense worthy of non-judicial punishment.

Colonel Roach must've sensed his unease. "At ease, Marine, nobody's gonna give you a ninja punch tonight."

"Thank you, sir."

"Why don't you and your fiancée take your seats?" Roach suggested.

"Yes, sir."

Taking her by the arm with his left, Cassidy took back his now-sheathed blade with the right then walked her to a table full of onlookers and well-wishers.

"Now that we've gotten that part out of the way," Roach beamed. "This chow hall is yours tonight. Eat, drink, be merry and remember, you've earned this," he said, the smile never leaving his face.

This time the crowd roared back at him, fairly pinning back his ears with the ferocity of their approval.

From his seat, Harper leaned toward Nealen. "How many days do we have till we fly out of here?"

"Day after Christmas, sir."

"It's a day too many," Harper declared flatly.

"Oh, I dunno sir —"

Even as another man's RPK came up, firing thrice, Sylvie was lighting up the enemy machine gunner, dropping Hondo's attacker dead in his tracks. Only then had Hondo Cassidy fallen back to her side.

"It was a long night. I can say that," Sylvie admitted at last.

"You did good work here," another soldier declared. He cocked his head to one side. "Looking for something?"

Sylvie's mind was leaping as she remembered the final blast of the Russian-made light machine gun. It had been meant for Hondo's chest, but Sylvie's rounds caught him as his finger was tightening on the trigger. Instead of killing Hondo, his bullets ripped through the haft of the upraised knife, separating hilt from blade in a jagged mess.

Which sent the blade flying all the way over... Sylvie's stride picked up as she ran forward to a spot near the edge of the position. *Here! Haha found it!* She held her prize up, then looked seriously at the soldiers.

"Where did they take the bodies that were here?"

"I think they're prepping them over by the burn pit."

"What about their weapons?"

"I think those are in the same space."

"Good. I'll need at least two of those," she ruminated, surveying her surroundings with a far keener eye than before. "While I'm over there, handling that, I need you to find me brass from right here."

"How much?"

"All of it. Yeah that'll do, all of it. When you come off post, bring it to the machinist shop. I'll be waiting for you, understand?"

"Yes, Sergeant."

"And tell no one."

"Yes, ma'am!"

Chapter 38

When Johnny Comes Marching Home

Smoking was still verboten indoors, but chewing tobacco could do in a pinch for feeding the nicotine addiction which afflicted most marines with too many years under the gun. Michael Roach had liberally distributed this and several other forms of pogue bait as the NCOs and officers of two platoons sat down with him in the Staff and O Hooch.

They were a haunting, motley sight, Michael Roach observed as he listened to their comments about the deployment, the firefights at Bourne, and most importantly, the Siege. Nearly all of them were bandaged, bruised or still recovering from being concussed.

"Gunny, final thoughts on the night?" He said at last.

"If I thought it was possible, I'd say pull a company of riflemen and have them learn how to be the next best thing to Air Cav."

"Gunny and I kicked it around afterwards," Nealen explained. "The security platoon did great work stepping in, but a single reduced platoon isn't nearly enough when you've gotta hold that much frontage."

"I think we need to consider C-RAMs, everywhere," Harper observed.

"You think it would've stopped the rocket attacks?" Mike asked.

"Maybe, sir. At the very least counter-battery radar with a better power supply."

"I hear you. It's a hard sell to people who only see the line-items in a budget."

Harper grimaced. "Understood, sir."

Mike looked left, toward where Hondo, Kramer and Pistol reclined against the bulkhead. "Speaking of people and budgets, Sergeant Cassidy, did you know that you've had charges sworn out against you?" Mike asked.

"Sir?"

"It seems you made quite the impression on the Honorable Minister Smythers of Reigate," Mike deadpanned. "She's preferred assault charges against you to Interpol."

"Ya know sir, I'm really good at remembering people I've hit, for one reason or another. I don't remember so much as wiping lint off one of her business suits."

Roach shook his head. "This was for attacking two of her personnel."

Hondo shrugged. "Okay. Good for her?" The room laughed at his clear lack of concern. "Seriously, Sir, I'm not exactly sure what you want me to do about it."

"I'm just making sure you know. Because I'm putting you in for a Navy Cross."

Hondo's chair hit the floor as the other men present gave him a cheer and Kramer slapped his shoulder in delight. Hondo stared, shocked.

"Sir?"

"Do the math with me, Cassidy," Mike ordered. "You salvaged a machine gun from a destroyed guard post, repelled an enemy assault accounting for the squad coming through the gap. Lyon's told us about it, and the ballistics people confirmed it during the hot wash. After saving Sergeant Lyon's life, you dropped five more sappers in the wire with your rifle while rebuilding the position. You and Lyons then dropped another two dozen before Nealen could make it through the wreckage of the helos to your position. She also informed us about how you charged out with a knife which accounts for three."

The other men in the room stared at Hondo in awe. "The 240 had a stoppage and they were too close to do anything else," he said.

Mike held up a placating hand. "Far be it for me to correct you on the matter. Graves Registration showed me their bodies. Very neat work."

"Thank you, sir."

"At this point, even if we split the count equally, you've accounted for thirty Taliban. Which is when we get to your direct fire mission."

"I just did what needed to be done."

"No." Mike shook his head. "You did it despite the clear danger you exposed yourself to in the process."

"Any of us would've done that, sir," Hondo protested.

"Hell no!" Kramer declared. "I've fought alongside you, remember Sangin?"

"Uh huh."

"Brother, every time bullets started flying there you ran to get it stuck in. Didn't matter how much, you moved to the sound of the guns."

Cherney spoke up from the side.

"You had to know you were inside the shrapnel radius. Anybody who's been to the Section Chief's Course would know that. I certainly did. But you still shot it."

"And you stayed standing the whole time," Tolliver added.

"Accept it Sergeant Cassidy, you're built differently," Harper interjected.

"Says the man who brought a sword to a gunfight," Pistol said casually, drawing chuckles.

"It worked at Little Round Top," Harper replied.

"Both actions were precisely what we needed to win," Roach persisted. "For that reason, my office is putting you in for the Navy Cross as well, Lieutenant Harper."

This brought on another round of cheers, and Harper smiled.

"Oh. Thank you sir."

"The BBC was broadcasting your speech live, before you broke the Dishu Brigade. A friend at Recruiting Command assured me that if I didn't put you in, they would."

"Nice to know I'm appreciated, sir."

"Indeed, and you should receive confirmation of your award within the next month. However, I do not believe Cassidy will receive his."

"I don't expect they'll be back, but I figure our people need a break just in case they do."

"You sure?"

"Using sabots to take out snipers is a perfectly acceptable use of munitions."

"God, what a joy it must be to have such largesse of supply." Henessy chuckled dryly before he keyed his radio mic once again.

"Yell if you need anything, I'm going to make sure the prisoners stay where they are."

"Roger. Kaag out."

\#

"James, a suggestion, if you will," Phil Bishop declared as all three TV men took a brief respite. The network had sent a message informing them to take a break, and they were using the opportunity to the fullest.

Looking over at his bearded producer, James Cochrane cocked an eyebrow.

"Do tell."

"We started reporting this last night, when it all began. We went live just before they broke the Taliban on the counter-attack."

"Aye."

"There's a lot of lads here from families back in America. Families who will be on pins and needles until they get a phone call that the lad in question is alright."

"I imagine they would be," James mused.

"My wife is going to be having kittens until she knows better," Timothy remarked.

"What's say we have the lads and lasses swing past wherever we're reporting, give their name and rank, and where they're from."

"I like it." James smiled broadly. "MOD can't get mad at us for doing so."

"They can't?" Timothy asked.

"Nope. Their rule only applies to the dead so Next-of-Kin can be properly notified by the servicemember's chain of command."

"I didn't know," Timothy admitted.

"Not a worry," Phil assured. "Those messages went up just after The Charge, once Nealen and Mayne could get a count on their people."

"Oh. Yeah. That mess."

"Would you believe they didn't lose anybody in that?"

"How?"

"Body armor. Though there are some very bruised ribs right now."

"I'll say." Tim shook his head. "Amazing."

"Time to be getting back on spot."

"Make sure you tell Nealen and Mayne about sending their people past while we keep the tape rolling," James said.

"On the way," Phil declared. "We are live in five, four, three, two —"

#

In the end, only one dead man's name had been uttered aloud on camera. An orphaned boy from Newquay, with neither mother nor father to see him off the mortal coil. So it had been reported to Captain Fitzsimmons as she sat in the Command Post, contemplating the price of what her lads and lasses had done.

But that orphan had not been alone when he paid out the last full measure of his devotion. And so the duty fell to his sisters, a platoon of women who thanked their lucky stars that Joseph Pilsen was a man of courage when it counted. His action might have been singular, but they ensured he did not die alone or unloved.

Phil Bishop caught the high sign from Gallagher and nodded to James, then whispered into his throat mic so only Timothy could hear.

"It's time," he said, voice thick with emotion.

Two tired, dirty formations of men and women shook themselves out and came to attention, waiting.

"Company! Pre-sent Hah-rms!" Mayne bellowed.

Back in England, the broadcast presenters watched as rifles came up, held just so.

Out of the medical tent, a stretcher, draped with a Union Jack was borne on six pairs of female shoulders, escorted by a burly sergeant with magnificent mustachios and a stiffly solemn face as he called the cadence.

"James, what can you tell us about this? What happened?" Susanna Reid, face of *BBC Breakfast* back in Manchester asked politely.

"Susanna, I watched the man on that stretcher throw himself onto a grenade," James replied huskily. "He took the whole blast with his chest."

Across England, viewers reacted to that news with shock, and sadness. Hats came off heads in diners and in train stations, in businesses people rose to their feet as the sight of that banner-draped body took on a profound meaning. Then, a new voice was heard as an American Marine stepped forward to stand beside the now-unmoving stretcher.

"Have you news of my boy Jack? " he began, in a voice which refused to break beneath the strain.

"Not this tide.

"When d'you think that he'll come back?"
Not with this wind blowing, and this tide.

"Has any one else had word of him?"
Not this tide.
For what is sunk will hardly swim,
Not with this wind blowing, and this tide.

"Oh, dear, what comfort can I find?"
None this tide,
Nor any tide,
"Except he did not shame his kind —
     Not even with that wind blowing, and that tide.

Then hold your head up all the more,
     This tide,
     And every tide;
Because he was the son you bore,
     And gave to that wind blowing and that tide!"

"Why?" Susanna choked out in a news studio shocked silent as the grave. "Why would he do that?"

"Because he was protecting a bunker full of his comrades. They're carrying him now."

Behind James, the American stepped back, and the British sergeant began barking commands. Six women who had been in that bunker bore the stretcher up toward the waiting Marine helicopter.

"That seems…" Susanna's voice drifted off as she watched the body disappear inside the cavernous hold.

"Farfetched I know," James said carefully. *"But I was there."*

"You were?"

James paused, staring into the camera with eyes which had seen too much, ears which had heard too much, and a heart which bore witness to the greatness of human courage. Behind him, Henry Pistol marched his six charges back out of the Super Stallion and into ranks alongside their comrades.

"I watched him die, saving my life and the lives of the forty-seven women with us," James said.

"That's… I have no words."

The helicopter's rotors began to spin, RPMs climbing as the triple set of engines roared to life, before the massive beast rose into the sky one last time. Cobra gunships quickly joined it in a steady formation. Timothy's camera tracked the movement, before returning to center on James Cochrane.

"In the last several hours, I have been a firsthand witness to the incredible courage and devotion of many young men and not a few young women. Perhaps the bravest of these was a young lance corporal from Newquay. His name was Joseph Pilsen, and he went out a damn good British soldier. This is James Cochrane signing off from Dishu, Afghanistan. Thank you, and God Bless."

\#

Hondo Cassidy fell heavily into his rack, wondering how long he'd been awake now.

The caffeine is finally starting to wear off, I've drained my bladder, showered, and with the sheer amount of reinforcements which we've got running around here, I don't have anything to worry about unless the Taliban are hiding a nuke nearby. Why, why do I feel incomplete?

His thoughts trailed off as a door swung open and feminine voices were heard.

Wonder what that's all about? His brain thought in a detached manner.

"Girls in the hooch!" a Marine shouted.

"One of those damn rockets took out our heater. It's two degrees outside, and we've no warm air in our tent," a woman declared.

That sounds oddly like Maresley, Hondo thought.

"That sucks."

"We're crashing in here with you lot until it's fixed," an equally cheerful voice declared.

And why does that sound like Sylvie? He wondered further. *No worry, I've been meaning to talk with her —*

The poncho Hondo had wrapped around one side of his rack pulled back, revealing a familiar face.

"Hey good-lookin' whatcha got cookin'?" a pretty brunette with entrancing eyes a man could drown himself in asked as she sat down on the edge.

"Hey sweet baby —"

He had no time to finish the line before Sylvie's lips were on his and they were falling back onto the thin mattress with a creaky groan of the springs beneath.

Cassidy let her mouth explore his, hands slowly caressing her curvaceous form, appreciating the lithesome beauty's presence now as a calming balm to his exhausted soul. He'd worried about her after they split up for the night to attend their separate duties. Now, she was back, safely in his arms once again.

"I missed you, Hondo," she told him, finally.

"Missed you too," he confessed. "In fact, something I need to get off my chest."

"Better not be me," she informed him mock-seriously as she looked down at him, letting an idle finger drag across the coarse stubble on his tired cheeks.

"Never you, dear woman. Not now, not ever," he assured.

"Then what is it?" Sylvie asked.

"I love you," he said quietly.

Around them, interesting sounds were emanating from the other racks, rising in their intensity. As softly as he spoke now, Sylvie had almost missed his declaration. She had not been prepared for it. Not at all.

But looking into those intense green eyes, she saw the truth of his words. Hondo Cassidy loved her. And she had no idea what to say. Her mouth struggled to form words her brain could not assemble. Before the words could finish forming, he laid a calloused finger on her lips.

"I don't need you to say anything. I just need you to know you matter more to me than any other woman in this world. I want you, I desire you, I long for you. I love you."

Again with that simple statement, which filled her soul and emptied her head of all thought except that this man, the one who'd put it all on the line for her when it mattered the most, desired her. They were words she'd never expected to hear in this godforsaken slice of hell's own blast furnace.

And yet, they had been uttered.

He was no longer awake. No, he had finally fallen asleep. As if saying that gave him reprieve to relax. Giggles and groans and grunts arose around her, and Sylvie smiled at the irony.

First man to take me to bed, and what's he do? Fall asleep before me!

She played with a tendril of tightly curled black hair, wondering for a moment if a baby sired by this man would be blessed with such locks.

He looks so peaceful when he's sleeping. I think I'll join him.

Laying her head down in the center of his chest, Sylvie Lyons let her thoughts run out on the deep tide of dreams, and in short order, she too slumbered. The long night of madness surrendered at last to a new dawn.

Chapter 37

Mama, He's Crazy

Father David Pascoe was no stranger to conflict. An Anglican priest by profession, the redoubtable Englishman had joined the Army nearly thirty years prior. Coming to Dishu with the relief forces had not even been a question when the Duty Sergeant informed him of it. The squaddies were his sheep and he their shepherd. Even if the only duty he could perform was to give Last Rites, he would give them his full care and devotion. He would have it no other way.

Since his arrival at Dishu, he'd been busy doing exactly that for the troops. He'd worked as a grief counselor before he'd joined the priesthood. Putting it to use here seemed to be the wisest course.

Some of the troops came on their own, others came carried along by their fellows. He'd pretended not to hear them as they drew near. *The Padre is here to help, he's one of us, and you can trust him. Sit down, talk.*

The newest person to visit him in the makeshift office space was an interesting study: quiet, heart-stoppingly beautiful, and very nervous.

No, not nervous. Unsure. She's sitting on a decision and trying to weigh it out.

"Good afternoon, Father."

"How are we doing, Sergeant?"

"I —" she paused. "Father, it's been seven months since my last confession, would you hear it, please?"

Pascoe smiled gently. "Of course my daughter."

Producing her rosary, Sylvie Lyons went through the steps of a religion she had devoutly followed since she was a small girl. It centered her, calmed her, and steadied her against the matter she was desperately seeking answers for. Finally, finished, she put the rosary back in its place under her shirt, and faced the priest with determination.

"Father, I need you to know I'm not ashamed of anything I've done since I came here. The killing was bad business, but it comes with being a soldier. I knew that when I took the shilling."

"Good. A lot of you young 'uns don't always get that." He studied her face for a moment. "What concerns you?"

"Father, I'm in love with one of the lads."

"Are you sure about that?"

"I'm —" she breathed, "fairly certain of it, yes."

"Good. Certainty is a good thing. Where is he from? London, Leeds, Birmingham?"

"Wyoming. In America."

He blinked, smiled slowly.

"One of the Marines then," Pascoe prompted.

"Yes."

"Would it surprise you to know you're the first one who's admitted such, and not confessed to misbehaving?"

Sylvie sighed. "Not really. We're not plaster saints around here."

"No, no you're not." Pascoe agreed. "Barracks don't allow for that to happen."

"It gets worse, Father."

"How so?"

"He's Mormon."

"They let Mormons in the American Marines?"

"When they're built and act like him, they do."

"Tell me about him."

Carefully, Sylvie explained how she had come to find herself attracted to the wild, angry man. "He's hell-on-wheels with guns. I watched him use a machine gun like he was born to it. Same with a knife."

"He can use a knife?"

"Aye. He swears he's good with knives and guns and nothing else, but the man does know how to cook. It's what he's done for us since he got here."

"Wait. I saw a Mess Sergeant who brooked no arguments about who ran it and the rules of his mess. Including the difference between cookies and biscuits."

"A stout man, with a chest like a barrel and shoulders where he ought to have a neck?" Sylvie suggested.

Pascoe laughed. "Of course, it's the one with shoulders on him like an ox! Couldn't expect some scrawny lad to sweep you off your feet, now could we?"

Sylvie sighed. "Romance was not what I anticipated when I came here."

"Ah," the Father's eyes twinkled merrily. "I would just as soon chalk it up to Himself having a sense of humor. He is prone to whimsy now and again."

She told him about Cassidy's confession to her, in the aftermath of the fighting, and he steepled his fingers as he listened.

"Well then. Have you told him how you feel?" Pascoe asked seriously.

"No." she shook her head.

"Why not?" the priest asked.

"I don't know how."

"It's rather simple really —"

"I think I want to marry him!" Sylvie said desperately.

"Now we see the real reason you're here. Tell me something, have you thought about your career if you do wed?"

"Sort of," she admitted.

"You'd have to decide who keeps their career and who gets out of uniform. You cannot stay apart and the marriage work."

"I'm up for Staff in a few more years," she admitted slowly.

"And yet, it seems you're unsure of it."

She nodded. "The politics of this whole mess have made me mad."

"That's fair," Pascoe assured, and sipped his tea for a moment.

"It is?"

"Yes. Nobody expects you to always be happy with how things are in the Army. Just because people think you're a myrmidon doesn't mean you are."

"Hondo says that too."

"Hondo? That's his first name?"

"Yes. It's the name his uncle gave him when he adopted him."

"Is he a well-read man?"

"Yes. Part of how we got together. He knew poetry my Grandpapa used to read to me when I was little."

Pascoe sipped at his tea again. "What do you know about Mormons?"

"They don't drink tea," Sylvie stated.

"Or alcohol. Or smoke. And they love big families."

"Big?"

"Five, six, even seven children," Pascoe proclaimed calmly.

"You're joking!" Sylvie said in surprise.

"Not even slightly. I assume you know how babies happen, correct Sergeant?" He asked.

Her cheeks colored brilliantly. "I ugh... I do."

"We in the clergy like to joke that our Mormon friends are trying to make up for lost time. Tell me, how old is he?"

"Almost thirty-one."

"Oh good. Prime age. Now, have you spoken with him about the matter?"

"Not yet, Father."

"You might want to let him know what you're thinking. It typically helps," he explained.

"I'm afraid of ruining what we have."

"Dear girl, that's where you've got to learn to gamble."

"But what if he says no?" Sylvie protested.

"Why would he?" Pascoe asked.

"I — I don't know."

"By all appearances, he's set his cap for you. He was willing to make the first move. And, he demonstrated vulnerability. Hard mannered men like that don't let just anybody in."

"Second time I've heard that now," Sylvie muttered.

"Might be a point to that. Especially as Himself is prone to whimsy."

#

Sylvie stopped near the door to her private workshop, examining Nealen's Redan in daylight.

"Morning Sergeant, how ya doing today?" a soldier asked.

"Alright, thought I'd come see what it looked like in daylight."

"You saw it in the dark?"

"I was sitting right inside here doing my thing when they blew the wall."

"Good damn." He looked her up and down, spying the name tape on her vest. "You're that Lyons?"

"What do you mean?" Sylvie harshly demanded.

"Everybody here has heard about how you and that Marine held this during the Siege. Was it really as bad as it looked on the camera footage?"

Her mind ran back to the wild moments when the Taliban had broken through while she was clearing a stoppage in the machine gun.

Cassidy hadn't hesitated to step forward, pistol and facón *knife in hand. She'd screamed at him to get back even as she cleared the stoppage and got the belt back in place, but he hadn't listened, caught up in a savage fury.*

One of the assaulters tried to parry the blood-stained knife. His face took the blow, blood spurting as the point punched through his eye.

Hondo yanked on the haft, ripping it up and out as he searched for targets.